Shadow

Book 3 of the Preternatural Chronicles

© 2019, Hunter Blain. All rights reserved. The contents of this publication, or any part thereof, may not be reproduced or transmitted in any form or by any means electronic or mechanical, including photocopying, recording, storing in an information retrieval system, or otherwise, without the prior written approval of Hunter Blain.

Contents

Epigraph		V
1.	Chapter 1	1
2.	Chapter 2	3
3.	Chapter 3	11
4.	Chapter 4	22
5.	Chapter 5	29
6.	Chapter 6	42
7.	Chapter 7	54
8.	Chapter 8	59
9.	Chapter 9	67
10.	Chapter 10	73
11.	Chapter 11	79
12.	Chapter 12	82
13.	Chapter 13	93
14.	Chapter 14	106
15.	Chapter 15	131
16.	Chapter 16	142
17.	Chapter 17	168
18.	Chapter 18	188
19.	Chapter 19	205
20.	Chapter 20	248

21. Chapter 21	259
22. Chapter 22	262
23. Chapter 23	273
24. Chapter 24	296
25. Chapter 25	298
26. Chapter 26	311
27. Chapter 27	315
28. Chapter 28	319
Epilogue	328
Afterword	339
Also By Hunter Blain	341

Epigraph

"Our doubts are traitors, and make us lose the good we oft might win, by fearing to attempt."

—*William Shakespeare*

"I am the author of my life. Unfortunately, I am writing in pen and cannot erase my mistakes."

—Bill Kaulitz

Chapter 1

Water dripped incessantly every few seconds in the dark, freezing prison. There were no windows in Queen Mab's dungeon, so Oberon—the once king of all of Faerie—had no idea how much time had passed since his imprisonment. Had it been years? Decades? Only the water kept him company.

Oberon refused to scream or lash out, knowing Mab would relish any show of emotion. Instead, he sat in meditation, dreaming of what he would do once he escaped. As he closed his eyes, his estranged wife flowed to the forefront of his thoughts, and he remembered.

Oberon had danced with the idea of absorbing the Unseelie Court for centuries. Though he had proclaimed himself King of all Faerie, he had known in the back of his mind that it was only in name. Everyone had been aware of Queen Mab and her unquestioned rule over half of Faerie. Therefore, the time had come to stop fantasizing over being the one true king. The time had come to attack and make it a reality. No one would dare question or doubt King Oberon. Not even in private.

Tatiana had argued with her husband over the necessity of the Winter and Autumn Courts.

"We could rule them *better* than that bitch sitting on the throne," Oberon had roared in his blinding anger. Tatiana had simply stood with arms crossed and glaring at her husband. Taking a deep breath, Oberon had softened his tone and pleaded, "Imagine it; Spring and summer in perpetuity! Flowers would always bloom, while full trees would wave in the warm wind! We can make it that way, wife."

"There can be no light without darkness, dear husband. We need the winter and autumn just as they need the summer and spring. It is this perfect dance of balance and equality that gives way to life in Midworld."

"Who cares about Midworld!" Oberon had bellowed, losing what small semblance of control he had had over his emotions. "I *want* that throne, and there's nothing you can do to stop me!" As Oberon had turned to leave and prepare his private army, he had been surprised when his opinionated wife had said nothing. Now he knew why. She had betrayed him by warning Mab about his intentions of overthrowing the Unseelie Court. Mab had been waiting with Tatiana by her side. The loyal army of King Oberon had faltered and kneeled before the combined queens of Faerie, leaving the king alone to face the Unseelie.

Oberon had refused to accept his fate and had battled everything that had been thrown at him. Frost giants wielding ice clubs, elves with blue eyes and skin casting dark magic, shrieking banshees, and even a cyclops had fallen to Oberon's blade and prowess. It wasn't until Tatiana had stood in front of him as he swung his sword that he had hesitated, allowing for Queen Mab herself to cast the powerful spell that had frozen the king in place. All of Faerie had known about his defeat and subsequent imprisonment.

"Bitch," Oberon barked through bared teeth. His face was sore from scowling for so long in the darkness. "You're going to pay for this, dear wife—*both* of you will."

Oberon could feel his fists shaking as wrath built a fire in his core that made his skin crawl.

"Maybe I can be of assistance," purred a smooth, female voice from the darkness.

Startled, Oberon's eyes shot open only to be flooded with absolute blackness. Two amethysts appeared a few feet away from him, followed by a gleaming smile of sharp teeth. Oberon was perplexed at how teeth could shine in the complete absence of light.

"Who might you be, specter?" Oberon asked in the tone of someone who was used to being the authority in the room.

"A humble servant of the one true king of Faerie," cooed the voice as the smile grew to a full Cheshire grin.

Chapter 2

"It's been taken care of. The limo driver's family has received a sizable life insurance check that they hadn't known about."

"Thank you, Da. I mean it. I-I don't know what I'd do without you, man," I admitted in a heartfelt tone.

"They'll be financially secure for generations to come," Da explained without making eye contact with me. This wasn't the first time he had had to clean up a sizable mess.

I noticed his reserved tone and distant posture.

"It was an accident," I lamely tried to explain with my hands out and palms up in a gesture that pleaded understanding.

"Your lack of control and forethought is not an excuse to murder the innocent. I had hoped the incident with the boy and his mother would be the last." There was a razor's edge to his voice that cut deep. Da had been my guiding light for over fifty years, and it hurt to bathe in his disappointment. I would have preferred screaming outrage to this.

"I—" I started, my words getting caught in my throat.

"—need to go see Father Thomes and ask for forgiveness," Da suggested tersely while returning his attention to the spreadsheet on his iPad.

I took his *subtle* cue and left my Fortress of Solitaire without another word, shame stealing my voice.

The night was warm and humid, with thin clouds rolling overhead. Instead of sprinting to the church, I decided to walk and assess my thoughts. Father Thomes was going to be less than pleased with me for killing another completely innocent human. Lilith, how much tar had I thrown on my already blackened soul this time? Thirty years of trying to bleach my sins might have been undone in a few moments of careless rage.

Some time passed with me dragging my feet before I looked up and saw the church of Father Thomes Philseep. Taking a deep, preparing breath, I stepped onto the landing and stood before the heavy front door.

As usual, the door began to open without having to knock. It was downright spooky that he always knew when I was at the front door. I just assumed Da let him know when I was coming, but then again, my friend and mentor did have holy abilities that I personally didn't know the limits to.

Father Thomes stood at the front door wearing his traditional priest getup, complete with the white collar atop his black robes. Lately, he had a slight hunch to him and kind of shuffled as he walked, signifying that my mortal friend was, indeed, aging. It felt like the blink of an eye since we had first met nearly three decades ago. He had already been middle-aged then, but now, I constantly questioned how much longer I had with him.

A thought struck that first made my worry grow before souring and sickening me: Did we have enough time to undo the damage I had done with the limo driver? It disgusted me that I was more worried about my own selfish desires than the well-being of the priest who had risked everything to work with a vampire with over five hundred years of sin on his soul.

Father Thomes, who had been smiling, must have seen something he didn't like on my face because his jovial expression faltered.

"What is it, my son?"

"Forgive me, Father, for I have sinned," I exhaled slowly.

Many words could be used to describe me: buff, witty, merciless, and sexual tyrannosaur; but contrite was usually not one of them. So when Father Thomes saw my expression and heard the tone of my voice, he knew I had done something catastrophic.

Feeling the situation, Father Thomes nodded somberly while letting the door open all the way. I followed him inside as he shuffled toward a stone staircase that led deep into the ground, the door creaking shut behind us as if on its own volition.

After making our way to the bottom, Father Thomes walked to the end of a lamplit hallway with doors on either side. Turning a knob on the wall above the fireplace, a warm flame sprang to life, dancing its excitement at being born.

Turning, Thomes slowly sat with a groan in his favorite padded reading chair. The thought had never occurred to me until right then that maybe the wooden pews where we normally had our conversations were too uncomfortable for his elderly frame now.

Thomes sat and looked at me expectantly.

If I could sweat, it would look like I had just gotten out of the shower, I was so nervous.

After a drawn-out, deep inhale that I held for a moment, I released my breath and relayed the whole story. I held nothing back as I described how I had mentally decimated a mortal's mind while in a fury, at which time I had had to make a decision.

"I just don't know if it was the *right* choice, Father Thomes," I said with a furrowed brow while his stony face processed my blunder.

"John, I know we agreed that I would forgive you for your sins when I first took you under my wing, but this…this is egregious, even for you."

My heart sunk as he spoke. I could feel my shoulders slump as my gaze lowered to the ground in submission. I stared at the floor as the light from the fire danced across the rug.

"Deus, Pater misericordiárum, qui per mortem et resurrectiónem Fílii sui mundum sibi reconciliávit et Spíritum Sanctum effúdit in remissiónem peccatórum, per ministérium Ecclésiæ indulgéntiam tibi tríbuat et pacem. Et ego te absolvo a peccatis tuis in nomine Patris, et Filii, et Spiritus Sancti." As Father Thomes finished the passage for absolution of sin, he made the sign of the cross. I wanted to sob, knowing I didn't deserve forgiveness, but relieved to receive it.

"Amen," I said softly while screwing my eyes shut, feeling the relief wash over me.

"There is still much to be done for penance, John."

With a grateful, understanding tone, I said, "I know, Father. The physics of religion. For every action there is an equal and opposite reaction, and all that."

"I'm glad you understand, my son."

After a closing pause on the subject, I decided to change the topic so as not to press my luck on forgiveness.

"How's he doing?" I asked, sitting up straight again in my seat and thumbing back toward the hallway. I was already feeling like my old self again.

Just a few doors down the hall from where we sat was my maker, Ulric, who had tried to kill me a few times too many. Father Thomes had promised to watch over him and keep him in his vampire-specific cell. This would ensure that he didn't die and make me the last vampire, which would cause the apocalypse. You should already know this unless you are some sort of roulette-playing sadist who picks up a book series at random.

"The blood supply has been an invaluable asset." Father Thomes was referencing the blood bank that my five-inch faerie companion was in the process of setting up for me. "Though he isn't drinking as much as I would like."

"I am honestly surprised that he is drinking at all. Figured he'd be all depressed and stuff," I said, feeling the warmth of the flames blazing in a fireplace that was so big a person could escape through it—I should know.

"We came to an understanding," Father Thomes said without a trace of levity. It made my blood run cold...er that he could force Ulric to act according to his will. Then again, I couldn't be that surprised—the dude had God on speed dial. Plus, our first meeting had been a quick but epic battle that had showcased the immense power he could wield.

"He sleeps most of the time, waking only to feed," Father Philseep continued.

"Yeah, he sure does enjoy his catnaps." I thought about Ulric's affinity for slumber and how it had ultimately tipped the scales of power in my favor. Even though he had been more than two hundred and seventy years older when he had made me, he had been asleep for almost four hundred years in his combined lifetime. It was also worth mentioning that the last sleep he had partaken in had been forced by me when I had burned him alive and left nothing but a skeleton, or so I'd thought. Now I knew that some small portion of him had remained—probably the brain—and that he had slept while on the brink of death until he had been somehow brought back—perhaps by lazy writing or something.

Looking back on that fateful night in London, it had been for the best that I'd put his fire out before his body had been wholly consumed, otherwise Armageddon could have started right then and there. At least now I had allies and a better understanding of how to stop the final battle between Heaven and Hell. On the flip side of that optimistic coin: if the final battle did commence, then all souls that have ever existed, whether above or below, would be collateral. So, delaying the end of times by a few years could be regarded as a moot point, if not negligible, in the grand scheme of things. Either way though, a lot of people were counting on me.

"How is Locke adjusting?" Thomes asked, referring to my warlock archnemesis turned tentative ally.

A few weeks ago, we had had a glorious battle indeed, worthy of a series on HBO—BUT only with the prerequisite that the final epic battle was so dark that no one was able to see what was actually happening. Oh, and the big bad guy we'd spent years learning to fear was killed while serving zero purpose. Winter must've been a guy because it had left as quickly as it had come, with the recipients left unsatisfied and alienated.

But back to what I was saying: Locke had killed my family when I was still human, and I had spent several years tracking him down as a vampire before realizing he had probably died of old age at the very least. PLOT TWIST—He had been sent back to Earth to serve as Satan's lackey and to piss in my Cheerios. I hadn't known at the time that he was the same commander who had killed my mother and father, because the Devil had burned his face, forcing Locke to wear a mask. Plus, he had changed his name from Commander Godwin to Nathanial Locke, the warlock. How lame was that? Fast forward a tad bit and I ripped Locke's head off, finally avenging my family, only to have said head delivered to me on a cardboard platter. Oh, and it had still been alive! Creepy, right? Locke had sworn he hadn't had a choice and regretted everything he had done while begging us not to let him go back to Hell, and blah blah blah.

I'd been really trying to better myself lately, seeing as how I was over five hundred years old and should probably put the nightlife behind me and mature a smidge. Ask me if it had been easy to forgive Locke.

Go ahead.

Fuck no, it hadn't. What kind of stupid question was that? Seriously, did you even read the series in order? Anywho, I had forgiven him—as best as I could—and also helped him make a new body. He was really *growing* to love it.

"Locke is doing fine, actually. He's relearning his powers in his new body, and even doing the dishes," I said with a serious face. "Though I did have to buy a step stool so he could crawl up to reach the sink...and the fridge...and the toilet." The corners of my lips tugged up in a smile I only kind of tried to conceal.

"It's alright to hide your pain in humor, my son," Father Thomes said. That struck a little too close to home. "Forgiveness is a journey that takes time. You have taken your first steps, which is the hardest part."

I took a deep breath in contemplation, then said, "What if he is lying and using me as a pawn in his chess game? I mean, I *feel* like he is truthful in his intentions, but what if he is growing in strength only to betray me later to Satan?"

"I don't think that is the case, John," Father Philseep said while staring into the fire. He was thoughtful, as if weighing the words in his mind before speaking them aloud. "The best way to find out if you can trust someone, is to trust them."

His words were heavy with wisdom, and I was taken aback. The Archangel Gabriel's words also flashed in my mind like an annoying pop-up banner that you tried to click away so you could get back to the video of the kitty playing with the puppy—I MEANT PORN. Yes, dark and nasty porn, not that cute thing I said.

Record scratch—Cut scene to me in my coffin, bathed in the light of my phone, watching YouTube videos while saying in a high-pitched voice, "Aw, cute wittle puppers can't get up the stairs. Hehe."

Gabriel's words resonated and mixed with Father Thomes', "*You are free to make any decision, in the entire universe, that you wish. It is the consequences that are unavoidable.*" I could choose to trust Locke and face a potential betrayal, or kill him and never be able to utilize his vast powers for the Light.

Sighing, I said, "I think you're right. The fate of the universe is at stake, and I need to have as many allies as possible."

"What about your personal growth?"

"That too, I guess," I responded, knowing he was right but still in a cosmic battle with my pride. "Long shot here, but do you know anything about the Shadow Court of the Fae?"

"I'm afraid that is out of my realm of expertise, my son."

"Thanks, Dad," I said sarcastically. "I figured you didn't, but wanted to double-check. Seems I've made some new friends."

"That sounds about right," Father Thomes said in such a way that I didn't know if he was being sarcastic or a hundred percent serious.

"Yeah, yeah. I'm super popular right now."

He got serious again after seeing my face. "Are you worried?"

"You're just going to say something along the lines of 'God only gives you as much dick as you can handle' or something prophetic like that."

"Not in precisely those words, but the message is the same."

I looked at him, worry evident in my eyes, "I'm scared, Thomes. Taylor told me that the Shadow Fae want to blanket all of existence in darkness." A lump of frustration and brimming fear lodged in my throat, threatening to choke me. "They know I am the key to making that happen. He said they will send everyone and everything they have at me."

"Who is Taylor?" Father Thomes asked, intrigued.

"He's an elf from the Seelie Court. They are friendly to this plane and want the continued existence of...well...everything."

"Ah," he said, hesitating. I wasn't sure how much the padre knew about the Faerie plane, but it was safe to assume this was a lot of information for him.

"Let me see if I understand this; there is a whole, what did you call it—court—that wants to kill you in the hopes that all of creation will be cast into darkness?"

"That's a bingo," I said as I leaned back in the chair, letting my butt slightly hang off the edge of the seat in exasperation at hearing my predicament out loud.

"How interesting," Father Thomes said calmly, absorbing the situation with surprising ease. "Do they have a leader?"

"I don't know. Da and Locke are researching that as we speak. Why do you ask? Thinking I should try and negotiate or something?"

"In every hive, there is a queen. Remove the queen, the hive ceases to be."

"You're saying kill the leader?"

"The fate of creation is on a precarious line, teetering dangerously first to one side and then the other. How long until we fall?" The father looked at me intently. "It is time to stop being reactionary. We need to take charge and end these threats before they have the opportunity to mount an offense."

"The best defense is a good offense, right?"

"Oh, I don't know. I don't watch sports. But it sounds good."

Freshly energized by our conversation, I stood up and said, "I like it, Papa T. I'm going to get a plan together with my team of misfits and save the world by killing some Fae bastards!"

"Go get them, tiger," Father Thomes said with a genuine smile.

"Pl-please don't say that again." His smile didn't fade as I turned to walk down the hall toward the spiral stone staircase. I slowed, briefly, as I walked past Ulric's cell, the red button on the wall next to the door glowing faintly in the lamplit catacomb. One press and the gates of Hell would spill open, commencing the final battle. My mouth salivated as I stared at it.

I shook my head, hard, and turned my neck to see Father Thomes standing in front of the fire, his features hidden by the shadows cast by the flames. His rigid posture conveyed enough without even seeing his face. Though I couldn't see his eyes, I knew they were watching me intently. He trusted me but was still wary of my nature, as he should be. My Predatory Self (or PS, as I called him) and I were mostly on speaking terms and had an understanding, but he had proven time and time again that giving him full access to the steering wheel of my mind was not the best idea. Conversely, he had saved my life more than a few times by doing just that. PS—can't live with him, definitely can't live without him.

I waved, and without waiting for a response, turned to make my way up the stairs, the pull of the red button calling to me like the rising steam of a cartoon pie on a window sill.

What the hell was that, man? I asked PS in the control room of my mind. He shrugged, not even close to the wheel. *Wait, was that me, then?* I asked myself out loud in my head. Pausing for the briefest of moments, he shrugged again. *O...kay then. Not worried at all.*

I was.

Chapter 3

It was starting to grow hot outside, even at night. Houston had some of the most brutal weather that could change on a whim. The humidity was the worst part. It could be a hundred degrees outside with 90 percent humidity, and people would pass out from heatstroke. It got cold too, but not below-zero cold like way up north, and not for very long. In my opinion, Texas had nine months of summer followed by three months of fall, winter, and spring all rolled up together.

All of this didn't really bother me, seeing as I was a badass vampire that didn't play by anyone else's rules except my own, and sometimes not even my own. Depweg and the twins, on the other hand, were more alive than I was, and were susceptible to the elements. Man, I was thankful I wasn't a werewolf because I bet that fur made it HOT. Excuse me, *werwolf*, with the first *w* pronounced with a *v* as the Germans said it. I *did* first find my BFF Depweg during WWII as we murdered a lot of Nazi shitheads, so I respected his decision to go by his motherland's pronunciation. I could sympathize though; I *hated* it whenever people called me Jonathan. What's in a name? Respect, that's what.

After absolving me of my sins, Thomes and I had discussed recent events, puppies vs kittens, and the existential crisis that was being a merciless vampire working with a holy priest, and after sitting in a reading chair for that long, my loyal trench coat had started riding up on my shoulders a tad. I repositioned the black leather, remembering—fondly—how I had stolen it off a superdead Nazi officer. Who had killed him? A powerful vampire whose hot button was the slaughter of innocents.

I felt the smooth leather that had once been covered in patches; there had been so many that it had resembled a quilt at one point. After one of my latest adventures, though, I had all but shredded this piece of antiquity to ribbons; luckily, I had a personal seamstress on staff who kept my attire alive.

Da was a five-inch faerie who told everyone he was a freaking angel. The only kind of angel he could be at five inches was one of those that sat on your shoulder debating with a five-inch demon on your every decision. Plus, the S.O.B. could shift planes, and I had never known an angel or demon to be able to do that. Then there was the fact that he's FIVE FREAKING INCHES. All the angels I had ever encountered were, like, over ten feet tall in their natural form.

Anyway, Da was amazing about keeping both my trench coat and gray beanie alive—two of my most prized possessions. He had somehow brought my coat back from the dead, and it looked almost brand new, but it still had the innards of the original. Truth be told, it had been patched so many times before the most recent restoration that not even Da could claim it was the original trench anymore. Just knowing the inner lining was untouched for the most part helped keep the emotional connection.

Walking down the crumbling steps of the church, I made my way through the brown grass and jumped over the once black wrought iron fence. Turning toward Valenta's Saloon, I started jovially walking down the street, whistling Dixie as I went. I was actually whistling an incredibly complex instrumental song from a group called Animals as Leaders. I hit every note with perfect pitch, something that would have been impossible for a mortal's lips, which I am *oh*, so humble about, mind you. The technical prowess of this particular band had blown even my preternatural mind, which made it more fun to whistle. The lead guitarist for that band was, without a doubt, a supe.

A breeze tugged at the loose black hair that spilled out from the back of my gray beanie. I was aware of the heat and humidity outside, but not bothered by it in the least. Not sweating was one of the many perks of being an immortal.

The air smelled clean, as the city had been drenched in rain during the day while I slept. I enjoyed smelling the rain-soaked grass and seeing the blades glistening with beads that glinted in the moonlight as I walked.

A rust-colored Pit Bull Terrier trotted up to me, tongue flopping as it panted. I immediately crouched down and began petting it enthusiastically while asking it if it was, indeed, a good boy. The stray enjoyed the attention as I grabbed one of my thumbs with the other hand and ripped it off at the base.

"You hungry, boy? Who's a hungry boy?" I asked in a playful, cooing voice, extending my hand out with the thumb as an offering. I knew he was probably hungry, and I could grow my digit back nearly instantaneously when I wanted. The pretty Pit sniffed and then delicately took my offering, chomping it and swallowing after only a few bites. My thumb regrew and I ripped it off again. I loved dogs.

After feeding my new buddy a handful (get it?) of digits, the Pit began to sniff the air. A deep growl emanated from its chest as it turned around in all directions, trying to find the source of the smell it did not enjoy.

"What is it, boy? A squirrel? Did little Jimmy fall down a well?" The stray did not respond. Instead, it began barking at a wall that should have been illuminated by one of the city's streetlamps, except this one had burned out.

"Odd," I said out loud to both the Pit Bull and myself. "Those are LEDs and should never burn out, huh, boy?"

Two glowing purple orbs blinked into existence. They moved from side to side until I got the distinct feeling that they had locked onto me. A Cheshire grin of jagged, gleaming teeth spread out of the darkness, forming a creepy U shape. The Pit yelped and sprinted down the road, slipping in place as it tried to get traction and flee.

I willed my senses out as I let PS put one hand on the wheel in the control center of my mind. I could feel my canines flex and elongate into surgically sharp points as my eyes shifted from a vibrant purple to a crimson red. The world became clear as day, and what I saw shook me to my core.

"The...fuck..." was all I could manage before the silhouette of a gargantuan reptile slithered toward me on impossibly fast legs. It ran to me faster than I could blink an eye before abruptly standing straight up, its mass growing from that of a nimble lizard to a hulking beast. It was like watching a shadow puppet show where things morphed seamlessly into other creatures.

I had to crane my neck to look at the eyes of the phantom. I was frozen with indecision and surprise when the huge beast backhanded me with enough force to send me sailing across the street and into an industrial warehouse wall. Luckily, my bones slowed my crash, exploding into dust.

As I slid down to my butt, my head dropped as I croaked out one of the manliest phrases that had ever come out of my mouth in my five centuries of life, "Owwy."

I lifted my head in time to see the beast stomping over to where I sat, the smokelike shadows billowing in its hand coalescing into a dagger that had no distinguishing features. The entirety of the monster, short of its glowing purple eyes and glistening teeth, was featureless. It was like in *Peter Pan* when the hero had had to fight his shadow.

Gritting my teeth, I willed my bones to heal as a bloodspear grew from my hand. I didn't know how much energy to put into the manifestation, so I dumped a lot just in case. This thing scared me. There was no conversing with the shadow monster; it simply attacked without the usual monologue. That meant this mofo meant business.

The silhouette strode forward, dagger in hand, as I thrust my spear into its unarmored stomach. It stopped abruptly, looking down at where the weapon met its incorporeal flesh. Its Cheshire smile diminished into a toothy grin in annoyance at the attack, but then reformed with vigor. The shadow beast looked back up at me as it stepped to the side, my spear sliding through its body without any damage being done. Stabbing my own shadow would have resulted in precisely the same outcome.

"Welp...shit," was all I could manage before the beast bent down to stab me in the face. As the blade was inches from its target, a car squealed down the street with its HID high beams on. The creature recoiled and shrieked in furious pain. I dodged the blade as the monster violently jerked, allowing only the smallest cut to crest my earlobe instead of my runway model face. My ear began to tingle where it had been cut.

"Get in!" a familiar voice yelled from the car that screeched to a halt at the curb. I ran toward the pink Rolls-Royce, sliding over the hood in supercool cop show fashion. I maybe put too much effort and slid off the hood, where I continued to travel over asphalt on my ass.

"John!" the voice cried out again, a bit more urgently this time. I recovered and scrambled on all fours to the passenger side door as the shadow monster bellowed its rage. I yanked open the door while risking a glance over the hood to see the monster start sprinting toward us, spittle flying from its mouth as it screamed. My ass touched the seat and Lily put the plastic to the rubber, as the saying should go nowadays.

Without looking up from the road, Lily pressed the button that brightly illuminated the inside of the cabin as the monster swung its blade at the windshield. Another cry of pain pierced the night as the shadow weapon disappeared in the light of the car's interior.

As we fled at alarming speeds, I used all my centuries of linguistic skills to eloquently state my concerns on what had just happened: "THE FUCK WAS THAT SHIT?!" I said in a totally calm, collected, and non-high-pitched voice.

"Shadow Fae," Lily answered quickly as she concentrated on the road ahead. "You've done it now, lover."

"The only thing I've 'done,'" I said with air quotes, "was not die." We took a turn at Mach-Jesus and I was thrown into my door. My hands fought feverishly to grab the seat belt and latch it on.

I looked over at Lily—my Fae friend with benefits—and noticed she kept glancing at the rearview mirror with consternation on her face.

"What are you looking for?" I asked, worried about the answer.

"That," she barked while nodding at the mirror. I turned to look out the back window to see a dark wave coursing down the street, knocking over light poles that shattered against the asphalt. It took up the entire width of the street.

"*Holyshitwhat'sthat?*" I asked in one syllable.

"Already been over this, John. Now be quiet, please. I need to focus." We hit a speed bump in an affluent neighborhood, and orange sparks illuminated the street around us in a flash as metal struck the road. The impact rocked me, snapping my neck, and I sat back in my seat facing forward, gripping the oh-shit bar for dear unlife while trying my best not to whimper. I failed. Of course, I wasn't scared about a potential crash; it was the part that came after we stopped that terrified me.

We drove through a housing development phase of the neighborhood and an idea struck me like a twist to the nipples.

"Pull in there!" I cried out, confidence returning. Lily did as commanded, pulling into the driveway of a house that only had its outer walls built up by 2x4s. "Get to the middle of the house!"

We ran onto the concrete pad of the house, and I began focusing on the wooden frames around us, exciting the molecules. Smoke began to escape the frames, growing in size until the wood caught on fire. The flames reached upward, clawing at the night sky and illuminating the world around us in a fiery haze. The black wave rushed toward the house, swallowing Lily's car before screeching in pain as the light swallowed the darkness at the edges. I took note that the shadow singed where the light touched it, sending up acrid smoke.

The amorphous wave circled the house once, searching for a way in, before it coalesced into a single small house cat with glowing purple eyes. Its features were still absent, sending chills down my spine at seeing a 3D animal with the characteristics of a flat shadow.

"How long until dawn?" I asked, panting.

"Three hours," Lily answered, looking at the smartwatch on her arm. I absently wondered if those worked in the other planes. "What's the plan?" she asked.

"We wait," I said, sighing at what was to come next.

"For what?"

"The sun to rise."

Lily turned and looked fully at me, her worry no longer captured by the immediate threat before us. "What does that mean for you?"

"I don't know. I'm kinda winging this," I said as I tugged at my now numb ear absentmindedly. "I could probably try busting up the concrete and hiding underneath, but the mortal workers might find me tomorrow and either dig me up to see what happened, exposing me to sunlight, or just pour fresh concrete over me without asking questions. Either way doesn't sound like a fun time for me."

"What are you doing?" Lily asked, walking to stand next to where I was messing with my earlobe.

"I don't know. Feels weird."

"Move your hand," Lily commanded. I complied, trusting she knew something I didn't.

"What...what is it?" I asked, anxiety creeping in.

"Oh no..." she exhaled, apprehension in her features. She grabbed my ear, and ripped it clean off my head.

"OW, FUCK!" I cried out in surprise. She held the ear up to my face, where I saw it had turned black around where the blade had cut. Watching closely, I could see the decay slowly starting to spread. "Oh shit," I exhaled with bulging eyes that shot between my detached ear and the shadow cat that was cleaning itself just outside the light of the flames.

"Let me see your head," Lily ordered, dropping the ear and grabbing my skull with both hands, turning it to better see in the light. Her squinting eyes examined it thoroughly before she released me with a sigh of relief. "We got it before it spread."

"Got what?!" I asked sharply, rubbing where my ear had been. I willed a new one in place before stopping to stare into Lily's eyes.

"The darkness."

"Look," I started, annoyed, "if this was a damn movie or book, that would be a cool thing to say, but Netflix hasn't called me back yet, so you need to explain, like, now."

"The Shadow Court wants the entire universe cast in darkness. Every star extinguished until light no longer exists."

"Got that already from Taylor," I said before pointing to my ear. "What does this have to do with it?"

"Taylor? You mean TalGoid?"

"That's the one. Funny how immortals like mortal names, huh, Lily?" I winked as I said her name.

"So the Seelie Court has joined the fray? Things must be worse than I thought." She drifted deep into her thoughts as she spoke, her eyes focusing on nothing as she looked inward.

"Hi. Hey there," I said, waving my hands in front of her unfocused eyes. "Um, my ear?"

She snapped out of her zoning and, without missing a beat, said, "Shadow faeries have weapons that can extinguish the light of any living being." When I just looked blankly at her, awaiting further information, she clarified, "Your soul, John. The darkness was consuming your soul."

"Consuming how? Like turning me into one of them or just flat out killing me?"

"I don't know how it works with creatures outside of Faerie. The Shadow Court has been banished to the darkest reaches of the Fae plane and is under constant watch and key."

I thought on her words for a moment before saying, "Okay, couple things. One: either I become one of them or my soul just straight up dies and I blink out of existence? B: how can you keep shadow things contained?"

"I don't know what would happen to you, John, but we can be sure that it would be bad," Lily explained calmly. "To answer your second question: under the Faerie sun, they are corporeal and susceptible to our weapons. I'm not sure what would happen in Midworld. Those who are infected by the darkness in Faerie also become a part of their endless army. They can even bring back the dead. This is the primary reason for keeping them away from the mortal plane."

"Pretty damn good reason," I said as I locked eyes with the cat and spat a loogie toward it. It landed with an audible thwomp in front of the shadow monster, who hissed in response. "Hmm, emotional for an assassin, isn't it?"

The flames stayed consistent as they continued to eat the frames around us. The fire was small enough that hopefully mortal authorities wouldn't show up, but still bright enough to keep the Shadow Fae at bay.

"Safe to assume it won't leave until the very last second before the sun rises?" I asked while crossing my arms in displeasure.

"I can't say, but I would be willing to bet on that," Lily answered.

"What if," I started, spitballing ideas, "you took me to the Fae plane?"

Lily's eyes grew wide at my outlandish suggestion. Ulric had told me long ago, when I had first been made, that in their plane, supernaturals were to the Fae what mortals were to supes on this one. With their home field advantage, I'd be helpless. To add sprinkles to this cake, there were supes who had fled this plane to try and avoid the apocalypse that would destroy Heaven, Hell, and the Earthen plane. These supes were no doubt aware of my role in the upcoming war and would turn me in for favor with the Fae. Plus, I had broken the rules a little bit back, so John was free game around the supernatural community. Fun to be me!

"I've actually never tried to bring a person with me before. Usually we go through a door," Lily said, concern evident in her voice.

"Don't suppose there's a door just lying around, is there?"

"Unfortunately, not."

"Nah, that'd be too convenient." I thought for a moment. "What if we use chalk to draw a door and then knock three times?"

"That's a movie reference, isn't it?" Lily asked, sighing.

"You're right. We don't have any chalk," I said, ignoring her lack of movie knowledge. There had to be an answer, so I used all my brainpower to think.

"Are-are you trying to, um, poot?" Lily asked.

"Poot? The hell is—Oh, you mean fart? That's what I look like right now?" Lily nodded slowly. "Well, haven't we learned something new today," I said to myself in just above a whisper. I had figured I had a supersexy contemplation face, like the model in the cover of a magazine where he is looking off to the side, too busy and important to care about the camera.

A real idea pinged in my brain like a microwave waking your roommates up at three in the morning because you had forgotten to hit cancel at the one second mark. "Can't I just piggyback as you shift? You know, hitch a ride?"

"I would slide through and you'd simply fall on your ample behind."

"Yeah, I squat. That's why my ass is so plump," I boasted.

"Sure it is."

"Fat jokes aside, how does shifting planes work, exactly?"

"You aren't fat, my dear. Just thick."

"Is that thicc with two *c*'s, like the cool kids say?"

"With a *c-k*, I'm afraid." Ouch, my pride. "I wouldn't have you any other way, my big teddy bear," Lily purred as she ran her hands over my ultra-athletic body. The shadow cat just outside the light began gagging, loudly, as it coughed up a black, featureless hairball. Dick had comedic timing.

With the moment ruined, Lily continued, "To answer your real question: It is a part of our faerie DNA. We resonate at a frequency different than humans and supernatural creatures that are not of Fae origin. At will, I can create and slide through a hole in this plane and into my home plane."

"Is it like a seventh dimension or something?" Lily looked at me with a tilted head and mouth open, so naturally, I continued, "You know, the first dimension is a dot, like on a piece of paper, but only the dot exists. The second dimension is the same piece of paper but you can draw from edge to edge—up, down, left, and right, but on a flat plane. The third dimension is what we live in—3D *Ooooo!*" I waved my hands like I was a performing magician, effectively making my point. Lily didn't react, so I continued my TED Talk. "The fourth dimension is where you can leave and enter a place in time like walking down a hallway and choosing a door. Once you get to the fifth and sixth dimensions, oh boy—you are able to see all of time and even *possibilities* that could conceivably exist across all space and time; but only in this universe. Seven and up is where you get to alternate realities, parallel universes, and other planes. Is the Faerie plane actually one of the eleven dimensions?"

"Say 'dimension' again and I'll make you rip out your own tongue," Lily said sternly.

"Noted. But seriously. You said you can open a hole in this dim—" Lily's eyes narrowed at me, "—*plane*, and into Faerie. Right?"

"Yes."

"And you do so by your DNA that resonates at a particular frequency unique to faeries?"

"Not all faeries, just the Fae. Where are you going with this?" Lily asked, intrigued at my train of thought.

"To open this hole between the planes must require a lot of training and focus to build that mind connection. Someone like me probably couldn't learn this ability in the next thirty minutes, if ever. BUT—and bear with me now—what if *you* opened the hole and I slid through with you?"

"Do your cells have my DNA to act as a key?"

"They could," I said, opening my mouth and allowing my fangs to elongate. My *point* made (puns for everyone), I closed my mouth and continued, "I consume enough of your blood to have your DNA coursing through my veins before it is filtered out, and then you open the hole and slide on through with me holding onto you. Voilà," I finished with jazz hands.

Lily stood looking at me, her mouth hanging open. "That is one of the sexiest things you have ever said." She ran her hand over my cheek in admiration.

"I'm not just huge bulging muscles, you know. My brain is also buff."

"Mm-hmm," Lily giggled while poking a playful finger at my gut that was slightly hanging over my belt. Emphasis on slightly, damn it.

She moved her wavy blonde hair away from her neck and stepped into my embrace. We pressed our bodies together as I leaned down to kiss her neck. She smelled like spring flowers on a gentle breeze, and it made my hairs stand on end.

My fangs pierced her skin, and Fae blood began flowing into my mouth. It tasted like what I imagined the finest wine to be—sweet and rich on my tongue.

Lily's ancient blood hit my stomach and began coursing throughout my body. A moan of euphoria escaped my lips, which were still firmly attached to her succulent skin. Lily began breathing heavily but controlled as I drank her life essence.

"That should be enough," Lily said with a hint of weakness. I couldn't hear her clearly; it was as if I were on a mountain top and she was yelling from the valley below. I was submerged in the purest elation as pleasure tickled my every nerve ending.

"I said, that's enough," she repeated with commanding bravado. I heard her that time and tried to pull myself off, but my Predatory Self had grabbed the wheel while I had been lost in my jubilation, and refused to let go.

Stop, NOW! I yelled into the face of PS, whose only desire was to keep drinking the powerful, delicious Fae blood.

Normally I would fight PS to establish dominance, but we had been working on becoming a team and growing together. I took my hands off the wheel and placed one on his shoulder. *Dude, please. I trust you.*

PS looked at me with eyes that slowly began to focus and then yanked his hands away from the wheel. I nodded once at him and smiled my approval; I knew how hard that was to do.

I grabbed the wheel in my mind with both hands and pulled away from Lily's neck before saying, "I'm sorry, Lily. My Predatory Self was harder to control than I thought he would be."

The two holes in her skin closed as she looked me in the eyes while still in my embrace. "It's odd when you say 'Predatory Self.' You know that, right?"

"Probably. We can chat on it later. My body is already beginning to filter your energy from the blood."

"Where does the blood go once you've used it?" she asked, amused.

"Later! Go, go, go!"

Lily beamed her brilliant smile and then the world slid around us. It was like we were on one of those flat escalators at the airport; the scene seemed to move around us instead of us through it.

The world began to smear as if a fresh oil painting had been turned sideways, giving way to a new scene.

I blinked and we were in Faerie. Everything was bright, and I glanced up to see the sun bathing everything in its light.

Chapter 4

I yelped in panic as I dropped to the ground, covering my head with my trench coat. Lily laughed and explained, "Not your sun, lover."

My eyes were squeezed shut and my jaw was set for the pain I was fully expecting. I opened one eye, squinting at how bright everything was, and looked around. My other eye cracked open, and I slid the coat back into position, exposing my skin to the sun of Faerie.

"How interesting," I said, mesmerized as I looked around. The colors were so bright and vibrant. My mouth hung agape as I slowly spun around, taking in the warmth from the sun and the beautiful scene.

"Welcome to my home," Lily beamed, pride showing on her face.

I manifested a pair of bloodsunglasses, or at least I tried to. Lily saw the look of concentration on my face and watched with amusement as I struggled.

"You're in Faerie, lover. Your powers won't work here, including healing, so please tread carefully."

I instantly felt as helpless as a newborn deer after his mother's been murdered by a hunter. I think I got that metaphor from somewhere that'll come to me later.

"There are rules you have to follow, John," Lily said with complete seriousness. "Please pay attention." As she spoke, she formed a pair of black sunglasses that she handed to me. I put them on, in awe of her power; then again, I was in her world.

"First, don't offend anyone. The Seelie Court will not attack unless provoked."

"That's...asking a lot," I said, being just as honest with her as I was to myself.

"However," Lily continued, "the Unseelie Court can, and will, attack for any reason—or for no reason at all. Keep that in mind."

"Um...okay?"

Lily continued, "Do not take anything from anyone. Do not ask or answer questions, but do it in a way that isn't rude."

"I wanna go home," I whispered to myself as I began to breathe heavily. I had never felt this naked in all my unlife. It was as if I were mortal again.

"Not yet, dear sweet John. We have a task to complete."

"And what task is that?" I asked.

"We need to find out how the shadow got out," Lily said with a set jaw. She was clearly not happy.

"Ah, okay. Can we, ah, make it quick?" I crossed my arms over my chest, feeling exposed.

"Of course."

We started walking through Faerie toward a city in the distance. Where we had come out was a beautiful wooded area, teeming with life. Little fairies (using the traditional Disney-esque spelling) buzzed in the air like the lightning bugs on Earth. They stopped flying to stare at us before continuing their seemingly random flight patterns. Lily saw me staring.

"They are mostly harmless, given you stay on the path. The sprites live in the moment without a care in the world."

"BAMBI!" I cried out while snapping a finger and surprising Lily.

"Pardon?"

"Huh? Oh, nothing. Something I was thinking about earlier."

"Right..." Lily let the word drag as her brain filed that away and shifted gears back to what she was saying. "Stay on the road and look forward. You should be safe while you are with me."

The woods started to thin, giving way to a field of the brightest green that rivaled any tourist attraction or movie of my plane. I was mesmerized as we walked over a stream on a bridge made of stone and wood. We were stopped on the other side by a particularly nasty-looking troll that put a hand out as he blocked the road.

"Toll," the toll troll said around tusks that protruded from his bottom lip, affecting his speech.

I looked him in the eye and said, "Fuck off," in my most nonoffensive tone.

"John!" Lily chided as the troll began to chuckle under his breath.

"I got this," I said as I strode past Lily and to the soon-to-be-dead troll. As I got face-to-face with him, I pointed my finger at his chest and was about to open my mouth when the back of his hand struck my face and sent me flying backward. I hit the green ground of the field and began rolling from the inertia. Stars swam in my vision as the world spun around me. I propped up on my elbows, head reeling, and tried to focus on my attacker. I heard a distant cry from somewhere a mile away. It was muffled, but I could make out "ON" was being said. With my noggin feeling like a bobblehead on the dashboard of an off-road jeep, I looked at Lily, who was frantically motioning at me.

I shook my head once and noticed nothing improved. The world was still spinning and my jaw was beginning to ache something fierce. I lifted a hand off the ground to cup my face and fell to the side. Oh, right—my arm was holding me up.

I shook my head again, and the world that was spinning slowed and leveled off, becoming still again.

"John!" I heard Lily frantically cry out. "Get out of the grass!"

"What?" My words came out slurring and made my face sting with pain. "Like in *Jurassic Park*?" Something tugged at my coat's collar, drawing my attention. It was a sprite. A cute, adorable, innocent-looking sprHOLY SHIT IT HAS FANGS. The sprite opened its little mouth much wider than what should have been physically possible and chomped down on my coat, taking a clean chunk out of the durable leather. I gulped. Another fairy of the Disney spelling landed on my boot while two more landed on my pelvis. They looked at me curiously, twitching their innocent little heads, then opened their horrific mouths.

"NO!" I yelped in panic as I swung my hands wildly at my crotch. I was *not* about to test the whole not-being-able-to-heal thing on Little John. My swung connected, and the little fairies tumbled through the air, shrieking their tiny rage. I kicked the last one, which had already chomped onto my steel-toed boot, and scrambled to get up. More balls of light swarmed toward me as I sprinted, rather slowly, to where Lily stood. I looked at my legs, which weren't a blur, and tripped over my own feet. My face smashed into the grass, breaking my sunglasses as I slid.

"Get up!" Lily yelled in frustration as she stepped into the grass, stomping over to where I was struggling to rise. This pain was all new; sharp and debilitating while my body was sluggish and weak, as if filled with cement. I rose on all fours as Lily approached. I tried getting up, but I was still dazed. She strode over to me and grabbed my trench coat at the collar. I was a kitten in his mama's jaws as Lily dragged me to the road where the troll remained, arms crossed and a smile on its face.

"What...just happened?" I asked between pants as something thundered in my ears.

"You have no power here, John Cook. I told this to you, and you refused to listen, almost getting yourself killed."

"Why am I so heavy?" I asked, standing up and looking down at my thick legs.

"Your body is powered by magic, whether or not you want to believe that simple fact," Lily scolded like an angry school teacher explaining why I couldn't eat the glue.

"But I know how my energy works and why I need blood. I can explain it scientifically—it's not magic!"

"Magic is just science we don't understand yet, while science we do know is still magic. Do you understand?" Lily asked.

"Not really," I answered loudly. There was a drum beating close by. How was no one else hearing it?

"Just because you know how something works doesn't mean it's not still magic," Lily reiterated.

What she was saying congealed in my brain, changing my lifelong perspective on the concept of what was magic and what was science. I was taken aback by that. This was all too much information at one time for my nonpreternatural brain to handle. First the counterintuitive rules, then the realization that I was Bambi in this plane, followed by the fact that everything I had known to be fact was now in question. I was used to my mind solidifying the information it took in in an instant without having to try and commit anything to memory. I was using an atrophied muscle I hadn't even thought about since I'd been a mortal on a farm in Ireland. I took in a breath and choked on something warm. My fingers investigated my face, only to pull away covered in blood.

"What the..." I exhaled in disbelief.

"As I said, you can't heal while in Faerie, not even minor wounds, and your nose is broken."

"Can I go home now?" I all but whimpered, feeling the blood running over my lips and into my beard.

In front of us, the troll was shaking from all the mirth he was partaking in as if he were at a chuckle buffet—all you can freaking eat. My fists clenched and Lily placed a tender hand on my shoulder in a gentle warning.

My Fae companion and guide turned to the troll, stuck out her chest while lifting her nose before saying, "Perhaps you know not with whom you speak, insignificant troll."

The troll stiffened while chuffing in anger as it turned to fully face its offender. It gritted its teeth, lifted its hands to grab at a spear on its back, and then froze. A look of confusion crossed its face, followed by one of recognition, before it dropped to its knees while slapping its hands on the ground in a show of submission.

"Pl-please forgive me," the troll stammered fearfully. "I didn't know it was you, Mistress."

"Mistress?" I asked with a nasally voice while pinching my nose closed.

"Later," Lily whispered.

"Please, pass undisturbed, Mistress," the toll troll whined out. As he finished speaking, he crawled on all fours to the side of the road, daring to enter the lush green fields of death.

"Thank you, my dear," Lily said as she walked past, a swagger in her steps. I followed closely behind, holding my leaking nose while a strange metallic taste rolled down my throat. It tasted...funny. Like pennies instead of a fine wine.

"Lily," I said, "Am I still a vampire here?"

"Don't be silly, sweet John. You are still you, just without all the fun extras that you have grown accustomed to in your universe."

"That makes sense; I have been accused of being extra before." A thought struck me. "So this *is* a different dim—" I started before Lily twirled on her heels to look me dead in the eyes, daring me to finish that sentence. "...u-universe. Different universe. I knew it!"

"Congratulations, John. Do you want to say the night sky is full of stars next? Both comments would be on the same level of magnitude."

"No. I'd like to say 'the night is dark and full of terrors,' but that might get me sued."

Lily shook her head as she walked just ahead of me.

"Hey, I could have gone with a *Star Wars* reference when you said 'magnitude,'" I said with air quotes. She ignored me as we walked at a fast pace toward a castle in the distance.

"Is that Oz?"

"No more movie references," Lily said.

"That's like asking me not to breathe."

"You don't need to breathe. You only do so to make obscure movie references and annoy me."

"That's not true," I said, feigning hurt feelings. "I annoy everyone equally. I'm an equal opportunity annoyer."

"You are doing quite the job right now. Top marks."

"I think I need to breathe now, Lily. I don't like it, but it does feel...kinda good."

"Hmm, how interesting," Lily purred.

"Seriously, where are we going?" I asked, wanting this to be over.

"I am taking you to the Seelie Court."

When she didn't continue, I asked, "Why?"

Sighing heavily like a parent whose child won't stop asking questions, Lily answered, "So you can tell them about the Shadow Fae that attacked you tonight."

"Me? Why me? Won't they listen to you?" I asked nervously.

"This is your responsibility. The Seelie Court has reached out to you already and extended friendship, have they not? They will be most curious about the events that unfolded tonight and how they came to pass."

"Can't I just send an email or something?"

"Your cowardice is a turn off," Lily said while keeping her gaze forward. That stung, but she was right—I was being a little bitch. Time to man up.

We walked for an hour or ten minutes—I'm terrible at time management—and the castle grew as we approached. And I didn't mean in just perspective—it *grew*.

The castle was imbedded in a tree that enveloped the sky with its reaching, full branches. The temperature, which had been warm to me, dropped to a pleasant coolness as we entered the shadow of the magnificent tree. It was then I noticed I had been sweating profusely.

The castle jutted out of the middle of the tree several hundred feet in the air, as if an army of history's most talented woodworkers had carved it out of the bark. Under the wooden castle, a village—no, a modern *city*—grew like shrubs on the forest floor. Right angles and buildings as tall as any on the Earthen plane surrounded the tree on multiple levels that swirled upward like a spiral staircase. The closer we came, the higher and wider the tree grew. Every step forward brought the city five steps closer.

I was aware that Lily had turned her head to view my reaction. "There is more magic in Faerie than you can possibly fathom. It is best to have an open mind and a shut mouth."

Normally I would have a wheel of quips in my mind that I would spin and then spit out, but I was in genuine awe of the size of this tree, and I was running out of breath. The tree reached miles into the sky and had a circumference that spanned a proportionate amount in relation to its height.

At the base of the tree was a gate made out of thick roots that organically opened to reveal a blinding light. As the tendrils slithered away, we stepped into the light and onto a bustling city street. I blinked and turned around to see a waist-high wall carved from the bark, the vine gate having completely disappeared. I nearly tripped over my own feet as I backed away from the ledge that was hundreds of feet above the ground below. I had just been on that ground a few steps ago! Oh, man, I did not like feeling like a mortal almost as much as I did not like green eggs and ham.

As I backed blindly away from the ledge, I bumped into someone that responded by backhanding me to the ground like a redheaded stepchild.

"Watch it, fool," the citizen said, turning his head forward and ignoring me. I stood, fists clenched, and was about to say something when I remembered how easily the troll had overpowered me.

I inhaled deeply, held it, and whispered, "Three, two, one; one, two, three. What the heck is bothering me?" It helped me gain control but also brought to the surface that I wanted to burn everything around me down. I was scared, and the desire to punish the powerful creatures around me was near overwhelming.

Between gritted teeth and eyes screwed tight, I whispered to myself, "Control it, John. Use your mind for once." I opened my eyes and saw the city, but not Lily. Looking around for my companion, I saw a cornucopia of Fae wandering the streets in modern clothing. Most had a rectangular device displaying…were-were they…yes, they were freaking cell phones…in Faerie. I wonder what network they used? Fae Mobile?

Some citizens had plain T-shirts and baggy pants, while others donned full business suits that glinted like scales in the sunlight. Wait, sunlight? I shielded my eyes with my hand and looked up to see the sun shining through the canopy of lush leaves as if they weren't there. Though it felt cooler, the light was basically as bright as having direct line of sight.

"What the…?" I mouthed, "Oh, right—magic." I lowered my hand and squinted ahead to the upward slope of the city. Lily had mentioned I was to do this alone. She always had to make things difficult for me. Walking toward the castle, I gulped at the thought of what awaited me at the end of the spiraling road.

All Fae-phones went off at the same time in the equivalent of an Amber Alert. I froze as countless Fae stopped where they stood, looked at their phones, then locked their gazes on me like a lioness identifying the weak gazelle.

Chapter 5

"Hello," I said lamely as I slowly waved my open hand in a half circle in greeting. The crowd of pointy-eared elves, tusk-mouthed trolls, beautiful nymphs, stubby dwarves, and several other varieties of Fae all glared at me. No one said anything or moved as assessing eyes glided over my vulnerable body.

Another alert sounded in a cacophonous crescendo that made me feel like I was the star of a horror movie. Eyes shot to screens before returning back to me. Those on the street moved to the sidewalk while never taking their gaze from me. After a moment of standing awkwardly with my back to a wall, I got the hint and stepped onto the road. Glancing up the massive spiral, I located the castle and audibly gulped at the impossible distance.

"Shiiiiiiiit," I exhaled in a long breath. I didn't want to spend another moment around these scary ass denizens. I dropped my head and began walking timidly as heads slowly turned to follow me.

Following Lily's advice, I kept my eyes on the ground directly in front of me so as not to accidentally offend anyone, which would equate to full permission to do me harm, right? This was the Seelie Court, wasn't it? Yeah, it was the Unseelie that could attack for any reason. Why was I having trouble remembering? My brain was operating like it was the middle of the day, but, you know, on the other plane. As I walked the incline, I became increasingly out of breath and my profuse sweating grew to a torrential cascade down my back. My heartbeat thundered in my ears as...wait...the fuck? Breath? Sweat? My *heart*beat? Oh God, I was a mortal. WAIT! "Oh *God*?"

"What's happening to me?" I asked myself between heaving breaths.

My mind raced with the implications of being *human* again. Even the word felt wrong to use. I looked inward, only to realize that I couldn't appear in the control room of my mind. I was stuck behind my eyes.

Dude, what's going on? I asked my Predatory Self. Silence was my answer. On the precipice of losing my shit, I screamed in my head, *PS! DUDE, ARE YOU THERE? YOU CAN'T LEAVE ME ALONE HERE!* A breeze blew across the street, kissing my skin and tugging at my trench and hair that spilled out from my beanie. There was no other sound both externally or internally, except for my thudding heartbeat.

Lily's words came back into my mind. I was still *me*, but without the extra stuff. I assumed she meant my vampirism and all the abilities that went with it, including PS. I felt more alone in that moment than I had ever felt in my entire life and unlife combined. It hadn't occurred to me until that very moment that I relied on PS for both his strength and his companionship. Granted, he didn't speak much, but that was just fine with me because I sure as hell loved to talk.

I became light-headed as everything compounded on top of each other, pressing on my chest until I couldn't breathe.

BREATHE! I sucked in a lungful of air after realizing I had been holding my breath while deep in thought. My nose was swollen shut, so I gaped like a fish out of water until my head cleared. I panted heavily before setting my jaw and continuing my journey to the top. My nose had stopped bleeding, but that bitch still throbbed with each pound of my pulsing heart. I was growing tired of this and wanted to go home.

As I rounded the corner, the castle gates came into view. I screwed up my face in bewilderment and turned around to look over the horizon; I was considerably higher than I had been moments before. Keeping my mind open and mouth shut, I quickly accepted Fae physics by turning back to the castle and making my way toward the enormous gate. A sliver of brilliant light poured from the bottom of the wooden gate as it slowly lifted open. Chains rattled as a door the size of a vertical football field was hoisted into the outside wall of a castle that extended several hundred yards into the blue Faerie sky.

When the door cleared enough room for my six-foot frame, I crossed the threshold. As I did, the gate stopped and reversed to close again with a ground-shaking thud. My anxiety upped in intensity a notch as I became a bird trapped in a cage.

"Welcome to Faerie, John," a familiar voice announced.

"Taylor!" I greeted my pointy-eared acquaintance. "It's so freaking good to see a friendly face!"

"Curious about how you arrived," Taylor said with a slight crinkle in his brow, "but, it is good to see you too, though it has been quite some time. Come, she is waiting."

"Who?"

"The queen of the Seelie Court," Taylor said devotedly.

"Cool," I drawled out. "Have you seen Lily by any chance?"

"Pardon?" Taylor asked as he tilted his head and raised one eyebrow.

"Nothing," I relented. "What's this queen's name?"

"Queen Tatiana of the Summer Court."

"Where have I heard that name before?"

"Our queen has become well known across your plane due to her affinity for helping humans. There are countless stories about her deeds spanning centuries of your literature."

"Neat. Glad I came to this court and not that other one. What was it again?"

"Unseelie, made up of the Winter and Autumn Courts."

We started walking to the castle as we chitchatted.

"What about the Shadow Court?"

Taylor stopped walking and looked at me with a stony face. "What about them?"

"That's kinda why I'm here, man. I was attacked by this huge shadow monster tonight."

"On the mortal plane?" Taylor clarified.

"Yeah."

"And you survived?" His eyes searched my body, looking for evidence of our battle.

"It nicked my ear, but I removed it before the darkness spread."

"Darkness? Who helped you? How do you know these things?" he probed.

"A friend. They told me I needed to come here and explain things to, I assume, your queen."

"Rightfully so," Taylor said while deep in thought, eyes drifting to the ground. After a moment, his head snapped back up and he said, "Right, let's carry on. She awaits." Taylor increased his stride, forcing me to increase my walk to a canter.

We walked through impressive wooden double doors that swung open from the middle. An ornate green rug spanned the width of the hallway we stepped into and ran the entire length. As I looked down, I noticed that it wasn't a rug but rather thick moss that had vines growing along the edges in a geometric pattern.

"Whoa," I said in awe.

"Magnificent, isn't it?" Taylor responded, pleased. "Just wait, you haven't seen anything yet."

"I don't know," I started, thinking about the castle that grew into a magnificent tree the closer you got to it, "I've seen some shit."

Taylor answered with a simple smile. We continued down the hall, which smelled pleasantly of flowers, and entered a large throne room. It was impressive to say the least; wooden pillars made of thick vines that twisted around one another held up a dome-shaped ceiling. Stars lit up the dome and seemed to move. Actually, they *did* move. The scene shifted from a pristine night sky with stars that shone like dense clouds to a roaring ocean with huge waves crashing on a rocky shoreline.

"So, you are John. She was right after all," said a confident, sultry voice that instantly seduced me.

"Who? Lily?" I asked, having heard this introduction before from Ulric. "Wait, let me guess; it's not for me to know."

"Mmm, I like this one," the Seelie queen said as she leaned forward in the impressive throne that grew in the middle of the circular room. My eyes started at the open ceiling, where the living throne began at one point, and followed its length downward, where it expanded in girth. The seat of the throne sat halfway between ceiling and floor. Precisely carved wooden stairs lead to the throne where she sat. The queen was wearing a form-fitting moss dress the same color as the hallway floor. An ornate crown made of twisting vines perched atop her beautiful brown hair. Flowers grew sporadically around her crown and even in her hair. Amethyst eyes glinted in the light, reminiscent of my own—only hers seemed alive compared to my own undead ones.

"Play nice. She could be your greatest ally or your most fearsome enemy," Taylor whispered as he leaned close to my ear.

I looked at him in challenge and said, "You do know the Devil himself is after me, right?"

"The Devil," the queen barked, "is not of this plane, and thus, has no power in Faerie. *I* am the Alpha here."

Deciding it was best to make friends rather than new enemies, which I was *so* good at, I said, "Queen Tatiana, please forgive my tongue. It is a great honor to be in your presence." From my peripheral vision, I saw Taylor nod slightly in approval.

"Oh, John, I would do more than forgive your...tongue," Queen Tatiana said with a seductive smile that turned my knees to jelly. My mind shot to Lily, and my stability returned. I was accustomed to the effects Fae women had on me and was used to fighting for my senses.

"Curiouser and curiouser," Tatiana purred as she crossed her legs, placing an elbow on a knee and stroking her chin. Without preamble, she uncrossed her legs, stood up swiftly, and began descending the stairs. She flowed gracefully, as if floating on a breeze, a warm smile cresting her face. She stopped right in front of me, the top of her head coming to my nose. Standing within my bubble of personal space, she began squealing like a schoolgirl while jogging in place. Then she threw her arms around me and squeezed, tight.

"Ow," was all I could manage. My body was a mess from my legendary fight with the troll. Maybe next time I wouldn't use the his-fist-to-my-face style of martial arts to make it a fair fight.

Pulling away, Tatiana looked at me and said, "You look terrible, John." She sniffed the air in front of her, crinkling her cute button nose as she did.

"I *feel* terrible. I-I think I'm human again. And that smell is me, I think. I can't really smell anything at the moment," I said with a voice that was still nasal. "I'm just not myself right now."

She burst out with a throaty laugh, doubling over in mirth. Holding her belly, she looked up at me and said between fits of laughter, "You...you're still you...sweet John." Regaining control over herself, she stood straight up and placed a hand on my cheek. "Different universe, different rules. Once we get you back to Midworld, your powers will return. Until then," she said while closing her eyes. Warmth spread from her hand and over my face, startling me.

"Stay still, please," Taylor instructed.

The warmth spread over my head and down my torso, expanding to encompass my entire being. It felt wonderful. My nose popped painfully, making me clench my teeth and groan. The pain quickly receded, and I took in a deep breath through my nose. The cool air felt awesome going down my nostrils as it filled my lungs. Breathing through your mouth was one thing, but man, it was infinitely better to inhale through your nose.

The warmth retreated from my fingers and toes, then arms, legs, torso, and finally my head. It left me feeling complete and healed, almost like my old self again.

"Wow," was all I could manage as my hands explored the injuries I had sustained. Taylor nudged me lightly with his elbow. I turned to look at him, and he nodded toward Tatiana.

"Oh, right. Thank you," I said to the queen of the Seelie Court.

"You are very welcome, John."

At that moment, I became aware of the smells in the air. I was mesmerized by the ocean spray that misted in the air above the throne, bringing with it the aroma of salt, wet rock, and sand. It was intoxicating to my human nose. As a vampire, I smelled everything individually, but this, this was one smell blended together that rode in waves—as a wave crashed, salt would dominate the air, then the wet rock and sand as the water receded; but still one smell. The ignorance I experienced at that moment was, indeed, bliss.

I must have closed my eyes and began sniffing the air like some sort of dog because Tatiana began to giggle.

"Huh? Oh, ya, the, ah…" I started tripping over my words as I pointed upward, "smells good…ceiling, I mean."

Tatiana's smile turned slightly predatory as a new scent invaded my nostrils.

"Oh," was all I could moan as my body responded eagerly to the pheromones that excited every nerve in my body. Did anybody else's pants get tight all of a sudden?

"Are you enjoying your sense of smell?" she asked as her fingertips glided over my chest and down my belly.

I began sweating again as I nodded. Damn, it was a lot harder to fight the urge as a mortal.

"Is there anything I can do to repay the favor?" I choked out before I instantly realized that I should *not* have asked that of a Fae noble.

Her eyes purposely scanned my body up and down before saying, "Oh yes, there most certainly is." I gulped audibly, which made her smile deviously. I felt a pang of guilt that what my body was doing was wrong, and I fought harder.

"You are unsure," she said, scrunching up her brow in playful concentration. "Does your heart belong to another?" My mind shot reflexively to Lily.

"I-I don't know," I stammered weakly. I didn't know what Lily and I were, only that I was falling in love with her—if I wasn't already there.

"Most interesting indeed," Tatiana exclaimed as her features relaxed into neutrality. Dropping her scent and control over my weak, mortal body, she said, "Now, to business. What is it you came all this way to tell me, oh damned one?"

I shook my head to clear my clouded thoughts. "The Shadow…" I started before being interrupted by the portal above the throne shifting to complete darkness. The light inside the throne room was swallowed by complete blackness. Someone yelped like a little girl. (It was probably Tatiana and definitely not me.) Candlelight erupted around the perimeter of the room where the pillars stood. On the throne appeared a large man dressed all in black. Queen Tatiana gasped in shock as she saw the man.

"Oberon," escaped her lips just above a whisper.

"Oh no," Taylor breathed in dismay, taking a step closer to his queen.

"Hello, wife," Oberon said, disdain dripping off his words. His voice was authoritative and suited for the head of the table at a huge corporation. He sat relaxed on the throne, one leg hanging off an armrest. Oberon had a chiseled jaw—that made me jealous for some reason—black hair that was slicked back, and black eyes that matched his outfit. He wore a two-button suit, silk dress shirt topped with an ascot, and slacks, all the color of the void swirling above the throne. The candles slowly died back down, the point having been made.

"Oberon, what have you done?" Queen Tatiana asked with profound concern in her voice.

"What have I done?" Oberon asked accusingly. "What have *I* done? I've done what should have been done eons ago." As he spoke, he aggressively got to his feet and began stomping down the stairs toward us. Taylor edged closer to Tatiana. Oberon shifted his gaze from her to him, taking notice of his posture, and then flung an arm out to the side. Though Oberon was still several yards away, Taylor yelped and flew into the darkness. It was as if he had been struck by a semitruck that echoed a terrible, bone-shattering crunch as it hit, making the pit of my stomach drop. I couldn't see where he had landed with my mortal eyes. Unfathomable fear and helplessness blossomed in my chest, creeping up my throat to choke me. My breathing became labored while my ears thudded with each pounding heartbeat. My mouth hung open and eyes grew wide as Oberon approached us. I did my best to fold in on myself in an attempt to be less of a target.

Tatiana stepped forward, putting herself between me and Oberon. Anger exploded from her in a torrent of words, "How *dare* you show aggression to me and mine. I am the queen of this court and will be treated as such. You are in my domain."

"Something that I learned in the darkness, dear queen, is if someone has to say what they are, then they are weak," Oberon said, eyes gleaming. Even the whites of his eyes were black. "Actions demonstrate more than words ever will."

"Be sure to taste your words before you spit them out, husband," Tatiana warned, hands opening at her sides. The air shimmered around her, displaying her raw power. "I am all-powerful in my bailiwick."

"You were..." Oberon said as he pulled a familiar gladius from the sheath at his side. He gripped the white handle with gold trim and held it down at his side, the blade at an angle to the floor.

My eyes nearly popped from their sockets as I recognized the angelic sword from the alley. It had nearly cut me in half the last time I had seen it.

"Oh...shit..." was all I could manage as the blade was ignited with flames the color of the darkest night. They weren't heavenflame or hellfire, I assumed because he wasn't angelic in origin. Instead, it was like he had poured his own hatred and malice into the sword, producing the flames in the plane where he was strongest.

Sensing danger, Tatiana threw her hands out, lancing pure energy toward Oberon in a crackle of power. Her husband swiped at the attack, catching it with the blade and burning it to nothing in an instant. As Oberon brought the angel blade back down, white armor lined with gold formed on his body, hidden by an intricate glamour—it was like watching someone film a pile of ashes being blown by a strong wind, and then playing the footage in reverse. The armor appeared from thin air and formed around him; all but the gauntlet I had in my *Battlefield Earth* collectors cup cabinet at home.

Tatiana cried out in despair as the celestial armor was corrupted before our very eyes. White and gold started bleeding to black and red. Oberon laughed as he stepped forward, the flames from the blade licking the air with black fire.

"John, run!" Tatiana cried out as she lunged for Oberon, grabbing his sword arm with one hand and his throat with the other. She didn't need to tell me twice. I turned and plunged into the black veil where Taylor had been slung. As I did, I heard Tatiana shriek in pain from behind as I stumbled through the darkness. I dropped to all fours, crawling like an infant, searching for Taylor. My hand found warm liquid on the moss at the entrance to one of the hallways leading to the throne room. Feeling both relief and terror, I crawled forward until my hands found Taylor's limp legs. I could make out a light at the end of the tunnel that barely illuminated Taylor's form. I stood, picking him up in a fireman's carry. He let out a weak moan that made my chest relax in relief. I knew for certain I would not have survived an attack like that in my current predicament.

I struggled carrying the tall man down the hallway and away from danger. Daring a glance, I turned slightly as I ran to try and look into the throne room. The abyss stared back at me. Silence screamed through sheer walls, deafening me. My heart thundered in my chest, threatening to rip out of my rib cage. I tasted blood as I heaved lungfuls of air. I was out of breath from both panic and being a not-so-fit mortal again.

I tripped on my own feet, my thick steel-toed boots weighing me down. From the angle I was running, I fell on top of Taylor, who didn't groan this time.

"Shit, shit, shit, shit, shit," I cried out as I struggled to get to my feet again.

A whooshing sound followed by that of a thunderous impact resonated behind me. Frozen, I turned to stare at the throne room, which was only visible through a shrinking hallway. Flashes of light streaked from the ceiling to the floor of the throne room, growing in numbers until a continuous wave poured down. Purple eyes fiercely glowed where the flashes landed in the darkness. First a few, then hundreds opened all at once, illuminating the throne room in a purple haze.

"Shiiiiiiiiiiiiiiiiiiiiiiit," I exclaimed calmly and not at all in the most mind-shattering terror of my entire existence. With a surge of adrenaline, I grabbed Taylor, put him over my shoulder, and sprinted for the exit. Sweat stung my eyes as I ran. Blackness started to swallow the edges of my vision. I didn't know if this was from the fucking invasion of the shadow creatures doing some evil Fae magic behind me, or I was just out of shape. Probably a little from column A and a little from column B.

As we cleared the threshold of the hallway and ran toward the gate out of the castle, I screamed at the top of my lungs, "OPEN THE GATE!"

An explosion tore through the castle behind me, sending a shock wave out that nearly made me kiss the ground with my face. I dared not turn around this time, having learned my fat-guy-running-with-a-very-tall-man-on-his-shoulders lesson about balance and inertia. From the corners of my vision, I saw blackness spilling like a rushing tidal wave over the organic wooden walkway of the castle's exterior.

At that point, I was breathing so hard that my dry throat was making wheezing noises. The muscles in my legs and shoulder ached from where I bore Taylor's weight, but I kept running for dear life. I couldn't feel my legs anymore, but they kept pumping one after the other, so I was thankful.

The door grew closer as I ran, but it did not open. I took in a breath that was so deep it teased breaking my ribs apart, and shrieked in sheer adrenaline-laced panic, "OPEN THE FUCKING GATE! I HAVE TAYLOR!"

Gears rumbled as the door began to lift skyward. I dared a look to the side and saw the castle walls were being painted in hungry blackness. It grew and ate the life of the wooden structure as if the darkness were alive and had an appetite that was insatiable. Obsidian stone grew like a dry sponge being submerged in water, replacing the living wood of the castle with lifeless, smooth rock. I briefly wondered how Oberon could get obsidian before I remembered it was just volcanic rock. Obsidian didn't expressly mean it was from Hell, though the black stone forged in the fires of Hell was something to be feared.

A leaf brushed my face as I ran, causing me to look up. As I did, green leaves shriveled and dried, turning brown before leaping to their deaths in a mass suicide. Paper-thin corpses blanketed the sky, blotting out the light with their impossible numbers.

Cries of confusion and dismay echoed throughout the city streets as the citizens of the Seelie Court spilled onto the streets and into the darkness. It reminded me of the night of September 11th when I awoke and watched humans on TV screaming as planes crashed into the World Trade Centers. The hollow expressions that crossed the faces of the Fae as the impossible happened before their eyes was relatable and universal across all planes. Their entire existences had revolved around this tree they called home, and now it was being deformed, destroyed, and violated before their unbelieving eyes.

Taylor stirred and I stopped running to set him down on the sidewalk.

"Tay-Taylor, snap out of it," I wheezed between gasping breaths as I doubled over and grabbed my knees. I thought my sides were going to split open. Taylor's head rolled on his shoulders before he locked his gaze on me. I watched as his eyes went from glazed to focused with preternatural speed, which sent a pang of jealousy and longing for my abilities. Being mortal sucked.

Taylor sat up straight and started looking around, the events unfolding before his eyes keeping him on the precipice of his stupor. One of his hands snaked up to his head where I noticed a massive purple-and-green bruise that bloomed under his alabaster skin.

"Taylor!" I yelled into his face. "Focus!"

His eyes locked on mine again and he nodded once.

"Get me to a door. We have to get back to Midworld. It's not safe here anymore."

To accentuate my point, an ominous dark globe started to slowly eclipse the Fae sun.

"Um, buddy?" I said, turning to look at Taylor whose eyes were glued to the star that was now fully evident through the bare branches of the dying tree. "I'm willing to bet that we wanna be outta here by the time that Death Star blots out the sun."

"Agreed," Taylor said urgently, standing up on unsure legs. He grabbed my shoulder for stability before saying, "Come, there's a doorway close."

With me as his crutch, Taylor began wistfully walking down the street and away from the castle, which was now completely made of black stone.

"What's happening?" I asked Taylor.

"Oberon has embraced the darkness," Taylor uttered sorrowfully. "But how? He was supposed to be in Mab's prison."

A thought crossed my mind, making me cringe. As we came to one of the skyscrapers, I stopped and asked Taylor, "Hypothetically: what if he had the gladius of an angel?"

Taylor whirled to look at me, eyes blazing. "What do you mean?" he demanded as he grabbed my shoulders in a death grip and shook me once.

"I kinda maybe killed an angel, got superhigh off his blood, and lost the body. Oberon had his weapon and armor—minus a gauntlet I still have back at my place."

Taylor squeezed harder, making me yelp, before taking in a deep breath through his teeth and saying, "We will discuss this later. For now, we must get out of Faerie."

"Why?" I asked, fearing I already knew the answer.

"Because he has freed the Shadow Court. Darkness will consume everything...and everyone." At the last part, Taylor spoke barely above a whisper. My heart broke at what I had done.

"Consequences I can't avoid..." I said, trailing off in thought. The Archangel Gabriel's words ricocheted around my skull.

Ignoring my state, Taylor pulled us inside the building and ran to a metal security desk. I was taken aback at how everything on the inside was modern; tile, metal, glass, even the furniture looked familiar.

Taylor pulled a key from a chain around his neck and stuck it into a slot. A plastic cover lifted up, revealing a red glowing button. Taylor slammed his fist down on it, and an alarm that was near deafening bleated outside. My hands shot to cover my ears before they had the chance to start bleeding from the sheer decibels of the alarm. In the corner of my vision, I noticed the front doors lifting up, creating a massive entrance through which citizens began spilling in. They formed several lines and began filing in front of a large half-circle structure that was behind the security desk. It was made of vines interlacing around one another, with sigils etched into them. As I watched, the air in the center of the wooden structure began to shimmer.

"Remember your glamours!" Taylor yelled over the din of mumblings and the alarm. At his command, each creature morphed into a human as their concealment spells were cast. It was impressive to see everyone in Faerie being able to do that with ease.

Once completed, the Fae walked in unison into the portal to Midworld. They reminded me of a synchronistic army as they paraded. Left foot, right foot, left, right.

Taylor manned his post, ensuring his fellow Faerians all made it to safety. My respect for him instantly grew at that moment. I stood by his side, awaiting further instructions.

Screams of terror and agony pierced the air. Even muffled by the alarm, it made my hairs stand on end. The line continued as if nothing had happened, though some heads did swivel nervously toward the back by those who were closest to the screams. I looked out the open entrance and saw what had caused the cries. Darkness had swallowed the street, the sun almost consumed. Black figures stood on the street, their purple eyes and sharklike teeth the only things I could distinguish in the shadows. They each carried crude weapons and were attacking the Fae that attempted to make it into the building. Elves manifested sleek swords, bows and arrows, and golden armor. Dwarves summoned giant hammers and axes with metallic armor. Trolls pulled spears out of thin air and threw them with grace and skill as they moved behind the armor-plated melee creatures.

A seed of hope was planted in my chest as the defending Fae formed a line in front of the entrance, protecting their brothers and sisters who were fleeing through the portal. Hammers crushed featureless bodies as arrows pierced chests, swords removed heads, and spears found new homes in torsos. The shadow monsters displayed no fear as they chaotically charged forward to their own slaughter.

The seed of hope blossomed into a smile on my face as I shook my fists in front of me in excitement that we could win this.

The sun was consumed then. The light faded, with only the office lights offering illumination just outside the building. The line of Fae defenders, who stood just outside the reach of the lights, inched closer to one another nervously as their heads searched back and forth, seeking their attackers. A black goblin-looking creature leaped through the air and was met with a troll spear that soared right through him. The featureless goblin with purple eyes and gleaming, jagged teeth landed on an elf and began tearing it to shreds with his clawed hands and fanged teeth. The elves and dwarves on the front line turned to attack the shadow beast, but only succeeded in stabbing and smashing their fallen companion. The elf's blue blood was slung over the line as his friends lifted their weapons to continue their attack of the shadow monster. My smile dropped to a frown and my heart tightened as I realized the weapons of the Seelie Court had no effect on the Shadow Court now that the sun had been swallowed.

The lights in the building flickered a few times before fading out, as if the power had been cut to the building. Only a red flashing light above the portal provided any illumination now.

"John, we must go, NOW!" Taylor screamed at me as he grabbed my coat and hauled me to the doorway. The alarm had died, leaving a painful ringing in my ears.

I turned my head and watched as more of the line was yanked into the darkness, where their screams pierced my ears—forever staining my mind and haunting my dreams.

The last of the citizens made their way through the portal as Taylor turned to the remaining defenders and yelled, "Destroy the gate!"

Without hesitation, the defenders turned and ran toward the portal. Just before Taylor and I went through, I saw the few remaining brave soldiers lifting their weapons as they swarmed the living vines of the half circle, ready to sacrifice themselves to close the portal forever. Behind them, a wave of featureless bodies surged in, filling the office building like a powerful tidal wave.

Chapter 6

We exited deep inside a dark cavern. My strength rushed back through my veins like a trail of gunpowder being ignited. I closed my eyes, clenched my fists, and moaned as raw power enveloped my entire body.

A loud pop reverberated through the cavern as the portal was permanently shut. I opened my eyes in surprise at the sound and saw Taylor lower his head in reverence.

"They gave their lives so that we may live," he said as a tear rolled down his bruising cheek.

"They didn't even hesitate, man," I responded in awe. I wanted to yell and jump at having my strength back, but now wasn't the time. I wouldn't be here if it wasn't for those who had sacrificed themselves.

"It is the greatest of honors for them to give up their immortality for their brothers and sisters." Taylor turned to the Fae refugees, speaking loud and clear for all to hear. The cavern gave his voice a bravado that seemed fitting for the occasion. "Let them be remembered for the heroes they were. May they find peace in the Veil."

"Peace in the Veil," the crowd echoed in unison.

"What are you going to do now?" I asked Taylor.

"There are contingencies in place." I watched the events unfold once again in the theater of my mind, confused at how the footage seemed to be from a faulty VHS tape rather than my usual crystal-clear clarity. As I watched in rapture, I focused on how the last defenders destroyed the portal rather than simply walking through and saving themselves. The door was right there! The absolute discipline was beyond impressive. I wouldn't be able to convince myself I would have done the same thing in their place.

I turned to PS and said, *Put that shit on YouTube and watch the world's armies shit their collective pants with envy. Am I righ—DUDE! You're back!* I cried out, having forgotten for the briefest of moments how I had lost him. I gripped PS in a bear hug and squeezed him tight. *Thought I lost you, bro!* PS returned the embrace and shuddered, relief evident. *Were you with me while I was in Faerie?* We broke our embrace, but I kept my hands on his shoulders for fear that he would be taken away from me again; PS shook his head in answer. *So, it was a blink from the burning house to now?* He nodded. *Well, let me catch you up, brother.* Still in the theater, I played the events scene by scene. They were fuzzy with missing frames. I could only assume it was from the fact my mind had been human at the time; but they were clear enough to get the picture.

Once we went through the portal, I shut off the projector, looked at PS, and said, *What do you think about that?* PS crossed his arms, lowered his head, and shook it from side to side, indicating that nothing good would come of this. *I hear you, man. They got out because of me. I killed the stupid angel, and that king guy somehow got the gladius and armor.* Something crossed my mind like a bolt of lightning. *But not all of it! The gauntlet! I don't know why, but that gauntlet is the key. Can you feel it too?* PS nodded once in agreement, looking from the ground to me with hope in his eyes. *Dude...I* started, feeling the emotions come on strong, *it's good to have you back. I-I think I've taken you for granted all these centuries, and I'm sorry. I'm not me without you.*

PS smiled at me. Then his skin started changing from a dark tone to a lighter one and said, *Nor am I, without you.*

Did-did you just talk? I stammered in disbelief.

I did. You have come to accept me as a part of you rather than a disease that must be compartmentalized. With that self-realization comes a new chapter in your existence.

Neat! I said enthusiastically. *It's like I leveled up or something!*

I have only one thing to say, my friend.

What's that, dude?

WHAT THE FUCK TOOK YOU SO LONG?! PS screamed at me while waving his hands in the air.

I...don't...know? I responded lamely as my voice went up in pitch. Then a puzzle piece fell into place. *Dude, I barely accept myself for who and what I am. How the hell did you expect me to consider you—the very personification of my vampirism—as a part of me?*

Fair enough, he said, visibly relaxing. I noticed his eyes had gone from a constant red to a deep purple. They weren't as light as mine in color, but they were a heck of a lot closer than they had been before.

By the way, what would you prefer to be called? I'm sure PS isn't ideal for you.

How right you are. PS was lazy and lacking in imagination. It really showed how you truly felt about me. I think people put more effort in naming a pet rock than what you gave me . I felt ashamed at how right he was. *Call me Baleius.*

Baleius, huh? What is that, like a demon name?

I do believe myself to be of demonic origin, though I don't remember anything before merging with your soul. I just like the name.

Sounds like a World of Warcraft *character,* I joked, then realized what he had said. A demon had merged with my soul? I had always thought as much, but it was unsettling to have it confirmed. It's one thing to think and another to know. *Why do you look more like me now? I mean, if you're a demon or something, why are you so damn good looking?*

PS...I mean, Baleius, looked down at his hands, turning them over in midair. I was about to interject when he began poking at his super ripped abs and said, *I don't exactly know. This is all new to me as well. My mind was a prisoner before. Only the most primitive part of me was allowed through. Now I am freed. You will have no more control problems from me, John.*

Good to hear. Funny, one of the primary reasons I kept you at bay was for that very fact.

The irony is not lost on me. But here we are. Now I will be able to assist more thoroughly. Here is the first of many recommendations to come: how to fly.

I know how to fly, I said a little more aggressively than intended. *It just takes a lot of energy to condense the air molecules under my feet while simultaneously spreading out those above my head to create lift.*

Would you like me to continue? Or are you not done interrupting me? Baleius asked with a playful smile that told me he knew something I didn't.

But of course, my good sir, I replied in a fancy British voice.

Wings, he said simply. His smile remained as if he knew I wouldn't catch on immediately.

O...kay? Yeah, man, that'd be great if I had wings. Though they might make me a tad conspicuous. As I finished, I brought up my thumb and index finger and smooshed them together while squinting my eyes.

Bloodwings, Baleius clarified with a smile that was now beaming to the point of blinding.

Blood...wings... I said to myself while letting my gaze go unfocused and dropping my hand. Lilith damn it! That's so obvious! I turned to him with a fake smile and said, *Well, I mean, if you wanna do it the easy way...or whatever.* I turned away in a casual, inconspicuous pivot while mouthing "Fuck!"

Taylor is looking at you, by the by, Baleius informed me.

Oh shit! I said as I pulled out of my mind and regained control behind my eyes.

"Sorry about that. Had a personal moment. So, where were we?" I said to a dubious Taylor.

We walked through the cavern and to the mouth where sweet, sweet moonlight greeted us. I gazed at my beautiful moon, basking in its pale light.

To those of you on Reddit asking: But-but Mr. Vampire, the light from the moon is just the reflection of the sun's rays! Why come isn't you being, um, deaded by it?

I would answer this: Listen here, you blouse-wearing poodle walker. You drink water, right? Well, what would happen if I stuck a funnel down your mouth and emptied a fifty-gallon drum of said water into your body? I'll tell you what would happen: I'd laugh maniacally while yelling to "hashtag this." Oh, and you'd die. Get my drift? Everything in moderation.

And—if I am to be completely honest on this—I think it also has something to do with the unfiltered natural sun cleansing the world of unnatural magic.

Shifting my eyes from my gorgeous moon to the area around us, I sniffed, noticing an unfamiliar odor emanating from the desert around us. I glanced around and saw nothing but sand, a few shrubs, and mountains. Wherever that portal had taken us, it was definitely not Houston.

"Where are we?" I asked while placing my hands on my hips.

"Nevada."

"Always wanted to go to Vegas," I said absently.

"It's only a few hours' drive from here. We have safe houses set up all over. Las Vegas has always been a place where the Fae can feel at home."

"Freemont Street?" I asked in reference to the famous—and infamous—street performers.

"Some. Most consider that below them, though. Cirque du Soleil is more to the liking of the Seelie Cou..." Taylor trailed off as his words sunk in. A single tear ran down his cheek as he looked up at the moon. I vaguely wondered if he saw the rock in space the same way I did.

"Taylor," I said sympathetically as I placed a hand on his shoulder, "the Seelie Court lives because of you. Look around." I motioned to the surviving members who were making their way to a row of tour buses at the base of the mountain we were on. Tan-colored camouflaged tarps covered the row of buses, held in place by steel cords attached to concrete anchors. With rehearsed precision, Fae refugees unclasped the anchors, pulled the tarps off, and rolled them up while others formed even lines by the bus doors. Keys attached to chains around necks were pulled free and inserted into the doors, opening them for the awaiting faeries. I noticed there were several buses that weren't being utilized, and realized with a shudder why that was. I did my best to keep an optimistic facade for my friend in need.

"I suppose you are right, of course," Taylor relented from his self-punishment.

"Taylor," I said, my hand still on his shoulder, "they are looking to you now. You saved them, and you are the closest thing to a leader they have now."

"Tatiana..." Taylor exhaled with a trembling voice, more tears of sorrow brimming in his eyes as his bottom lip quivered. He fought to maintain his composure for his people, but was steadily losing the battle.

"Hey, listen," I commanded as I grabbed both his shoulders in a tight grip and turned him to face me squarely. "Now is not the time to wallow in self-pity; now is the time to lead. Your people *need* their leader more than ever before. We will get Tatiana back. You have my word."

That is a tall order indeed, buddy, Baleius whispered in my ear. *How are we going to stop that which we cannot attack?*

We'll figure it out later, hush, I whispered back before I apprehended what I was doing. *Why am I whispering?* I continued to whisper.

Taylor looked up at me with red-rimmed eyes that were hardening with his resolve. "You're right. We do what we must. Thank you, John. Your words are kind." Taylor motioned to the buses while clearing his throat. "Would you care for a ride?"

"As much as I would like to see Vegas, I'm afraid I have an impossible task ahead of me. The Shadow Court wants me dead. I couldn't even kill one wittle kitty cat, and now they're all free. How many of them are there, by the way?"

Taylor stiffened at the mention of the cat before answering, "Countless, John, and that cat is one of the fiercest creatures in all of Faerie. Do not regard the shadow assassin lightly. I have heard tale after tale about that elusive feline. I don't know how much of it is true, mind you."

"Neat," I said while inhaling through my teeth. As I exhaled, I asked, "Any advice, at least?"

"Yes—run," Taylor said with complete seriousness.

"That helps...NOT!"

"Your sarcasm aside, I speak with sincerity with my suggestion. One scratch from the assassin, or any of the Shadow Fae, and you could be infected."

"Hypothetically," I started carefully, like a man asking his wife her thoughts on a threesome, "what if, and bear with me now, I had no choice but to fight them. What then?"

Taylor observed my eyes, searching for any clue that told him I was just kidding and would most definitely follow his valuable instructions. There wasn't any. Rubbing his forehead with his palm, he gave up and said, "They are invulnerable when cast in darkness. Only the light can open them up to attack."

"What about silver, iron, and the like?" I probed. "Doesn't that stuff usually work against faeries?"

"Yes, iron and silver can work on *some* of the Shadow Court when not in direct light; but not all."

"Also neat," I drawled as I ran a hand through my thick beard in concentration. "What about holy weapons? Do those work?"

"What did you have in mind?" I could tell I was pushing the limits of the stressed-out Taylor.

"Like, an angel gladius?"

"I couldn't attest to the efficacy of celestial weapons against the Fae."

"What if you were a betting ma...elf. Elf is what I said."

"Then I would wager weapons made by the creator of the cosmos might be effective against all they are wielded against."

"I knew that," I said.

No, you didn't, Baleius retorted.

"Shut up!" I barked out loud.

"Pardon?" Taylor asked, clearly confused at my outburst.

"Oops! Sorry, wrong number." Taylor just looked at me with a single raised eyebrow. Then something stuck in my mind like a bug in your teeth while riding a motorcycle (or while running preternaturally fast down a country road).

"Hey, Taylor? Uh, you mentioned the creator of the cosmos. Can I...can I ask, ah..."

"What my stance is on God?"

"Ye-yes."

"I recognize him for what he is; the creator of everything. Though I do not subscribe to the man-made religions," he answered honestly as we stopped by a bus that was only half full. "What about you?"

"Me?" I asked, trying to buy time to formulate my answer. I think Taylor caught on to that fact and didn't answer the redundant question. "I suppose Catholic, to a degree. I *do* go to church," I said with a slight chuckle, as if I were the only one aware of the inside joke. Which, of course, I was. Taylor simply regarded me patiently.

"I, ah, have a unique relationship with God, I suppose. I work with a priest who guides me toward the Light, bleaching my blackened soul as I do. I mean, I would like to meet God when I die, but I don't really talk to him now or anything."

"I think I understand," Taylor said. Now it was his turn to place an understanding hand on my shoulder.

Glancing at my bare wrist, I said, "Welp, look at the time. Gotta fly!" As I finished, I willed blood out from between my shoulder blades, up and over my trench coat. The blood extended out and then down at a ninety-degree angle before forming into thick bones. From the bones grew leatherlike skin with swoops at the bottom akin to a bat's wings. Once complete, I extended the wings in a truly impressive wingspan that made Taylor gasp and take a few steps back. I gave them a few test flaps, and dust shot out like waves on the sand.

Let me take control until you get the hang of them, Baleius suggested. *Plus, you will look like an imbecile if you falter after awkwardly avoiding the understanding Taylor just tried to give to you.*

Good idea, Dr. Phil. All you, I said as I let go of the steering wheel of my mind and let the demon in my head take over. Without another word, he lifted my head to the sky, brought my wings straight up, crouched at the knees, and shot up into the air. Once I cleared the ground by several yards, I flapped the massive bloodwings once and soared into the clear night sky. A few more flaps and I was at the cloud line and above the mountains. I leveled out, turned to the east, and began flying home.

Holy...shit, I said to Baleius. *This is so fucking awesome. I'm flying, dude!*

We, Baleius responded before laughing in enjoyment at my childlike glee. *There is so much more for you to learn,* he said. I became even more excited at the many lessons that were to come.

Hey, I started to ask, turning around to face him in the control room of my mind, *how do you know so much? I mean, you said you didn't remember anything before me, right?*

The only way I can adequately explain it is to say that it is in my nature to know. I am what gave you these abilities.

You don't remember anything before me? And what you do *remember while with me was seen through a mind that was only partially free?*

He stopped focusing on the scene outside the windows of my eyes to look at me with an unsure expression. *I don't really know how to convey my thoughts. I remember the events taking place—I was just unable to communicate. My reactions were also limited to their base modalities.*

Something hit me then. *I had a dream recently. In that dream, there was a group of demons sitting around a fire. I approached them, and they told me that fallen angels in the beginning could choose either brains or brawn.* I was pacing back and forth in front of the windows, trying to piece everything together as I spoke. *But! He mentioned that a select few had been able to maintain their angelic brains and brawn—or something like that. I was interrupted before I got anything more.*

Are you implying, delicately by the way, that I gave you strength in exchange for mental fortitude?

Exactly! And for some reason, now you have been unlocked like a secret character in a video game. And I didn't have to pay $19.99 to get you! Score!

I've been free all of fifteen minutes and I am already exhausted.

Yeah, that happens a lot, I said dismissively. *Do you have a better explanation?*

At the moment, no, Baleius admitted.

Who knows, man; maybe in a future book?

That's annoying. Why do you do that?

What? Break the fourth wall? I asked innocently.

Precisely. It is not an endearing quality and only provides confusion to your friends and allies.

Meh. I like doing it. You knew what you were getting into when you said "I do." Baleius responded with complete silence while turning his head to stare out the windows, allowing his consciousness back outside. I stood and looked out of one of the portholes in my skull and gawked in wonder as we pierced through a cloud and came out on top. It was what every God-fearing man described a typical Heaven as; white fluffy clouds that carpeted below as far as I could see, and a star-filled sky above. Over the desert, there wasn't any light pollution, allowing me to see every star, every galaxy. It reminded me of the centuries leading up to the inevitable invention of the light bulb—man had always had a fascination with harnessing the power and light of the sun. The constant illumination poisoned the sky and choked the stars.

As I watched, I had an urge I needed to act on. I wanted to feel the wind on my skin.

Can you teach me how to use the wings? I asked hesitantly, like a nervous child asking the teacher if he could use the bathroom.

Of course, Baleius responded, taking a step to the side so that I could place a hand on the wheel. *Notice the pattern; flap, upward drift, level off, lift wings before we start dropping, and flap again. After you are at the height you wish, extend the wings to soar.*

I did as instructed, but it felt weird. I tried to use my arms to flap, which equated to us starting to fall back to the cloud cover.

Focus, John. They aren't a part of you like your appendages. Moving your muscles will not make them work.

I focused and flapped out of sync, which threw me into a disorienting roll toward the ground. I came out the bottom of the cloud cover and rushed toward the ground below. As I tumbled, the brown earth swapped places with the clouds to become the sky before twirling back into place for a split second.

Okay, you take control, I said nervously as I stepped away from the wheel and motioned to it. *I don't know what'll happen if we hit the ground from here.*

If we hit and your brain is rocketed from your skull on impact, we'll die.

Take the Lilith-damned wheel! I pleaded.

No. This is a lesson you must learn.

I stood looking at him, searching for signs of submission. When I didn't see any, I belted out a quick scream of frustration while throwing my hands up and letting them drop onto the wheel.

The greedy earth rushed to embrace me. The only thing missing were pouty red cartoon lips that made sultry kissy motions beckoning me to my doom.

Is this where your story ends, John? As a smear on the desert floor? I wonder how long it will take the animals to eat our flesh—if such a thing is even possible. Either way, the morning sun will surely remove your remains from the face of the Earth.

That pissed me off. I was *not* going to saunter off into eternity because I couldn't control my own manifestation.

Concentrating, I felt my wings and made the right one extend to level off my rolling. As I leveled off, I imagined my wings flapping once. They obeyed, and my descent slightly slowed. I repeated the thought again and again until I was flying steadily a few hundred yards above the ground. The pouty red cartoon lips frowned in disappointment then stuck out their tongue and blew me a raspberry.

"WEEEEEEEEEEE!" I cried into the night as the wind attempted to deafen me by rushing past my ears. I felt my beanie start to slip as I picked up speed, forcing me to manifest my medieval bloodhelmet. This served to keep my loyal headwear in place, but also protected me from things in the air that might slam into my face, like birds. I'd had my fair share of run-ins with giant bugs at ludicrous speeds and did not want to see what a bird would feel like.

I tucked one wing in and did a controlled roll this time, screaming in pure joy as I did. Untucking the wing, I leveled off and tilted the top of the wings upward, which sent us into a wide barrel roll. At the crest of the loop, we lost momentum and began falling straight down. I pulled both my wings close to my body and oriented on the ground before extending them out to their full, magnificent glory.

I was so delighted that I sang a tune from my favorite Disney movie, "A whole neeeew wooooooorrrrrrrld. A new fantastic poooiiiint of view."

Really? Aren't you supposed to be some badass vampire that rips his prey limb from limb? Baleius goaded.

Aaaaand the cause of the apocalypse. Don't you dare forget that.

Oh yes. How could I have forgotten.

I was really starting to get the hang of things when the first signs of dawn reared their ugly tendrils.

We will have to find a safe spot to rest, Baleius said. *And don't even think about trying to outrun the sun. I honestly have no idea how you aren't ash by now.*

Agreed, but only because I have no idea where the fuck we are, I admitted. If I did, I'd probably try and beat the dawn. I stopped flapping and began gliding down, my eyes scanning the ground for a suitable location to rest during the day.

Wait! I exclaimed more to myself than to my new verbal companion. *I have an idea.*

Do you mean a plan? Baleius snickered to himself.

Oh, Lilith. Is this what I'm like?

Yes indeed, my friend. Now, about that plan?

I carefully pulled out my phone—OtterBox case or not, I didn't know if it could survive a plummet from several hundred feet up—and selected my Hilton app. I had to open and crash the program several times before I decided to give up.

Hmm. That's odd, I mused to Baleius.

What is it?

The phone isn't working. I just got the damn thing! Baleius didn't respond.

I put my phone into the inside pocket of my trench and oriented on a major highway.

There is bound to be a hotel along the road.

Within seven minutes of flight, we located the sign of a Holiday Inn.

Damn, I lamented.

What is it?

Not a Hilton. I have so many points with them.

Any port in a storm, Baleius responded.

As we soared—covering vast distances in record time—I truly appreciated Baleius.

Dude, I began with awe in my voice, *I wish I had learned to fly long ago. We got here in no time.*

There will be many lessons to come. But for now, let's get to the room.

Just as the sun was beginning to peak over the horizon and caress the clouds, I landed in the parking lot. Well, I say landed, but one might be able to successfully argue in a court of law that I crashed and tumbled as I hit the ground at Mach speed—and they would win.

Yeah, sorry about that, Baleius said. *You were doing so well, and I thought you had it.*

Grabbing the wrist that had broken my fall, and itself, I yanked it back into place with a crunch to let it heal. *Next time, don't trust me to know what I'm doing. I only look and sound confident; inside my head is a monkey playing with electrical wires on the space shuttle.*

Well, while we are on the subject, Baleius said hesitantly, *you might have landed with giant wings in a parking lot surrounded by cameras. Giant wings that are still out, mind you.*

Shit! I barked, willing the manifestation to quickly retreat into my back along with my bloodhelmet.

Nothing to be done about it now. Dawn is upon us. We will simply have to hope that no one will have any reason to view the footage.

As we walked toward the front door, a thought struck me. *Um, hey...you weren't present every time I, uh...was intimate, were you? 'Cause before, it was like doing it in front of your dog. But now...*

Yes, but that is a discussion for another time. Morning is upon us.

As we walked through the sliding glass doors, a young black female looked up from her screen to regard me with wide eyes and a gaping mouth. Huge glasses slid down her nose as she gawked, her gaze shifting from me back to her screen, which showed the parking lot in astonishingly crystal-clear resolution.

Chapter 7

"Um, hi?" I greeted in response to the speechless caramel-skinned young woman in front of me. A white plastic name tag had "Tiff" stenciled on it. "Checking in?" I said as she continued to gawk.

"Y-you..." she stammered, pointing at my shoulders.

"Had wings, right. All an illusion. Can I check in, please?" I said quickly, turning my head to regard the light creeping toward the building. It was like watching a tsunami in slow motion. I didn't have time to handle this.

There is an easy way to ensure she doesn't speak, Baleius offered.

No! She's innocent. Besides, who's going to believe some teenager?

She was looking at the screen. What do you think was on it?

Shit. You're right. What are our options? We only have a few minutes.

I have a solution. Extend your hand toward her, and follow me. I extended my hand with my fingers stretched toward the stunned clerk before retreating inside my mind. Letting Baleius take control of the wheel, I followed him out of the control room, down my arm, and into the woman's head.

With Baleius as my guide, I followed him to the storage room I was used to seeing whenever I *successfully* entered someone's mind. In the center was a single file cabinet that represented short-term memory. As I opened it, I immediately saw what we were looking for.

There's the recent memory file, I said, pointing.

In a moment. First, we must get her to erase the footage.

I-I can do that? I asked, intrigued. Ulric had never completely shown me how to control a mortal's mind. On the one occasion he'd attempted the lesson, I had drove the human completely insane. A still image of a man tearing his own face off sped through my mind like the flash of a gun at night—violent, bright, and gone as quickly as it arrived.

There is much you can do, John. The older you become, the more power you'll come into. The more power you accumulate, the more abilities will be available. Now focus. Baleius ascended through the ceiling of the storage room we were in with me in tow. Like a pair of specters, we entered the control room of her mind, which was in sharp contrast to my own. Where mine was monochrome and minimalist, hers was full of anime posters, bright colors, and furniture comprised of giant beanbag chairs.

The hell is this? I asked, looking around in amazement.

Her unconscious decor.

I mean, mortals have control rooms as well? How did I never know this?

You know now.

Can I do this too? I inquired, pointing to the decorations.

You want anime posters? Baleius asked, walking up to a beanbag positioned in front of her eyes and inspecting it. He was clearly more interested in the mission at hand than he was in entertaining my man cave fantasy.

No, dude. Movie posters! Batman. Batman Returns. Robocop. Predator...

I get it, Baleius interrupted, turning to face outside her eyes as he sat down. *Now watch.* His eyes went unfocused, and the scene outside started moving. I walked to the eye-windows and saw a hand in front of me with fingers outstretched. It was surreal looking at my own body.

I was a passenger watching a movie scene unfold before me. The camera panned, locking onto the computer. Caramel-colored hands came into view and began flying over the keyboard. The file containing the latest date was located and opened.

"Hmm," Baleius hummed through his host's lips.

What?

Using his own mouth—or should I say, metaphysical mouth—Baleius said, *The date is off.*

Probably just a lazy typo or something.

Inside the folder were several files that were labeled with the areas they covered and today's date. The parking lot file was opened, and Baleius began skimming the video by clicking the play bar.

How do you know how to do all this? I asked, turning to look at Baleius in his comfy-looking chair.

I don't. But she does, he said while his eyes remained unfocused.

Interesting, I said to myself as I returned my gaze to the scene outside. Baleius had found the part where I landed like a graceful butterfly, and was rewinding it over and over. Empty parking lot, peaceful, super buff vampire smashes into the concrete and rolls with limbs flailing. Rewind. Empty parking lot, peaceful—*DUDE! I get it!*

The girl began laughing as she watched the screen. Her laugh was odd because it was a male demon's chortle but through the vocal cords of a mortal female.

When Baleius was done with his torture, he commanded her hand to grasp the mouse, hover over the delete icon, and click. The screen went back to the other folders, and Baleius clicked "Live" to return the cameras to normal.

Might want to check us in and get a key card, I anxiously suggested as the morning light began to enter the lobby. Baleius made the hands fly as if he had been working as the front desk clerk for months.

Got it. Follow me, and we'll snag the memory on our way out, Baleius said as he stood up.

Hey, why wasn't she in here? I asked, looking around.

You mean the mental representation of herself?

Yeah. Why's the room all done up if she isn't here to enjoy it?

Did you have a mental copy of yourself when you were mortal?

Uh, I don't think so, I said as I thought back.

You had no need, or even the mental capacity, until I came along.

Makes sense, I suppose. Still doesn't explain the decorations.

Unconscious, just as yours is.

Aw, man. My subconscious is boring.

Your subconscious isn't an early twenties young woman who enjoys watching anime in its original tongue.

You mean without the dubs? I questioned, unbelieving. *Who does that?*

Tiff does, Baleius said as we floated through the floor below. We located the memory and popped the file like a bubble.

That was easy, I commented.

It was a short-term memory not yet solidified to long-term. Easy to do when fresh.

What about when it becomes long-term?

Still doable, but you risk damage to the mind. Synapses are created and branched to other memories, forming a delicate network. Destroying one could cause a cascade of problems that might become irreversible.

Good to know. We flowed out of her essence and back up my arm and into the control room. I noticed that it was now filled with framed movie posters and comfy leather furniture fit for a bachelor's pad.

Neat! I exclaimed in pleasant surprise as I ran around the room admiring all the epic movie posters. On one, Arnold sat astride a motorcycle brandishing a lever-actuated shotgun. Next to it was a man in a parka with lights shooting out of his face for John Carpenter's *The Thing*. Another had a picture of Jodie Foster's head with a moth where her lips should be. I all but skipped to the other side of the room to admire a poster of Pinhead holding the Lament Configuration. I giggled as I saw Bruce Campbell on another poster in front of a dark castle with a chain saw for a hand and his shirt ripped, revealing a super buff, airbrushed body.

Perhaps you can enjoy your posters another time?

Right, I acquiesced. *At least what happens in the control room is sped up.*

Forgive me if I don't trust someone with the fatal flaw of time management.

Yeah, I put all my points into charisma, I said as I walked to the wheel.

Baleius stifled a bark of laughter as I took control.

The first thing I noticed was that the morning light was spilling into the lobby all the way to the tile in front of the desk. I grabbed the key card, parkoured over the desk, and hurriedly made my way to the elevator bank. The doors opened immediately after pushing the up button, and I stepped in to select my floor. I was having trouble keeping my eyes open as the dawn swallowed the Earth.

Stepping out, I took note of the room map and made my way to my door. Light shone from under the door.

"Shit," I muttered to myself.

Pull your beanie down to cover as much of your head as you can. Let your coat sleeves hang past your hands and lift your collar. Hold—and I can't believe I'm having to explain this to you—the coat up in front of your face.

Well, if you want to make sense... I trailed off as I unlocked the door and did as suggested with my attire. Hesitantly, I opened the door and was bombarded with sunlight strucking my trench coat. I groaned as the heat nearly overwhelmed me.

Hurry, Baleius commanded.

I shuffled toward the window with my coat acting as a shield from the hungry sun. My sleeve slid up, and my wrist was set ablaze. I screamed through a clenched jaw and tight lips, willing my fingers to not drop the coat.

Once I felt my elbow hit the wall to the left of the window, I used my free hand to grab the blackout curtains and tugged them closed. Letting go, I put my free hand behind the shield of my coat and moved to the other side to repeat the process. The room filled with the smell of charred flesh as I closed the curtains. I ran to the bathroom, sharply sucking air through my teeth, and put my blackened wrist under the sink to run it under cold water. I groaned in pain as strands of John-jerky flaked off to land in sharp contrast to the white porcelain. On top of everything, I was exhausted as I fought to stay awake.

You're fine. Get some rest. We have much to discuss tomorrow.

"Like what?" I asked out loud as I yawned while walking to the queen-size bed.

The fact that the time stamp on the security footage was set at 2029.

I barely heard him as I fell face-first onto the bed, losing consciousness in an instant.

Chapter 8

I awoke with a start, aggressively pushing myself into a seated position on the bed. I was vaguely aware that my wrist had healed during my slumber.

"What the fuck do you mean 2029?!" I asked in near-panicked frustration.

That's what the camera system showed, Baleius responded while deep in thought.

No way, man. No freaking way. We were only in Faerie for a few hours, right?

Yes. We need to find Taylor or Lily.

Oh shit, I exclaimed as comprehension hit.

What is it? Baleius asked, giving me his full attention.

What if I was right and Faerie really is one of the higher dimensions?

I don't follow.

In all dimensions after the third, time is a huge proponent. When we shifted planes, we went into one of the last three or four known dimensions, where they have their own set of universal laws and physics; including time.

Baleius didn't say anything, suggesting that I should continue my theory.

Look, say we are in space just outside the event horizon of the black hole, Cygnus X-1, and I jumped out of the ship and floated toward the center. If I turned to look at the universe as I floated, millions or even billions of years would pass before my eyes the closer I got to, and crossed, the event horizon. From your perspective, I would appear to be frozen in time, unmoving for millions or billions of years until I crossed the point of no return. Then I would simply vanish from your perspective because light wouldn't be able to travel from me to your eyes anymore. Time is relative to the person.

I see. Time in Faerie passed normally for us, but back on Earth it was accelerated.

Accelerated from our point of view, but normal for them. Oh, Lilith, everyone probably thinks we are dead.

I don't think so, Baleius said confidently.

Why's that? I demanded in frustration. *Surely my friends would've noticed we were gone for ten fucking years?!*

The world is still here, he stated flatly.

Ah, right, I relented. *Hmm, I think I understand the premise of* Peter Pan *a little more now.*

How so?

Kids stay young in Neverland and years pass between visits, right?

I think I understand where you are going. But we need to get in contact with our allies.

Oh no...

What?

Father Thomes...he was already old before we fled to Faerie. Baleius didn't answer, which told me as clear as words that he agreed with my right to be concerned.

Let's get going.

Wait, let me check something first, I said as I pulled out my cell phone again. "No Service" was displayed at the top. *Shit. I guess I can't get mad at Da for not paying my cell phone bill for ten years with no use.* An idea came to me then. *Maybe I can connect to Wi-Fi.*

I went to the settings and searched for the Holiday Inn signal. There was none to be found under Wi-Fi.

That's freaking weird, I said as I closed my useless phone and replaced it in my pocket.

All the more reason to return home quickly.

We headed out of the room toward the elevator, rode to the first floor, and exited into the lobby. An older Indian woman with a bindi on her forehead looked up from her computer to smile and bid me farewell. I waved with a forced half smile and stepped through the automatic doors.

Please step away from the building far enough so that the cameras can't see you this time, Baleius suggested.

I walked to the edge of the parking lot and into the open desert until I felt confident the cameras wouldn't see me bust out my vamp-wings.

Focus on making the wings just as they were last night. Don't deviate or they might not be able to sustain flight.

Got it.

I closed my eyes and pictured the wings in my mind, willing blood to snake out of my back. They peeked out from under my collar and slid down my coat and into place before starting to form my bloodwings.

Very good, John, Baleius said in approval as crimson wings extended several feet in either direction.

I looked up at the night sky, found the stars I was searching for, and oriented on home. With an explosive flap of my bloodwings, we shot into the night.

I followed the major highway, swooping down to glance at road signs and making changes in direction when necessary. I knew I was getting closer to home when the humidity started to build, thickening the air. Though something was off.

Does it feel a tad chilly to you?

I don't really pay attention; but now that you mention it, it is somewhat noticeable.

Hmm.

After a few hours of gliding just under the sparse cover of clouds, a welcomed sight came into view—the bright lights of Houston. As we soared closer, I noticed the city had expanded outward. Roads that I thought would always be under construction were complete, only to be replaced with other highways beginning their own expansions or reworks.

A few more minutes of flight and I was descending to the cemetery I had called home for over thirty years. A sigh of relief escaped me as I took note that it was still well maintained. It would have been a real shame to have a parking lot paved over my Fortress of Solitaire...oh, and all those graves too, of course. But mostly that first thing.

I landed at the mausoleum and began moving the marble door as my wings retreated back into me. Hope washed over me as I saw that the hidden entrance was still closed.

Ma-maybe they still live here, you know? I said more in a reassuring statement to myself rather than as a question to Baleius. *If they had abandoned the place, they probably wouldn't have bothered closing the door behind them, you know? Not with the big marble door at the front.*

There's only one way to find out, Baleius said quietly. I could feel the unease in his voice, which only compounded my growing anxiety.

No, they wouldn't have left me.

It's been ten years, John. It would be in the realm of unreason for them to hold out hope for that long. Control your emotions and let's push through.

You're one to talk about emotions, I remarked childishly.

Considering the situation I was in, I would confidently say I handled myself exceedingly well. Do you think you would be able to fare any better?

Knowing I was in the wrong and had been a dick to him, I ignored the question and pressed the false stone to open the hidden door. I made my way down the steps and to the front door of my home. Fear gripped my chest and tightened my throat as trembling fingers reached for the handle before stopping just before touching it.

Should...should I knock? The question irked me. This was my home, damn it. I grabbed the handle and pulled the door open, relieved to see it wasn't locked. Stepping inside, I flipped the switch on the wall next to the door, and light bathed the kitchen and attached living room in a white/blue hue from the LEDs.

I didn't recognize what I was staring at. The white marble had been redone to black quartz. The walls and cabinets had been repainted dark colors. Crown molding had been added. In the living room, comfy bachelor furniture had been replaced by sophisticated works of art. The couch on the wall was dark leather with big, fashionable buttons all along the leather cushions. The buttons created deep recesses, making the cushions look incredibly thick and comfortable.

On the wall across from the couch was a huge, paper-thin TV. I stared in awe as I approached it, unbelieving how impossibly thin it was. There weren't any cords running to it. Placing my ear against the wall, I tried to see just how thin the TV really was. It was as thick as a poster that comes rolled up in a cardboard tube.

Below the TV sat an expensive-looking entertainment center with a console the size of a remote control. An X was stenciled on it. It also had no wires running to it.

"What the fuck?" I asked out loud.

A cannonball of invisible force slammed into my stomach, sending me flying back into the kitchen where I smacked into the metal front door.

I lifted my head to reveal glowing red eyes and bared teeth with two sharp fangs as I searched for my attacker. I spotted him immediately and pushed myself off the wall with enough force to fly through the air toward my small opponent.

Halfway to my target, I noticed the frame of a small boy standing in a doorway with hands glowing green and purple.

"John?" asked a voice in slow motion as I soared toward him. I shot my hands to either side of the metal door and willed two pillars of blood to explode out of my hands. As they hit the frame, I steadily solidified the pillars, slowing my speed until I stopped right in front of the young boy.

"L-Locke?" I stammered, looking him up and down, letting my eyes return to their violet color.

Locke's glowing hands went out, and I was able to see his face. The head of a man on a ten-year-old body. The man-child stepped forward and wrapped his arms around me as I willed my blood to retract into my palms. Then Locke did something unexpected: he began sobbing. Unsure of what to do, I put my hands on his shoulders and waited for the storm to pass.

"Where have you been?" Locke asked between heaves of pain and relief.

"That's what I'm trying to figure out. I spent a few hours in Faerie before the Shadow Court attacked and came out ten years later," I said before adding, "Why are you crying?"

"It's bad, John. It's so bad," Locke said as he broke the embrace and wiped tears from his face. "I also didn't know if you were dying somewhere, with the apocalypse about to start at any time. Ten years. For ten...years...I thought about the end coming any minute. Imagine going to sleep not knowing if you would wake up again."

"Or worse, if you were on the toilet," I jested, trying to alleviate the tension. Locke chuckled as he wiped his face clean. "Where is everyone?" I asked, turning my head to look at open doors leading to empty rooms.

Locke looked at the ground as his bottom lip trembled.

"Dude..." I exhaled. "Don't leave me hanging like this. Where's Da?"

"Da...shifted planes to go look for you...and never came back."

"Oh, Lilith...the Shadow Court." My mouth hung open in dismay as realization stole my breath. My head grew light, making me woozy at the thought of what could have happened to my friend. Shaking my head to clear it of the mounting worry, I asked, "And Depweg? Where's he?"

Locke's lip stopped trembling and he took in a slow, deep breath as his gaze lifted to latch onto mine. In purposeful, pained movements, he shook his head back and forth while never breaking eye contact.

The anxiety in my chest exploded like a world-destroying nuke as I stepped back with eyes bulging. My feet struggled to find purchase as my leg bones disintegrated, leaving behind unstable jelly unable to bare my weight any longer. I collapsed to my knees, my hands sprawling out to catch my fall. Tears blurring my vision, I asked in a shaky voice with an excess of air surrounding the words, "Wha-what happened?"

"With you gone, no one was willing to stop the evil from spreading. No one except Depweg and the twins. Reluctantly, Father Thomes paired with them, and they tried to pick up where you left off. For a while, they did good, until word spread of what they were doing." Locke paused at the end, unsure of how to continue.

"Dude, tell me what happened to my best friend," I barked angrily as tears streaked down my cheeks. This was too much.

"A hunter set a trap that no one saw coming. He-he got them." His eyebrows were knitted together as he broke the appalling news.

Those three words slammed into my chest like a stake being hammered into my heart.

"How do you know they're dead?" I asked as my head became heavy, forcing my gaze to lower from Locke to the ground.

"I don't; but there was a lot of blood. I gave up hope when I saw distinct drag marks in the pools of blood."

Something is off, Baleius said quietly.

My strength returned and I lifted my head to study the warlock. "Why didn't you keep looking? And why do you seem so shaken up about *my* friends being missing or dead?" I accused aggressively, anger bolstering my words. My eyes glowed red with my building rage. "You never liked them, you sick fuck. You tried to kill us!"

Locke took my onslaught with grace as he spoke. "You were gone a very long time, John. We had plenty of time to grow close after we gave up looking for you. Jonathan Depweg was my friend. My only friend. The twins always kept me at arm's length, but not Depweg. He forgave me, and he became a brother to me." Locke had tears that flowed in unison with my own.

My fury subsided. I was attacking Locke as a means of distraction, and he didn't deserve it. I looked at the ground in my shame and anguish.

"Do you know where they could be?" I asked while squeezing my eyes shut, knowing it was a long shot.

"No," Locke said, shattering my hope. "But I know who took them."

My eyes shot open to meet Locke's as I barked out, "Who?!"

"His name is Ludvig Mansson, and he is truly terrifying."

"What kind of stupid name is Ludvig?" I asked, hating whatever name Locke would have given.

"He's a Swedish supernatural hunter who's more than proficient at what he does. Be careful, John. He's adept against many foes. Many of the few remaining supes in the region have gone missing."

"Where can I find this Swedish meatball?"

"I'd suggest watching the news and getting ahead of any stories about humans being killed in particularly gruesome ways. He is sure to be hunting the few supes that didn't flee to Faerie."

"I don't have time for that," I said, biting on my thumbnail as my mind wandered. "What about if we set our own fucking trap? Make it *look* like there's a pack of wolves, or something similar, killing humans in Houston."

"I thought you were worried about your soul?" Locke asked cautiously.

"I don't have to kill innocents to leave a trail of bodies," I said dryly. "How long ago were they taken?"

"About a year," Locke answered.

"A...a year? Oh, Lilith. Even if they are alive..." I trailed off as my mind meandered into the darkness of horrific possibilities. "How do you know he hunts *all* supes and isn't, like, a werewolf hunter or something?"

"Valenta told me. It's one of the few places I'm not scared to go to because of how close it is. The bar has been empty since the warlocks aided in the mass exodus from Earth, so I'm one of his few remaining customers and points of contact. Val confided that he suspects it's Ludvig."

My face scrunched in an angry microexpression that only lasted a nanosecond at the reminder of how Locke had opened a portal to Faerie. Countless supernaturals had met their fate at the hands of Queen Mab, who didn't take kindly to trespassers.

It was good to hear Val was still around, though. I'd be willing to bet he would be harder to remove than an Alabama tick. No, not ol' Val. Unless he wanted to, he wasn't going to move for anyone or anything.

After a few moments of heavy silence, a thought struck like a blacksmith's hammer on an anvil.

"Father Thomes?" The words were barely audible as I spoke his name. I must have swallowed a lemon or something because there was a huge lump in my throat that prevented me from swallowing.

"He's alive, but not doing well. After what happened to the pack, his health declined dramatically. I think the guilt at losing you and then them wore on his soul. After you, then Da, and finally the pack, I decided to lie low. I try to send help his way—you know, for groceries and stuff. They report back to me."

"I should go see him."

Locke nodded with tight, flat lips. "I will reach out to my people and see if I can find out where Ludvig is."

I turned and made my way toward the front door, pausing for a moment to look into my empty room.

"I-I thought you were dead," Locke said as I stared into the void. It was dark.

Twisting my neck to regard Locke, I said, "It's okay. I'm just glad someone is still here."

Locke nodded once and crossed his arms protectively over his chest—at a loss for words—as I exited my broken home.

Chapter 9

Not wanting to waste any time, I sprouted my bloodwings and shot into the night. As I passed over Valenta, I had to fight the urge to not land and talk to him in desperate search for answers. I knew it was more important to reach Father Thomes and let him know I was still alive; or undead, if you wanted to be technical.

The church came into view and my heart sank. Wooden boards covered several broken windows, probably from delinquent teenagers. The wrought iron fence had lost its battle with rust and had fallen toward the church. As I began gliding to the ground, I noticed the gargoyles were gone. A quick glance around the property and I saw something that made me do a double take; there was a small area covered in broken stone near the back gate. Chunks of earth were missing, as if peppered by mortar fire, where the crumbled bodies of the gargoyles rested.

I landed by the front porch and ran up to the door as my wings retreated back into my body. As my knuckle touched the door, a bolt of lightning lanced out from a glowing sigil above the entrance. I was thrown several feet back into the yard, crying out in agony as every nerve in my body was overly energized.

I lay in a heap on the ground, wheezing in pain as white smoke rose off my cooked body.

"Smoked vampire does not smell good," I croaked, feeling the heat dissipate from my skin.

It was a ward, Baleius said.

"No shit, Sherlock," I retorted into the night. My head cleared, and I pushed myself up to a seated position, my fingers feeling the dry, crusted dirt beneath them.

Is there another way in? Baleius asked.

I think so, I answered in my head as my gaze climbed the walls of the church to the chimney. *I'm willing to bet that isn't protected.*

I stood on unsure feet as my body continued to heal from the intense attack. My body had stopped wafting smoke as I walked to the edge of the church wall. Looking up, I crouched and leaped to the roofline. I had meant to land on top, but hadn't put enough strength into it, forcing me to grab the edge before I fell.

Damn, that ward freaking hurt!

I pulled myself up, putting in more effort than I liked, and began making my way to the chimney. As I approached, I gingerly tapped the structure with my fingertips to test for another ward.

Yeah, I didn't think he would have been able to make his way up here to plant the ward. Excellent thinking, John.

I pulled on the chimney cap, separating the aluminum with ease, and sat on the edge of the brick. With my feet dangling down the dark hole, I began letting myself descend slowly toward the basement. Accumulated ash easily broke free with my touch and filled the small space with gray/white dust. I had to squint my eyes and close my mouth as I went deeper.

I reached the bottom and hesitantly stuck my head out from the fireplace to look around, shifting to my preternatural eyes to see clearly in the dark. Once I saw it was clear, I stepped into the parlor where Father Thomes and I had sat not long ago…except it was long ago for a mortal with a finite amount of sand in his hourglass.

What's wrong? Baleius asked. *Why have you stopped moving?*

I-I'm scared of what I'll see once I find him. He was already so old, I trailed off to a whisper at the end.

Baleius didn't answer, giving me the time I needed to gather my resolve. Setting my jaw, I started down the hallway, pausing in front of Ulric's prison. I took a step toward the door before catching myself. Father Thomes was more important. Plus, the world was still here, so he clearly had to be alive.

Wait, why is the world still here? We were gone for ten years, right?

Hmm, I was wondering that myself. Perhaps you weren't the last? Besides Ulric, I mean. Maybe there are those who slumber, Baleius suggested. I nearly slapped myself in the forehead for not considering that plausible scenario.

We can pontificate on that later.

Pontificate? Really? Baleius prodded. *Perhaps you mean "ponder"?*

That's what I said. Ponderficate.

I see what you are doing, he said in an understanding tone. *Face your fears and let's find the priest.*

His name is Father Thomes Philseep, I said a tad more angrily than I had anticipated. I supposed the little man who lived inside my head was right; I was scared.

Turning away from Ulric's prison, I made my way up the spiral staircase until I reached the main floor where the cathedral was, along with Thomes' personal chambers.

Stepping into the big room, I looked around, assessing. Jesus was now sitting on the stage instead of being hung up. I could see a crack on one of his arms where the cross had fallen, presumably landing on its side. Looking at the wall where he had once hung, I could see where an anchor had deteriorated and then failed, leaving a hole in the wall. Behind that, a sizable chunk of the wooden stud had been torn out in the collapse.

My ruby eyes locked onto the chambers of my friend, and I slowly made my way toward his room. If I had a heartbeat, I was sure it would be thudding in my ears like a metal band's bass drum. Regardless, my nervousness built on top of itself like those zombies in *World War Z* as they tried to get Brad Pitt.

After what felt like an eternity, I stood in front of Father Thomes Philseep's room and knocked the theme to *Terminator*.

A cough answered, followed by a weak, raspy voice that called out, "John?"

My throat was so tight that I could barely answer. "Yes, Father. It's me. I-I've been on vacation," I attempted to jest.

"Come in, my son. Please, come in."

I grabbed the brass handle, turned it painfully slowly, and entered the chambers. A single candle resting on a nightstand tried in vain to light up the modest room. Shadows danced in unison with the tiny, orange flame. My eyes saw everything clear as, ironically, day, but I was confused why my friend would allow such dim lighting.

As if in response to my thoughts, another candle was brought to the first, the wicks meeting to give life to a second flame.

My only mortal friend held up the new candle to get a better look at me. His stark-white hair looked alarmingly thin where it still remained. Liver spots had aggressively multiplied and migrated from his hands all the way to the top of his deeply wrinkled head. His skin was almost as thin as his hair. I could see tendons and veins that were basically covered with the flesh equivalent of Saran Wrap. Arthritis had deformed his hands drastically, creating lumpy appendages that barely registered as human.

Cracked lips worked as my friend spoke, "Where..."

"I was in Faerie for a few hours."

Father Thomes cocked an eyebrow at me, prompting me to explain.

"Best I can figure is that it's a different dimension, and time was different for me. I even lost my vampirism over there. Had a heartbeat and everything. Weird shit."

"Did you at least have fun on your vacation?"

"Um...it's pretty bad over there, now, and I think it's probably my fault. Maybe...definitely. Yeah, I did it."

Father Thomes strained to sit up and prop a few pillows behind his back. "You brought about the destruction of an entire dimension?"

"Well, it sounds bad when you say it like that. And I don't think it's all the way destroyed—more like taken over? Yeah, that sounds about right."

"Oh, John, you just can't help yourself. How did you manage such an impressive blunder?" Father Thomes began a coughing fit then before reaching with trembling, deformed hands to grab a glass of warm water on the nightstand. He took several large gulps, sighing in relief as he set the glass back down.

"Um...remember that angel I allegedly killed? You know the one. Remember how I lost its body and, ah, sword? Turns out the Shadow Court maybe got their hands on it and apparently used the angelic weapon to free their army," I told him with a hint of embarrassment. "Hmm, when I say it out loud, it sounds pretty epic. Kinda like a straight-to-Netflix movie."

"Netflix doesn't exist anymore."

"S'cuse me? Come again?" I said, doing a dramatic double take.

"I think they combined with another streaming service."

"Weren't there only, like, three before I left? Isn't that illegal? A monopoly or something like that?"

"Their prices are pretty good, so no one complains. Besides, now there are several smaller streaming services."

"Ah, good ol' consumerism."

Though the banter felt natural to me, it had been a decade for my mortal friend, who was knocking on death's door. The awkwardness was palpable.

"I'm sorry I wasn't here, Thomes. But I'm here now. I need to fix this."

"How can you fix time, my son?"

"Oh man, you're right," I exhaled as I unconsciously sat on the edge of his bed, my legs suddenly unable to carry my own weight. My gaze shifted to the wall as I thought about the impossible task in front of me.

"I'm glad you're here now, at least. I was always saddened at the thought of not getting to say goodbye before I passed."

His words crashed into my heart like a speeding semi into a stalled smart car. I turned my head to look my seasoned friend in the eyes, then the world went blurry.

With air unable to squeeze past my tight throat, I mouthed, "No," as the waterworks were notched to eleven. Taking in a deep, steadying breath, I said, "I knew this day was going to come, no matter how hard I tried to push it out of my mind. It was always there, like that aunt you hate but are forced to see on holidays."

"It's okay, John. I know where I am going once I pass."

"What if you don't have to pass…" I said in a knee-jerk reaction. It was more a thought than an actual question.

"My son, even if I wanted to, you know I can't accept your dark gift," Father Thomes said calmly.

"How can you be so at ease? Dying is literally my worst fear right now."

"Because you don't know for certain where you will go."

"Well, killing that innocent limo driver sure didn't make things any easier…"

"You have asked for His forgiveness and received His mercy. Now you must forgive yourself."

"I-I can't."

"You don't feel you deserve forgiveness."

Looking down at the ground, I wiped my face and said, "I don't really know, but that sounds about right." Unable to blow my nose, I inhaled sharply and swallowed the saline snot.

"Always remember, John, that He is listening. When you are ready to forgive yourself, you'll be able to ask for His divine help to find peace of self."

"Thanks, Thomes." An idea burst into my mind like a bolt of lightning in the dark. "Hey, what if there was a way for you to live longer without endangering your soul?"

"John, I…" Thomes started before I interrupted him.

"Think about it. If I can somehow prolong your life, we can keep the apocalypse at bay. I can't do it alone, and I think you know that. Right now, you're all I've got. Well, besides a mini-Locke who's afraid to leave the house."

"Can you blame him? Jonathan and the twins were powerful, resourceful, and intelligent, and they were taken," Thomes said as his head hung low in shame.

"Hey, it wasn't your fault. Don't pull that crap right now. Only one of us gets to be a self-defeating drama queen."

Thomes looked up smiling and said, "You said it, not me." He thought for a moment before saying, "What did you have in mind?"

I put a hand on his gnarled knuckles and said, "Let me reach out to someone and see about keeping you with us a little longer. At least until we make sure evil is totally defeated."

Reaching over to his nightstand, he pulled open a drawer and retrieved a necklace. Thomes handed it to me and said, "This will help protect you."

"From what?" I asked, looking at the silver crucifix. I could feel it hum with holy power.

"Many things, my son. It is time you signify your allegiance to the Light."

"The irony isn't lost on me."

He chuckled, which turned into a hacking fit. I sat helplessly watching my friend catch his breath.

"The silver will protect you from divination and even ranged attacks, like curses. It will also allow you to pass through the church's defenses. Lastly, it looks snazzy on you."

"Snazzy, you say?" I replied, hanging the pendant around my neck, the reflective silver in direct contrast to my black shirt. It felt...odd. I didn't know if it was a mental hurdle or the fact that it was made of silver. Then again, I did carry the kukri around with no problem. "I'll wear it with pride, Thomes."

I rested my hand on his and smiled. He put his other hand on mine, nodded once, and said, "It's good to see you again, my friend."

Chapter 10

I left the home of my friend—my compass to the Light—and stepped into the cool Houston night. I knew what I had to do, and nothing was going to stop me.

Sprouting bloodwings, I shot into the air toward the clinic of my friend, Doc Jim.

What makes you think he's still there? Baleius asked, annoying me.

I don't know for sure if he is, but I need to check all my bases. It's like I stepped into the polar opposite of It's a Wonderful Life. *Where the fuck is Mr. Potter? I'm gonna tear him limb from limb.*

We arrived at the clinic within a few minutes.

Lilith, I love these wings!

A word of caution: being in the air exposes you to the mortal world. Radar might pick you up if you fly too high, prompting a response from the human authorities, potentially even the military. Normal citizens might record you with their easily accessible phones, which would, once again, draw attention. While in heavily populated cities, maybe we should, how do mortals put it, take the bus?

I'll take that into consideration, I said as my bloodwings were drawn back into my body. The building still looked in good working order. The parking lot was well attended, with only one rogue weed defying the odds to grow through the asphalt. Cupping my hands around my eyes, I peered through the glass door to see a dark, but clean, waiting room. I rang the after-hours doorbell and moved my hand back to my face to better see through the glass. The LED streetlights outside created glares over the tinted black mirrors that were the door and windows.

A light flipped on behind the reception desk, and I breathed a sigh of relief as an only slightly older Doc Jim shuffled into the lobby. He fidgeted with a key chain, searching for the right one to unlock the door. As he found it, he stuck it into the door and looked up to see who was at his door. He froze, squinting his eyes and leaning forward to better see.

"Oh, right," I said as I lowered my hands from my face and stepped back, allowing him to view me better. Doctor Jim Hunt's eyes went wide behind his glasses as he rushed to unlock the door. He opened it and I walked into the lobby as he stepped back, looking me up and down.

"You haven't changed at all," Doc Jim said.

"Long story short: I was out of town for a few hours and came back to a world where I'm missing ten years." Patting my pockets, I said, "And I don't know where I put them."

"It's good to see you. Things have been..."

"Bad?" I finished for him.

"Awful," he corrected. "Not to boost your ego, but things started going awry with you gone. Jonathan and his pack tried their best to keep the peace, and for a while they did well. Word spread about merciless wolves prowling Houston with egregious sinners as their targets."

"That's what did them in," I said somberly. "They brought too much attention."

"Being a preternatural vigilante does seem to have its risks."

"Pimp'n ain't easy," I said with a half-hearted smile.

"What brings you here, John?" Doc Jim asked, cutting to the chase.

"A few things. First, checking up on my allies to determine the consequences of my absence. Second, to see what information you might have on Ludvig Mansson."

"The Hunter?"

"Well, the werewolf hunter at least," I corrected.

"I'm afraid his talents go beyond just werewolves. He is known across the world as the Hunter. Unfortunately, not much more is known about him besides his affinity for hunting all supernatural creatures, regardless of their moral compass."

"To be fair, there really are only a few of us that even have a moral compass. But why isn't there more known about him? It doesn't make sense that the entire world has heard of him, but that's it."

"There have only been a handful of beings that have escaped him. A very *small* handful, mind you. It is more than likely that your friends are..."

"Dead," I exhaled as my head became too heavy to hold up. It felt as if my chin resting on my chest was the only thing keeping my head from rolling off in my despair.

"I really need to work on my bedside manner."

"No," I said, forcing my gaze to lift and meet his. "I appreciate your honesty. Being told what you want to hear does no one any good. Never be afraid of the truth with me. Though I can admit I can be emotional at times."

Doc Jim chuckled at that while nodding in agreement. I looked at him in silence for a moment, edging on uncomfortable, which prompted him to ask, "What is it?"

"The third thing I wanted to ask is, do you have access to anything that will prolong a mortal's life? Maybe even reverse the signs of aging, or at least heal things like arthritis?"

"I-I don't think I have anything like what you are looking for," he said, hesitating and dropping his eyes away from mine.

He's lying, Baleius said impatiently. *Look at him. He has barely aged with a decade added to his life. Compare that to your priest friend who appropriately aged.*

"Doc, we just talked about honesty. I meant what I said," I told him calmly, but with an edge of coldness. If he was going to bet where my loyalties were strongest between my mortal allies, he was not going to like the answer.

"I am being honest. I don't have what you want for the priest."

We can make him give it to us, Baleius suggested aggressively. *I can show you.*

No. He is still a friend, and I don't want to cross that line.

Even if it means Father Thomes dies?

I answered with hesitant silence.

I can show you how easy it is to extract information.

I know how to do it, I scolded Baleius.

You know how to find some information, yes. But I can show you how to force a mortal to give up even the most precious of secrets, those that would be impossible to find without their consent.

He is not a bad guy, Baleius. I refuse to treat him as such.

Then why is he hiding the information you need to save your friend?

Baleius, I started, on the precipice of losing my patience. *I'm sure he has his fucking reasons. Now cut the shit.*

Just looking out for you, my friend, Baleius said in placation.

"Help me understand, Doc."

"He's close to death, isn't he? That's why you are pressing the issue."

"Yes, and I need him to live a little longer to help prevent the fucking end of days. Understand?" My voice was flat, devoid of emotion, but came across more sternly than I meant it to.

Doctor James Hunt looked at the ground and slowly began nodding his head, as if coming to a conclusion he didn't like.

"Follow me," he said, walking past me and pushing through the double metal swinging doors that led to the back. The familiar sanitized smell of the OR permeated the air. Something tugged at my attention; silence. No dogs barking, cats meowing, or birds chirping.

"How's business?" I asked, looking around.

Doc Jim had made his way to a stainless steel cabinet that he unlocked with a key. Sliding it open to search inside, he said, "The day job is fine. A little slow right now, but not as slow as the night job. It would seem the supernatural community is thinning quite noticeably."

"Why do you think that is?" I asked, already knowing the answer but curious as to his thoughts.

"If you take what's happening paired with the prophecy that you appear to be the center of...well, it's not good."

"Someone is clearing out those with the abilities to fight. Mortals stand no chance against demons by themselves."

"That's what I'm afraid of. I can't help but feel you being here, now, was also deliberately planned."

"Lily," I breathed.

"Come again?"

"She showed up right when the shadow assassin did to conveniently save me. Hmm," I put my hand on my chin in thought as I looked up at the tiled ceiling.

"What is it?"

"I don't understand something. I figured out how to get to Faerie, not her. It was my idea that I talked her into."

"Are you entirely sure?"

My heart, which had barely healed from its trust issues with my Fae lover, cracked again as I sighed and said, "No. No, I'm not. She knows me completely and is fully capable of manipulating me if she wants to." The pain must have been evident on my face because

Doctor Jim walked over to me and placed a hand on my shoulder. His other hand held a clear glass vial with a stopper.

Handing the vial to me, he said, "This will prolong the priest's life for a while, but not indefinitely. I assume that's why you didn't gift him with immortality."

"He is a man of God and is ready to go to Heaven. I convinced him that I need him here to save all of existence. I think he also realizes that if Hell is released, he isn't safe in Heaven. No soul is safe."

Doctor Jim nodded with unfocused eyes, feeling the gravity of what I had just said.

"Say, Doc, what's in this?"

"Tell him it's a concentration of resveratrol that'll help prevent his chromosomes from being cleaved, resulting in an extended life."

"How does that extend life?"

"After about the age of twenty-five, humans' internal clocks switch on and slowly begin the death process. Chromosomes are attacked by something called telomeres, and basically the ends of them are cut with every replication. Eventually, the cells cannot divide anymore and the person dies. Of course, this takes several decades to occur. Vision loss, hair growing white, taking longer to heal, all symptoms of aging. The contents of that vial will alleviate certain ailments related to aging while preserving the DNA, for a time."

"Neat," I responded, pleased. "I'll pass along the information." Looking up from the vial, I said, "Thanks, Doc. You might have just saved all of eternity."

"Glad to do my part. I won't charge you this time."

"Good, because my phone isn't working anymore, so I don't have access to my cryptocurrencies." A thought struck. "How are they doing, by the way?"

"Bitcoin went up to over a hundred thousand each a few years ago, leaving me with a very comfortable retirement when I decide to take it."

"Awesome! I probably have billions now!"

"Well, there were some new regulations that came out as a result, and bitcoin was outlawed in most countries. Last I checked, it was now only worth a few pennies each."

"FUCK!"

"Indeed. But surely you have more baskets to put your eggs."

"Yeah, I did. Da set that up for me...an-and he's missing. He went to Faerie in search of me, not knowing the Shadow Court had taken over."

"Faerie is gone? How's Taylor?"

"He's in Vegas with what remains of the Seelie Court."

Doc Jim nodded his head before he said, "I am sorry about your friend."

Does that not strike you as odd? Baleius threw in. *He asked about Taylor first after you mentioned your faerie friend is missing.*

I wanted to lash out at the demon in my head, but he had a point I couldn't refute.

Let's play this one close to the vest, for now.

"Thank you for your help, Doc. I need to get this to Father Thomes," I said, holding up the vial, regarding it in the sterile light of the OR.

"I'm glad to see you back, John. I'm ashamed to admit that I didn't realize how much the world needed you."

"Flattery will get you everywhere, cutie-pie," I replied with a wink. "But seriously, I think it's me who has caused all of this. Funny, isn't it?"

"What's that?"

"That the world needs me *because* of me."

"Well, I'm here to help, if I am able. I kind of enjoy having existence right where it is."

With a tight-lipped smile that I forced, I turned and made my way out of the clinic and into the parking lot.

What is he hiding? Baleius whispered in my brain.

Not now, dude. First, we save Thomes.

And after that?

I'm going to save Depweg and the twins before going back to Faerie to find Da.

Speaking purely from a position of self-preservation, I don't fancy that last part.

Then you better help me figure out a way to kill those fuckers, 'cause we're going.

Chapter 11

Father Thomes was snoring by the time I made my way back to the church. The crucifix necklace he had given me allowed me to pass unscathed through the wards. I placed the vial on the nightstand, careful not to wake my friend. He would know what it was when he woke up.

I listened to his shallow breathing for a moment before realizing how weird it was to watch a grown man sleep. As quietly as I had entered, I left the church with a feeling of accomplishment; Father Thomes would live, even if only for a little bit longer.

I closed the giant wooden door behind me as gently as I could before stepping out into the yard. I walked around the building, stopping to stare at the divot the angel statue had created when it had tried to kill me. Fool hadn't known whom it was messing with. With ease, I had defeated it in battle with nary a scratch. His catlike gargoyle buddy hadn't faired any better. The might of John the Vampire was the stuff of legend, and no stone guardians were going to stop me.

It's embarrassing that I know what you are thinking right now.

You can read my freaking mind?!

I don't have to. You are unconsciously smiling, nodding, and clenching your fists, all while lifting your chin in a show of confidence. Don't lie to yourself; they nearly tore you completely apart like a stuffed toy given to a Pit Bull.

Damn. That was a good analogy. Or was it a metaphor? I was too lazy to dig through my brain city to find out.

Shall we continue? Or are you not done self-aggrandizing? Baleius scolded.

I responded with silence as I made my way to the back of the property. There, near the fence line, were the remains of the church's stone protectors.

You would think he would have found better guardians after I defeated them so easily last time.

What should concern you is, if your priest friend had the ability to resurrect the stone guardians after they ripped you apart, why didn't he do it again?

If I remember correctly, you were there with me getting de-legged like a Thanksgiving turkey, buddy, I chided. *But you're right. May-maybe he's too weak now?* I asked with growing concern.

I kneeled down around one of the burnt holes in the ground, examining the damage for clues. Looking up from where I was crouching, my gaze wound a path to the back door of the church. I stood and made my way there, searching for signs of attack.

I looked above the door and saw a ward that mirrored the one at the front entrance. I turned my head to regard the yard and came to a conclusion.

Multiple attackers, I stated to Baleius.

I agree, actually.

Gargoyles are destroyed, which means they made it this far, but no bodies. I'm willing to bet one of them was turned into an all-organic, gluten-free lightning rod, and his buddies had to cart away the corpse.

That adds up, Baleius concurred.

"Who would want to attack a priest?" I asked aloud, looking around for answers.

Come now, John, Baleius sighed in annoyance. *You can't be surprised that, in your absence, he was attacked. How many scores of cultists, demons, and aggressive supernaturals have you killed?*

I don't know. At least five.

But you see my point, yes?

Yes, I see your stupid fucking point, I barked with all the words coming out strung together like cursive. *You're saying it's my Lilith-damned fault he was attacked.*

All I'm saying, Baleius continued calmly, *is that you had to have anticipated retaliations at some point. With you gone, what better chance would they have?*

Suckers didn't realize how powerful Father Thomes is.

Was, Baleius corrected. That stung. My friend did seem barely able to even sit upright in bed, much less defend his church. *He doesn't even seem strong enough to conjure his stone defenders back to life.*

Well, I'm back and won't let anything happen to him. We need to see Val to make sure he spreads the word that Father Thomes Philseep is off-fucking-limits.

Chapter 12

I walked to Valenta's Saloon, my mind racing with my new reality. Ten years had never seemed like a long time to me before until they had been taken away in an instant. How the hell had Ulric slept so long? Maybe I had never noticed the passage of time because I hadn't had mortal friends to gauge against. What I did know was that some major moves had been played on the chessboard of eternity while I'd been looking away for only a relative moment.

"Fucking cheaters."

What was that? Baleius asked, confused.

Hmm? Oh, nothing. Just lost in thought.

Baleius accepted my answer, but I could feel his eyes on me. I couldn't blame him.

I approached the saloon and walked through the double swinging doors. The inside was empty. Completely…empty. Valenta stood behind the counter reading an ancient book with a red leather cover. The title was unreadable, the ink having deteriorated long ago.

"Serving clam chowder again?" I asked in greeting.

Val's eyes shot up from the book in instant recognition. "Boy, where'n tha Hell ya been?" he drawled, making his way to the other side of the bar. Val then did something I wasn't expecting from him. He hugged me. It was a tight, strong, pat-on-the-back kind of hug, reserved for the manliest of men.

Separating, I said, "Took a brief vacation to Faerie. I wouldn't recommend it."

"Fer a decade?" Val asked, putting strong emphasis on the last word.

"It turns out Einstein was right: time is relative." Val awaited a more thorough explanation, so I told him what had happened.

"Sounds ta me that tha time delay was intentional. Don't it?"

Lily flashed through my mind before I said, "Unfortunately, I've been arriving at the same conclusion."

"Well, it's damn good ta have ya back, boy," Val said, slapping my shoulder lightly. He made his way back to the other side of his bar and said, "I got somethen fer ya," before disappearing into his back room. I sat at the bar and waited. I looked around at the empty, dust-free tables, impressed that he took so much pride in his bar, even without the business.

After a few minutes, he emerged again holding a familiar sight. My mouth salivated as he set the bottle of Jack and Blood on the bar. A clean, empty glass was set down next to it. Val popped the cork and poured me three fingers worth of the delicious enchanted liquid.

"Oh, man, I would kill for a drink right now," I proclaimed, grabbing the glass and bringing it up to my nose. The aroma was intoxicating. Goose bumps sprang along my arms and neck as I took my first tentative sip. I wanted to savor every last drop.

"What's yer plan now, John?" Val inquired.

"I need to save Depweg and the were-twins from the Hunter. Then I need to go back to Faerie and find Da."

Val's eyes shifted in thought before settling back on me. "What's yer plan ta get back?"

"Welp, sure as shit not going to ask Lily, that's for damn sure. I'm confident Taylor might be able to help me, if I can find him in Vegas." Val didn't respond, which was not uncommon for him; but something was off. "Why? Do you know of another way?"

Val thought for a moment before coming to a conclusion, "I do."

"...fucking and?" I said, slamming my drink on the counter in my frustration. Some of its contents sloshed over the side and onto my hand. Without thinking, I brought my hand up to my mouth and licked the precious liquid off.

"Ya have ta understand that a promise was made."

"Val, we're talking about the end of everything. You fucking understand me? I need all the help I can get."

"An' what happens if ya die o'er there?" Val replied sternly. "Didn't ya jus' get done say'n the Shadow Court took o'er?"

Fuck! He's right, I said inside my mind, hoping Baleius might offer some insight.

That's not his decision. Why don't you make him tell you?

I'm beginning to think we can both learn from one another.

In regards to what? Baleius asked, annoyed.

He's a friend, dick. We don't force our allies to bend to our will. Got that?

And if Da is in trouble? Perhaps dying at this very moment? What then, hero?

I started to see red at his audacity, but part of me knew he was right. I closed my eyes, took a deep breath, and said, "Three, two, one; one, two, three. What the heck is bothering me?"

"Pard'n?" Val asked.

"Sorry, Val. Having an internal debate," I said as the thought about Da being hurt sunk in, adding grease to the tight grip I had on my temper. It started slipping. "As a matter of fact, Val, it's specifically about you preventing me from saving my friend." My voice grew in intensity as I lost the battle with my rage. I felt my left eye twitch a few times as I struggled to keep my face from baring teeth.

"I think ya'd better reassess tha situation, boy," Val said, eyes beginning to glow white. My own eyes shifted from purple to red as Baleius placed a hand on the wheel without my noticing.

"You aren't going to do shit, barman," I taunted while standing up to full height. "You said it yourself; I die, the universe ends. So put those fucking eyes out before you learn what I'd be willing to do to save Raziel."

I hadn't meant to call him by his angelic name, but it had an odd effect on Val. His eyes went out and mouth dropped open.

"Raziel? Da is Raziel? Why didn't you tell me?" Valenta asked, all pretense of an accent gone. He began hyperventilating as his eyes went unfocused, and he began looking around and pacing.

I slowly started stepping away from the bar as Valenta began growing in size.

"You're a fucking angel?!" I asked accusingly, my own eyes growing into white saucers with red centers.

Valenta, now full angel size, locked his eyes on me with a scowl. They glowed a fierce white, with plumes spilling upward like a Jacob's ladder. "Where is he?" Val demanded.

"I-I don't know!" I stammered, unbelieving. "Like I said, I just know he shifted planes looking for me several years ago. Once the sun was blotted out, the Shadow Court was impossible to harm from what I saw. Th-there's no way he made it far."

"He's an angel, foolish child," Valenta boomed with a voice that reverberated through the walls.

"For real? He wasn't lying?"

"I had wondered for some time where Raziel had gone to after the battle with Samael. It would appear he has been busy."

"What reason would he have to be on Earth? And why the hell are *you* here?"

"Gabriel must have sent him to keep an eye on you, abomination." As he finished his thought, a million interactions between Da and me flashed through my mind in an instant.

"It-it makes sense," I began. "He has tried to guide me toward the Light for so long. Heh, I called him my Devil's Advocate. I think...I think I always knew. I just couldn't believe an angel would want to be my friend, much less help me." Something tickled the back of my mind. "Hey, Val, why would he pretend to be a five-inch faerie, but then tell me the truth about being an angel?"

"Would you have acted differently if you had known he was an angel?"

"What do you mean?"

"You have been trying to do good, correct?"

"Yeah. Da has helped immensely."

"Precisely my point. You did those things you considered good because you wanted to. Had you known Da was Raziel, it would have changed your behavior. You might have always been hesitant to fully embrace your good side because you would have thought you *had* to instead of *wanted* to."

"Then why tell me the truth?"

"Raziel doesn't lie."

"Heh. Sonofa..." I said, shaking my head in wonderment.

"You need to get my brother, abomination."

"Dude, why do you feathery fucks keep calling me that? It's getting old."

"You don't know, do you?" Val asked.

"Know what?!" I demanded. "That I'm a human with a demon fused into my soul and DNA?"

"That's not for me to say."

"What's stopping you?"

"Destiny is stopping me. I am not here to interfere in the affairs of man. Your future is in your own hands."

"Why are you here, then?" I asked, crossing my arms in front of my chest.

"I know you, John. This will not be dropped until I relent. So, I will save us both time and frustration by telling you as much as you need to know."

"Good. Because right now, you and I have some trust issues to work out."

"I didn't agree with Father or Samael. I believe in live and let live without intervention. I was neither jealous nor infatuated with the humans Father created and wanted no part in their petty squabble."

"Whoa. Pretty bold to call God petty."

"You and Samael would get along."

"Huh? How so?" I asked, confused.

"I didn't call Father petty. I said their disagreement was petty. Please try not to put words in my mouth, you hairless monkey." He smiled at the insult, more in friendly jest than contempt at my transgression.

"You gonna continue the story?" I suggested.

"I thought it was evident, but sure, allow me to dumb things down for you: I didn't like either side's stance and went out the back door while they fought. I have been content to live among the humans since the dawn of your time."

"My time?"

"Wasn't it you who pointed out the relativistic nature of time? The universe was created long before humans were even an idea in Father's imagination."

"Right. I knew that," I claimed. "Go on."

"I can't make it any dumber for you," Valenta said with a straight face.

"Well, *try*. Let's start with what's your angelic name."

"Though it is unimportant, the name Father gave me is Varhmiel. I abandoned my name and title when I left the Silver City. My name is Valenta. I chose it. I like it. It's mine."

"Respect," I said while nodding my head in appreciation. "I knew I liked you for a reason."

"What's your next question? I know you have one," Val prodded, planting his hands on his hips.

"What have you been doing all this time?"

"Protecting the supernatural community."

"Yeah, why's that?"

He shifted his weight onto one foot in agitation before saying, "Maybe I feel akin to them. Maybe this is my entertainment. Maybe it has something to do with the fact that I want no part of mortal lives, and the supernaturals don't fall into the category." His agitation was shifting toward aggression.

"Dude, I get it. Calm your tits, alright?" I told Val while holding my palms out in false surrender. He responded by narrowing his eyes. "I love how you're the one mad at me. Hey, raise your hand if you didn't lie to your friend about your entire existence." I struck my point home like a hammer on a nail by dramatically throwing a hand into the air.

"I never lied, child. I simply didn't tell you, or anyone else for that matter, what I truly was. To use your language, it was never your fucking business, bitch."

"Oh shit!" I exclaimed, putting a fist up to my open mouth and tittering. "That was awesome. Okay, we are friends again."

"Oh, good," Val said as he began shrinking back to man-size. As he did, I became aware that he had looked comical behind the bar at his full height.

"I would ask what's up with the accent, but I'm afraid you'd use my own logic of blending in against me and make me feel like a dummy."

"Smart," Val said with a grin. Then his face went flat in an instant as he turned and began walking toward the back room doors. "Follow me."

I did as instructed and followed Val into the kitchen. Once through the doors, he turned and headed toward the darkened corner where a metal door led to the basement. He waved his hand over the doors and whispered something that could have been mistaken for Latin, though it was a dialect I had never heard.

The door popped and slowly began opening.

"This way," Valenta directed, taking the steps made of stone.

"Follow me. This way," I whispered to myself, making an exaggerated face and bobbing my head back and forth in mockery. "Any other cliché phrases you wanna add?"

From below came a muffled, "Shut the fuck up and get down here."

"Oh, damn. Didn't know angels could curse!" I said, taking the steps two at a time until I reached my guide.

"And why's that? They're just words you people made up."

"What do you mean 'you people'?" I told him in an urban accent.

"You are exhausting," Val said, pinching the bridge of his nose.

"I get that a lot."

He stopped then, turned, and looked at me with a wrinkled brow. "And yet you continue down the path of incessant pestering. Why?"

"I'm me. Take it or leave it. I'm not going to pretend to be someone else or walk on eggshells."

After a noticeable pause, his features relaxed before turning to continue his walk through the tunnel.

It was a damp, cool, concrete tunnel with a perforated grate as the floor. Our footsteps echoed against the walls. Some water was evident underneath the grate in a thin, silver line against the lights overhead. Along the walls were metal shelves illuminated by fluorescent ballasts. A variety of goodies sat on the shelves, with the first three bays entirely occupied by bottles of liquor. My eyes latched onto my familiar Jack and Blood, and I unconsciously licked my lips. The next bay had different meats that had been dried and preserved.

After that were sections of shelving containing military-style lockboxes.

"What's in—"

"Don't ask," Val interrupted. It took me by surprise, and I looked at him in a new light.

"Got it," I answered as my eyes went back to the boxes that were now near irresistible. They appeared to glow like a birthday present you were dying to open. You know the one. I wanted, no, *needed* to open one or all of them.

My footsteps slowed, prompting Val to turn and aggressively clear his throat.

"What lies ahead is more precious to you than any trinket in those chests."

"Then you won't mind if I take a gander," I said as my hands caressed a case. I could see from the corner of my eye that Val had crossed his arms in agitated waiting.

I slowly opened the closest box, expecting a golden light to emanate. None came. Inside was a foam liner with holes that perfectly held its contents, one of which was a mason jar filled with salt and flakes of something else. I gingerly lifted the jar and peered inside, slowly moving the container in my hands. Intermixed with the white grains at a 10-1 ratio were reflective flecks. Some were darker, while others reflected the light brilliantly.

"Iron and silver," Val answered my silent question flatly.

My face slightly contorted in a frown as I nodded my head in both admiration and fear while muttering, "Not bad." I wasn't sure what creature would need a salt circle infused with both iron and silver to be contained. Salt was predominantly enough to contain even the strongest of demons.

Setting the jar back in its place, I picked up a sealed glass case that held an old, long, rusty nail.

I shot a look at Val and said, "No way."

"Yes. One of the nails from the crucifixion of Jesus of Nazareth."

"How do you have it?"

"Boy, I'm an angel who's been on Earth since before Eve took a bite of the forbidden fruit. I was there when Christ died for your sins. It took everything in me to restrain myself from freeing him, damn what Father had to say. Mankind didn't deserve his love after the atrocities they committed."

"Thought you didn't care either way," I said softly, aware of the delicate eggs on which I walked.

"There is a difference between staying neutral and not acting. How was I supposed to let God's son be tortured for countless hours for a species that didn't appreciate the gift? I had taken a step forward and was about to summon my gladius when, in the middle of his agony, he stopped screaming and looked right at me; but only for the briefest of moments. It was long enough for me to understand that it was what he wanted."

"He *wanted* to die a historically gruesome death?"

"Of course not, John. What he wanted was to save all of mankind, no matter the cost."

I looked back at the nail, feeling the weight of its significance in my hand.

"Where are the others?" I asked.

"I don't know. They could be anywhere."

"Aren't some of them on display somewhere? Like, doesn't the church have them or something?"

"Their authenticity cannot be concluded. I believe the church simply uses them as a symbol, regardless of their origin. Humans crave symbolism in the divine."

"Hmm," I exhaled while putting the nail back in its slot. "How do you know this one is real?"

"I watched as they removed his body. A Roman guard pulled the nails out and set them, carelessly, in a bag. To him, Jesus was another criminal that deserved punishment, just like all the others before him. He didn't care about the significance of those pieces of metal, and treated them as such. One fell to the ground as he fumbled while putting them all in his bag. He even looked down at it and shrugged, not even caring enough to take the time and bend down to retrieve what he had dropped. As he moved on to the other bodies, I simply walked over and picked it up before disappearing into the night."

As he finished, I noticed an empty slot where a spearhead had been.

"What's this?" I asked, pointing to the empty space.

"It was the Spear of Destiny," Val breathed out, letting his head hang low and arms uncross and fall to his sides.

"You mean the spear that killed Christ?" My eyes shot from him to the case and back again. I could sense his trepidation. "Where the hell is it?"

"I was forced to make a trade a while back."

Whirling on him, I cried out, "What the feck did you trade it for? What could be more important than the Spear of Destiny? Doesn't that have like superpowers or something?"

Fierce eyes lifted from the ground to burrow a hole through my head. "I have my reasons," Val growled in warning.

Throwing my hands up in placation, I said, "Got it. Understood. Noooooo problemo."

I closed the lid to the crate and walked to Val, who had resumed his way down the stone corridor. In short order, we arrived to a circular room at the end of the tunnel. Within the rock walls of the round room were doorways that led into smaller rooms. I counted seven in total.

Val continued straight ahead into one of the rooms, where a wooden arch was the only item in the chamber. It had the depiction of a castle growing in the middle of a tree that reached into the clouds etched into the wood.

"This is a doorway to Faerie, isn't it?" I asked, pointing at the carvings Valenta had made into the wood.

"Yes."

"I always wondered where you got your enchanted consumables from." Turning back to where we had come from and hooking a thumb in the air, I asked, "Where do the other doorways lead to?"

"Never you mind. If you want to find Raziel, here is your path." Val touched the wooden arch, and a portal shimmered into existence. Darkness was on the other side. Like a foreboding kind of dark that signifies it might not be the best decision to go into it.

"You, ah, wanna come with?"

"I cannot interfere."

"Neat. Super neat. Just…just plain neat," I said defeated as I took a step toward the gate.

"What are you doing?" Val exclaimed, somehow turning the gate off before I could cross the threshold. I couldn't see a switch anywhere.

"Um, going in?"

"Alone? Might I suggest rescuing your werewolf friends first?"

"Right. That's a good idea," I exhaled, letting my nerves settle.

"John," Val began with a concerned face, "you really need to think these things through. If you die, all of creation is at risk. Do you understand?"

"I, ah, I..." I tripped over my own words before the truth came pouring out. "I have no idea what the fuck I'm doing, Val. I question my every decision because there's so much riding on me. I-I can't bear the weight of the entire world and every soul that has ever lived. I mean, seriously, how could anyone be responsible for more souls than what's even fathomable? You might as well ask me to count the grains of sand on every beach in the world."

Val nodded his head, accepting my answer. "We are never given more than we can bear, John. You carry a weight that only you can endure."

"I don't know about that, man. Depweg has a pretty solid head on his shoulders," I responded as I crossed my arms and shrugged my shoulders.

"I'm sure that he does. But, if I may ask, when was the last time you saw him under extreme duress?"

"Define extreme."

"I don't think I need to, and you don't need to answer. It's a moot point regardless. As long as you realize you are meant to carry this burden because you *can*," Val said. "I'm confident your friends will have their parts to play as well."

"I hadn't really thought about that," I admitted as we walked back the way we had come. If I was the king on the chessboard of eternity, my friends made up all the other crucial pieces. They would lay down their lives to protect me. Some would even sacrifice themselves to give our side a slight edge. And that's what really kept me up at day.

"People see the good in you, John. They see the evil too, don't get me wrong on that. Whether you realize it or not, you inspire those around you."

"I do? If I have good *and* evil, how do I inspire them?" I asked, genuinely intrigued at an angel's answer on the matter.

"You fight your inner demon relentlessly. Did you know that you are the first supernatural to resist his predatory nature and use his abilities for the betterment of mankind?"

"What? That can't be true," I said, disbelieving. "What about Depweg? Or, heck, even Locke, for Lilith's sake."

"Your friends came after you, so you are still the first. Besides, ask him what he was like before meeting you, John." Val stopped and stared into my eyes then, signaling an entire encyclopedia of information with just a glance. "The reason he is who he is today is because he found you when he did. It stands to reason that if you had come across him even one day prior, you would have killed him without a second thought. That situation with the Jewish boy and the werewolf hunter really shook things up for him. And if I were to be honest with you, I don't think his sanity would have held if you hadn't stumbled upon him."

The back of my neck tingled, and I could feel the hairs stand on end as I thought of how close I had been to never knowing my best friend.

Val noticed as I shuddered at the thought and reassured me by saying, "Everything happens for a reason, John. Remember that."

I didn't know what to say as we made our way back through the room of portals and past the crates. I glanced at the one I had opened, feeling the significance of its contents. Though, to be fair, right now everything felt significant to me. I was dealing with a lot of emotions, thoughts, and self-doubt that I could do this.

After we were back in the bar, I poured myself a much-needed shot all the way to the brim of the glass. I called out, "Skol," to the empty bar before downing the drink. I was going to need all the confidence I could muster.

Chapter 13

It took almost an entire week to lure out the Hunter—Ludvig Mansson. All I needed was a consistent trail of decimated bodies that looked as if they had been torn apart by enormous dogs. It was kind of fun to artfully manifest bloodwolves from my hands to eat the flesh of evil men, of whom apparently there was a surplus. By the same token, I took note that there was hardly a supe to be found in the region, which resulted in an excess of fair game for me. It was morbidly akin to hunting wolves completely out of an area, resulting in deer overpopulation. The world needed a checks and balances system or the scales would tip.

After the flesh was consumed by my bloodwolves, I would absorb the blood from the meat while passing the muscle, bone, and skin to the ground. So as not to be suspicious, I would then bag all of the leftover meat, leaving only the bones, and take the flesh to one of the many feeding grounds. There was plenty of wildlife on the outskirts of Houston that wouldn't waste a free meal. I smiled, then, in remembrance of the alligator pets I once had many years ago. After I had been tracked down due to my predictable behavior, I had decided it was best to spread the love when I needed to dispose of my edible evidence.

Having set the trap, my waiting paid off in the form of an impressively large man wearing a black leather trench coat—how cliché. At least my coat had been taken off a Lilith-damned Nazi officer during the war of duba-duba-aye-aye. That shit's unique, unlike this Van Helsing wannabe. He was a few hundred yards away through the thin cover of the trees, walking toward a clearing. My eyes shifted to full predatory red once it was clear that my bait had been taken. I crouched lower on the tree branch, about fifteen feet off the ground, watching and waiting for my time to strike.

A wide-brimmed black leather hat sat upon a head whose face was covered with red-lens tactical goggles and some sort of breathing apparatus. All his clothing was black, including his gloves which had carbon fiber knuckles. An assortment of items decorated his utility belt, including three skinny vials next to the belt clasp. A sword hilt poked out the top of his coat while he brandished an odd-looking short barrel rifle. It resembled an elephant gun with the muzzle expanding outward near the end of its length.

I watched as he walked a little too confidently through the woods where my trap had been set. My senses were on high alert. Everyone had warned me that this guy was no mere mortal. He had skill and the wherewithal to employ dangerous toys for any and all occasions. My vision tunneled on my target, prepared for any attack should he notice me before I pounced. He was a fairly good distance from me, lending me some assurance that he wouldn't be able to strike from that far, even with his firearm.

The Hunter's head was on a swivel as he methodically scanned his surroundings, ready for any supe to attack.

I didn't think, however, that he was prepared for a vampire as old and strong as I was. Considering that he couldn't have possibly hunted any of my kind—and most myths were just that, myths—I was confident that—

"He's here!" a younger voice called out from behind the tree I was crouched in. I shot to my feet, turning around in surprise as I did, and was greeted by a blast from what resembled a shotgun. A slug smashed into my iron-infused body armor, hurling me out of the tree where I slammed into the ground, tumbling for several feet. I was going to kiss Depweg for giving me the chest plates and carrier vest once I rescued him.

"Never go hunting without it," I groaned to myself as I drunkenly got to my hands and knees. I felt my sternum beginning to heal with audible pops. Looking down at my chest, my fingers examined the silver slug that was imbedded in the armor. I was both impressed and terrified that the shot had been near perfect center mass.

Gritting my teeth in indignant rage, I located the attacker, who had racked another round into the weapon and was leveling it in my direction. I hesitated for the briefest of moments as I noticed it was just a kid, probably not even sixteen years old.

My attacker did not hesitate as I did and squeezed off another round in my direction. Pushing off with my hands and feet, I leaped into the air and spun while bringing my arms in close to my torso. While performing my acrobatics in midair, I felt a tug on my coat, along with a ripping sound. As I landed, I quickly risked a glance at my poor trench and noticed a brand-new hole. Kid or not, I had to stop this threat.

I shifted my weight, getting ready to blur in a big circle to flank my attacker, when a bola wrapped around my torso from behind. My arms were pinned to my sides, throwing off my balance, as I began to run.

Shit! They set a trap for me!

The irony is not lost on me, Baleius said. *Now focus. What is this material around our chest made of?*

I looked down and noticed it was a simple steel rope connecting the metal ends, and puffed out my chest while extending my arms as I ran. The bola snapped, and I barked in laughter at my win, right before smacking headfirst into a tree.

You are truly embarrassing, Baleius sighed.

Dude, shut up. I got this, I exploded at him as I quickly stood up, embarrassment flushing my cheeks.

An explosion from a firearm sounded as a net made of silver smacked into my back, pinning me against the tree I had just made friends with, chest first.

"Why...the fuck...can't I...break silver or iron!" I screamed through a clenched jaw as I pushed against the tree.

Quick footsteps crunched the leaves covering the ground behind me, growing closer. From the sound, I anticipated my attacker was around thirty paces away and closing.

How the hell did he get so close, so fast? I asked Baleius.

I smell magic about him.

He's a fucking supe?

I don't know, but we can worry about that later. Stop trying to break the chains that bind.

How else do you expect me to get out of this? A thought struck me then, and I positioned my hand in front of my chest. I punched through the wood with ease and began clawing at the tree, tearing it to shreds as if it were made of popsicle sticks. Once enough of it had been turned into toothpicks, the net began to loosen, allowing enough slack for me to bend slightly at my knees and jump up. I took the rest of the tree with me as I leaped through its corpse, clearing my silver prison.

While in midair, I grabbed the tree, which was around three feet thick at its circumference, and turned my body to face the attacker that had flanked me.

Ludvig the Hunter had stopped advancing and stood with his arms and legs out to either side, ready to react to whatever I was about to do.

Using my preternatural strength, I threw the tree like a bulky spear toward the Hunter, who took me by surprise by standing his ground.

As the massive spear sailed toward him, Ludvig took one step forward until the left side of his body was the only thing facing the tree, and pulled a sleek sword out of a scabbard on his back. The sword ran the full length of his spine and hummed with magic. I could see runes etched into the blade that reflected the moonlight. Ludvig swiped upward just before the tree hit him. There was a silver arc of light that extended from his swipe, and the tree split in two. The remains sailed past the Hunter on either side of his body, sending up an explosion of dirt as they smashed and then slid on the ground.

Holy...shit...that was cool, I admired inwardly.

While still in midair, I willed and then threw out a bloodspear attached to me by a bloodrope. I had anticipated his ability to block, so I pulled the spear back at the last second as Ludvig swung his enchanted weapon. As he did, he left himself open, and I sent another spear out with my other hand toward his exposed side. The Hunter didn't even flinch in surprise as the needle tip of the bloodspear approached his body. Instead, he moved at a speed that even I had trouble tracking and cut my weapon with ease. The loss of energy stunned me, but I hadn't thrown a ton of energy into the attack just in case he had holy or enchanted armor on.

I recovered as I hit the ground just in time to pull a Neo as a silver arc sailed toward me. I bent at my knees and landed on my back with a thud, which was a more realistic homage to the movie—I *could* have stayed bent at my knees and basically floated in midair, but just didn't want to.

The arc passed over my body, clipping a handful of my hair that was trailing above me as I fell. I shot my legs into the air with preternatural strength and flew upward feetfirst like a missile. As I soared, my incredibly fast attacker pulled a stick from inside his Van Helsing duster and pointed it at me. An arc of lightning forked out in the blink of an eye and wrapped around me like a python about to squeeze the life out of its prey.

"The fuck?" was all I could manage before the arcs started tightening around me. Before they could start tickling my nerves, I pulled the silver kukri from the sheath on my back and placed the holy metal into the mass of the lightning.

There was a deafening pop as the spell broke, leaving me unsinged as I flew through the air toward my surprisingly skilled opponent. With my free hand, I willed a bloodrapier—the favorite weapon of my maker—and brought it to bear as I landed a few paces in front of Ludvig. I lunged with the tip of the sword aimed at his throat, still unsure if he had body armor, and he parried reflexively. I anticipated this and turned my body to swipe at his sword arm with the silver kukri. He dodged the attack by pivoting his entire body, bringing the magic stick up as he turned. The tip was glowing white as a smaller arc of lightning shot out and licked my knife-wielding hand. The muscles in my forearm contracted and released a hundred times within the span of a second, forcing me to lose my grip on the weapon, which dropped to the thick foliage of the ground.

As he disarmed my knife hand, I pivoted my body and lashed out at his lead leg. My bloodrapier struck home and cut a small gash into his thigh.

He responded by sending a gale of frozen wind out of his wand that blew my head as if I were trying to give a nuclear-powered leaf blower a blow job. My eyes froze in an instant, blinding me. My cheeks billowed out before freezing as well, leaving me with a face that screamed fierce…probably.

I stumbled backward, waving my hands frantically in front of me. Ludvig began his approach, positioning his silver-infused sword for the final strike. As he lunged, I sidestepped and stabbed him through the bicep of his sword arm, using my preternatural sight to aim at his heat signature. He dropped the weapon, but not before punching me in the face with his wand hand. It hurt. Like it actually hurt me. I've been hit by countless foes—which admitting now feels a bit odd; doesn't exactly make me sound like a pleasant fellow—and very few could rock me like Ludvig just did.

Once again, my ample backside found the dirt as my brain struggled to reboot. My bloodsword retracted into my body on automatic reflex as I rolled onto my back, my skull hitting something hard on the ground. Whatever was under my head hummed with power.

I brought my hand up to my skull in a show of stunned confusion and grabbed the hilt of the silver kukri. I opened my freshly thawed eyes and looked at Ludvig. Though his face was hidden by his tactical goggles and breathing apparatus, I could tell he was pissed. His left hand, still holding the wand, grabbed his bicep, where blood flowed freely. I smiled and reached out with my will to grab hold of his oozing life energy, and pulled. The Hunter's blood began flying toward me like a crimson snake slithering to its new master. I began to stand as his powerful blood became mine, leaving him stunned as more and more poured from his arm like an opening nozzle. Lilith, it was unbelievably potent.

As I reached full height, I drew in a breath and slashed my prey's other arm with the kukri. As new blood poured from the gash in his forearm, the wand slipped from his weakening grasp and toppled to the ground.

Behind us! Baleius cried out, pulling me from my blood bliss. Dropping the focus on Ludvig's blood, I made a one-eighty turn and was met with a whip infused with silver. How the hell did these guys afford so much of that holy metal?

The whip roped around my throat, and I was tugged, yet again, to the freaking ground, but face-first this time. I felt like John Wick in the third movie where he keeps getting kicked through glass displays over and over and over again…and over. As I fell toward the ground, I produced my own bloodwhip in ironic contrast to the holy metal, and lashed out at the kid. My own rope found its target, wrapping around his tender neck. I leaped back up to my feet as the fledgling supernatural hunter gasped in fear as I willed spikes to begin forming along my manifestation. As I did, I cut his whip with a quick swipe of my razor-sharp kukri, letting the pieces fall to the ground.

A sheet of white-hot pain exploded down my arm as an enchanted sword cut through my bloodwhip, stunning me as if I had grabbed an electric fence powered by a fission reactor. I had thrown more energy into the manifestation than I had originally meant to, not fearing the chance of hitting enchanted or warded armor from the kid's exposed neck.

As every muscle tensed in nerve-shattering pain, I began falling backward to the ground, as if I were a plank of wood. Ludvig, who was standing in front of me and a step to the side, grabbed my coat and pulled me close to his covered face. In a thick, Swedish accent, the Hunter said to me, "What de hell are you?"

"Ha, *Predator*," I said weakly in reference to his unintentional movie quote.

It didn't take long to regain my faculties, but I decided it was best to play possum for a moment. Maybe I could get a few answers.

"Magni, to me," Ludvig called out without taking his face from mine.

Foliage crunched underfoot as the teen approached. I lazily shifted my gaze from the huge man holding me to look at the smaller…I guess he was a trainee? My blood manifestation had lost cohesion and had basically melted all around the kid's neck and shoulders, giving him a crimson ascot.

I got a clear view of the boy then; red spots of acne sprinkled sporadically over his pale face. He had a small nose under eyes that bulged when they saw my face. He was familiar somehow.

"It-it's him!" Magni cried out, pointing a shaking finger at me.

"Who? De vampyr?" Ludvig asked. "You're sure?"

"I'll never forget his evil face. That monster killed my mom."

I straightened then, figuring out where I knew him from. "The boy," I mouthed in disbelief. I put my hand on Ludvig's chest without thinking about the action and shoved him away with ease, as if bating away a fly. He flew for several yards before hitting the ground, tumbling. From the corner of my vision, I was aware that he had recovered with unbelievable reflexes, but I didn't care.

"I-I'm sorry!" I stammered, tears brimming in my eyes as my mouth gaped open. I had thought about this moment countless times. "I didn't mean to!"

Magni—the boy I had turned into an orphan during a blood rage—looked at me and said, "I don't give a *fuck* what you meant to do, monster. YOU KILLED MY MOM!"

My world spun as he spoke; the weight of his words was more powerful than any weapon imaginable. I collapsed to my knees, dropping my head to my chest in shame as Magni unslung and brought the shotgun up, aiming at my vulnerable head.

"Wait!" Ludvig called out, running to stand between the barrel of the shotgun and my head. "You can't kill him." I lifted my eyes toward him in wonderment, my head still too heavy to raise.

Tears spilled freely from Magni's eyes as he snarled at his master, "Why the hell not, old man." Hot blood bloomed under his pale face, painting it a rage-red.

"Because you'll cause Ragnarök," Ludvig the Hunter said calmly, weathering the storm of his student.

"I don't care!" Magni shrieked in teenage defiance. "He killed her! HE-KILLED-HER!" His voice trailed off into sobs, letting the shotgun barrel fall to the forest floor.

"My mom was killed in front of me, too," I shared with a trembling bottom lip. "I-I have no excuse to give you, Magni. I-I didn't even know your name. Da told me you were being taken care of, but wouldn't tell me anything else." I found strength in the chance to explain and stood up, taking a step forward. This prompted Ludvig to turn and place a hand on my chest in a blatant warning to keep my distance, not only for Magni's sake, but my own, too. "I've thought about that night, so much." I began sobbing then. "I-I wanted to reach out, but Da wouldn't let me. He-he knew I'd just make things worse. I deserve your hatred!"

"Who's Da?" Magni asked, wiping his nose with the sleeve of his black shirt. "Raziel is who took care of me."

"They are one and the same. It turns out that Da was the angel Raziel...for both of us," I said, sniffling. "And right now, he's in trouble."

"Where is he? What did you do, monster?!" Magni demanded, snapping out of his sorrow at the realization that his watcher had gone missing. A touch of jealousy struck me then, barely noticeable but still there, like a train horn in the dead of night from miles away.

"In the darkness of Faerie," I informed them. Ludvig shot me a cursory glance before returning his gaze to Magni, who still held the powerful shotgun. He knew the importance of keeping me alive, and a grieving teenager could produce a problem. The kid saw how intently his teacher was looking at him and slid the weapon over his shoulder.

Ludvig removed his goggles and breathing apparatus before turning to look at me. He had a square jaw, dark blue eyes, and tuffs of coarse blond hair that stuck out from under his fancy hat.

"What do you mean, darkness?" Ludvig asked in his thick, southern Swedish accent. It wasn't the stereotypical speech pattern associated with Swede's on TV and movies. Where theirs was an inflection roller coaster within every sentence, Ludvig's was more akin to the near monotonous German.

"The Shadow Court escaped their prison and took over all of Faerie," I informed the duo.

"Ah, I see. Dat might explain the colder climate." I noticed how he had trouble pronouncing the "th" sound of certain words.

"Huh?" I asked dumbly, not paying much attention to the chill in the air. For a vampire, it was more of a sensory fact than something that was noticeably felt—at least when compared to a human. I could withstand temperatures ranging all across the spectrum and barely notice. It was more like when you smelled something distinct from far away; you knew it was there, but it wasn't overwhelming. As a mortal, I could remember walking outside from a warm house into the freezing temperatures and having my breath taken away and muscles almost seize up. "How long has it been like this?"

"It started over nine years ago. Maybe closer to ten."

I gulped. Ludvig noticed as I did, forcing his brow to wrinkle.

"If what you say is true, vampyr," Ludvig started, using the Swedish word for my kind, "Den dat means de Unseelie, run by de Winter Court, have taken over. Dis is not good." He looked at me intently then, as if just remembering something, and asked, "Why do odders say you are good? A good vampyr makes no sense."

I remembered my first meeting with Father Thomes back in 1990. He had told me that honesty was the key to trust. Inhaling deeply, I began my story.

I told them about how my parents had been killed because of our land. About how I had watched my mother's last moments in the brazen bull and how I could still smell her burnt flesh. How I had been offered a chance to avenge them. I kept my eyes on Ludvig as I spoke this part, glancing tentatively at Magni, who clenched his jaw as his eyes stared daggers at me. I wanted him to know about my mother so I could help him understand how truly regretful I was for my actions.

I recanted my disagreements with Ulric about using our abilities to help people and only drinking from those we deemed bad. About how my constant desire to be good wore on Ulric, who had refused to change his ways after being alive so long. I told them about our battle in the backstreets after I had worn out my welcome with my master, and how I had accidentally caused the Great Fire of London as a result.

I told them how Lily had come into my life after Ulric. About how she had saved mine and Depweg's life and then enacted a life debt on us. She had removed all her commands before I was to face Ulric, which I'd thought was a show of affection and trust; but now, the possibility that it had been just another form of manipulation and control had crept into my mind. On top of that, she hadn't issued any more commands to either Depweg or myself since then, even though we were still in her life debt. We would probably be under her spell until the end of time, or until we saved her life somehow.

I went over how she had helped save me from the shadow assassin by letting me piggyback a ride to Faerie. I confessed to feeling like that had been the cause of the decade-long time dilation, though I couldn't fathom her reason why. I wish I knew what she was playing at because my heart was becoming more and more scarred.

Next, I poured out how I had met Depweg during World War II, and how we had shared an affinity for killing Nazis. I noticed Ludvig's face experiencing microtwitches, indicating I had touched a nerve.

Then I shared how I had met Da when I had needed him most, just like Magni had. I realized, now, that he was my literal guardian angel sent to help me grow toward the Light. I missed him terribly at that moment.

"My goal was to save my best friend, Depweg, and his pack from you two hunters, and then go pull Da's ass out of the fire." Ludvig and Magni looked at each other for a moment, exchanging an entire conversation with just a glance, before turning to regard me.

When they didn't speak, I asked meekly, "Is-is he still alive?" My voice caught in my throat as I spoke, terrified of the answer.

Ludvig took a big breath before saying, "Depweg is still alive, yes. We have had numerous conversations, and I am conflicted wid what to do wid him."

I exhaled the breath I had been holding, relieved that Depweg was still alive. "And the twins?" I asked.

"Yes, dey are still alive," Ludvig confirmed. "I have dem at a cabin in de woods."

"Where is it?"

"I'm sorry. I don't fink I am ready to tell you dat, just yet."

Sudden anger built up in my core like a flash flood, white-hot and hungry for vengeance. "And why the hell not?!" I shouted, losing my temper immediately. They had my friends, and I wanted them back, now.

You could kill them both, you know, Baleius said, feeling my trepidation. *They won't be able to fight back without ending the world, and they know it.*

Thought I told you to quit with that shit, I barked at him in response.

You said for your friends. The man and the boy are not your friends.

Dude...just, lay off, would ya? Trying to be a good guy over here. Stop putting poison in my head.

Baleius didn't respond, but stepped away from the wheel now that he was no longer needed. I returned my attention to the supernatural hunters before me.

"Look, I like your werewolf friend, but he is still a werewolf. I hunt all supernatural creatures—"

"And help Satan in return!" I fervently interjected.

"What do you mean?" Ludvig asked, perplexed at the connection.

"Supes are required to hunt and kill all demons for a multitude of reasons. Satan tricked most of the supes to flee to Faerie by having warlocks create doorways at all the major ley lines in the world, leaving the Lilith-damned world defenseless. Now you...you come along and kill our last remaining defenders."

"It's not our fault!" Magni interjected in a near panic, the way children did when they were trying to eloquently describe why their parents shouldn't be mad at them but knowing they couldn't, which only exacerbated their frustration.

"Care to explain how killing the last of the supes is not your fault?" I regretted my choice of words the second they left my big, stupid mouth.

Magni's expression melted and turned to solid stone before he stated with a coldness that sent shivers down my spine, "I guess my mother never taught me better." It was like looking at an abstract version of myself. There was nothing behind his eyes but disdain for me.

Seeing the situation beginning to spiral, Ludvig stepped in and said, "Any of de remaining supes dat we killed, were a credible danger to humans. It was as if dey had no accountability anymore. One of dem even dressed up as a clown and ate children up norf."

I forced the volcano of rage in my chest to subside, which was easy to do as I struggled with the word "norf." It took me longer than I cared to admit to realize that he had meant "north."

Closing my eyes and rubbing them with my fingers, I asked, "You're telling me that the supes that didn't go to Faerie thought they could do whatever they wanted with everyone gone?" It was known that the supernatural community policed their own. Stood to reason that if there was no one around to uphold the law, then why bother. Heck, the reason why humans didn't go around killing each other for transgressions like cutting each other off in traffic—or even just breathing loudly—was because it was illegal to do so, with stiff consequences.

"Yes," Ludvig answered, confirming my theory.

"A clown, you say?" I asked, letting my hands fall away from my eyes.

"He said his name was Pennywi—" Magni began.

"Sh-sh-sh-sh-shhhh!" I shushed urgently, holding my finger up and looking around dramatically. "Do you want to get sued?" I stage-whispered. Magni frowned at me before he caught on and made the drastic mistake of letting the corners of his lips curl up in a smile before he realized what was happening and forced it back down. Ha! I was basically in. He was going to like me, and forgive me, and say, "It's okay you killed my mommy, Mr. Buff Vampire, because we're bestest friends now." Probably.

"So..." I started, unsure of what to say. "What now?"

"In regards to?" Ludvig asked.

"I bet you're fun at parties, aren't you?" I poked at him. Magni stifled a quick giggle. Ludvig glared at him briefly before returning his hard eyes to me. "I mean, big guy, that you can't kill me, and I don't want to kill you, right? And you have my best friend who *I know* you know is a good guy; it's why you haven't killed him yet. Did he tell you he was working with a priest to do God's work?"

"Your God means liddle to me, vampyr. I am Swedish."

"What the fuck does that mean, huh? You're a Viking who worships Odin? Is that it?" I was growing annoyed again while simultaneously being distracted by his delicious, flowing blood.

"Dat is a stereotype. Most Swedes are agnostic or affeist, actually."

"Aff-e-what now?"

"Affeist. You know, dey don't believe in de afterlife."

"Oh! ATHeist!" I said with emphasis on the "th" sound. He remained impassive.

Focusing on what he had said, I responded with, "Fine. It's also a stereotype that all supes want to be evil or rule over mankind. Depweg is one of the finest men I know, and you have him locked up like a damn prisoner. So I'll ask again." I let my eyes glow a fierce red. "What now? And keep in mind I'm only asking to be civil."

Magni let the strap of his shotgun slide off his shoulder as he subtly took hold of the weapon.

"It would seem you have us at a disadvantage, yes?" Ludvig said calmly.

"Appears that way, doesn't it, bub?"

"I assure you, dere is no need for aggression."

"Hey, who attacked who first?" I demanded.

"We didn't know exactly what we were hunting. And you have been gone for a long time now, haven't you?" he countered. "We only knew dat someding was killing men and making it look like werewolves."

"Yeah, about that. How did you know I had set a trap?"

"We found some of de drained flesh."

"Neat," I exhaled, shaking my head at my lack of planning and surplus of laziness.

"What is dis, neat, you say? Is dat not a word for someding good?"

"Oh, man, just shut your pretty mouth," I chided while shaking my head in exasperation. Then I lifted my head and let my red eyes underline my point. "Take me to Depweg, pretty-fucking-please."

"Like I said; dere's no need for aggression. I will take you to him," Ludvig said, signaling a truce. Having a verbal understanding, he focused on healing himself by placing a hand on his bicep and closing his eyes in concentration. A warm glow emanated from between his fingers; after he was finished, he repeated the process on the gash on his other arm. I noticed his bleeding had not only stopped, but the skin beneath was fully healed.

Aggression? I just wanted to see my friend. Didn't seem unreasonable to me. Maybe it was a little harsh, but...Something tickled my brain and I looked inward to see that Baleius had placed a hand on the steering wheel.

*You son of a...*I said, slapping his hand away.

I was just offering my assistance, should it be needed, Baleius told me innocently.

I know what you were doing, I retorted quickly. *Look, you can't go around killing everybody you disagree with.*

Why not?

Damn it, dude! Now's not the time. Just—just stop being a dick to everyone, I ordered, fatigue at having to explain everything taking over. I was beginning to see what people meant when they referred to me as exhausting.

My eyes shifted back to purple and my posture relaxed. Ludvig and Magni took note of this, relaxing their own stances in return. We were basically at a standstill; I couldn't kill Ludvig without losing the opportunity to save my friend, and he couldn't kill me without killing everybody in the feck'n universe. And the kid, well, I didn't think I was physically able to harm him at all now that I knew who he was. Even with what was at stake, if he put the gun to my head, I didn't think I could stop him from squeezing the trigger and ending my existence. I deserved his wrath. I deserved to be punished.

"Sorry about that. Now then, let me try again," I said before clearing my throat. "You seem like a reasonable fellow. How about taking me to see my ol' buddy, Deppyweg?" I asked with a smile that I hoped came across as friendly.

Chapter 14

It didn't take long to make it back to the Hunter's decked out van. It was a four-wheel drive monster with off-road tires, limo tint windows, and blacked out, well, everything. In the cover of night, it would be hard for most creatures to distinguish the vehicle.

"Shotgun!" I called out as I jogged to the passenger door.

"I don't think so, monster," Magni answered flatly, brandishing his own shotgun as he approached confidently.

"At least you didn't rack it menacingly," I relented, moving out of the way.

"Why would I do that? It's already locked and loaded. Racking it would expel an unused shell."

"I...never mind," I said, not feeling like explaining the typical movie trope. I slid open the side door and was greeted by a BDSM's wet dream.

Chains hung from the ceiling, while black hoods, handcuffs, and zip ties were organized on the side opposite the door.

"Neat!" I proclaimed, impressed.

"You keep using that word," Ludvig said as he shut the driver's side door and started the ignition.

"Are you gonna say that 'I don't think ita means what you think ita means?'" I asked in a terrible Spaniard accent.

"What? No. Why did you say it like dat? Dat's not how I sound."

"'Dat's not how I sound,'" I mimicked perfectly. "It's from a movie! Lilith damn it, you guys are terrible at this!"

"What'd I do?" Magni asked from the passenger seat, annoyed.

"Ugh, nothing! Just take me to Depweg," I said before adding, "Pleeeeeease," with extra syllables.

Ludvig and Magni glanced at each other, unsure of what to make of the situation. After a moment, Ludvig typed the destination into the GPS and put the van into gear before pulling onto a dirt road that led out of the wooded area.

"Hey, kid, can I ask you something?"

Magni turned his head to look at me with a confused scowl, pondering what I could possibly ask, and then turned forward again before saying, "What do you want?"

"Is your name really Magni?"

"No. And yes. My name was Collin until Ludvig adopted me."

"Interesting choice," I said while nodding my head.

"It means Mighty in Old Norse. Collin was but a child. Magni," Ludvig started, glancing appraisingly at his student, "is worddy of that name."

I mouthed "worddy" a few times until it clicked. "Oh, worthy."

"Dat's what I said."

"I mean, it's honestly a badass name."

Magni didn't respond. I understood his situation. Here I was, the monster that had killed his mom, offering a compliment. Pretty sure there was no self-help book on how to handle that situation.

"Can I, um, ask you another question, Magni?"

He didn't answer, but turned his head to stare at me.

"How…uh…how did you meet Da—I mean, Raziel?"

"Raziel saved me…from you," Magni began with venom in his voice. Then it softened as his mind relived the memories of the one who had been there for him when he had needed it most. "Then he made sure I went to a good place that cared for me. I didn't like it at first, because it wasn't my home. It was a school and a dorm with kids that had money—I mean, their parents had money. It was hard, at first, but Raziel visited me every day after my studies were over. He would talk to me about supes, and tried to help me understand why you killed my mommy…my, um, mom," he corrected himself, feeling vulnerable at the childlike term "mommy."

"Every day?" I asked, feeling somewhat dizzy that I had never known how much my actions had forced Da's hand.

"Yeah, every day. He would leave at sundown and always say, 'Remember, I won't always be here; but I'll always be with you.' It made me feel…calm, like I wasn't alone anymore. Then I met Ludvig—who adopted me—and Raziel stopped coming. The last time I saw him, I asked him why, and he said I was in good hands now, but that he would always watch over me."

"Yeah, that sounds like him," I choked up for a moment, remembering when we had first met; but now was not the time for that. "Thank you for sharing that. I had always wondered what he had set up for you. He always told me that you were in good hands and that I should stop asking."

"Raziel told me that you get into a lot of trouble. After a few years of visits and talking about you often, I thought I had forgiven you. I-I wanted to meet you, but he told me that wasn't a good idea. He said the people you care for get hurt; like a lot."

That rocked me back in my seat, and I became light-headed for a moment. I had always known that to be true, but to hear it out loud—and that one of your dearest friends had said it—was hard to process.

"He was right," I told him just above a whisper as I let my chin rest on my chest. I closed my eyes and took in a steadying breath. Something the kid had said resonated, and I had to ask a question that I really didn't want to know the answer to. "Do you?"

"Do I what?" Magni asked snappily, squinting his eyes in an expression that clearly told anyone who saw it that he had no idea what I was talking about (teenagers, am I right?).

"F-forgive me," I stammered.

I could see the side of his face smooth while his head bobbed with the motion of the van.

"I thought I had...until I saw you. It felt like I was in the car again." His expression hardened, and he turned to face me with anger in his eyes. "Do you have any idea how many times I woke up in the middle of the night, screaming? Huh? Do you? Or how I got really good at hiding my sheets in the school's laundry after I had pissed them? I kept seeing your red eyes and your fangs covered in my mom's blood trying to get me. Do you understand what you did to me, you asshole?!" He was on the verge of frustrated tears as he looked directly into the eyes of the being that had shattered his whole world.

"Yes," I croaked out. "I know exactly what I did, and it has haunted me as my biggest failure."

"Why...why did you do it? Why my mom?" he asked with a rage-filled expression that was quickly giving way to sorrow.

"There's a lot to know," I said as I began to tell the story about how I'd been made, including my constant battle with PS. Then I told him about how I had been hurt to the point of rapping at death's door, and how PS had pushed me off the wheel while I had been at my weakest. "Your...*mom*," that word felt so heavy in my mouth, "didn't do anything to deserve what happened. It wasn't her fault. It was mine. I let my Predatory Self gain control. I'm so sorry, Magni. I promise I will do everything in my power to make it up to you!"

Magni turned around, not wanting to let me see his tears, and stared out his window.

After a few minutes of painful silence, Ludvig chimed in.

"How is it you aren't like the odder supernaturals?"

"I've thought about that on countless nights," I said as I looked out my own window. Trees passed by as we drove down the trail. "I keep coming back to my...parents," I said slowly, my eyes flicking to Magni as I said it. "I told my maker, Ulric, that I didn't want to hurt the innocent. I fought him for years on the subject, until he grew tired of my apparent weakness and tried to kill me. Well, that and I figured out he had been lying to me, and knew I was going to leave him whether he wanted me to or not. I am not inherently evil just because I'm a vampire. Being a vampire just enhances who you are, and I think it's the same with most supes that started off as humans. If you're an asshole when turned into a vampire, you're an asshole vampire. Though I will fully admit that the dark gift makes it hard to be a good guy sometimes. The way I see it, most vamps have—or had, since I'm the last one —" I started, deciding to leave that Ulric was still alive out of the conversation for now, "a bad reputation because only the incredibly strong of will who can fight their own Predatory Self or the evil ones who *thought* they were always in control made it more than a few days or weeks. I can tell you that, according to Ulric, I was an anomaly among the immortals."

As I spoke, I realized I had the supernatural hunter's full attention and decided to take advantage.

"I'm not the only one, you know. The weres you have are good people as well. Depweg is the best of us, far more noble than I could ever be, and the twins follow him as their pack leader."

"Why do you fink dey are still alive?" Ludvig asked, glancing at me in the rearview mirror.

Silence grew again as we all considered the words that had been shared between us. After a few moments, I decided it was time to pull out my wild card and change the subject.

"So, what are you, Lude?" I asked in as jovial a tone as I could. "Mage? Wizard? Sorcerer? What?"

"He's a paladin," Magni threw out impatiently. Ludvig shot him a look, prompting the teenager to respond as most do. "What?"

"No way, man. Paladins can't throw elemental magic like that shit back there," I said accusingly, pointing my thumb over my shoulder.

Ludvig returned his gaze to the road, shaking his head and sighing, before he said, "Technically, I'm a hybrid."

We stopped at the end of the dirt road, which intersected a paved street. When he didn't continue, I pushed the issue by saying, "Gonna finish that thought there, buddy?"

Ludvig looked at me in the rearview mirror and said, "I'm a paladin who has learned the ways of elemental magic."

"Uh-huh, I got that. Where did you learn it from?"

"From wherever I could."

"Stop playing coy and spill the beans. Are you a wizard, Harry?"

"I don't understand," Ludvig informed me.

Magni started shaking his head and said, "It's a movie. Just—just tell him so he'll shut the hell up, please."

"By Odin's beard!" the big man started, agitated. "I learned from mages and wizards dat were willing to teach me."

"Ha! I knew it. Wait, how is a Viking also a paladin?"

"I—" Ludvig began as a large tree crashed down in the road right in front of the van. We smashed into it hard, abruptly stopping our momentum. Well, I said "our" momentum, but I wasn't in a seat attached firmly with a safety harness; so while Ludvig and Magni halted with the van, I, on the other hand, went flying through the damn windshield. It's okay though; the ground has always been there to catch me when I fall.

As I tumbled head over heels, a thought went streaking through my brain; *could this night get any worse.*

I think we all know the answer to that question.

I righted myself, landing in a movie-esque superhero pose, only to be kissed on the cheek by another tree that was swung like a baseball bat.

Stars burst into life within my vision as trees dropped from the sky only to disappear into the ground. As I hit and skidded on the road, I realized that the trees weren't falling; I was just flying sideways.

"Ow," I tried to say as I rubbed my face, noticing half of it was crushed in like a soda can underfoot. A quick focus of will, and bones popped back into place, filling my beautiful mug back out.

Get up, now, Baleius ordered, striding over to grab hold of the wheel with me.

Good idea, I responded, commanding my legs to get to work.

For a vampire as old as you are, you sure get knocked down a lot.

Yeah, as if you were expecting to be hit by a damn—

The tree sailed downward in an arc toward where I stood. I couldn't see what was holding it in the darkness. Rolling backward, I dodged the brunt of the attack, but was still struck by smaller limbs that did no real damage.

I burst through the branches of the tree and into the air. With a bloodlongsword in hand, I searched with shifting red eyes for my attacker. Holding the thick trunk was what appeared to be a pitch-black arm. I couldn't see any features other than the fact that the outline was darker than the rest of the surroundings. Even in the dead of night, the moon provided enough illumination that even a mortal could make out the white and yellow stripes on the road. What I struggled to stare at was an absence of all light, creating an outline against the surroundings.

Still in midair, I followed the arm up to the body, and finally, the head. A pair of glinting amethysts stared back at me while a Cheshire grin spread as I realized what I was facing. The glowing purple eyes and white teeth were the only distinguishable features on the huge shadow assassin.

Knowing in an instant that my blood weapon would pass harmlessly through the monster, I freed my right hand and smoothly reached for the silver kukri sheathed at the small of my back. The monster was overconfident and let me get closer, knowing I couldn't hurt it with my preternatural attack.

As I swung the huge sword downward with my left hand, I used the momentum to pivot my body while in the air. While my body turned, I slid the kukri out and slashed at the monster's face.

A roar erupted from the monster, like the sound of squealing metal, as the blade cut through the Shadow faerie's flesh. The hand holding the tree like a bat released it and shot up to cover the wound. As it did, I landed in a crouch and slashed at the thigh of the monster.

Quickly assessing his situation, the shadow beast used its free hand to swipe down at my knife-wielding arm, forming its own manifestation as he did.

I sucked in sharply, squeaking as I did, as my hand and silver weapon dropped to the street. The blade clanged against the ground, and for some reason, the thought that I would have to sharpen it later flashed through my head; if there was a later.

Seemingly in slow motion, my wide eyes flew down to look at the stub of my forearm. The edge was black from where the shadow assassin had removed my hand.

Oh shit, I exclaimed to Baleius. *The darkness...*

Worry about that later, please, Baleius responded through intense concentration.

The beast roared again, but this time with as much satisfaction as rage.

I began bending at my knees and waist to pick up the silver weapon with my free hand when the monster let go of its face and grabbed the back of my neck. Massive hands wrapped around my entire head, lifting me into the air. In the back of my mind, I vaguely took note that the monster only had three thick fingers, including thumb.

As had been my luck as of late, the ground rushed up to boop my sexy body. I couldn't blame it; I was irresisti—My world went black as the now familiar stars bloomed into life. The feeling of being lifted and then slammed back down was a new experience for me. Right before I hit, the monster opened its fingers, allowing maximum John-to-road contact, before closing them around my head and lifting again. After three or four hundred times of this happening—it was hard to keep track—I eventually yelled, "WAIT!"

For some reason, the shadow monster stopped and brought me to his face out of curiosity.

"Fuck you," I lobbed a bloody loogie in defiance. It passed through the shadow creature to splat onto the asphalt. The feeling of careening to the ground came back with a vengeance.

As my body made a crater in the blacktop of the road, a plume of fire exploded into life, bathing the highway with a fierce orange light.

Immediately, the hand pushing my head into the ground went incorporeal as the Shadow faerie shrieked in agony. I used the brief reprieve to roll over and through the monster toward the source of the fire.

Ludvig bared crimson teeth as his wand spewed flames toward the monster. I could see bone peeking out of a split eyebrow that streamed blood down his square face. It looked delicious.

Stop it! I cried out to Baleius.

Not me. We're hurt and need healing, Baleius responded calmly.

Crap. It looks so good.

As much as I would like to agree, we have a bigger problem to contend with, like our arm.

I was not expecting him to be the voice of reason. That monster must have done some serious damage for me to be this hungry. Willing a blooddagger in my remaining hand, I sliced my arm off at the elbow before the darkness could creep up.

Closing my eyes, I tapped into my reserves and pulled enough energy to clear my head from the thirst. Bones snapped, crackled, and popped back into place as I pulled from my blood savings. I was aware of how my chest cavity filled out where the impacts had crushed my body between my armor plating. The thought of those commercials showcasing s'mores oozing out between two graham crackers flashed through my mind. Finally, my arm grew out from underneath the sleeve of my poor trench coat that now ended at my elbow.

"Holy shit. That thing fucking hurt me bad, man," I huffed to Ludvig. "What do we do?"

"I'm not...really...sure," Ludvig spit out between his red teeth.

A thought stuck out. "The silver hurt it!"

As if on cue, Magni hobbled out of the van and made eye contact with me, using his shotgun as a crutch. I held out my hands, nodded to the gun, and he threw the weapon to me, collapsing to the ground and wincing as he did.

"Hurry. I can't hold dis much longer," Ludvig urged. A quick glance toward him showed veins ready to burst from strain.

I turned to face the monster and racked the shotgun. A shell ejected as I did. I slapped myself mentally for pulling the noob gun move.

As I lifted the barrel to point at the shadow assassin, who was dancing just out of the range of light the flame provided, Ludvig yelped in exhaustion and dropped to one knee. His flame went out as he went down, prompting the shadow monster to charge.

I squeezed the trigger and the shotgun kicked in my grasp right as a shadowblade cut through the weapon between my hands, splitting it in two. As the useless firearm fell to the ground, I noticed trees were visible through a punched-out hole in the darkness that stood in front of me. Purple eyes widened and looked down at the gaping wound that did not bleed. Hands roamed over the hole, disbelieving.

The eyes blazed in fury and indignation as the beast sucked in a long breath. I stepped back as the shadow assassin bellowed into the night, sounding like the horn on a train. The teeth in my skull vibrated from the sheer force while broken glass danced on the ground.

On either side of me, I could see Ludvig and Magni covering their ears as they screamed in pain.

As quickly as it had started, the monster ceased its call into the darkness.

Ludvig and Magni pulled their hands away from their ears and gawked at the copious amount of blood streaking their palms.

"Ludvig! Are you okay?" I called out. He didn't respond or even give any indication he had heard me. I turned my head to look at Magni, who was staring at me, fear in his eyes.

I called out to him and he yelled in return, "What? Oh no! I can't hear!"

"Fucking shit," I cursed, turning back to the monster who was holding his wound with both hands.

He's hurt! Where's the knife?

Behind him.

I took a step forward before Baleius cried out, *Wait! Something's wrong…*

I felt it too. The trees all along the road seemed to move, but there was no breeze to be felt in the cool air.

"I got a baaaaaad feeling about this," I said to myself as the shadows on either side of the highway started writhing like pits of maggots.

"Ludvig!" I cried out, waving my arms frantically as I ran to where he stood lost in a daze. He looked up at me and scrunched his face in confusion. I pointed at the tree line aggressively. His eyes followed, growing stern as they took in the incoming threat. I was impressed; I felt my own eyes were wide with fear as the shadows started morphing from that of the trees into savage, featureless monsters.

He moved his coat flap out of the way with an elbow and reached for one of the vials on his belt. I could see they were made from a dense polymer of some sort to prevent breakage. Ludvig slid one from its slot, pulled the rubber stopper, and downed the liquid in one gulp.

He quickly slid the empty vial back into its place before closing his eyes and clenching his fists. Veins pulsated along his neck, snaking up to push through the skin covering his face. A guttural roar came from his huge chest, reminiscent of a heavy metal singer. I took a nervous step back, not knowing what to expect. Did I say nervous? I meant I gave him his space to do his own thing out of respect. A respectful step back.

From the tree line, dark forms rose from the ground, all with purple eyes that seemed to lock onto me. I gulped—but once again, out of sheer respect and not nervousness. I wasn't scared of these…terrifying, featureless monsters that I couldn't hurt but which could tear me to shreds. The silver kukri flashed through my mind, and I had never wanted anything more desperately than in that moment. It was how mortals described being stranded in the ocean with sharks swimming just beneath the surface; completely helpless and unknowing of when that final strike would occur.

Ludvig held his wand while wild eyes darted between targets. It was like he was on some sort of enchanted speed. I saw that the wound on his eyebrow had completely healed, leaving behind unharmed flesh that had fresh blood all around it. I wondered if his hearing had recovered as well.

"Silver and light!" I called out to Ludvig. He shot his gaze over to me, nodded once with bared teeth, and returned to watching as the Shadow faeries finished their entrance into our world. With his free hand, Ludvig grabbed the hilt of his sword and pulled it from its sheath. Wand in one hand and sword in the other, he was ready for battle.

I turned to look at the kid, who stood trembling. He was unarmed and clearly not trained enough to stand toe to toe with these shadow asshats. Hell, I wasn't either if I were to be honest with myself—good thing I wasn't.

We need the knife. How are we going to get past Bubba there? I asked, referencing the giant shadow monster standing on the road.

I have an idea, Baleius announced.

You mean a plan? I snickered. I just couldn't help myself. Baleius ignored me.

Ignite the dry leaves along the road.

Huh? I can't do that...can I?

We don't have time for your self-doubt. Give me the Lilith- damned wheel, he said, all but knocking me away. As I relinquished control in my mind, I looked out the window of my eyes and returned my consciousness to the battle about to start. It was odd having my Predatory Self in full control; sort of like when someone tossed something at you and by nothing but reflex alone, you caught it. It was still *you* doing the actions, but without your consciousness having to think.

With Baleius in control of my body, I dropped to a crouch, hands curled at either side of my waist like I was cupping invisible tennis balls. I waited for my chance before I made my move.

The world went still then. No one moved as both sides assessed the other.

Warn him about getting cut, I instructed Baleius, who had full control over my body. He didn't respond or do as commanded. The only sound was Magni's panicked breathing of.

I SAID—I began, raising my voice, until a rogue breeze blew onto the battlefield, somehow signaling to everyone that the fight was on.

Howls of delight rang from both sides of the road as the Shadow Fae rushed in like two tsunami waves competing on who could swallow us first.

I screamed in fierce concentration as my hands exploded upward, palms facing the stars. A line of flames several feet high ignited on either side of the road as if a line of gasoline had been lit.

Howls of hunger changed key to screams of pain as the flames lifted higher into the air, feeding on my energy and the dense, dry brush along the roadway. Tree to tree and everything in between was washed in brilliant orange light.

The shadow giant bellowed in rage and charged forward, wisps of smoke peeling off from where the light burned his incorporeal flesh. I was exposed where I stood, holding my attack for as long as I could lest we be overwhelmed by an enormous wave of claws and teeth.

I watched as the bringer of darkness approached like a freight train at full speed. Amethyst eyes fuming with rage as razor-sharp teeth chomped at the air. I kept my hands up, focusing on the flames keeping the horde at bay. I tried to pour more energy into exciting the molecules of the air to produce a brighter flame before the beast could decimate my sexy, supermodel body, but the creature was already committed and nothing would stop it from reaching me. I could see the flames down the road through the hole in its torso.

Jump! I cried out to Baleius. He didn't respond or move. *Dude, are you listening!*

When the beast was a few paces out, a familiar shadowdagger formed in its hand. It lifted the weapon up and brought it down toward my head, intent on splitting me in two.

A silver-infused sword startled me as it swung in an upward arc right in front of my romance novel face. It slashed through the dagger, which evaporated into smoke as it lost contact with the monster. The beast reared in pain, and I dropped my hands to jump through the hole at its center.

As I landed on the other side into a roll, I heard Ludvig grunt in pain. I dared a glance over my shoulder and saw him tumbling backward on the ground, his sword clanging to the ground off to the side. The monster's gigantic foot set back down after, presumably, kicking the Hunter away.

Turning my head, I located the silver kukri and rushed to it. As I grabbed the weapon, shadow monsters started jumping through the diminishing flames that I had lost my focus on. A few were incinerated from the still powerful tendrils of flames that snaked up toward the sky at random intervals. My fire was just as stubborn as I was and refused to die. Someone get me a "Proud Dad" bumper sticker.

I turned and began running toward the shadow assassin, who was moving toward Magni. Ludvig was still recovering from the massive blow he had sustained.

As I ran, several Shadow faeries leaped through the dying fire and began scrambling toward me, sharp claws beating on the asphalt like the pounding of rain on sheet metal, but my focus was on Magni; that is, until I saw some of the Shadow faeries leaping onto the big monster and being sucked into its flesh. The bastard was healing by using the bodies of its soldiers!

Cheater! I cried out as I watched through the windows of my mind.

While running, I stuck my free hand in front of me and willed the molecules to ferociously excite in my grasp. I poured my energy into the manifestation, knowing it was either lose the energy or die. A ball of plasma with the scaled power of a star radiated light in all directions, searing the shadows that leaped toward me. The light cut through the faeries like water dissolving cotton candy, evaporating them in the intense power of the microstar.

With every action, there was an equal and opposite reaction. I didn't know if that fit, but it sounded good. Why was I saying this? Well, you see, the flesh from my hand began melting off as I tried to contain the power of my John Star. Bone pierced through liquefying skin.

YYYYYEEEEEEOOOOOOOWWWWW! I cried out as nerves sang their song of torment like a church choir. But it had the desired effect. Shadow monsters stopped swarming us to retreat into the darkness, allowing me to run up to their leader, who was rearing an arm back to strike a petrified Magni.

The light struck the beast and he turned right as my hand—which had been reduced to brittle bone under the unforgiving heat—fell off. The light winked out as my hand shattered on the ground like dried dirt; but some of the light had damaged the beast, who shrieked in rage as it turned to swipe at me. He was missing an arm, and half his face was decimated, leaving bubbling skin that I could make out now. Good. Let the bastard burn.

As the monster swung at me, I brought the kukri up and removed his swinging arm before halting in front of the beast and slicing in the opposite direction at his waist. There was a low-pitched wheezing sound that escaped the monster as its top half fell to the ground like a thick tree which had been expertly cleaved by a lumberjack. Well, I did have the beard already. Lumber-John. I liked it.

I grabbed Magni and dragged him to where Ludvig was sending torrents of flames into the darkness. I noticed the Hunter's face was crazed, with spittle shooting from between his lips as he laughed manically. He had gone berserker or something.

Letting go of Magni, I placed my hand on Ludvig's shoulder, trying to get him to flee with us. He whirled on me with eyes blazing and bloodshot, forcing me to deflect his wand hand with my elbow as he brought it around.

"We have to get the fuck out of here!" Baleius shouted through my mouth. I concurred wholeheartedly.

Ludvig's crazed eyes locked onto Magni and his features visibly relaxed a tad. He returned his gaze to me and nodded. The blood on his face was dry and cracking from the intensity and heat of his attack.

"Keep them off us," Baleius commanded through my mouth as impressive wings sprouted from my back. I saw that they were bigger than normal, and was about to ask why when I grabbed Magni and brought him close. I reached for Ludvig with my other hand before remembering it was a bubbling goo on the pavement. I could feel Baleius focusing as he tried to heal it, but nothing happened.

Shit. That ball of light prevents me from healing?

It was plasma, Baleius told me, frustrated. *I didn't anticipate having to use so much energy.*

Good to know, I said, filing away the information for later use. Something snagged my attention and grew in the back of my mind like the sirens of an ambulance approaching from a distance. I looked back out the viewport of my mind and noticed I was panting heavily.

How much energy did we use on the plasma ball? I asked Baleius, turning to where he stood at the wheel.

Too much, he answered weakly.

How much do we have in reserves?

I don't know, and I don't want to try and use any more. It'll take a while to build back what we have lost.

Are you sure I can fly with the weight of these two? I know the wings use up a lot of energy to provide lift.

What choice do we have? Baleius barked, exhaustion wearing his patience as thin as roast beef from the butcher.

Oh, I don't know—what about the Mage-a-din all hopped up on Berserker-flavored Mountain Dew?

We don't need him, Baleius responded sharply, agitated at the thought of needing aid from anyone else.

Well, carry on, then, Mr. I-don't-need-no-man.

Baleius ignored my jab while letting his consciousness spill back into my body.

I reached for Ludvig, wrapping my nub under his armpit and against his chest to secure him.

I looked to see the shadow assassin was grabbing his lower half and bringing it to meet his torso. I watched in anger laced with awe as the shadow flesh started stitching itself back together as more of its soldiers sacrificed themselves to their master.

So that's what it feels like, I said, suddenly having empathy for every opponent I had ever faced.

I was about to rocket into the night when Ludvig cried out, "Wait!" as he broke free and rushed to his sword on the ground. He sheathed the weapon, pulled his goggles down over his eyes, set his breathing apparatus in place, and finally tightened the drawstring on his fancy hat.

"You done?" Baleius said through my mouth, annoyed. When Ludvig nodded, we resumed our escape position, and I leaped into the night.

Magni screamed in terror as the ground rushed away from us at an alarming speed. Over his cries, a piercing screech sent waves along my wings. I almost lost my balance trying to hold on to the heavy Ludvig as both hunters struggled to cup their heads after the cry almost ruptured their eardrums. I dared a glance back and saw something that would probably haunt my dreams for the rest of my life—if I made it past the night, that is.

Two glowing orbs trailed plumes of purple smoke as they soared to catch us.

Shit! I cried out.

"Shit," Baleius echoed out loud, a tad calmer than me.

As I watched in terror, two rows of white teeth birthed into existence under determined eyes. I couldn't see exactly what was chasing us, but I could perceive what the darkness blotted out as the body moved. Streetlights and a ground that was illuminated by the moon were obscured as enormous wings flapped.

A purple mist enveloped the crashed van we had left behind before orienting on us as we fled.

Oh, Lilith, that's not mist...those are eyes!

Be quiet, Baleius commanded, focusing on the situation at hand.

An army of amethyst eyes rushed to join the two giant orbs of the big shadow monster. The Shadow Fae had taken a cue from their leader and morphed into nightmarish birds that had razor teeth in their beaks. They were catching up.

I helpfully offered sage advice to Baleius in the voice of Jeff Goldblum, *Must go faster! Must go faster!*

We're too weak! Baleius yelled back, his air of calm and control beginning to crack. *We need to drink one of them.*

No way, man! Don't do it. We have to have something in our reserve tank.

Are you willing to risk permanently losing the energy we have spent centuries building? Baleius asked harshly.

What's the point of having it if we don't use it? After a moment, I added, *But...you know, don't lose it. Okay?*

In response, Baleius grunted before opening the floodgates of my reserves, sending a rushing wave of tremendous power throughout my body.

As the shadow monster opened its jaws to snap at my feet, I abruptly changed direction and dove downward, spinning as I went. Magni passed out from the g-force and went limp as the still hopped up Ludvig fought to aim his wand.

"Hold steady, damn it!" Ludvig yelled over the din of screaming, furious shadow birds and the rush of wind. I obliged and leveled out; but from how I held him with my nub hand, I couldn't fly straight and turn him easily. He struggled to fire behind him, missing our pursuers entirely.

"Grab my belt, fool," Baleius barked out with my mouth.

Without hesitation, Ludvig stuck his hand between my ripped, six-pack abs and the thick leather of my belt, and turned while flying a few hundred feet in the air. I let my grip around him slip as he positioned himself. My ample belly pressed against the top of his hand—to, you know, keep him in place. I'm not fat.

Near freezing wind tugged at his legs and Helsing-style coat, making it difficult to aim.

Ludvig began laughing hysterically as he started throwing elemental magic at the purple-eyed birds flying at us. I looked over my shoulder to see a wall of amethysts blot out the stars. A blast of wind gusted out of Ludvig's wand, doing absolutely nothing to the shadows. Next, he tried fire, which kept them at bay but didn't destroy them. Magni continued to hang loose in my grip, his feet dangling at an angle behind him as we flew.

I can't keep this up forever. I'll run out of energy eventually! An idea shot through my head. *Let me grab the wheel.*

No, Baleius responded coldly. *This is no time to give you control.*

He was right. I'd probably drop Magni or fly us into a damn power line or something. *Fine! But I have an idea. Tell him to aim for their eyes.*

A look of recognition swept over Baleius' face as he said, *You're right!*

"Aim for their eyes!" Baleius shouted over the howl of the wind to the paladin mage.

Ludvig didn't need to be told twice. He sent out an arc of lightning that missed the first target he shot at. Another blast forked out and slammed into the eyes of a bird that had dared to get too close. It shrieked in surprise before exploding into mist, the stars becoming visible behind it before being replaced by another shadow.

"Woohooooo!" Ludvig cried out in sadistic joy as another beast exploded.

The shadow assassin didn't like what was happening and squawked its wrath. The wall of purple began to swirl as Ludvig continued his onslaught, taking out bird after bird as they gained on us.

The wall of shadows dive-bombed toward us, and I wrapped my wings around my body to fly downward like a lawn dart.

"I can't attack like dis!" Ludvig cried out as we plummeted back toward Earth. I was impressed at his dedication to the battle, but we were flying downward nearing terminal velocity, which harshly pulled his feet skyward from the air friction.

We need to make it toward light, I said to Baleius, who didn't acknowledge my statement.

As we approached the ground, I unfurled my wings and soared just below the streetlights. The wall continued its kamikaze trajectory before the front line was swallowed by the bright LEDs. A few made it through, being shadowed by their dying brothers' bodies, and struck home.

One shredded through a portion of my wing, while another took off one of my legs, narrowly missing my passengers.

I screamed in pain as I was struck. We began to lose altitude from the hole in my wing, the speeding road fast approaching and eager to catch us.

I positioned my wings perpendicular to the road to create drag and slow us down. As I did, the hole in my damaged wing split open like a stubborn bag of potato chips, tearing from tip to tip. We began to tumbled toward the ground.

"Drop!" I cried to Ludvig, sucking in my gut to free his hand after our speed had decreased precipitously. As he did, I pulled Magni to my chest and wrapped my wings around us. We smashed into the pavement with bone-shattering force and immediately began tumbling, the road tearing my manifestations to shreds. Pain radiated down my spine from where the asphalt had ripped my energy-laced wings from my body. I held Magni tight in my arms, absorbing as much damage as I was able, and cursed as I felt my beloved trench coat start tearing now that my wings were gone.

We came to a stop, and I immediately sat upright, letting Magni lie on the ground, protected for the time being by a bright streetlight shining above us.

Still in control of my body, Baleius willed a silent chain saw to existence and smoothly removed my leg above where the darkness was spreading. It was odd seeing a working chain saw without the accompanying roar of the combustion engine. Then again, I knew we didn't need one to make the blades work.

Holy shit! A freaking chain saw? How had I never thought of that?

I do not know. The mechanics are quite simple.

As he spoke, I used some of the precious energy to heal my foot and then my hand. It took some intense focus and energy, but my ball scratcher grew from my wrist, making me whole once again.

Right then, just as I was feeling like things were looking up, something massive slammed against the top of the pole and sent the light housing exploding into the night. Along the road, streetlights on both sides of the pavement were met with the same fate. With each crash, the night swallowed more and more of the world around me. A feeling of dread swelled in my chest alongside the growing darkness of the night in a twisted dance that I couldn't escape.

Ludvig hobbled over to where I sat, stuck out his hand, and said with a delighted smile, "De fight is not over yet."

We clasped forearms and I got to my feet, kicking off my remaining boot as I did to even out my stance. Fighting in one steel-toed boot would have been troublesome, or at the very least, distracting.

We turned to face the shadow assassin as it landed and morphed back into the massive featureless monster. All I could make out besides its eyes and teeth were thick limbs that blocked the moonlit scene behind them.

Purple eyes swirled above us like water circling the drain, watching the culmination of the show.

They know we have nowhere to go, I mused, feeling the last of the hope I had wither and die. I walked to the wheel in the control room of my mind and locked eyes with a Baleius who had fear in his eyes. *If we are to die, mind if I drive?*

The demon or pure mental personification of my vampirism or whatever he was, removed a hand from the wheel and took a small step to the side. I stood next to him, grabbed the wheel, and said with an empty smile, *I hope the apocalypse is as much fun as all this has been.*

The monster before us didn't attack. Instead, he turned his head to regard a portion of air next to where he stood. He placed one of his three dense fingers at a point in front of him at shoulder height, and then dragged a claw to the ground. The air split open like flesh that had been cut, curling at the edges from the release of tension. Out stepped a formidable boot of black armor etched in red linings. A similarly covered leg appeared after, followed closely by a bare hand and then the rest of an impressive body.

"Oh...poop..." I lamented as King Oberon snapped his fingers, stitching the portal behind him closed.

"Hello, John," King Oberon said jovially as he pulled his helmet off. A warm smile spread over his face as he rested the piece of armor in the crook of his arm. His gladius was sheathed at his side.

"What have you done with Queen Tatiana?" I demanded.

His smile faltered for a moment before returning. "Why do you care about the affairs of the Fae?"

Magni began to stir, moaning and grabbing his head with both hands. He had been put through a lot of g-force as we evaded the denizens of the Shadow Court.

Ludvig kneeled in front of him and reached for his head instinctively, ready to heal his ward.

"Don't," I whispered without moving my mouth. "Not yet."

Ludvig glanced at me through his tactical goggles and then back at Magni, understanding my meaning. He simply stroked the boy's hair like a caring parent would. It sent a pang of guilt through my heart that I had put this orphan child into the exact situation that Da had done his best to avoid. I destroyed everything I touched. It was my curse.

"I don't," I proclaimed loudly to Oberon. "I care about my world, though. You've fucked things up."

"Oh? Have I, now? In what way, vampire?" he scoffed like a dickhead boss sarcastically asking why you deserved the raise, knowing he wasn't going to change his mind.

Ludvig stood up and addressed Oberon with confidence, "You have disturbed the nature of fings. Balance must be restored." It nagged me that he sometimes interchanged "th" sounds with a "d" or "f" instead.

"I don't remember asking you to speak, mage," Oberon chided Ludvig, his eyes pulsing a fierce purple in warning.

Good. He doesn't know he's a paladin. Can we use that? I asked Baleius.

I'm not sure yet.

"What do you want?" Ludvig asked the King of Shadows, ignoring the previous comment.

"Ah, the direct approach. I admire that from a man with a mask," Oberon exalted in delight.

"Did-did you quote that on purpose?" I asked, confused. *Batman Returns* was one of my all-time favorite films.

In answer, Oberon extended his hand, palm open, and sent a blast of purple energy toward me. His eyes blazed as he lost his temper and screamed, "Where's my gauntlet, you insect?!"

Ludvig dodged to the side, grabbing a woozy Magni as he did, while I somersaulted in the opposite direction.

That's why we aren't dead yet, I said to Baleius, who nodded in agreement. *We have leverage.*

Give it to him in exchange for our lives.

What? No way, dude. If he wants it that badly, it's got to be for a damn good reason. Maybe it unlocks his final form or some other anime-type shit.

So what if it does, Baleius countered. *If we die, the end of everything occurs.*

And if he gets the Lilith-damned gauntlet, then he has no reason to keep us alive. Didn't Taylor say the Shadow Court wants to cast the entire fucking universe into darkness?

Live today. Fight tomorrow, he said with a tone of finality. He wasn't wrong, but he sure as shit wasn't right, either.

"Why do you want it?" I inquired, knowing full well what the answer was.

Oberon went from rage beast to calm and collected in an instant before saying, "Do you have ANY idea how awkward it is to walk around in an outfit that's missing a glove?"

I wanted to like this guy; but the whole destruction-of-the-universe thing really put a damper on our relationship.

"And if I give it to you?"

"You can't!" Ludvig interjected urgently while sticking a hand out as if to stop me.

"He can and he will. If he does not, then…" as he spoke, Magni started sliding over the pavement toward Oberon's open hand.

"NO!" Ludvig cried out as he grabbed hold of one of the boy's legs. He was pulled to the ground and dragged along with his protégé, refusing to let go.

As they reached Oberon, they were each hoisted into the air by an unseen force and into the king's open hands. Oberon closed his fists and held them both by their throats. I hadn't realized before just how huge the Faerie king was until I saw him compared to the taller-than-average Ludvig. Oberon held him at eye level, but Lude's feet dangled almost three feet off the ground.

King Oberon looked at me, then, and said, "Their lives, for the gauntlet." To accentuate his point, he began squeezing their necks. Their feet kicked the air uselessly as he held them steadfast.

"Okay! Okay," I shouted as I brought both of my hands up in pacification. Oberon's grip relaxed enough for the hunters to stop kicking the air wildly.

A plan started to form. It was crazy. It was stupid. It was going to work…I hoped.

"It's a good thing he's not a paladin, or he might *heal* himself if you hurt him," I called out, putting emphasis in my words.

"He can't heal if he's dead," Oberon returned. "Where's my gauntlet?"

"It's at home, in a display case. I have a *light* on it," I said, once again emphasizing certain words. As I spoke, I put a hand behind me and formed a loose fist as if I were holding something invisible.

This is going to suck, I warned Baleius.

What are you doing? Just give him the damn armor!

Two things, I started. *Stop being a little bitch. And the armor was at home the last time I saw it ten years ago, so I can't exactly give it to him right now, can I?*

You're going to get us killed…

Probably, I admitted, focusing on the middle of the swirling mass of Shadow Fae above us.

I took in a deep, steadying breath, pulled an alarming amount of energy from my vastly depleting reserves, and yelled, "HEAL!"

Ludvig stuck each of his hands out to point at King Oberon and the shadow assassin and sent out a blinding flash of light. It was ironic that a healing spell—which would normally aid anything it was cast against—provided a bright illumination that hurt the creatures of shadow.

Oberon and the shadow beast roared in surprise and pain as Magni and Ludvig dropped to the ground.

A cacophony of squawks came from above as the swirling mass of shadow birds positioned themselves to attack. As they did, I threw the hand that I had been hiding behind my back into the air and sent every ounce of energy I had into the ministar I created. I screamed with exertion as the death star—that I had totally stolen from Locke—sailed into the sky, swallowing scores of shadow birds as it ascended. The higher it got, the more energy I poured into it, letting it grow and grow.

I was brought down to one knee, unable to keep myself standing as I forced everything I had into the manifestation that meant life or death. I bared my teeth as I felt the cords on my neck pushing against my shirt and damaged coat from the strain. My vision began to dim at the edges as pure energy, which had taken centuries to build, flowed forever away from me.

Fierce light shone in all directions, dissolving the shadow monsters who cried out in pain before their screams were abruptly cut off. I was both alarmed and surprised when I felt myself get lighter from the gravity the star was creating. Within seconds, the sky was free from all shadows, leaving behind only the shadow assassin and King Oberon, who were far enough away to withstand the light from the star. Either that or they were too powerful to simply dissolve.

I squinted and saw that Oberon was only shielding his eyes from the light while the shadow assassin's featureless flesh began to bubble noticeably.

I dropped the rest of the way to the ground, completely exhausted, as my limbs became too heavy to hold up. My death star hand dropped stiffly to the road in front of me. I was surprised when the star remained in existence, pulling on everything around it for a moment while setting the very air around it on fire. The wind screamed in my ears as the atmosphere was sucked into the star, feeding it. My coat flaps began dancing in the air around me like puppets controlled by frantic strings while my hair struggled to free itself from the prison that was my gray beanie.

Then the microstar began to shrink, slowly at first and then rushing in on itself. There was a blue burst of light that extended in all directions like embers from a dying fire. Leaves, sticks, and other assorted vegetation fell from the sky as the gravity died with the orb made from pure energy. I was going to have to be careful of that in the future if I ever regained the immense power it took to create such a manifestation.

It hit me, then. All the centuries I had spent amassing the energy from each kill, gone in a single moment in time. I felt naked.

I let my gaze drop from where the real stars filled the sky again to land on Ludvig and Magni, who were battling King Oberon and the shadow monster.

Ludvig had given his wand to Magni in the fray, and the young hunter was attacking the shadow assassin with a mixture of flames and lightning. Though his attacks were nowhere near as powerful as Ludvig's, he was smart. After a spout of fire to push the monster back on its heels, he would send arcs of lightning at the amethyst eyes before switching back as the beast approached again.

King Oberon had drawn his angelic gladius and was dueling Ludvig. The Swedish hunter parried with his own enchanted sword, doing his absolute best to deflect the celestial weapon rather than attempt to go blade to blade in a direct block. They were incredibly skilled swordsmen that moved at preternatural speeds.

"Holy shit," I breathed, realization dawning on me that Ludvig could have cut me in two with ease. He had restrained his true power with me, which would have caught me off guard. Now I knew the extent of his ability. Lilith, no wonder he had gotten Depweg AND the twins all at once.

Magni waved a sheet of fire in front of him, disguising his next move. As the shadow assassin bellowed in frustration while inching backward, an ice shard pierced through the veil of flames and struck one of the beast's eyes. The monster screamed in response, but this time it was comprised of fear and pain rather than rage.

King Oberon feigned a power strike at Ludvig, who ducked on pure reflex. As he did, Oberon kicked out at blinding speeds, impacting his opponent square in the face and crunching it sickeningly. Ludvig's limp body flew backward as if struck by a truck, blood trailing the air as he soared.

As Oberon brought his foot back down, he turned his free hand toward Magni, who was about to lash out at the beast's other eye. A ball of purple light exploded from the

Faerie king's palm like a sci-fi weapon and passed through Magni's forearm that was connected to his weapon hand.

Magni sucked in a sharp gust of air as his hand thudded to the ground, still grasping the wand. His remaining hand grabbed at the smoking flesh that had been seared closed. His eyes went wide before glazing over and eventually rolling back into his head as he started falling to the ground. As he fell, the shadow beast grabbed him in both hands and brought the unconscious hunter up to his face. Strands of saliva strung from his upper and lower jaws as he opened his giant maw wide.

The boy whose mother I had viciously killed inched closer to the gleaming teeth. The orphan Da had tried to keep me from in order to protect him from my poisoned kindness had had his arm blown off. The teenage hunter who had dedicated his life to preventing others from experiencing the pain I had forced him to endure had watched his master get defeated in battle. Magni, who had had his childhood stolen and had been thrown into a world that would make most men cower in a fetal position, was about to die…because of me.

"Waaaaaaaiiiiiit!" I bellowed at the top of my lungs, nearly passing out from the exertion. King Oberon held up an arm that was bent ninety degrees at the elbow, signaling the monster to halt. The shadow assassin stopped moving as if a pause button had been pressed. Oberon smiled at me, knowing full well what I was about to say. "Spare them, and I will give you the gauntlet."

King Oberon's arm didn't waver as he seemed to consider. Of course, it was all just a show of control because he didn't give two shits about the kid and only wanted to complete his celestial ensemble.

After a few more seconds of feigning indecision, King Douche dropped his hand and said, "Deal." He then turned to the shadow beast and said, "Lolth, drop the boy. However, if the vampire attempts to deceive us, kill both his companions."

Lolth, the shadow assassin, tossed Magni's unconscious body to land and tumble to where Ludvig lay still. I rushed to them, dropping to my knees to cradle Magni's head. I looked down at where his arm ended in blackened flesh that steamed in the cold air, placed my hand over it, and began to concentrate.

What are you doing?! Baleius demanded urgently. *We don't have the energy for this sentimental nonsense!*

Shut up, I commanded coldly. I didn't care what it cost; I was going to heal this boy.

Blood oozed from my hand, slower than normal, and began coating his arm where it ended. My hand began to tremble from the exertion as the blood formed a small pillar to where his hand would be, then began expanding outward. I imagined his forearm, wrist, palm, and finally his fingers before sending enough energy to repair his flesh.

Black bugs began to swarm my vision as everything I saw steadily shrunk to a tiny pinprick. My head swayed, and a part of my concentration was shifted to not toppling over on the street. Once I felt his heartbeat in his fingers, I knew I had done my job and began retracting my precious blood back into my hand.

I examined my handiwork as my vision returned and the bugs slowly cleared, escaping to first my peripheral vision, then outside the scope of my sight entirely. Though a few had remained behind to dance in front of my eyes sporadically. Stubborn bastards.

"Where...is it?" Oberon asked impatiently, so eager to finally have his winning moment.

"It's at my lair. You'll find it locked in a cabinet," I said, defeated.

"Oh no, I will not find anything, imbecile. You are going with me," Oberon said with a touch of ire in his voice. He then turned toward Lolth and snapped his fingers. If I had had any energy left, I would have used it to shit my pants as Lolth lowered into the ground as if on an invisible elevator only to reemerge behind me. With a hand imperceptible in my current state, Lolth backhanded me and sent me flying away from the hunters. Magni had just begun to stir right as the enormous beast rose from the shadows on the street and grabbed the hunters in each of its massive hands.

As quickly as it emerged from the darkness, it disappeared again, dragging Magni and Ludvig into the abyss. Magni's high-pitched shriek was cut off as his head was swallowed by the shadow.

"Magni!" I screamed.

"Don't worry about them. Simply an insurance policy, should you change your mind."

"Where are they?" I demanded, stumbling to get to my feet. I tripped and landed on the road, feeling the asphalt tear at my cheek. I was surprised to find it hurt. I lifted myself up on hands and knees, a hand rubbing my stinging face as I looked up at my aggressor.

"In *my* Faerie," Oberon said coldly, emphasizing that the plane was now his.

"What about Queen Mab?" I asked, both out of curiosity and in an effort to buy time in the hopes of formulating a better plan.

"Dead," he said with a show of teeth. "She left me to rot in my prison instead of choosing to aid her rightful king. She paid her insolence with her life, as will those that refuse to bow to Oberon, King of *all* Faerie."

Oh, man, he referred to himself in the third person. He's completely insane, I said to Baleius.

Being a prisoner for a length of time can do that to a mind, Baleius responded flatly with more meaning than he had probably meant. I did a mental double-take and decided to let that comment go for the time being.

"It is time, Jonathan. Take me to what I seek," Oberon commanded as he made his way over to where I was still on my knees.

"It's just John," I stated weakly, as if I were out of breath. "Question: what happens when you complete your set? Do you get, like, plus one to all defenses or something?"

"Why explain that when I can, instead, describe in agonizing detail what will happen if you don't take me to my prize?"

Fuck! He had deflected my attempt to get him monologuing. I knew I should have rolled more points into charisma. Whatever he wanted with the celestial armor, I could guess it meant a similar fate on Earth as what had befallen Faerie.

Oberon grabbed the back of my collar and lifted me up as easily as hoisting a pillow off the couch. A whine escaped my throat before I could stop it at being dominated like an ant beneath the magnifying glass of a bored child.

"Now then," Oberon said once we were nearly touching noses. "Where to?"

Chapter 15

Oberon looked skyward and began to levitate into the air with me in tow like a child's teddy bear. As we reached high enough to view the city's landmarks, Oberon instructed me to point in the direction of my home. I did as commanded, feeling as vulnerable as a beat dog; but I did, however, try to take advantage of the long journey to the end of everything.

A few times, I attempted to trick my captor into revealing something, *anything*, about what his post-glove goals were.

"So, ah, how about that Midworld, huh? I think someone should come along and just, I don't know, *do* something to it. I just don't know who could do anything to a big ol' place like Earth or how they would do it. Hmm. What do you think, Obi? Can I call you Obi?"

He answered with stern silence.

After the third attempt, Oberon halted midflight and lifted me to face him. Anger cracked his otherwise stony face as he smoothly grabbed my throat under my chin with his free hand. The hand that had been holding my collar moved to rest on top of my shoulder near my neck. With a grimace of barely controlled rage, he pressed down on my shoulder while my head was held firmly in place by my jaw. Confused eyes went wide once I understood the error of my ways as a series of sequential pops started between my shoulder blades and raced up my spine to my skull. With each ruptured disc, my teeth rattled and my jaws cracked. My skin burned like fire where it was being stretched to the point of ripping apart.

Oberon licked his lips in eager anticipation as moans became yelps that became screams. My toes started to tingle as I gawked into fierce eyes that watched me with a burning intensity. I had seen that look on my own face before and knew that Oberon was having an internal debate on if he actually needed me alive to retrieve his prize. From how his eyes grew wider the closer I got to decapitation, I understood which decision he had made.

My legs went numb below my waist, and my fingers began to tingle as my vertebrae began to break apart.

"Okay! Okay!" I desperately cried out between teeth that were being smashed together. My frontmost pearly whites cracked and then shattered under the pressure before Oberon stopped.

Oh, thank Lilith.

Might I suggest keeping your mouth shut for the remainder of existence? Baleius chided frantically in my ear. *I rather enjoy being not dead.*

Without so much as a word of warning or gloating, Oberon grabbed my collar again and lowered me back into place. He resumed flight as I continued to reluctantly point toward the cemetery, my hands alternatively rubbing my neck and jaw. I didn't have the energy to heal my ruptured discs, cracked vertebrae, or shattered teeth. I fought back tears of pain and humiliation; I wasn't going to give this sonofabitch the satisfaction.

We landed at the entrance of my home, Oberon keeping his tight grip on my collar to support my paralyzed legs. I pointed to the marble door, and Oberon used his free hand to punch the stone. It flew into the room, tumbling over the throne in the center before resting against the far wall. I gulped before pointing with tingling fingers to the hidden entrance. He tore it off its hinges with ease, and we started our descent into the Earth.

I opened the door to my home—trying to prevent the powerful king from destroying that too—and Oberon threw me inside with enough force to somersault over the couch. I cried out as the floor smashed into my broken face, sending a dizzying wave of nausea through me. It scared me how much King Oberon's attitude and demeanor had changed since the street battle. This close to his goal, the time for bravado was over.

As my vision cleared, I noticed a fancy glass vial plugged with a cork under the table just inches from my face. There was a dark red, viscous liquid inside that called to me.

"Gabriel," I mouthed as my numb hands reached for the vial and removed the cork with nearly limp fingers.

Behind me, Oberon began tearing open cabinets in search of his prize. He noticed the locked cabinet and, with a bark of joy, ripped the door off.

"What is this?" he demanded angrily. "Cups? What in the seven Hell's is *Battlefield Earth*?" He turned to face me then, noticing the vial that I had placed to my lips, and was smashed in the face with a bolt of fire from across the living room. I suckled on the vial with all I had as my eyes looked weakly in front of me to see Locke in a defensive stance. As he stood, green fire circled the floor in front of him before crawling up his body. When the fire went out, Locke was donned in full epic battle robes with plates of iron and obsidian covering his torso along with his upper arms and legs. An obsidian helmet that looked like a dragon's face covered his head as eyes began to glow a fierce purple that swirled with green.

"Warlock!" Oberon bellowed as he recovered. Using my hand to move my head, I saw him conjuring a ball of absolute darkness into his hand. I took note that it was different than his usual purple energy attack.

"He's after the gauntlet!" I cried out as the beginnings of power began entering my veins. It had been angel's blood what my friend had left for me. My vertebrae popped as they healed, and teeth formed anew. Discs reformed, and feeling returned to my hands and feet. I took in a deep breath and my eyes shot open wide and full of energy, like a dying man injected with adrenaline. It wasn't what I needed to completely refill my depleted reserves, but it might be enough for me to live.

I leaped to my feet as Locke rolled to the side and dodged the shadow ball. It slammed into the wall where he had been standing and evaporated it like cotton candy thrown into molten lava. Locke had a new window to his room curtesy of the Shadow King.

Locke's eyes shot to the wall and back to his opponent before he began chanting, causing all the light in the room to begin flowing to his hands like water down a drain. As the light built, Oberon moved into a defensive stance.

"Come on then, magic child," Oberon challenged with a growl.

Locke worked skillfully as he extended his hands and an ethereal sledgehammer appeared in his grasp. With a confident smile at one corner of his lips, Locke smashed the ground in front of him.

The entirety of my Fortress of Solitaire shattered as if made of panes of glass—the walls, floor, and even the ceiling broke apart as if my home had been a cube inside of a much larger room. As the world around us disappeared with the deafening sound of breaking glass, I realized that we were now on a platform with a deep pit all around the outside. There was a gap between the platform and the black stone walls where torches lined sporadically all the way around and then straight up. Where there had once been a ceiling now stood an intimidating stone dome at least fifty feet up. There were sigils all over the platform that I didn't recognize, as well as circles of iron spaced around the outside and center of the stage. Green fire erupted from the edges of the stage, removing all doubt that this battle was going to be for blood and bone.

"What the fuck?" I wheezed with a gaping mouth. Flames licked upward from the edge of the platform, spilling heat across the stage as they reached skyward.

The warlock took us to his training grounds; a mirror dimension of sorts, Baleius answered for me, having direct knowledge of Hell magic and its machinations.

Thought you couldn't remember anything before me, I stated flatly as a passing comment rather than a question. Baleius didn't answer, and I didn't care at that moment.

"I will use your skull for my wine, warlock," Oberon asserted with sickening confidence as he cracked his knuckles ominously.

I walked to one side of the platform, giving Locke and Oberon plenty of room as I continued to recover. Lilith, just how much energy had I used that not even *angel blood* replenished my tanks? Not just any angel's either, but the Archangel Gabriel's himself! I had a new substantial appreciation for my well of power now.

Locke chanted something as his fingers danced in the air, and a swirling vortex appeared on the ground just in front of him. Clawed hands reached from the purple-and-green swirling storm on the ground, lifting a demonic monstrosity the size of King Oberon himself from the abyss. The warrior had gray skin covering bulging muscles, with thick black chains wrapped around his waist, shoulders, and wrists. On his hip sat a scabbard that the demon reached for, pulling forth a skillfully crafted sword made of obsidian forged in the pits of Hell itself. Eyes glowed green on a face that held no emotions. This hellion was completely under Locke's control.

"Holy shit," I said in awe as the demon rushed Oberon, sword ready to strike.

King Oberon pulled out his celestial weapon and charged headlong into the demon's attack. Angelic sword met demonic blade, sending a shower of sparks cascading all around like an industrial grinder on metal.

Where the demon was all power and wild attacks, Oberon was patient, calm, and smooth like water. He flowed with the attacks, taking little strikes where he could while defending himself from the fierce blows that would split an elephant in two with ease.

Viscous black blood flowed from the conjured demon's gashes along his body, coating the floor in a dark mirror. The obsidian chains did their part and protected what they could, but Oberon knew what he was doing and was going to defeat the demon by a thousand cuts. Locke noticed this at the same time I did, and we both moved to attack.

As the swordsmen fought in the middle of the platform, both refusing to give up any ground, I moved in from Oberon's left while Locke went to his right.

I manifested a bloodpike while I saw Locke clasping his hands together and separating them to reveal a long wooden staff complete with floating stones at the tip. Each stone was different and hovered around the end like a planetary model.

Locke chanted something to himself, and one of the gems—a sapphire—glowed bright like a cell phone in a darkened theater before blue lightning shot out to strike Oberon in the chest.

He saw it coming and gritted his teeth, betting that he could take whatever power was behind the tiny warlock. King Oberon was both right and wrong. Though the bolt of lightning didn't kill him, it did lift him off his feet and toss him back several feet. This allowed the demon to strike at a spot between the angelic armor as the Shadow King's body shifted from the attack. Oberon roared in fury as he recovered, landing in a roll, and was back to his feet like it was all a skillfully choreographed Las Vegas show.

Locke shot out another arc that Oberon reflected with his gladius, sending forks of lightning in all directions. I barely dodged a small section of the blast as I charged forward. The demon, who was in melee range of Oberon, was not so lucky and took the brunt of the warlock's attack. He crumbled to the ground in a curling mass of smoldering, bubbling flesh. The obsidian sword clattered to the ground beside me before sinking into the ground to join its master in Hell.

I gotta give it to Locke; he didn't even hesitate. He removed his hands from the staff—which simply levitated just off the ground in front of him—and his fingers danced again. Two portals opened up this time. Locke's brow was coated in sweat and exertion as four clawed hands reached from the darkness and into the pit.

Oberon saw his chance and rushed impossibly fast toward a vulnerable Locke. I threw my pike at his rushing legs, willing the manifestation to morph into a whip as it reached where I thought he was going to be. The bloodwhip wrapped around Oberon's legs and he started to fall as I yanked with my borrowed angelic might.

He swung his gladius at my bloodrope, but I had anticipated this and had already willed the weapon back toward me as I ran to catch my falling opponent. I willed a shield and hammer into each hand and leaped to swing at Oberon's head. He saw the attack coming and decided to go down in a roll rather than fight to remain on his feet and catch his balance.

My hammer shattered stone where it struck, and I had just enough time to bring my shield up as Oberon kicked out at me. The force was stronger than anything that had hit me in all my existence, and I was thrown backward, sliding toward the edge of the flaming pit. I quickly turned both manifestations into ice climber's hooks and attempted to stop by slamming them into the stone beneath me. A pang of doubt entered my mind as the edge of the platform continued to rush toward me even as the spikes dug into the stone floor and tore matching lines several inches deep.

Then a section of stone near the end folded in on itself, creating a curb that I smacked into. I quickly got to my hands and feet and saw Locke with one hand out toward me, the cords on his neck standing out in sheer focus and willpower.

Holy shit. He caught me!

Focus! Baleius yelled.

Two more demons had been spawned in the time I had given Locke, but they were several feet smaller and covered in obsidian armor from head to toe. They had maws that snapped hungrily at Oberon as they charged on four thick legs. They reminded me of attack dogs covered in full battle armor as they stampeded.

Locke grabbed his staff again, and a ruby began glowing this time. He screamed as he hoisted his weapon into the air and slammed it into the ground, sending a rushing wave of crimson-colored flames that ran between the hellhounds.

Oberon leaped into the air, easily avoiding the attack. But Locke seemed to have anticipated this. As Oberon sailed over the wave, it collected and shot upward like a geyser to strike Oberon head-on. He screamed in surprise as the hellhounds took hold of both his arms while still in midair. With their collective weight, they slammed him down to the stone platform with enough force to shatter bone. The flames continued to shoot skyward around him, bathing him in an inferno while at the same time having no effect on the hounds, who had been created in Hell where fire reigns.

I got to my feet and ran toward the fray, leaping with the intention of landing on my Faerie meal. As I did, I called out, "Locke, NOW!" while morphing my hooks into twin daggers with armor-piercing tantos at their tips.

Locke took my cue and released his flame attack right as I landed on King Oberon's stomach. His arms were being stretched out to either side, which created beautiful gaps in his armor that I took full advantage of. I stabbed one dagger into his exposed armpit and the other into his stomach and began siphoning his ancient life force with as much gusto as I could manage.

His blood rushed into me, filling my body with power that made me scream in triumph. Baleius and I lost focus on everything else in the world as we drank deep from his well of enormous power in an attempt to refill my own.

In my elation, I didn't hear Locke calling out to me. After a few seconds of bliss, I drunkenly glanced toward the noise to see Locke waving his hands frantically and screaming at me. With a huge effort of will, I focused on the now, tearing myself from my blood stupor, and heard what he was saying.

"Move! Now!" Locke called out. As he did, I looked back at my target who had freed himself from one of the hounds and was swinging his gladius in an arc over his body. With only a nanosecond to act, I threw myself straight up in an explosion of stone just as the blade passed where I had been and through the other hound. With his other hand freed, he grabbed the throat of the remaining hound and squeezed its throat like a paper cup. A yelp was cut off as the beast fell to the floor, its tongue rolling out and black blood oozing as it spasmed.

Locke focused his will on a dark emerald. It glowed and a jagged beam of green shot out to latch onto Oberon's exposed flesh. Light began flowing from the Shadow King and into Locke's staff. I noticed he made a face of pleasure much like I did when feeding.

What the hell is he doing?

Siphoning his soul, Baleius said appreciatively.

While this was happening, I reached the cusp of my ascent and began falling back to the stone platform below, daggers ready to go again. Even with only a few seconds of feeding, I felt amazing, incredible even. I let my legs lift into the air as I began shooting downward toward my target like a bunker buster ready to bring some freedom to one of those countries that ended with "-stan."

As I did, I had a front row seat as Oberon grabbed the beam of green light with his gauntleted hand and reversed the flow into himself.

Locke gasped and fell to one knee as his own soul started being siphoned out.

"NO!" I cried out as bloodwings manifested and flapped once to reach my target faster. Oberon wasn't expecting this and recoiled as I crashed into him. I wrapped my wings around us both and pulled his arms in tight to his body. I jammed my daggers into his back in search of exposed flesh, and found one slit. Blood flowed as Oberon struggled mightily to free himself.

He raised his head back and slammed it into my forehead, stunning me. He did it again and again until I went limp and slipped to the ground in a daze.

A flaming green skull flew into and exploded on Oberon, impacting him hard enough to send him back a few paces. Another struck, and he took a few more steps backward. A third attack struck, and Oberon was a single step away from falling into the hungry flames of the pit before he regained his senses and grabbed the next skull that flew toward him with his armored hand. He smiled as he looked from the skull to Locke before taking one long step forward like a baseball pitcher. With a grunt of effort, Oberon lobbed the flaming skull back at Locke, who could do nothing but collapse to both knees in fatigue as his ironic fate approached.

I ran at preternatural speeds, my trench coat flaps cracking like whips, and stood with arms outstretched and eyes screwed shut between Locke and the flaming skull. Waves of green flames washed over my body, which wasn't protected by celestial armor like Oberon's, and I collapsed to the ground shrieking.

Oberon smiled, realizing his victory, and began making his way to where Locke kneeled and I writhed around, trying to extinguish the intense flames that were making my skin bubble. I noticed my silver cross was glowing with heat, burning through the remaining tatters of my shirt. A thought crossed mind; could I have just died if not for the pendant Father Thomes had given me?

As the last of the flames were frantically pat out by hands I could no longer feel, Locke sighed in exhaustion, and the world streamed around us like water down the drain. In its place was my Fortress of Solitaire, untouched by the battle minus the initial blasts.

"Goooooood," Oberon said, sounding like Emperor Palpatine. I stood to face him and willed a gladius into my hands; but nothing happened. He laughed as he saw the look of confusion on my face before backhanding me across the room and into the metal wall.

Oberon leaned down, wrapped a hand around Locke's tiny neck, and hoisted him to eye level. He turned to keep his eye on both Locke and me without worrying about an attack from behind. He removed his helmet with his free hand and placed it in the crook of his arm.

"Well fought, warlock. Now, where is the gauntlet? No more games." His cheekbones cast shadows up his skull that blotted out his eyes except for two purple glints in the darkness.

"Do you give your word that you will leave once you have it?" Locke croaked on the edge of choking while sweat streamed down his forehead.

"You fought bravely, and I respect that. So, I agree to your terms. Give me the gauntlet, and I will depart," Oberon promised.

"And you won't harm us," I added quickly.

Oberon's eyes shot to me, and his brow furrowed for only the briefest of moments before returning back to its placid, regal state. "Of course," he agreed, coldly this time, though.

Locke tried to turn his gaze toward me before giving up and saying over his shoulder, "John, it's in my room, behind the painting."

I walked to Locke's room before Oberon called out, "No tricks, vampire, or I'll make this one suffer an eternity in my dungeons." To emphasize his point, he tightened his grip around Locke's throat, causing him to cry out in a rasp.

I went into Locke's room, saw the painting on the wall above his bed, and went to it. As I stood in front of the work of art from H. R. Giger, I looked down at my burnt shirt and noticed the silver pendant had charred a cross into my flesh.

"Thank you, Father Thomes," I said under my breath as I grabbed the edge of the painting. It opened on a hinge, and there, on a shelf in the wall, was an iron box the size of the gauntlet. Underneath was another shelf that had an old-looking garment box with a black bow on it. I retrieved the iron box and walked back to the living room, where Oberon was waiting with an unreadable face. I set the box on the coffee table and stepped back.

"Open it," Oberon commanded tersely.

As if handling a ticking bomb, I undid the latches on the top, allowing me to lift the lid. Inside was the beginning of the end.

The fingers of a pearl white gauntlet etched in gold stuck out as if awaiting a handshake. Oberon smiled and dropped Locke to the ground, who gulped in long lungfuls of air intermixed with fits of coughing.

Oberon placed his helmet back on his head, reached into the box, grasped the gauntlet, and pulled it out. He wiggled his naked fingers and slipped them into the armor, which clicked into place over his forearm. As he finished, the red etching of the whole armor glowed bright, and Oberon gasped in elation as the celestial armor, forged in Heaven above, was complete again. I watched in horrid fascination as the gauntlet began to bleed from white to black as red snaked along the edges, swallowing the gold.

Oberon did something then that scared the shit out of me; he began cackling like a madman as his wide eyes looked at his identically armored hands. Oberon pulled his gladius out of its scabbard, and it ignited in a blaze of heavenfire along its length. His cackling crescendoed into a full-bellied maniacal laughter that reverberated against the walls. Black shadow flames began dancing with the white, red, and blue of the heavenfire, adding the energy of the Shadow Court to the celestial power.

The Shadow King Oberon abruptly stopped laughing, as if remembering something, and looked at me with an evil smile. As his grin spread, his head tilted downward while keeping his eyes locked on me until his eyebrows threatened to block his vision off.

"Hey! You gave us your word!"

Oberon spoke in a way that made my stomach clench, his voice low and methodical, "I intend to keep my word, foolish vampire. But know this; this world will bathe in the dark, and your human cattle will perish before you starve. Tell me, mosquito, how long can you go without blood? A year? A decade? Perhaps it will take a century for you to wither and die, going insane from the thirst before you perish." Oberon raised his face toward the ceiling, looking down his nose at me before he continued, "Do you see why I intend to keep my word? I want to witness the last vampire losing his mind from hunger before making a chandelier out of your bones." He let his eyes go unfocused as he stroked his chin in thought. "I think I'll place it above my throne so I can gaze upon you at my leisure. Mmm, yes. Ta-ta."

He then folded in on himself, leaving a shock wave that exploded all the glass in the living room, including my Lilith-damned *Battlefield Earth* collectable cups.

"Dude is artistic when it comes to bones, I'll give him that," I said to myself as my guts unclenched. We were safe...for now.

Locke caught my attention and I rushed to where he was dry heaving with bulging eyes.

"What can I do?" I asked, worried.

"In my room..." Locke trailed off. I grabbed hold of his slender arm near the shoulder and lifted him to his feet. We walked to his room, where he pointed to his desk. On it sat a wooden box with a glass cover displaying different stones in red velvet. He uttered a few words under his breath, and the box popped open with a hiss. Locke grabbed for a purple cluster, held it in his hand, and slammed the whole thing into his chest.

It burst in a small explosion of purple smoke which swirled around him until it found his face. The smoke snaked its way into every hole in his head, including his eyes, as Locke screamed bloody murder at the top of his lungs.

I stepped back in terror as I watched the events unfold. I had never seen anything like it before.

I was vaguely aware that the pieces of stone that fell to the ground were now green instead of purple.

Within a few moments, Locke stood up straight, whispered some words, and closed the glass case again.

"What the hell was that?" I asked in awe.

"A soul stone," Locke said, rejuvenated.

"A s-soul stone? Whose soul?" I asked, perplexed.

"Is that what we are really going to discuss now? Oberon has what he came for," he barked. "We need to seek council."

"Agreed. But first, we need to go get Depweg and the twins."

"I don't know if we have time for that."

"And I didn't ask, did I?" I cried out, surprising even myself. "Look, we are going to need their help. Can we agree that having three werewolves would be helpful?"

"Do you even know where they are?" Locke asked.

"Yes, I do. Now, let's go fucking get them, and then we can stop by Val's for some...*supplies*," I said with a wry smile.

Chapter 16

We walked through the kitchen and to the front door. I stopped by my cabinet and sighed heavily at the broken cups. Picking up a piece of glass, I looked at John Travolta's disappointed face and dropped the piece on the black countertop. Forest Whitaker gave me the stink eye from his place on the bottommost shelf; but that was to be expected.

Making our way up the stairs with Locke behind me, I asked over my shoulder, "What did you make of what he said?"

"Which part? It all sucked."

I pursed my lips while tilting my head before nodding in agreement, my eyebrows shooting up for a moment.

"I meant the part at the end, where I was going to starve."

"I wasn't really in the right mind while that was going on. He had nearly crushed my windpipe."

"So a soul stone healed you?" I asked.

"What did he say about you starving?" Locke asked, shrugging off my probing question.

"He said he was going to cast the world into darkness and that I would starve."

"That doesn't make a lot of sense. If he doesn't kill you, how can he start Armageddon?"

I shrugged in answer, a cold feeling making its way up my spine. He was going to watch me starve to death over decades, maybe even a century. I was incredibly thirsty at that moment, like how an alcoholic eyed the glass container on the store shelf just as the shakes began to manifest. My tongue glided over my dry lips subconsciously.

We made our way to the mausoleum, where Locke took in the damage Oberon had wrought. He shook his head as we walked outside. I picked the marble door off the floor and set it in place as we stepped outside. I wound up having to lean it against the entrance, but was confident no mortal would be able to move it.

Locke and I made our way to the parking lot where a sleek Tesla coupé awaited. It was gunmetal gray and looked like it was more related to a Lamborghini than to the Teslas I remembered. Had to remind myself that I had lost a decade in the blink of an eye when Lily and I had shifted planes to Faerie.

My teeth ground together subconsciously as I thought about her betrayal.

"Everything okay?" Locke asked hesitantly as we got into his clearly expensive vehicle.

"Hmm? Oh, not really," I said as Locke sat in silence, waiting for me to continue. "I don't know what Lily is aiming for, man."

"What do you mean?" Locke asked while pressing the ignition button. The only indication that the fully electric Tesla had turned on was a speaker system just outside the cabin that produced a powerful revving sound.

With ease, I typed in the destination I had watched Ludvig put into his van's GPS and hit start.

"I can't figure her out, dude. Like, what is her endgame with me? She says she is trying to help me, but then goes and costs me a decade. Lilith damn it, I bet she is responsible for that Lolth creature attacking me."

"Lolth? Did you say...Lolth?" Locke blurted out as he shot his head toward me, focusing on that one tidbit from my lamentations.

"That's what Omega Oberon said, at least."

"Oh, Christ," Locke breathed, shaking his head slightly and returning his eyes to the road.

"What?"

"Lolth...where do I begin..." he started, searching for the right words. "She is the goddess of the drow elves."

"What the fuck is this, Dungeons and Dragons? Who are the drow elves?"

I took note that the road we were traveling down, which used to be littered with ramshackle businesses, now was lined by massive warehouses. The roads had also been paved over with sleek, black asphalt. All streetlights were made of LEDs—the bulb of the future.

"The drow are a race of dark elves that are Faerie's version of demons. They live in darkness and want the destruction of the light."

"Alrighty then. So where does this Lolth bitch come in?"

"She is one of their gods. Books have been written about the drow pantheon, but few know the truth. What I can extrapolate from the few mentions of Lolth in my library, she is something to be truly feared."

"Neat! Super helpful!" I said in dramatic annoyance. "How do we stop them?"

"I'm afraid I haven't the first clue."

We pulled onto 288 heading toward Lake Jackson. I was impressed at how futuristic the cars on the road had become. A white truck with FORD lit up across the grill in color-changing lights zoomed by, the taillights a solid thin red line that were almost as bright as the bluish headlights. I lifted my hand to shield my eyes when the windshield darkened slightly, giving the light shining through a green tinge that didn't hurt my light-sensitive eyes. I lowered my hand as an idea struck.

"Light," I said absently.

"Come again?"

"I haven't even cum once, you greedy perv." Locke turned his head slowly to regard me with an expressionless face.

Sighing, I exclaimed, "Sorry. Anyway, light is a weapon against the Shadow Court."

"Except for King Oberon, who is of the Fae High Courts."

"Right, but he has adopted his gift much like I did with Ulric in that dungeon. Just because I was once mortal and still have human DNA, that doesn't protect me from my vampiric weaknesses."

"Are you saying a flashlight can take down the Faerie king?" Locke asked dubiously.

"Well, no. But I'm willing to bet dollars to blood that sunlight will fuck his shit right up," I said with growing excitement. I turned to face Locke, barely able to contain my delight. "What do you wanna bet that he hasn't figured out how vulnerable he is in the light? I mean, he knows its uncomfortable or whatever, but he probably thinks he's all but impervious now."

"Especially with the celestial armor."

"Yeah. S.O.B. has the whole set now, but maybe we can use that confidence."

"That's...not a bad idea at all, actually," Locke said while stroking his chin in thought.

"What? You're surprised I can come up with a *plan*?" I said, putting emphasis on the last word.

"You've reached your catchphrase limit, John."

We passed by an H-E-B and I pointed so quickly across Locke's body that he almost lost control of the car in his surprise.

"Stop there. I have a feeling we are going to need some stuff."

"Want to warn me next time, bud?" Locke exhaled, taking the exit to the grocery store.

"More fun this way."

We parked and made our way inside. Locke's battle armor had disappeared, leaving behind street clothes.

"Um, are acid-washed jeans back in?" I asked, looking at his pants. Above them was a multicolored windbreaker straight out of a Marky Mark music video.

"Unfortunately," Locke said, zipping his jacket up. There was a noticeable coolness in the air.

As we walked into the store, we were blasted by warm air and bright lights. The smell of baked breads and sugary desserts wafted through the air as we walked through the bakery section.

"After you," Locke said, waving his hand in front of him.

We walked toward the camping section, and I noticed the store was full of people even at this hour. They walked from aisle to aisle, periodically glancing at their hands. Around their wrists was a band of varying colors that projected a screen whenever the wearer made an L shape with their thumb and forefinger. Once their fingers were closed again, the screen disappeared.

"Neat! I want one," I said to Locke, pointing at a random patron's wrist. They eyeballed me, unsure of what to say as Locke and I continued past.

"Is that what you came here for? A new phone?"

"No, we came for..." I started as my eyes searched and then locked onto propane camping lanterns. "This!" I found the biggest one that promised the brightest light and grabbed all they had on the shelf, handing some to Locke to carry. I also pocketed some flashlights that projected a beam that could be seen from space, according to the bold letters on the package. Lastly, I grabbed a box containing glow sticks that you snapped and shook to create light.

Passersby took sidelong glances toward me, and I stopped to examine myself. My trench was missing the sleeve below and elbow and the back was sliced up from road rash. The shirt underneath was burned and I was quite sure I looked like a vagrant.

We were making our way to the front of the store when I passed by a rack of clearance clothing. I picked up the only men's black shirt they had and inspected the tag.

"Double XL. We are in business," I said as I draped the shirt over my shoulder. At least my burned shirt would be taken care of. I dared not replace the coat—that was nearly a century old—with something off the rack.

I yawned as we stood in line. Locke turned to look up at me—because I was over a full head taller than him in his young body—and scrunched his brow.

"Can't remember the last time I saw you yawn unironically."

He was right. I still hadn't replenished all my reserves from creating the giant ball of plasma. "Yeah, I took a cue from your book of spells and made a giant ball of death that burned a shadow army to a crisp. Took everything I had and more."

"Plasma?" Locke asked, interested.

"Yeah."

"Why didn't you just create light?"

"Because I...didn't think of it?" I admitted. "What do you mean?"

The cashier scanned our plethora of light-emitting products, not even caring enough to look up at us minus the initial, "Hello."

"Plasma is caused by one of many scenarios. How did you make it?"

"I poured raw energy into a sphere that expanded the more of my power I put into it. Once started, I couldn't stop until we were in the clear; but at least all those shadow bastards were incinerated by the light."

"You created pure plasma by superheating the air with your energy?" Locke asked as he finished paying by placing his phone wrist against the terminal. We grabbed our bags and walked toward the exit.

"Sounds about right," I confirmed. "I didn't know of any other way to do it."

"That's where you messed up. Whenever I created my plasma attacks, I did it by means of fission. I split the nucleus of a single atom and contained the resulting plasma in an orb of electromagnetism. That is actually the hardest part—containing the exothermic explosion and not destroying an entire city."

"So, if I understand this right, all I had to do was split a single atom to get the same effect?"

Locke's eyes grew wide and he became full of energy as he said, "Wait, wait, wait. Don't even think to try it, John. I practiced in a timeless void until I could get control over the entire process. If you try and create fission without the fail-safes, you could potentially destroy all of south Texas."

"Hmm," I responded as we set our bags in the trunk of the Tesla. I removed my coat and tore off the remains of my battle-worn shirt before putting on the new one.

"I'm serious!" Locke cried out, barely able to control the urgency growing in his voice. "I know you are able to excite molecules, as well as a few other party tricks, but that is a short step and a hop away from pulling an atom apart. If you are going to try, let me put you in a void first. Just please be careful. You have no idea of the powers you are contemplating."

"The moral of the story is I used too much energy on a simple attack," I said, changing the subject. It was best I didn't dwell on something as potentially catastrophic as fission, especially after being told not to. Telling me not to do something usually had the opposite effect.

"Right. You could have simply used the energy to create just light instead of the superheated plasma."

I rubbed my hand as Locke said this, remembering how the small plasma ball had not only destroyed my flesh but prevented me from healing for a bit.

I replaced my trench coat and walked to the passenger side of the car. We got in and he pushed the ignition button.

"Is there a reason plasma would prevent supernatural healing?"

"I suppose, yes."

"How?"

"Off the top of my head, the only thing I can think of is that the plasma could destroy every cell so completely that there would be nothing left to heal, as it were. Similar to a tree that has been burned in a quick fire or one that has been scorched from the outside in, all the way to the core. In one instance, the tree would be able to eventually heal and grow healthy again. In the other, the essence would be burned to its core, leaving behind charcoal instead of wood."

"I was thinking something similar," I said, rubbing my wrist. "Hmm."

"What?"

"I think it's interesting that I can, say, heal the burnt flesh of a mortal or even grow an entire new body using my energy, but I can't heal from things like plasma, iron, silver, or the sun. The list just keeps growing." I finished by letting the back of my head hit the headrest and sighing.

"Something I find odd," Locke said, "when I created the fission balls, UV radiation was produced as a result. Yet you weren't affected at all."

"Yeah, I haven't totally figured out exactly how the sun burns me." An idea struck me then. "I wonder if I can use my tanning membership?"

"Your what?"

"Long story. I thought that UV lights might do more than just increase my melanin production, if you know what I mean. Now I'm not so sure."

"Why…"

"Do I have a tanning membership? Or at least *had*," I finished for Locke. "Like I said, long story."

We pulled back onto 332, which led to 2004, and drove past farmland before pulling down a road and toward thick trees. The GPS showed we were another four minutes away.

"What was that place you took us to back at the lair?" I asked.

"It was a dueling arena I built between planes. I use it to practice my summonings and spells."

"Between…planes. Holy shit, dude."

"I'm taking my second chance very seriously. Plus, with you and then Depweg gone, I had no choice but to respond and grow stronger. I was dead serious when I said I wasn't going back to Hell, nor will I let Hell come to Earth."

"Welp, glad to have you on our side." A question popped into my head, and I asked, "Were you always a warlock? You know, even when you were Godwin?" As I said his name, I visibly shuddered, feeling a burst of negative emotions bubble up for a moment like a toilet on the verge of giving up.

"Technically, yes. But not really."

"Alright, not confusing at all."

"I had some abilities, but I didn't know what they were or how to really hone them. After learning vampires were after me, I decided it was past time to learn how to structure my powers. I sought out a teacher and learned all that I could, but it was actually Satan who unlocked my full potential while in Hell. Now we know why," he said, glancing at me with just his eyes before returning them to the road ahead.

"Jokes on him, then. But I gotta ask, what's with the soul stones?"

"Much like your source of energy is from blood, mine is from souls. Warlocks aren't exactly holy warriors."

"How were you able to use elemental magic?" I asked, remembering the staff he had used in our battle with Oberon. "Come to think of it, how is a paladin able to use elemental magic as well?"

"Elemental is the most basic form of magic. It flows all around us, and anyone with the ability to feel magic is also able to harness it. Humans do it all the time without realizing it."

"How so?" I asked, intrigued.

"There have been cases where humans have been diagnosed with an incurable illness, only to completely eradicate their sickness with only the use of positive thinking and meditation. I assume that whenever you create a manifestation you visualize the weapon and your body creates it. Am I right?"

"Pretty much," I admitted with a shoulder shrug in a gesture that said, "what of it?"

"They can picture their bodies destroying the tumors or reconnecting nerves or any number of other miracles, as some call them. The truth is they are harnessing the magic that flows around all living creatures on this planet without even realizing it. Just because I am a warlock doesn't mean I cannot access the energy that flows all around us. The same goes for—what did you mention—a paladin."

"How did you access elemental magic while in your arena?" I asked.

"I had to utilize my staff to use my stored energy and focus it. The gems are like a magnifying glass, with my energy acting as the sun in this scenario. It is necessary to focus."

"Can you teach me to magic?" I asked sheepishly, purposely saying it wrong. I honestly didn't know why I had such a hard time just asking for favors in a straightforward manner.

"I don't see why not. You clearly have a grasp on some advanced techniques."

"Sweet!" I exclaimed with fists raised in excitement.

The GPS chimed and we pulled slowly onto a dirt road. The path ran through a wall of trees that swallowed us as we drove into the yawning mouth. The road was bumpy and I had to hold the oh-shit handle to keep from popping up and banging my head on the roof of the car.

"You could have just put your seat belt on," Locke suggested as we pulled up to a house with a circular dirt driveway. It looked quaint, reminding me of Depweg's old cabin. A pang of guilt twanged in my chest as I thought about my friend's cabin—and Tiny Tim.

Sadness threatened to explode in my chest. Like any man would have, I squished down the emotions into a little ball in my gut.

We stopped in front of the house and I got out of the car. We went to the trunk, which was were the engine was usually located, and each grabbed a flashlight and lantern. A quick test revealed the compact flashlights were, indeed, powerful. I walked toward the front door, hissing propane lantern in hand.

"Check for traps," I said over my shoulder to where Locke followed. I let my senses flow around me as Baleius placed one hand on the wheel. My eyes flexed and canines elongated in my mouth as the world sharpened around me.

The lights were off in the cabin as I stepped to the front door. I heard the dry foliage crack underfoot as Locke made his way around to the back.

I grabbed the front door handle and tried to turn it. Locked. I placed the tip of my finger at the entrance of the keyhole and willed blood to first flow and then solidify, forming a key. I turned my hand and the tumblers engaged, unlocking the door. I repeated the process on the dead bolt above the handle and opened the door, letting it swing inward slowly with a long, creaking sound.

When nothing happened, I hesitantly stepped across the threshold. It smelled clean inside, yet a bit musky. I walked down a small hallway and into the living room. On a wall just inside the room, I saw that the AC was set to off. I blew air out of my nose in a semblance of a chuckle; Ludvig had seemed the type to not waste electricity when he wasn't home.

I sniffed and noticed the scent of musk had grown stronger. I walked toward the smell, using the aroma as a compass, until I came to a rug in the middle of the living room. I kicked it out of the way and was rewarded with a hidden door that led into the earth below.

"Here," I called out loudly to Locke. There was a sizzle and a pop as the back door swung inward. I looked up to see Locke holding a wand similar to the one Ludvig had. The brass door handle smoked from whatever spell or magic Locke had used.

He walked over to where I stood, and I got a clear look of his weapon. It had ancient-looking runes inscribed down its length that I hadn't ever seen before. They seemed to pulse with a neon green glow.

"Are they down there?" Locke asked, breaking me from my inspection of his wand—which didn't sound like I had intended it to.

I looked down and sent out my senses. "The door is canceling my abilities."

"Mine too," Locke said in agreement.

I kneeled and stuck the tip of my finger on the padlock keyhole. As I sent blood in, I recoiled in shock, standing and waving my finger as if burned.

"Iron. Why the fuck does iron burn when touched but silver doesn't?"

"Depends on the iron. If it is blessed, both iron and silver can burn on contact for specific supes."

"Of course. He's a paladin and can bless whatever the feck he wants." I stuck my finger in my mouth and sucked on the throbbing digit while staring at the door. "Well then," I said as I bent down, grabbed the handle, and ripped the door off with the protest of grinding metal. I threw the door on the couch and shined my lantern into the darkness below.

The smell of fresh blood began oozing into the room from the hole. Locke and I looked at each other, and without a word, I jumped into the abyss.

I landed some twelve feet below the floorboards of the cabin. Pillars of concrete were positioned throughout, offering support where the dirt of the earth would have if not for the hidden basement.

Holding the lantern above and just behind my head, I began my search. I didn't need the light to see, but preferred to keep it as a deterrent to any Shadow faeries. Locke came down the steps one at a time behind me, careful not to lose his footing. The unmistakable aroma of blood guided my nose, and within a few long strides, I came to a wall with a door. Locke came up behind me with hurried steps.

"Blast it open, now," I commanded Locke, who didn't protest. I stepped out of the way and he waved his wand in a rectangle around the door, and the concrete holding the metal began to liquefy. As he focused, I could see the door hinges on the other side of the wall. Once they were completely visible, he let his focus drop, and the concrete ceased melting.

Handing my lantern to Locke, I willed a hammer in one hand and a chisel in the other. I placed the tip of the chisel on the topmost hinge and hammered the rod out with a handful of quick strikes. I repeated the process two more times, returned my blood to me, and pulled the door from the hinge side. It didn't want to come at first, but then relented by collapsing to the ground with a resounding thud.

Locke handed my lantern back to me, and I willed a gladius in my free hand as I stepped into what could only be described as a cellblock. There were six rooms with doors made of iron. They stood three deep on each side of the pitch-black hallway. I could taste the blood that was in the air now, making my skin crawl with helpless frustration. I wanted to run to each room and throw the doors open, but I needed to control myself. Blood meant an attack of some form or another, and I could tell there was a lot of it. I approached the first door and noticed there was a latch at eye level. I slid it open to reveal an empty room.

I checked the cell next to that one, and it was also empty. The third door I came to, I noticed a pool of blood that glinted like a sea of rubies in the light of the propane lantern. A lump leaped from my stomach and lodged itself in my throat as I reached with trembling fingers to grasp the handle of the little window. I started breathing heavily as I braced myself.

I slammed open the cover and looked inside with the lantern next to my face, the hiss of the propane loud in my ear. I inhaled sharply in dismay as I saw what was in the jail cell.

Inside was the shredded torso of one of the twins. I couldn't tell which one it was because the face looked like it had been through a wood chipper. I saw what was left of the tattered workout stringer and deduced it was probably Dawson. Warm blood still oozed from his waist between uncoiled intestines.

"It's fresh," I said as if in a dream before snapping back into reality. "It's fresh!" I barked at Locke in warning, who immediately took a defensive stance, his clothes growing into the battle robes once again. His wand glowed a fierce hellfire green as he turned to face the way we had come. I put my back up to his, methodically scanning the darkness ahead of me for danger.

"In here!" a muffled voice cried out from one of the cells on the opposite wall. We sidestepped over to it, and I opened the cover. I was taken aback by how much older Joey had become. He had faint frown lines on his forehead and eyes that no longer held the innocence of youth. His hair was shaggy and greasy, and he had an unkempt beard.

"John?" Joey called out in as much surprise as relief.

"Yeah, buddy. It's me. Where's Depweg?"

"I think he's next to me," Joey said, pointing to the room closest to the end of the hallway. The door was open. The light from my lantern created shadows that swelled and danced as I approached the open cell. My wide, crimson eyes darted all around, desperate to find my brother. I made a tiny whining sound as I cleared the edge of the door and saw the room was completely empty.

"Well?" Joey said just above a whisper, sensing the tension and smelling the fresh blood in the air.

I stepped back to Joey's cell and said to both him and Locke, "Empty."

"Damn it," I heard Locke bark to himself. Depweg was his friend too. Probably his only friend.

I regarded Joey's door and saw there were two locks and a handle. I turned the latches on the locks, grabbed the handle, and pulled the door open. Joey stepped out and looked around the darkness.

"Where's Dawson?" Joey worriedly asked, looking between Locke and myself. In that moment, I knew the weight of the words I was about to speak was going to shatter his world and leave him in jagged pieces for the rest of his life.

"He-he's..." I tried to say. Joey stood as still as stone, his eyes demanding I finish my sentence. "He's dead." Joey rocked back as if I had given him a little shove, his eyes briefly rolling into the back of his head. Joey placed a hand on the stone wall to catch himself and began to breathe heavily. As he breathed, his nostrils flared, and his eyes followed the cause of the scent. Bulging eyes landed on a steaming puddle of blood that led into a cell on the opposite wall of his. He began to hyperventilate then, the cords standing out in his neck with every fierce inhalation.

He took a step forward with eyes the size of the full moon, prompting me to place a tentative hand on his chest.

"Please...don't. You don't want to see, man. Please," I said to Joey, my emotions mixing with my words and causing my voice to crack.

He either didn't hear me or didn't care as he continued to walk forward. I let my hand slide off his chest as he stepped past and into the nightmare of the rest of his life.

I heard his bare foot slap wetly into the pool in front of the cell, and I closed my eyes and shook my head. It was like watching a horrific accident that you were powerless to stop in slow motion. Nothing you could do, nothing you could say, nothing you could bargain or trade would stop it from happening. And it was going to be monumentally tragic.

Joey tried to suck in air at the same time he began screaming, and it came out a garbled waver. My heart dropped as my mind flashed to what Joey was seeing. Dawson's eyes were still open, glazed and unfocused.

Joey exhaled everything he had in his lungs before only squeaks came out. Then he sucked in air and began screaming incoherently, a mixture of despair and unimaginable pain that could only be brought to the surface after a lifetime of fear. His worst nightmare had been birthed like an atom bomb on his psyche, tearing his sanity to shreds. His twin brother...his best friend whom he had spent nearly every day with since birth, was dead.

A guttural chuckle pierced the air between screams, prompting Locke and I to quickly change stance and stand side by side facing the end of the hallway. There was a doorless frame with nothing that we could see beyond. We carefully walked forward as I reached into my pocket and grabbed a handful of glow sticks. I broke them all by bending them against my thigh and began shaking until the familiar green grew into life. I swung my arm in an arc and let the glow sticks fly into the room. Some hit concrete pillars, others bounced off stone walls and clattered to the ground. One flew and then bounced off something I couldn't see. It landed and rolled a few paces to a lump on the ground. My heart sunk as I realized it was Depweg, hunched over and bleeding from grievous wounds. His blood was black in the green of the glow sticks and flowed with sickening ease from gashes in his torso and arms.

"Depweg!" I screamed and took a step forward. Two glowing amethysts appeared in the air near the ceiling, followed by the familiar white of a Cheshire grin.

"Lolth," I drawled out.

"You know me, mosquito?" the goddess inquired. Her voice was cavernous while still maintaining some semblance of femininity. It was like a sound engineer had applied autotunes to it.

"I know enough," I said, hoisting my lantern to better light the room. Lolth recoiled before pursing her featureless face and sending a puff of air toward us. As if we were simply holding wax candles, the propane lanterns' light was extinguished in the gust of air, leaving behind a room that was sporadically bathed in the green of the glow sticks.

"Then you know it is pointless, insect. Oberon has the celestial key and is freeing my children as we speak," Lolth purred. Instead of reigniting the propane lanterns by clicking the red button on their bases, I decided to opt for the more powerful beam of the flashlight.

I squared my shoulders while reaching into my coat and said, "I don't give a shit what he's doing. You're both dead, you hear me? I'm going to kill that pixie Oberon, you, and all your shadow bastards too." As I finished, I pulled the military-grade flashlight out of my pocket, pointed at Lolth's smiling face, and pushed the button.

The light slammed into the Shadow goddess' face and immediately began peeling her flesh back like a hurricane tearing down a sand dune. She shrieked so loudly that I could feel my ears beginning to bleed. I was aware of Locke dropping to his knees and cupping his hands over his own ears as she screamed.

A blur of black fur bolted past me and crashed into the screaming monster's torso. Even though the ridiculously tall beast was crouching, it still toppled backward as the werewolf attacked her. Snarling jaws ripped at melting flesh, tearing huge chunks out of the shadow. Claws raked in unison like a dog trying to bury its favorite bone in the soft dirt. Black blood splashed the walls with each of Joey's rage-fueled attacks.

Lolth regained her senses enough to know how bad the situation was and grabbed Joey's skull with a hand, tossing him to the side. He landed on the stone wall on all fours and rebounded back toward his target, his eyes glowing the fiercest yellow I had ever seen on a were.

The Shadow goddess saw the attack coming and rolled behind a pillar, effectively breaking from the line of sight of my flashlight. As she crossed into the shadows, the light no longer impeded her abilities, and she disappeared into the darkness. It was unnerving to see the massive body vanish behind the relatively thin concrete pillar instead of coming out the other side.

Joey leaped as the last of Lolth's body disappeared, and passed through the thin air to land on the other side of the pillar. His head shot back and forth in search of his prey. When he couldn't see it, he brought his nose down to the floor and began pacing around, audibly sniffing as he did.

Locke cried out as an invisible hand wrapped around his head. I brought the beam of the flashlight around just as Lolth leaped through the ceiling and into the darkness. Locke dropped to the ground, clawing at the helmet that was crushing around his skull like a soda can.

I scanned the light all around me, trying to anticipate Lo—A hand shot through the darkness at my feet, slamming into my pelvis and slamming me into the ceiling with a crunch.

The flashlight went skidding off as I dropped it. Lucky for me, the beam pointed in my direction as it stopped, and Lolth screamed while dropping me. She fled around another pillar, disappearing again.

As I laid in a heap on the concrete floor, I willed my broken hips, legs, and ribs to heal, groaning with each pop.

I was vaguely aware that Joey was running back and forth in the room, sniffing the ground and air around him in search of his prey.

Locke screamed as he was pulled into the shadows, his cry cutting off as his head disappeared into the ocean of black.

Scrambling to my feet, I sprinted toward the flashlight and was rewarded with dismay as the plastic broke under an unseen mass. The beam winked out in an instant, filling my universe with the horror that is helplessness. Only the glow sticks barely illuminated the room, coating small sections of the walls and a few pillars in green.

Joey yelped from my side and I turned, searching with my preternatural eyes to see Lolth holding the skulls of my allies in each hand. She wasn't smiling anymore as she began to squeeze her fists tight.

"Wait! What do you freaking want already?!" I cried out with my arms outstretched in placation.

Lolth paused crushing Locke's and Joey's skulls long enough to answer, "I was only here to deliver a message. But only you need to receive it, pathetic insect."

"What is the message?" I asked as I slowly brought my wrists together, palms still open.

"We have something you want and are willing to trade."

I focused on the air in front of my hands, feeling the molecules in the air.

"Let me guess; whatever it is you have, you want my life in return," I growled between teeth as I prepared my attack. "NO FUCKING DEAL!" I bellowed as I willed my pure energy into the air in front of my hands, sending out a blast of light that blinded even me in its intensity.

Lolth shrieked in pain before disappearing behind another pillar. I couldn't see how much damage I had done to her, but knew it had had to be bad enough where she wouldn't come back for a while…probably.

Joey and Locke fell to the ground, both whining and groaning. As my eyes healed from the flash of light, I saw Locke grabbing his skull and Joey pawing at his while rubbing it on the cold ground. Locke was bleeding from his ears, nose, and eyes as he pulled out a purple stone that was smaller than the one back in his room. He crushed it in his fist and gasped as the soul rushed into him, healing his life-threatening wounds.

"Help Joey!" I called out as I rushed to Depweg, placing my hands on his gushing wounds. I willed my blood out, covering his entire torso, and focused on stitching his skin closed. I became dizzy and started seeing black and white dots bloom in the darkness, but I kept my focus. I briefly wondered how much energy I had used on my flash attack, though it hadn't felt like a lot. Within a few moments, Depweg had stopped bleeding, but he had already lost a lot of precious blood.

I willed my blood back inside me and then sat down with a plop, exhausted.

Locke rushed to where I sat and pushed past me to kneel by Depweg.

"Jonathan. Can you hear me?" Locke asked Depweg.

Even in my weakened state, a pang of jealousy shot through me. Jonathan? No one called him that. Wait, why did I care?

Hey, I said inwardly to Baleius, *you can let go now. It's over.* Baleius did as instructed without protest.

I stood on shaky legs and made my way to where Joey was circling the ground where Lolth had vanished into the darkness. He chuffed once and trotted over to inspect Depweg. Apparently, Joey's were-skull was stronger than Locke's human one and hadn't sustained as much damage.

"Hey, it's okay, buddy. He's going to be fine." I feigned confidence as I reached out to pet him. Once my fingers touched his fur, his jaws snapped at my hand. "Whoa there. I get it." Joey seemed to see me then, as if for the first time, and lowered his head while his ears folded back. "All good, man," I said while scratching him behind the ears. Then he began sniffing the air and hesitantly took one step toward the hallway where his brother's blood still oozed. Joey howled at the ceiling in a long, soul-shattering cry for his twin. It broke my heart. I got down to my knees and wrapped my arms around his thick neck in an embrace. He responded by turning from the hallway and resting his head on my shoulder. I could feel him shake with grief as he whined in unimaginable sorrow.

"I'm sorry, man," I said as I pulled away to look him in his dark, glistening eyes. "But I promise you this: we are going to get that bitch and make her, and her entire race of Shadow fuckers, pay. Every. Last. One of them."

He continued to whine with each breath as he buried his head into my shoulder and neck. I could feel his warm tears on the skin of my throat. I did the only thing I could think to do; I let him sob while embracing him. Locke kneeled by our side, lowered his head, and rested a hand on Joey's back.

I carried Depweg upstairs and laid him out on the couch to rest and recover. His were-healing wasn't as instantaneous as mine was, but it was infinitely better than a normal human's.

After searching around the house and shed outside, I found a folded up blue tarp and went back downstairs to recover Dawson. I had Locke wielding dual flashlights on my six the whole way before I noticed a switch near the entrance to the basement.

Setting my jaw and scowling, I flipped the switch and bright lights filled the basement prison.

"Lilith damn it," I sighed as I shook my head.

After Locke and I exited the basement, I kicked the trapdoor closed, which startled Depweg awake.

"No, NO!" Depweg cried out as he began crab-walking backward on the couch, trying to escape what wasn't there.

I was still holding Dawson, so Locke rushed to his side and put a hand on his chest while repeating, "You're okay. You're okay."

Depweg's eyes flicked around desperately until they landed on Locke. There was the briefest moment of confusion before recognition settled and Depweg wrapped his arms around Locke, whispering, "Oh, thank God."

"What happened?" Depweg asked as he pulled away. That's when his eyes found me and went wide for an instant before shrinking back into a scowl.

I had set Dawson down in the kitchen, still wrapped in the blue tarp. The droplets of blood striking the floor tugged at my attention.

Locke explained to Depweg about finding Dawson and the ensuing battle.

"Dawson," Depweg mouthed as he cradled his head in his hands. Then he shot his face up to Locke and asked, "Where's Joey?" Depweg alternated looking between me and Locke and back again.

"He's sitting outside. We felt it best to give him some space," Locke answered.

Depweg stood and walked to the back door. He turned his head to regard me without a word before stepping outside to console his packmate.

"It's not your fault," Locke said quietly as he read the situation. I didn't respond. A lot of things had happened with Depweg and I over the decades, and never once had he looked at me like that. Not once.

We buried what we could find of Dawson deeper into the woods surrounding the house. No one said anything. Joey stood stoically over the unmarked grave, the tears streaming down his face clearing lines in his dirt-covered face. I had suggested he get cleaned up while I buried Dawson, but he had ignored me, opting to carry his brother's decimated body personally.

I patted Joey's shoulder and began walking back to the house, Locke and Depweg close behind. Depweg was still weak from blood loss, but was not going to miss his packmate's funeral. Locke helped keep him steady as they traversed the trail.

When we were out of earshot of Joey, I asked, "What did Lolth want with Dawson anyway?"

"He didn't want him. His was simply the first cell he popped up in. He wanted me," Depweg said tiredly.

"Did she say anything?"

"No. He just grew from the floor like he was coming out of a freaking swimming pool. I tried to defend myself, but I couldn't even touch him."

"Her," I corrected.

"Right. Her." Depweg stopped walking, drawing my attention, and I turned to face him. "Where the hell have you been, John? Nine years. Nine fucking years."

My stomach dropped as I realized he didn't know it had been a year since he had been taken. He didn't have a beard like Joey, but his skin was hanging loosely from muscle loss, though it wasn't as much as I thought it would be. Ludvig must have fed them decently and provided basic toiletries.

Locke cleared his throat. When Depweg looked between him and me, Locke started to speak. "Jonathan, it's been…"

"You've been here a year, brother," I finished for Locke. With Depweg, I knew it was best to rip the Band-Aid off.

"I-I knew it had been a few months. But…a whole year?" Depweg asked, staring off into the distance. Pale moonlight reflected in pupils that had started to glisten. Then his eyes became focused again, and he looked at me with barely contained aggression behind his gaze. "Where in God's name have you been?"

"I was in Faerie, but it only felt like a few hours to me. King Oberon came and completely took over the entire plane, and I barely escaped with Taylor. When I got back, ten years had passed."

"We think Lily had something to do with it," Locke added. Depweg shot his eyes to him, then back at me. Understanding cleared his scrunched expression.

"Lily," he breathed.

"I have no idea why."

"What about the prophecy?" Depweg asked quickly.

"What do you mean?" I asked.

"For ten years—*ten years*," he spit out the words the second time, "Ulric was the last vampire to walk the Earth. Why didn't the apocalypse happen?"

"Oh shit!" I exclaimed, so caught up in the time dilation that I hadn't even considered the prophecy to the end of the fucking universe. "I don't know, man." I thought for a moment before I said, "Maybe we aren't the last two? Or maybe it has something to do with the two planes being parallel to one another and it not counting as me being gone?"

"When it comes to time, all options are on the table," Locke said thoughtfully. "I could easily believe either one of those theories."

"Let's focus on this later. We gotta rescue Ludvig and Magni."

"Rescue?! Did you say *rescue?!*" Depweg spit out.

"Jonathan," Locke started calmly, "Magni is the boy." Depweg stared at Locke, not catching on. Then Locke nodded subtly in my direction without taking his eyes off Depweg. "*The* boy...from the cemetery."

Recognition flashed across his face as Depweg turned his head to regard me. "He became a hunter? Humph, fitting," Depweg said sourly, looking at the ground as his mind worked.

"It also turns out that Ludvig is more on our side than what anyone could have guessed," I said carefully to Depweg. A year was a long time to have your fuse shortened. "He says you were the first supe he had let live this long because he wasn't sure if what you had told him was the truth. Think about it; a supernatural hunter that didn't kill a pack of werewolves. Instead, he-he talked to you, wanting to believe but unsure. It is unprecedented."

"Un-precedented," Depweg said slowly, tasting the words before letting them fall out of his mouth like the spit before a fierce vomit session.

"He's right," Locke said as the voice of reason.

Depweg regarded Locke for a long moment, his brow furrowing while lips curled into a snarl for a nanosecond before his features relaxed, giving way to reason. Closing his eyes, he nodded once before he resumed walking. Depweg didn't look at me, and I felt his blame permeating my skin like the flame from an out-of-control bonfire.

I followed loosely behind, giving Depweg a chance to process what must be done. I didn't think I needed to remind him that the entire known universe was at stake. I noticed that in his anger, he was walking more upright and with less assistance from the much smaller Locke.

Once we were inside the cabin, Depweg raided the kitchen and began consuming whatever meats he could, raw. I could hear his heavy breathing as he tore entire mouthfuls of animal flesh from huge slabs.

Joey walked in a few minutes after and went straight to the master bedroom without saying a word. The shower was turned on before being muffled by the bathroom door closing softly. Even an act as simple as trying to shut a door and then having to press on it a moment later because the force hadn't been enough to engage the lock showed how hurt Joey was. He barely had the strength to hold himself upright. I had been there, and knew that the darkness of every blink showed the gruesome still image of his brother torn in half. I wished I could take his pain unto myself, but even if I could, I had enough corpses in my closet to contend with. This would be a defining moment for the rest of Joey's life; he would either rise from the ashes of his former life and grow stronger, or let his sorrow eat away at him like an insatiable cancer. I silently prayed for the former.

Locke sat down on the couch next to me and spoke in a soft whisper, "What are we going to do about..." he trailed off, nodding his head toward the master bedroom.

"Be there for him," I said staring forward, remembering all those I had lost.

Depweg came into the living room then, his eyes still cold toward me. It wasn't fair. I hadn't known I'd lose so much time by trying to save my own ass.

"There's another reason we are going to Faerie," I said to Depweg, my voice filling to the brim with ice. I could understand his situation, but I wasn't going to be blamed for his actions that had led him to Ludvig.

Depweg continued to stare, awaiting my reason as he crossed his still massive arms across the acreage of his chest.

"Da is there," I informed the distant Depweg with a voice that portrayed the accumulated love I had for my faerie friend. Hidden in my words was also a tone that screamed that I didn't give two shits if he blamed me right now. He was going to get over it to save Da, and he was going to do so quickly.

Without uncrossing his arms, he looked first at Locke and then at the ground, nodding in understanding.

"I had a feeling you'd say that." He looked up at me then and said, "That was a long time ago, man. If what you say about Faerie is accurate, he's dead."

"Don't say that," I said, fiercely shaking my head. "Don't you fucking say that." I began to breath heavily as I clenched and unclenched my fists.

"You need to understand before we go in there that it is a distinct possibility. Otherwise, he would have shifted home, right?"

"Even if there is only a remote possibility that he is alive, it's worth the risk," I breathed through my teeth, trying to control my building rage.

"The entire world is worth the risk? All the innocent souls in Heaven? Hmm? Are they an acceptable loss for one person?" Depweg shot at me.

I didn't answer his rhetorical question. Instead, I stared daggers at him. I could feel my eyes on the verge of shifting while my gums tensed at my canines.

Stop it! I yelled at Baleius, only to realize that I was holding the wheel, alone. I turned to see him gazing through the windows of my eyes, paying me no attention. His hands were clasped behind his back in contemplation of the scene unfolding.

Without embarrassing myself further, I returned to the world outside. I tried to take control of my churning emotions and forced myself to relax. Depweg had just been through a year imprisoned in a jail cell, and one of his packmates had been murdered.

It was as if my anger was an oil fire on a gas stove. I wanted to just throw water on it and be done with the whole ordeal, but knew that it would only grow in fury and intensity. I had to remain calm, face the problem head-on or risk irreparable damage. I started by turning the knob of the stove off. Then, calmly, placed the lid on the fire to extinguish its oxygen supply.

I filled my lungs slowly, deliberately, as I regained control over myself.

"I'm sorry, man. Everything that has happened is my fault. I trusted Lily against my gut feeling and brought this house of cards down."

"Not sure I fully grasp the metaphor, but I appreciate your words. That being said, we both know Lily. The question prominent in my mind is: are you going to let her talk her way out of what she did?"

"Hell no!" I cried out, not believing the vehemence of my own words. Depweg cocked an eyebrow at me. "I-I don't know, man. I..."

"Love her," Depweg finished for me. His words struck hard, though I already knew it to be a fact.

"Yes," I conceded. "And I think she feels the same about me."

Locke interjected then, "Of course you do. She's a Fae. Manipulating emotions is their bread and butter."

"Guys, I really don't like being teamed up on, okay?" I said defensively, throwing my hands up, palms out. The stove was gradually being turned back on without my consent.

"You need to hear it," Depweg continued strongly. "She is going to give you some bullshit excuse about looking out for your well-being—"

"Or flat-out deny it," Locke added.

"—and you can't fall for it," Depweg finished.

"What if—"

"It wasn't her?" Depweg completed my thought aggressively. I got the sense that he was growing tired of the conversation. Well, that made two of us.

Letting my emotions slip, I fumed, "It's a damned good question to ask, dude! I was in Faerie while King Asshole swallowed the Lilith-damned sun! All while turning the fucking giant tree castle into a lifeless stone city! So maybe it was hi—"

"Yggdrasil?! Yggdrasil was destroyed?" Locke interrupted on the verge of hyperventilating. "Why didn't you say that sooner! Oh shit. Oh SHIT. This isn't good."

"Yggdrasil? Isn't that the world tree from Viking lore or something?" I asked, rage subsiding. I was beginning to feel like I was on a roller coaster of emotion.

"Norse, and yes. The world tree is real, connecting several planes of existence together. It has been described in several mythos; but I assure you, it is real." Locke thought for a moment before adding, "Wait, what did Lolth mean by the celestial key?" He stood and began quickly pacing back and forth in the living room as he thought out loud. "King Oberon has a celestial armor complete with gladius. With that, he can cut through the very fabric of reality and even time. We need to get there and stop him."

"Stop him from what?" I asked, fearful of the answer.

"I don't have the knowledge on the subject to complete the picture. But what I can say confidently is that whatever he is doing, it can't be good."

"Taylor told me that the Shadow Court wants to cast the universe into darkness. We thought I was the key to making that happen."

"Oberon promised to let you live if you gave him the gauntlet," Locke said.

"He doesn't need me to attain his goal. He has his key now," I said. "Besides, you remember what he said at the end."

"Not entirely. I was trying not to die at the moment."

"What did he say?" Depweg asked. I filled him in about how Oberon had subtly mentioned that I was going to die no matter what by him killing all humans on Earth somehow.

"So, what, is he going to cut the world tree down or something?" Depweg asked. "What would that do?"

"I don't exactly know," Locke said while deep in thought, "but if the tree connecting all reality together is destroyed..."

"I'm sorry," I said, throwing my hands up. "I'm having some trouble believing some Norse fairy tale about a damn tree holding the nine realms together."

"Said the vampire to the werewolf and warlock," Depweg countered.

"I..." I started, holding up my index finger as if to make a point. Letting it drop, I relented, "Point, match, Depweg."

"Let's use the same logic from the stories we have heard as compared to us," Locke thought aloud while grabbing his chin between thumb and forefinger.

"What do you mean?" I asked, confused.

"We know the stories about things like vampires and werewolves that are told by mortals are drastically overfantasized and altogether wrong. I mean, John, you are wearing a silver crucifix." The three of us looked at my silver pendant sitting brightly atop my black shirt.

"Lilith damn it!" I said as a finger found a hole in my brand-new shirt. "I just got this stupid thing."

"On the clearance rack," Locke added curtly before finishing, "But you see my point. Now, we need to take what we know and weed through the lore."

"Maybe I'm just a big, dumb idiot with a ripped physique, but what does this matter?"

"I see where he's going," Depweg said, leaning against the doorframe to the kitchen. "Maybe the tree itself doesn't *actually* hold several planes of existence together, but does, perhaps, act as a doorway."

"That theory holds water," Locke said. "It could be the power source that allows for portals, or maybe it acts as some sort of beacon for the Fae whenever they shift planes."

"Ah, I get it," I admitted. "The Fae could use the tree to traverse the mortal plane. That would explain how Lily always managed to pop in wherever we were."

Locke and Depweg both looked at the ground in thought.

"Let's assume it is some sort of access for anywhere on, at least, Earth and Faerie; how could Oberon use that against us?" Locke mused.

A thought burst to the front of my mind like a gunpowder explosion. I snapped my fingers, stood up, and said, "I got it! He will use the tree to free the drow army. We know, or at least it is said, that only the High Fae can shift planes at will. So Oberon's army wouldn't be able to use the tree because they are just normal Fae."

Depweg straightened from the doorframe as the conversation grew in energy and excitement. He added, "But what about the Shadow faeries?"

"The ones you can't see, except their eyes," I breathed out with unfocused eyes. My mind played the image of purple mist flowing up to the sky to chase us. Countless eyes had made up that mist and had almost killed me and the hunters. A subzero hand ran chilling fingers up my spine, making me shudder.

"Yeah, what about them? How could they get through but not the, what did you call them, drow?" Depweg asked.

"He brings up a great question," Locke said. "I feel like we are on the right track but are missing a key piece to the puzzle."

We all stood for eight or nine minutes, desperate for any thought to emerge. As the adrenaline faded from our conversation, I started to yawn. I plopped back on the couch, closing my eyes as I did. Something bothered me that I couldn't put my finger on.

"A lot has happened tonight," I said, feeling the lack of energy. "I need to eat. How much time do I have before dawn?"

Depweg looked at the clock on the wall.

"That can't be right..." he muttered to himself. Then he walked into the kitchen and glanced at the green digits on the oven and microwave. After confirming the time, he walked quickly to the window and peered outside. It was as dark as midnight outside.

"What?" I asked, growing worried with how he was acting.

"It's a quarter past nine," Depweg said, returning to the living room to pick up the TV remote.

"What?" I repeated. "How can that be? I've been up for several hours. Hell, the drive here alone was over an hour. How can only a few hours have passed since sundown?"

"It's a quarter past nine, in the morning," Depweg confirmed as the television sprang to life, displaying a local channel with nine o'clock news scrolling across the bottom of the screen. A man and woman wearing formal clothing that looked like it belonged in a sci-fi movie had stern faces as they read the news.

"Turn it up," I said, standing back up and taking a step closer to the TV.

Depweg pressed a button on the remote, and the newscasters' voices grew in volume.

"...are theorizing that an unexplained phenomenon has created a perfect solar eclipse spanning the entirety of the globe. Experts are perplexed at the lack of a physical astral body blocking the sun," the male newscaster said.

"We have breaking news as we go live to our correspondent, Michelle Gonzalez," the female announcer said.

"Thank you, Stephanie and Geoff. I have with me Dr. Lance Heinrik, who is an astrophysicist with a specialty in yellow dwarf stars," Michelle said as she turned her body to regard the man next to her clad in a worn-looking brown suit jacket complete with elbow patches. He had a black bowtie with red dots on it. "Doctor?" she said as she moved the microphone in front of the astrophysicist.

"Um, yes, um, thank you," Dr. Heinrik said with an Americanized German accent. "What we are experiencing is a rogue black hole that, for unexplainable reasons, has placed itself squarely between the sun and Earth. All light is being sucked into the phenomenon which, at best guess, is around the size of a basketball. The intense gravity, even by such a small event horizon, is trapping all the light from the much larger sun, preventing the sun's rays from reaching the surface of Earth."

"And how will the black hole impact those of us on Earth?" the reporter asked with practiced calm, even though she was practically talking about the end of our world.

"Uh...without the warmth and light from the sun...we-we're all going to d—" the transmission switched back to the reporters sitting at their desk, scrambling to shuffle through the blank papers that newspeople had as props.

The male reporter, Geoff, put a finger to his ear, regained his composure, and looked at the camera while crossing his hands in front of him before he said, "Thank you, Michelle. Coming up next: is the government tracking you using social media algorithms? Find out after this commercial break."

Depweg pressed a button and the screen went black. We all sat in stunned silence for what felt like several minutes, staring at the black screen which reflected our own blurred faces back at us.

"That's what he did with the armor and tree," I drawled out as I ran my palm over my face.

"What do you mean?" Depweg asked.

Locke picked up on what I was saying and explained, "He used the tree to find a point in space and created a black hole that was just big enough to swallow all light heading for Earth, but small enough to not destroy the solar system."

"Oh...fuck..." Depweg gracefully added to the conversation.

Oberon's last words to me held a new terror. I had no idea how long I could survive without consuming blood. I knew it took less than a week for me to start getting hangry, but I didn't know if that was because of my desire to keep my well of power fully stocked or because I would die without it. I guess I could sleep like Ulric had on more than one occasion; but that would only delay the inevitable. All life on Earth would end without the sun. The irony of that sentence was palpable to a vampire.

The shower was shut off in the master bathroom, and Depweg, Locke, and myself all exchanged glances with one another. It was funny to me that our biggest problem right now was how to tell Joey what we had just learned, as if in doing so, it would become a reality.

Joey came out of the bedroom and stopped by the couch in which Locke and I were once again sitting on. He looked around and no one made eye contact with him.

"What?" Joey asked.

"Um…" I started before Depweg spoke. It made sense for him to break the news, considering he was his pack leader.

"A lot has happened since we were imprisoned, Joey. Long story short, the Faerie king has somehow created a black hole between Earth and the sun, effectively cutting us off," Depweg said with militaristic determination, refusing to sugarcoat the situation.

Joey didn't say anything. After he had sobbed on my shoulder, his face had become a blank canvas, devoid of any emotion except for the scowl that had appeared when he had buried his brother.

"So what do we do?" Joey asked matter-of-factly, seemingly unfazed by the apocalyptic news we had just sprinkled on him.

"We are going to Faerie," Depweg said, glancing my way. In that brief moment, I knew he was relenting to the rescue of Ludvig and Magni. We were going to need all the help we could get to save the freaking world.

Chapter 17

"What's the plan?" Locke asked from where we stood around the kitchen island. I had drawn a map of Faerie as best I could remember from my dull, mortal's memory. I was confident in its general accuracy, but only barely.

Depweg had taken control over the situation, so he said, "First, we all need as much energy as we can possibly consume. I'm to the point where I think Plan Wild Card is perfectly reasonable." My eyebrows went up in surprise as I realized what he meant.

"What's that?" Locke asked.

"It's where we invade Huntsville prison and feast on the most violent offenders," I informed him. "We came up with it as a last-ditch emergency maneuver. The number of prisoners in there that meet our criteria is more than enough to replenish all my reserves. Then the weres feast on the remains. Hell, you can steal their souls as well. These guys are the worst of the worst. Child molesters, murderers, rapists; all ripe for the picking."

"Okay, good," Locke agreed.

Depweg continued, "Once filled up, we make our way to Valenta's to grab some of the artifacts John just told us about."

"Then take the portal at the back of his basement to face the Shadow Court," I said, dumping the rest of the flashlights from H-E-B on the counter. We split them up evenly after testing each one. "Make sure to light up whatever you want to kill before attacking. Joey proved that even the goddess, Lolth, can be hurt as long as bright ass light is on her."

"That means we need fire," Depweg said.

"I got that covered," Locke threw in confidently.

"And lots of it," I added.

SHADOW OF A DOUBT

"Any color preference?" Locke said with a mischievous smile.

"As best as we can figure, Da and the hunters will be contained at the base of the castle. We will have to open the front gate somehow."

"Oh shit," I exhaled while standing upright, my head dizzy with my realization.

"What is it?" Depweg asked, still all business.

"I-I lost my powers in Faerie. I was a fucking mortal, heartbeat and all. I don't know if you guys will have your powers either."

"Scheisse," Depweg cursed in German.

"What are we going to do, then?" Locke asked.

I leaned over and whispered in his ear before standing straight again.

"What?"

I leaned in again and repeated what I had whispered before straightening yet again. When he looked at me, I motioned with my hand for him to say what I had asked him to say.

"Um, okay. Um, what do we need?" Locke asked with a confused look on his face.

"Guns," I said in my best Keanu. "Lots of guns."

"Agreed," Depweg confirmed without giving my epic quote the recognition and praise it deserved. "I have a collection squared away that I had been building ever since...that night," he finished. I could see Locke shift uncomfortably where he stood. He cleared his throat once while keeping his eyes on the crudely drawn map before us.

"I was wondering where all those Sigs that we stole—I mean, borrowed—from those soldiers had gone."

"Armor, weapons, and ammo. I've added varying melee weapons as well. All silver and/or iron infused."

"I have a collection of alchemical grenades I have been working on. I can catch anything on fire, even water," Locke added helpfully.

"Neat!" I exclaimed, happy with myself for remembering what Faerie had done to my abilities BEFORE going in. Then I shuddered at the thought of almost leading the last of my friends to their unwitting deaths at the hands of Shadow faeries. The lack of one simple thought could have cost us everything.

"Right. We'll swing by my storage unit to get the weapons and armor, then wherever Locke needs to get his," Depweg said.

"No need," Locke spoke as he turned to face the back counters of the kitchen. He swung his arm in a perfect circle, and the air wavered before fading out. There, juxtaposed to the clean, crisp kitchen, was a wall of wooden shelves against stone. On the shelves were numerous devices that I had no idea what they were for. Locke reached up and grabbed an entire shelf of handheld orbs that contained a black-and-green powder. He began placing them into a bandolier that appeared across his chest and waist, filling each slot until he looked like he was ready to cosplay at the nearest steampunk convention. The leather straps perfectly held the grenades in place while offering protection against accidental damage—which I was all for. I wouldn't want to be in the car when we hit one of those bumps on the dirt road leading out of here and then BOOM, Tesla fire coffin.

As he finished, Locke waved his hand in the opposite direction, closing the portal to his stash. The cabinets and countertop were returned to their normal, HGTV state.

"Show off," I said while simultaneously being mildly impressed.

Locke smiled at the compliment before returning his gaze to the map.

"The throne room is here," I pointed at the center of the castle. "I would expect Oberon to be there."

"Why?" Depweg asked.

I was thrown off by the question. "Be-because that's what bad guys do? I don't know, man."

"So we are going to play this like Oberon is just sitting in his throne room, like the boss of a video game, rubbing his hands together maliciously?" Locke asked facetiously.

"Well...when you say it like that," I said, trailing off. I stepped back from the island and leaned on the counter behind me, crossing my arms as I did.

I inspected Joey then. It was hard to see the once young, playful Joey in such a somber mood. Frown lines were now permanently etched into his forehead. His muscles had already began filling back out from when Depweg had made him eat before we started over the plan.

Depweg continued, "We don't know where he will be. He might not even be on that plane. The plan of attack doesn't change, regardless. We get in, careful not to engage for as long as absolutely possible, get the hunters, and get out. Since we can assume they will be in the dungeon, we can go cell by cell and do a quick search and rescue for Da. If he isn't there, we make our escape and plan the next move from the safety of Valenta's," he laid out with proficiency. "One last thing," he added as we began to move away from the island, "expect the unexpected. Improvise, adapt, and overcome. Don't get caught like a deer in headlights."

I quickly stifled a chuckle that tried to escape as I pictured the Bear Grylls meme at his comment.

We stepped outside and I made my way to the Tesla, calling out, "Shotgun!" as I did.

Locke cleared his throat obnoxiously, and I turned to see him standing in the clearing between the house and the driveway. "Make a circle. There's enough of us here for this," Locke ordered.

"For what?" I asked as I turned from the passenger side of the car and walked toward the group. As I stepped into place, completing the circle, there was a slight pop in my ears. Locke began chanting as he stuck his hands out to either side of him, reaching for the hands of the dudes who stood next to him. I recoiled back, not wanting to hold my bros' hands. I was a man, damn it, and men didn't go around holding other dudes' hands.

Without breaking his concentration, Locke shook his hand in midair, signaling that I needed to grasp it. With a sigh and a chip to my manliness, I grabbed his hand and the hand of Joey, who stood next to me. We completed the circle, and the ground began glowing purple between us. I gawked in awe as a frame made out of bones and covered in those weird, glowing runes rumbled from the dirt. It extended into the air, the size of a normal doorframe, and began to fill with bones that flew from the ground as if drawn by a magnet, forming the door. Locke stopped chanting as it became complete.

"You can let go of my hand now, John," Locke said with a smile. I threw his hand away and wiped the clamminess off on my black jeans as if I had touched something wet and sticky on the edge of the trash can.

We all moved to look at the front of the door, and watched as Locke grabbed a skull where a door handle would be, and turned. There was no show of lights or even a hiss as the bone door opened. As it did, the Huntsville prison came into view. There were no fences, so I assumed we were already on the inside of the perimeter.

"Fuck, that's cool," I said softly in admiration. Locke beamed with pride as he stepped through first.

"Joey," Depweg said in a commanding voice as he began taking off his clothes. Without a word, Joey began removing his own clothing until they both stood naked in front of the door. Then they fell to their hands and feet and began the change. Bones popped as their faces grew outward and knees bent backward. Tendons elongated while fur sprouted over their entire bodies. Their human teeth grew into pointed fangs as their eyes shifted to a bright yellow with black slits. Within moments, a five-hundred-pound, dark brown wolf who stood eight feet long from his nose to the base of his tail shook his fur as if it were wet.

A smaller black wolf with a white patch on his eye stood next to him. Joey was around three hundred and fifty pounds and two feet shorter than his alpha, Depweg, but still terrifying to look at.

They leaped through the door and I took my cue to shift. Baleius put one hand on the wheel, and I looked at him in the control center of my mind and said, *Have fun.* Baleius smiled in return, and I felt my own change take over.

I stepped through the portal and then turned to see where we had come through. The bone door was gone, leaving behind a field of grass that led up to razor wire fence.

"Neat," I said to myself as I turned to catch up with the others. Locke had made it to the wall and had pulled out his wand. The runes down its length began glowing a faint green, and he waved it in a circle at the wall. The stone began to crumble like sand, leaving a hole big enough for us to walk through.

"Remember, I sap their souls, John drains their blood, and you two get the meat," Locke said. Depweg chuffed once and then I nodded in agreement. "This is the TDCJ housing unit, which is where death row inmates are held." That was good enough for Depweg's and my moral code to be satisfied.

Locke stepped through the hole that led to a hallway lined with cells. He lowered his head and began chanting before lifting his wand to the lights above him. There was a bolt of green electricity that jumped from his wand to the nearest light. Sparks shot out from the fixture before the lights on either side of that one followed suit a millisecond later. Within a few seconds, the entire housing unit was powerless.

"That'll buy us some time. Also takes care of the cameras," Locke said before approaching the first cell. He waved his wand, and the lock popped open. I slid the door out of the way as Locke entered to face a very confused older man dressed in a white jumpsuit. Without preamble, he waved his wand at the man and whispered, "Anima furantur." The prisoner, who had backed up against the wall, looked like he was being electrocuted as his muscles tensed up and a pained groan slipped from his mouth. A white mist started flowing from the man's eyes before pouring down his face and out toward Locke's extended wand. As the mist reached the halfway point, it began to darken from a bright white to a dull gray and finally a sharp purple before being sucked into the wand.

"Okay, John," Locke said as the mist began to trickle from the prisoner's eyes.

I stepped forward and held my hand up, palm forward. With sharp focus, I latched onto the frantically flowing blood of the victim—who had probably committed unspeakable crimes against his fellow men—and began siphoning it through his mouth and nose. I pulled the blood from the thin flesh of his esophagus and lungs, sending a torrent of crimson flowing through the air to disappear into my palm. It was completely unnecessary, but I wanted to look cool after what Locke had just done.

"Whoa," I heard Locke say from behind. I hid a smile as the last drops of life flowed into my being. The prisoner dropped to the floor, as pale white as his jumpsuit. I noticed with unease that his eyes were a glassy white after having his soul sucked out. I closed my eyes in drunken euphoria as the prisoner's life energy became mine, filling my body. But I needed more, much more, to recover what I had used with the plasma attack.

I opened my eyes and turned to see Locke had already moved on to the next cell. Locke said the soul-stealing phrase again, and there was a gasp from his victim as I stepped out of the way of Depweg and Joey. Their mouths began salivating as they licked their maws while approaching their meal.

As I entered the adjoining cell where a dark-skinned prisoner's mist was already starting to falter, I heard the sound of flesh being torn from bone coming from where I had just been. A shudder crept up my spine. I definitely preferred my method of eating.

The prisoner began slumping as his soul left his body, and I moved in to stab his liver with a blooddagger. It required less mental effort to siphon my dinner this way, plus it was faster. The hairs on my skin stood on end as the last of the delicious blood entered my body.

We repeated the process down the entire line, drawing confused shouts from the cells lining the opposite wall. It was pitch black inside, so the inmates couldn't see what was going on, but they could hear the cries of surprise as Locke latched onto their souls.

"Don't worry, your turn is coming," I warned to the remaining dinner plates with my best creepy voice. They began yelling while Locke started on the other side. Though they had no idea what was happening, they knew it wasn't good.

In short order, we had cleared the now silent hall. Only our footsteps and the clack of the werewolves' claws on the tile floor made a sound.

"I need more," I said to Locke, who looked at Depweg for confirmation. The large wolf looked up at me with questioning eyes. "I used up almost everything I had, and there's a lot to replenish." Depweg continued to stare at me before he looked at Locke and chuffed once.

"John, are you sure everyone past those doors meets your guidelines?"

Damn it. I knew he was going to ask that.

"Look, we are in a maximum-security prison. This isn't a white-collar crime place, alright? The scum in here did very bad things to wind up at Huntsville. Plus, if I don't replenish my reserves, I could die. So, in effect, I am saving the world by eating these men."

"If you say so," Locke said before he continued, "I'm full, though, so you're on your own. We'll be waiting by the portal."

"Got it. See you soon," I said as I pulled the locked metal door open with my growing strength. The locking mechanism broke as if made of aluminum foil. Lilith, it felt good to have my preternatural strength flooding back into me.

I made my way down a hall where another door stood, barring my entrance to the main level. I ripped the metal apart with ease as I stepped into the multilevel detention center for the maximum-security inmates.

A couple of the emergency floodlights had popped on, illuminating sections at either end of the long hall and in the dead center. Several inmates stood together in a group, squinting to peer into the darkness at whatever sound they had heard when I tore the door apart. It must have been terrifying from their point of view as the thick metal door was ripped to pieces like a finger through one-ply toilet paper. I let my eyes flash red in the darkness as I stepped into the floodlights, exposing a smile with two surgically sharp canines. I began laughing a low, throaty chortle that grew in cadence and pitch until it was a spine-tingling titter.

"What the fuck, man!" one inmate that was at the front of the pack and had the best view of what was coming called out. This was going to be so much fun!

"El Diablo!" another cried out from the building crowd.

I abruptly ceased my mirthful laughter, and my face went stony before I blurred forward and into the mass of blood bags awaiting their fate.

As I made my way to the dead center, I jumped twenty feet into the air, positioned my palms straight down, and sent out hundreds of bloodtendrils that lodged into the ground like tiny harpoons. The bloodspikes pierced whatever flesh they came into contact with and began siphoning the crimson goodness into me. From the viewpoint of the inmates standing on the steel platforms that ran along the cells on every level, it must have been like looking down at red Christmas trees, with the inmates as the ornaments and me as the cute angel on top.

I let out a primal scream from the rush of energy that filled my tanks like a silken tidal wave that crashed into every nerve in my body. After a few more seconds, I reached the bottom of the barrel of blood supply and let the tendrils shoot back into me. I landed in the middle of the pale bodies that were slumped over each other like discarded sacks of flour, and took a knee. I trembled with elation and power as I sent the energy back into my reserves, which was fucking hard to do. All I wanted to do was remain kneeling where I was and feel the power course through my veins; but I wasn't finished yet.

Screams filled the tall room as reality struck home for the prisoners. I giggled at the irony that was applicable to a lot of these prisoners, seeing as how they had probably caused great terror and pain to an innocent victim to have wound up at Huntsville's maximum-security wing.

As footsteps pounded on the steel platforms, I jumped up one floor and began tearing into my next round of meals. I stood in the middle of the landing, extended my arms to either side, and sent out two-inch-thick spikes through my palms. They flew out until they slammed into the walls on either side of the long hall. A few inmates were pierced, but several more were missed. So, I obliged them and granted them the experience of being consumed by yours truly by sending out row after row of smaller spikes, three feet in all directions of the two bloodpoles. That did the trick. Screams of terror grew into shrieks of agony as plump bodies were pierced in numerous places. Bone had been shattered into pieces where they had attempted to block the bloodspikes from doing what they must. I was confident that every pelvis on the landing had been turned into a fine sand. That was alright with me; let them suffer.

As I finished, I leaped to the other side and repeated the process before making my way up one more level. Within a few minutes, hundreds and hundreds of maximum-security inmates were relieved of their life energy; and I was that much stronger.

"Don't worry, boys," I said as I stepped from the platform on the top level and sailed to the ground, my trench coat flapping hard as I fell. "It's for a good cause."

I walked toward the hole Locke had made and was stopped by a flashlight and a staccato of panicked cracks from a firearm. Two bullets managed to turn into flat pieces of lead against my chest. My face turned down to watch them peel off and fall to the ground. Fingers probed the new holes in my black shirt.

"Son of a..."

My gaze shot toward the guard, who was fumbling with his spare magazine. I blurred forward, put my hand in front of his face, and whispered, "Sleep," before he could even register my movements. I sent my will into his body, found his control center, and hit the emergency shutdown that was normally reserved for a skull-smashing accident, like a car wreck or being knocked out by Mike Tyson.

I pulled my consciousness back, and the guard fell like a rag doll to the ground, allowing me to step over him and through the hole to the outside.

My skin felt hot compared to the air outside, and I was pretty sure wisps of steam were billowing off me. At least it felt that way.

With my preternatural eyes, I could see Locke and the weres standing at the position where the door had been. As I approached, Locke held his hand up, stopping me in place.

"Walk around," Locke said, moving his hand in a wide arc. I did as he suggested and saw why. The door came into view as I crossed the event horizon. I had almost walked right into it, though I was curious how that would have worked from a physics standpoint.

Locke turned the skull, pulled open the door, and revealed a reinforced metal storage door. We stepped through and Locke closed the door behind him this time. I walked around in a circle again, expecting to see the door slide back into view, but there was none this time.

"Fucking neat!" I exclaimed.

Depweg and Joey began the transformation back into their man-suits. As they did, I admired the quality of the storage facility we were in. We were indoors, but there were no cameras down the hallway like you would expect. It smelled clean inside, like I imagined a sterile environment would. My eyes went to the door in front of us, and I took note of the impressive locks.

As the weres completed their transformation, they stopped to pick up their wolf teeth. Depweg then placed a hand on the scanner next to the door. He brought his eyes to a retinal device, and blue light moved over his face from side to side. The hand terminal turned green and there was a hiss behind the door, followed by the sound of massive gears moving. I took a step back with my hands out in front of me as I mouthed, "Whoa."

The door swung open like a bank vault, and I noticed it was almost as thick as one, too. On its back side was a spiderweb of metal rods that contracted into itself once unlocked.

"Holy shit," I said in awe. "You two are something else."

"We had to step up our game when you left," Depweg said without a hint of smugness in there. He was simply speaking factually.

"Pretty hard to be me, huh?" I said jovially. The excess of dinner I had just enjoyed had put me into a good mood.

"Maybe we are taking things more seriously than you did," Locke said, mildly reprimanding me.

"Yeah, that sounds about right," I admitted as I followed the very naked Depweg into his massive storage unit. He was about three inches shorter than me but eighty pounds less, at a professional bodybuilder lean one-eighty. Veins ran across his lats and even his massive chest, not to mention the pipelines that ran down his arms starting at the shoulders. I could see the striations in his muscles as he moved.

Locke saw me gawking at my no-homo man crush and I quickly examined the ceiling, nodding appreciatively at the, uh, tiles and, um, lights.

After a few more awkward moments of staring upward, I shifted my gaze to the awesome storage unit in front of me.

It was at least fifty feet deep and twelve feet across, with tables lining both sides. Above the tables were countless guns of varying brands, calibers, and uses. In the center of the back wall was a Barrett .50 caliber rifle with an impressive scope assembly. I could tell at a glance that it had thermal optics as well as night vision. A suppressor stood out for a foot at the end of the already impressively long barrel.

Below that was a table housing huge magazines filled with ammunition tipped with silver.

"How the hell did you guys find this place?" I asked the room.

"I own it," Locke said. "And the cemetery," he continued.

"What?"

"Yes. I don't know why you never thought about it. That's why I wasn't afraid to park my car out front."

"I, uh, don't know why I never thought about it. Come to think of it, I don't even know how much wealth I have left since Bitcoin went tits up."

"I pulled it out for you," Locke informed me.

"Oh, thank Lilith!" I said, running up to Locke and throwing my hands around his tiny frame. I playfully stroked his hair a few times like a loving mother. I was surprised that he didn't protest. Then a thought struck. "Hey, wait a minute. You didn't pull it out for me. You wanted my money for yourself!"

"No shit, Sherlock," Locke admitted freely. "We thought you were dead. After Da disappeared, I found his meticulously detailed notes on your entire empire and made the necessary adjustments."

"So, I still have my wealth?" I asked hopefully.

"You are one of the richest men on the planet, John. I'm surprised you never utilized your resources more effectively."

"Eh, I let Da handle all that." As I said his name again, I felt a pang of guilt and anxiety tightening my chest. We were here for Da. Locke saw my face change as I thought about our mission, and I turned to regard the walls.

Depweg had donned an entire black tactical outfit and was lacing up his boots as Joey followed suit next to him. Depweg stood, grabbed an armored vest off the wall, and tossed it to me one handed. I caught it and watched as he repeated the process with Locke and Joey. I could feel the slight hum from the plates inside the carrier and knew it was steel with iron and silver mixed in. These puppies would stop most mortal weapons—barring armor-piercing rounds or anything more powerful than a .308—and ranged magical attacks. Everyone slipped on their vests and set the clasps in place, pulling on the straps to draw the armor tight.

Locke looked down at his comically large vest compared to the rest of the group. Even Joey, who was only five-four, had more than enough girth on his chest, shoulders, and back to secure the armor in place. Depweg approached the much smaller Locke and helped him adjust the vest's shoulder straps to cover his vitals instead of just his stomach.

I slipped my trench coat back in place and reached under the armor to pull my silver cross out. I let it rest on top of the vest instead of being crushed uncomfortably between my super buff chest and the unyielding body armor.

Locke donned his battle robes while Depweg and Joey began methodically grabbing weapons off the wall. They wrapped thick belts around their waists which dangled leg holsters that they clasped into place around their thighs. Depweg threw me an identical one and I mirrored their movements, though I had to readjust my silver kukri sheath so as not to be impeded.

They pulled Glocks off the wall and slapped in double-stack magazines of .45 caliber ammo before racking the slides. Then they smoothly slid the weapons into their leg holsters before securing the guns with a latch that went over the back of the slide. Depweg underhand tossed a Glock toward me with one hand and a magazine with the other. Monkey saw and monkey did. After my Glock had been secured, Depweg tossed me three magazines that I slid into the mag holder on the side of my belt near my left kidney.

Next off the table was a bandolier with thick loops that covered the entirety of the belt. Depweg slid in shotgun shells of varying colors. Some were white, others were blue, while the last ones secured in place were red.

"What are those?" I asked, pointing at the different colors.

"Silver slugs, iron pellets, dragon's breath," Depweg said, going in order.

"Um, dragon-what now?" I asked, doing a double take.

"Dragon's breath. It will coat anything you point the weapon at with fire."

"How is that legal?"

"Normal dragon's breath is perfectly legal. These on the other hand," Depweg said, pulling a red casing out of its loop, "are made with phosphorus." As he finished the last word, his eyes grew wide with glee.

"*That* is the coolest thing I have ever heard. Thank you for sharing that sentence with me," I said, basically wiping drool from my mouth. Lilith, I wanted to shoot a Shadow fucker with one of those.

Depweg grabbed a Benelli auto shotty off the wall and handed it to me before grabbing an identical one for himself.

I watched as he grabbed three shells in his hand and slid them expertly into the breach. He grabbed three shells of a different color and followed suit. Lastly, the dragon's breath was loaded before he engaged the bolt, chambering a round. The weapon was then slung across his chest, with the sling going over his left shoulder and under his right armpit. It hung loosely, pointing straight down to the ground.

Instead of the Benelli, Joey chose a Springfield M1A .308, also with a lengthy suppressor at the end of the muzzle. There was a drum magazine attached that looked like it could hold at least thirty or forty rounds.

The familiar Sig MPXs were next. Sleek rectangle suppressors had been affixed to the muzzles since the last time I had laid eyes upon the fully auto beauties.

Depweg pulled one down, slapped in a magazine, and pulled on the charging handle before sliding the one-point sling over his right shoulder. Doing this would allow the fully automatic gun to fall to his side as he pulled the shotgun off his chest. He filled the six empty slots on his chest with thirty-round magazines. A quick adjustment of the bandolier, and he was fully equipped with his firearms. Joey and I did the same before moving on to the melee weapons. My silver kukri remained on my lower back, but I slid a five-inch sheathed blade down my boot, securing it with a clip. Depweg and Joey put marine-style KA-BARs on their lower backs, followed by small blades that could fit into a closed fist at the front of their belts.

I looked up at the wall and froze as a full choir belted out epic a cappella music with lyrics in Latin. My eyes danced sensually over an iron katana etched with silver and recognizable holy markings in the handle. It gleamed in the light and seemed to make a *shling* sound as I gawked at it. With a tiny titter that escaped my mouth, I smoothly let my trench slide off my arms and land on the table next to me as I picked up the blade. I placed it against my back as Locke secured it against my plate carrier using the MOLLE straps. I replaced the trench coat and willed a pair of bloodsunglasses on my face.

"Easy there, Blade," Depweg joked as I posed.

"Not sure how to feel about that reference."

"That's not the look you are going for?"

"Ah, damn it. I guess he did corner the market on the swords-poking-out-of-trench-coats-while-wearing-sunglasses look."

"Be careful with that blade, Blade," Depweg remarked with a wry smile.

"I think I'll be just fine with it, Lassie." His smile faded quickly.

"I mean it isn't just iron, John. It's cold iron. Incredibly difficult to make right, but way more effective at canceling magic than regular iron or even silver."

"Unless it is blessed silver," Locke added.

I noticed Locke wasn't going for the firearms.

"Hey," I said, waving my hand toward him. "What's with the no-guns thing?"

"Oh, I don't need all that you have," he responded.

"Why? 'Cause you can't carry the weight?"

"Someone has to wield Big Bertha," Depweg said, motioning to the suppressed Lapua .338 on the wall. I gulped as I looked at the monster.

"It's as big as he is!" I called out.

"Right, but once he has the tripod out, he won't have any problems," Depweg explained.

"Ah, makes sense."

"It is surprisingly light," Locke said, hefting it with relative ease. It looked more like a skeleton of a gun than something that could blow a hole through a brick wall.

"Just under nine pounds unloaded. Recoil might be a little aggressive, but it's a fair trade off for the weight," Depweg said.

Depweg then handed Locke a few .22 caliber weapons that weighed considerably less than the heavy shit the rest of us were rocking. Lastly, Locke swung a backpack over his shoulders and cinched it in place before Depweg started loading it up with the Lapua-specific, five-round magazines.

"That's good," Locke said once he had reached his comfortable weight limit. Depweg zipped the backpack closed, and we were ready.

We stepped into the hallway and Depweg pressed a button to secure the bank vault door. Then we made our way outside and to a much larger storage unit that was attached to the parking lot. Depweg followed the unlocking process again, and the door swung open to reveal a truly awesome sight. The choir from before dropped their coffee and donuts and rushed to sing a drawn-out chorus made entirely of "ah" syllables. A fully customized military Hummer was bathed in the light of the facility's flood lamps. The thick windows—that I assumed were bulletproof—were tinted limo black. All-terrain tires supported a lifted frame with reinforced suspension for traversing off-road. I opened the rear door to see something that made the tip of my Little John tingle—a matte black chain gun was on a platform that could be rotated three-hundred and sixty degrees once the roof was popped open and the weapon was engaged. I followed the belt of the weapon, which contained silver-tipped rounds numbering into the thousands.

"Merry fucking Christmas to me," I said to myself before turning to Depweg, who was opening the driver's side door. "So, this is mine too, right?" I asked half sincerely.

"No. Get in," Depweg answered.

"Not going to call shotgun?" Locke chided as he climbed into the passenger side and closed the door.

"Nope. I'm breaking my habit in an effort to better myself and calling minigun instead," I said, climbing into the turret and clapping my hands repeatedly in delight. I could almost hear Locke and Depweg rolling their eyes from way up front.

Joey silently slid into the seat behind Locke and resigned himself to look out the window. I could feel his pain emanating as if there was a void extending a few feet all around him. It was dark and cold.

Depweg pressed a button and the car came to life similar to Locke's Tesla.

"Wait. Is this an electric Hummer?"

"Most vehicles are now with the discovery of sodium-ion batteries," Depweg informed me as we pulled onto the road.

"You'll like this," Locke said, turning in his seat to face me. "They can also be charged while driving by utilizing Wo-Fi signals."

"What, like 4G?"

Depweg and Locke chuckled as they looked at one another. It was pissing me off.

"Hey, dickheads. Ten years, remember? Fill me in without the assholery, please."

"Currently, we are utilizing 6G, which is actually faster than even fiber optics can provide," Locke said.

"That doesn't make sense. A signal produced from towers is stronger than a hardwired, fiber-optic line? Bullshit."

"Well, it's cheaper because the signal is sent directly from satellites, courtesy of Elon Musk. There is nowhere in the world where you can't stream, well, whatever you want," Locke said.

"The signal is coming from space regardless, brother," Depweg added. "Think of it like cutting out the middle man. Not only would hard-wiring be a huge expense, it is completely unnecessary. Everything, and I mean everything, is connected to Wo-Fi."

"I'm going to go out on a limb here and assume you two meant to say 'wo' instead of 'wi.'"

"Correct. Wi-fi was limited in range, with the signal dropping drastically as the radius grew. Wo-fi is worldwide. Plus, Elon has a sense of humor about these things. Wi-fi was a trademarked name, so he changed one letter—which is twenty-five percent of the word itself—and avoided the trademark litigation. If that hadn't worked, he announced on social media that he would have called it 'Not Wi-Fi.'"

I barked out a laugh. Lilith, I loved that crazy Mr. Musk.

After I wiped a tear and breathed out, "Whooo," from my laughter, the ride became awkward. I think we realized that the useless information we were talking about—though incredibly interesting to me—was to mask how nervous we were about the task ahead of us. Except for me, none of us had ever had to fight without our abilities, and the experience I had would be left off my résumé. Lilith, I hoped I would run into the bridge troll again. How dared he promote the toll troll stereotype. Racist.

Feeling the tension, Locke turned in his seat and said, "I never asked; when did you first meet Da?"

"Oh, man, it's a doozy," I said, clapping my hands and rubbing them together. "Meeting Da was a turning point in my existence."

I closed my eyes and it's 1965 in Indonesia. I'm standing on a riverbank in the city of Surabaya. The river is clogged with hundreds of bloated bodies with varying degrees of mutilation. Some have gashes in their throats from ear to ear, while others are missing their heads entirely.

I stare at the carnage with a mixture of emotions. The military were not biased by age or sex. Men, women, and children bob in the rushing waters, their lives taken because of politics. My mind flashes with images of my father on the ground, a knife sticking out of his bleeding thigh.

Disgust fills my heart as I make my way down the riverbank toward the source of the massacre. The bodies have stopped coming, signaling that the executions are over, but the night is young and more people are going to die tonight; I'm going to make sure of it.

After a few hours, I come to a bridge on the edge of a town that is covered in thick, viscous blood that has begun drying. The air smells metallic, even to me, as all the life energy in the blood has dissipated, leaving behind dead, useless liquid. Following the path through the layer of blood, I see hundreds of crimson footprints in the sand leading to a nearby building. I begin to approach as a voice comes from behind.

"Hello, Jonathan," a cultured British voice says.

I stop midstride and roll my eyes as I begin to turn around while saying in my native Irish tongue, "It's jus' John." With how much a pale white guy with a reddish beard stands out in Indonesia, there is no reason to mimic the local dialect in an effort to blend in.

I'm met with a faerie that is floating at eye level a few feet from where I'm standing. I don't know what to say.

"What do you plan on doing inside there?" the five-inch faerie asks.

"Kill 'em all," I respond coldly. My face is scrunched in confusion as I await the purpose of this visit.

"Why?"

"Who the hell are ya, pix?" I demand, crossing my arms.

"A friend," the faerie responds, ignoring my crude label.

I wait for him to continue before figuring out that is all I'm going to get for now. "The shite's killed innocents an' must be stopped 'fore they hurt more."

"Haven't you, yourself, caused innumerable harm to mortals all around the world?"

Anger flares as I uncross my arms and take a step forward to point directly at his smug little face. "Y'know me, faerie?"

"The vampire who sought revenge for his murdered family," the faerie answers confidently.

His knowledge of me is disarming, and I let my hand drop. At that moment, I couldn't explain why, but I trusted him. "I wan' to protect the innocent."

"Because you couldn't protect your father, and your mother?"

When he says the word "mother," I begin to see red; I struggle to keep my rage in check until I know why this faerie is here and how he knows me.

"Aye," I admit slowly, controlling my emotions.

"Thank you for your honesty, John. I am here to help you."

"How's tha'? Gon' bite their ankles, then?"

"By guiding you. For example, you could go into that building and take the life of every soldier in there. But it won't stop there. They are simply men who are following orders."

I look at the building where the soldiers are probably lying down after a successful mass execution. I really *really* want to punish them.

"Or, you could focus your attentions on those that give the orders and enact real change," the floating sage finishes.

My vision sweeps back and forth between him and the building full of murderers.

"I wan' to kill them," I admit to the faerie, my voice flat and stone-cold.

"A compromise, then. How about," he starts, pacing back and forth in midair as he strokes his chin, "we stop their commanding officers and maybe just the soldiers who committed the executions?"

"Listen here, pix," I say, lifting my finger to point at him again. "I a'ready have a code for whom I get to eat. An' these bastards," I continue, shifting my pointing finger to land squarely on the building full of soldiers, "meet tha' code fairly. Even those who didn' wield the blade are guilty for na stopping their comrades."

"Every soul deserves a chance at redemption. Wouldn't you agree?"

The thought of a clogged river flashes through my mind, and I say through a clenched jaw, "Any man will'n to murder women an' children deserves me wrath."

"Very well. I can concede that in this instance the crimes are egregious. And, I suppose, Rome wasn't built in a day."

"The fook does tha' mean, faerie?"

"Please, call me Raziel."

"That be an angelic name, faerie. Ya clearly are no angel," I say, making a point to look between him and the ground and waving at the empty air below him.

"Then, if I may inquire, what would you call me?"

"Seems to me tha' ya're tryen to talk me out of me actions, like a devil's advocate. Aye, Devil's Advocate—Da." I titter at how clever I think I am. "Your name be Da."

"Father help me," Da says as he exhales. "This will be harder than I thought."

"He's been doing his best to guide me ever since," I said with respect. "No easy task, I assure you."

Both Depweg and Locke laughed at my comment.

"We know," Depweg said, pretending to wipe a mirthful tear from his eye.

"Alright, alright. Enough of that," I said.

"Thank you for sharing," Locke said after a moment of silence. "Da means a great deal to all of us—yes, even me. We were growing close—well, closer—in your absence." After a pause, he added, "He really loves you, you know."

My throat grew tight and I nodded quickly.

"If he's alive," Depweg said, "we'll find him."

We pulled down the street that connected Valenta's Saloon and the church, and I almost asked Depweg to stop so I could check on Father Thomes. Instead, I opted to focus on the mission at hand, not knowing how much time we had before the hunters were killed.

The church passed by and I stared at the building that was falling apart with age. I decided right then to hire a crew to restore the church to its rightful glory—if we made it back.

A minute later and we were pulling into Valenta's empty parking lot. I was kind of bummed that I hadn't gotten to use the minigun in our brief ride. Then again, what had I expected? Maybe a rhino demon charging in out of nowhere? Preposterous, I tell you.

The four of us unloaded, and my companions followed me through the swinging doors of the saloon. An expecting Valenta sat behind the bar, reading a first edition copy of *The Vampire Lestat*. I appreciated the subtle irony.

"Didn't take you for an Anne Rice fan, Val," I said in greeting as we approached the bar.

"Breaks up the monotony of existence, son," Val drawled. "Can't be picky with genres when time isn't a finite, precious resource." I noticed he had closed the book without a bookmark or even dog-earring the page he had been on. He looked us up and down before nodding. "That'll do it, alright."

"Let's hope so," Depweg said.

"Might you have anything that could aid us in our quest? Say, downstairs?" I asked shamelessly.

"Mayhaps," Valenta said as he turned to push the door of the kitchen. "Follow me."

We obliged him. No one said anything as Val opened the secret door to his secret basement that held all kinds of secret artifacts that he had attained by secret ways. The four of us filed down the stone stairs after Val, Joey bringing up the rear. The sound of tactical gear rubbing against each other competed with the slap of our rubber soles as we walked down the hallway. The narrow stone walls seemed to amplify the noises we made.

Val walked to a bay of shelves and pulled the topmost case down, setting it on the ground with a loud thud. He unclasped the lid and opened it to pull out a single pebble that looked like it was made of ivory.

Val extended his closed hand out to me. I responded by holding my hand out to him, palm up. He dropped the surprisingly heavy pebble into my hand and said, "Dat there is a one-way ticket home. Speak your return words now, and when ya say 'em again, it'll bring ya right back to this spot."

I looked at the white stone in my hand, and only one phrase came to mind. It was from my second favorite Tim Burton movie starring Michael Keaton. "Home home home," I said as I brought the pebble closer to my mouth. It pulsed a white glow once before returning to normal.

"Good," Val said approvingly. "This way."

"Is that it?" I asked incredulously. "Not going to give us, like, a holy hand grenade or something?"

Val whirled on me, dropping his Southern twang as he said, "You think me stupid, abomination? If I give you—of all people—any of these powerful artifacts, I might as well be handing them over to the enemy. What good they might do you in your ungraceful hands is nothing in comparison to what evil might be brandished by the dark Fae."

I held my hands up in placation as I said, "Alright, alright. I get it. I appreciate the help you have given us, Val."

Locke found something interesting on the ground near his feet to look at as he cleared his throat uncomfortably. Valenta waited for another dumbass comment from me before turning to stride toward our destiny.

We followed him down the hallway and toward the room of portals.

"My God," Locke exhaled as he looked around, instantly recognizing what he was looking at. Joey kept his focused eyes forward, not interested in anything but the door that led to his revenge.

Val approached the same portal as before. He placed a hand on the doorway, and the air shimmered into a dark scene beyond.

With his drawl back, Val said, "B'careful, boy. Bring back Raziel. Y'hear?"

"We will," Locke answered before I could. He was starting to piss me off with the whole "friend of my friend" thing. I didn't like the feeling of being replaced, and I could admit that to myself.

You ready for this? I asked Baleius.

He looked me dead in my eyes and said, *Not really. But what choice do I have?*

None. I gave him a half-hearted smile before stepping through the portal and into the darkness of Faerie.

Chapter 18

As I stepped through into the Fae plane, a huge weight was applied to my body, pushing me toward the ground. I stumbled a few steps before catching myself against a wall made out of logs.

Leaning against the wall, I closed my eyes and tried to acclimate to my mortal predicament as quickly as I could.

I looked around and became dizzy before a burning in my chest told me to breathe. I sucked in a deep breath and felt my heart race as I started to hyperventilate.

"Breathe, John. In, one two, out, one two," Depweg said, rushing to my side and placing a hand on my back. "In, one two, out, one two," he said again.

I followed his instructions, and the black bugs swimming in my vision began to thin out before disappearing completely.

"Being mortal sucks!" I said between deep, controlled breaths. The air smelled like flowers and leather. I sniffed the air, confused, before my nose touched my shoulder. I continued to sniff as I moved my arm in front of my face, smelling the leather of my trench coat.

"You act like you've never smelled your own coat before," Locke said as he wiggled his fingers in the air, testing his powers. The air refused to crackle with his usual green-and-purple energy signature. He frowned slightly.

"Well, normally each smell is distinct and identifiable. Right now, everything is a mix of smells that I can't really tell apart. Just smells like leathery flowers or something."

"I understand what you're getting at," Depweg confided. "You'll get used to it in about five minutes and won't even notice."

"Odd I didn't notice before," I said to myself.

"Doesn't matter. We are here for a mission," Joey said flatly, bordering on aggression.

A small crackle of electricity shot between Locke's fingers as he focused.

"Hmm. Elemental magic is still accessible," Locke mused.

"That's good, right?" I asked hopefully.

"I must confess that I am quite the novice when it comes to elemental magic. I have always relied on, and perfected, my warlock abilities. Never seemed to have time for the more—basic—magic."

"Someone learned how to sprint before he could crawl," I poked.

Locke ignored me. He was good at that.

After checking our automatic rifles, we positioned them in hand with the barrels pointed down. We made our way outside—which was as dark as our plane—with Depweg in the lead and the rest of the team spread out in even increments in a straight line parallel to the road. Behind him was me, followed by Locke, with Joey bringing up the rear. I looked over my shoulder to see Joey's head on a swivel, checking all around. I was impressed at his discipline. Then again, I didn't know what I had expected from a packmate of the military man at the front of the squad.

Depweg signaled to spread out, but I quickly waved off the idea, remembering the fairies that had almost eaten me. He nodded, and the fire team remained on the road.

After several minutes of walking, I became alarmed that my knees had begun squeaking with every labored step. Sweat drenched my shirt, and I was tempted to remove my trench coat; but with nowhere to place it, I opted to endure rather than leave it behind. I was perturbed to notice I was the only one breathing heavily.

A few more minutes of walking, and we came up to a familiar bridge. As we crossed it, my old troll buddy popped out from underneath and stood, blocking our path. He smiled hugely as he recognized me.

I walked briskly past Depweg and straight to the troll, my thumb removing the latch on my Glock.

"Well, well, well," was all the troll got out before I placed the firearm against his forehead and squeezed the trigger once. One of his eyes rolled downward in its socket as a red mist plumed outward from the apple-sized hole in the back of his skull. The other eye stared straight ahead, going glassy and unfocused. For some reason, I thought about how odd it was that his head had been rocked forward—almost knocking the gun from my hand—as the bullet had exploded out the back of his head. He collapsed straight down before crumpling to the side of the bridge. I gave him a swift kick in the ass, and he toppled to the water below with a satisfying splash.

"Feel better?" Depweg asked.

"Much," I answered.

"I hope so, because you just announced our arrival," he finished, shaking his head while pinching the bridge of his nose. "No more surprises, please."

"Um, ten-four copy on that roger roger," I said, embarrassed.

"Fall in line," Depweg commanded as he continued toward the castle. He picked up his pace, and I wasn't sure if it was a tactical decision or a punishment for me.

As we approached the world tree, which was now made of stone—at least on this plane—Depweg held up his fist in a silent command to halt. We did as instructed, with Joey turning to face our six and kneeling, his gun at the ready.

Depweg scanned the horizon, choosing the best angle of approach. He made his decision and motioned forward. We headed toward the city but away from the main door. I wanted to question why not the simplest approach when I saw what Depweg had been looking for.

A side entrance—probably reserved for deliveries or some other necessary purpose—came into view. Rather than being impressive and flanked by high turrets on either side, it was just a simple wooden door. Depweg pulled out a small pair of expensive-looking binoculars and scanned the distance. He held up one finger, indicating a single target.

I squinted to see a lone Shadow guard standing at the ready five feet in front of the entrance, his head scanning back and forth. Seeing just one when I was already used to seeing scores was odd. His purple eyes darted restlessly in a one-eighty-degree radius in front of him. Minus the eyes, nothing else was discernible about him. Heck, the only reason we had even seen him was because 1) Depweg was expecting a guard at the door and 2) the purple eyes in the darkness were somewhat noticeable. Terrible design flaw.

Depweg turned to face Locke, who nodded in response. They had just had an entire conversation without a word, and that green monster in my chest lashed out to make me tighten my jaw. Baleius wasn't here, so I knew the jealousy was all me.

Locke unslung his hilariously large rifle as Depweg sat on the ground, cross-legged. Locke placed the middle of the long barrel on Depweg's massive shoulder and flipped open the covers on either end of the scope. I was expecting him to prime the lever, but all he did was move a switch near his thumb, taking the weapon out of safe. He sighted the target, took in a deep breath, and began to release it slowly. As he did, his finger squeezed the trigger and a muffled *pop* sounded, like briefly activating one of those air machines for your tires you could find at gas stations. I was supremely impressed at how quiet the report of the weapon was with the suppressor.

I looked to the target after my brief awe-fest with the Lapua and saw a head was missing from atop his shoulders. The body slumped to the ground before evaporating into the night air like a fart in the wind.

"That's helpful," I whispered. "No bodies to worry about."

Depweg held up a fist beside his head while looking right at me.

Locke charged the handle and released the empty casing, which he caught in midair and pocketed before returning the bolt, locking another round in place.

"Show off," I whispered as we made our way to the side entrance. Depweg shot a scowl my way, and I pantomimed zipping my mouth shut.

We hugged the wall, letting Depweg examine the door as we kept watch all around us. He approached the wooden door and cautiously pulled on the brass handle. It opened without protest as Depweg did a quick sweep with his Sig rifle. Once it was evident that the coast was clear, he motioned for us to follow him into the grounds.

Inside, it was eerily quiet for how big the area was. There was something about large spaces that you knew were supposed to be teeming with people that made my nerves stand on end. Ever been in a mall at closing, alone, when all the gates were closed and the lights were turned low? It felt...wrong. But I could only surmise I felt this way because I was a freaking mortal and balls deep in the Shadow Court–controlled Faerie.

Depweg looked at me and I pointed toward where I thought the path was that led to the castle. He briskly nodded once before sighting his automatic rifle in front of him and making his way forward at a slight crouch.

We made our way through the dark, empty city that had once been bustling with faeries of all flavors. I was surprised to find a lack of patrol from the Shadow creeps as we approached the giant entrance to the castle proper.

I hustled to walk next to Depweg and whispered, "How the dickens are we going to get to the other side of that wall?" As I spoke, my eyes walked up the massive stone barrier that stood between us and our friends.

Depweg answered by holding a finger up to his lips this time, dropping the military fist-up gesture in exchange for a layman's one. Annoyed, I did as told and fell back in line as we came to a spot on the wall next to the huge wooden gate. We formed a line as Depweg pulled something from one of the large pockets on the side of his legs. It was a thin can that looked like it could have been a Red Bull drink, only it had a small red trigger under the nozzle. He gave it a few shakes before placing the nozzle against the wood and pressing a release on the top of the can with his thumb. Safety disengaged, Depweg squeezed the red plastic trigger and coated the wood in a circle of white foam big enough to walk through. It grew slightly before solidifying in place.

Depweg placed the can back in his pocket before stepping to the side. He pulled out a rod the size of a pen and clicked the button on the side once in test. A small blue arc of electricity came to life at the end of the pen, which Depweg placed against the hardened foam. He clicked the pen once more and pulled his arm back quickly as the entire circle engulfed in a bright, white flame that hurt to look at. I shielded my eyes while stifling a cry of surprise as the circle began eating into the wood. Within a few seconds, it had eaten through the thick door before burning itself out in a sudden flash of light.

I rubbed at my eyes, blinking away the pain in my pupils. They had rushed to constrict at the blinding light.

As my vision slowly came back, Depweg addressed the group in a hushed whisper, "We probably don't have much time now, so let's turn on the high speed."

"Copy," Joey and Locke whispered in unison.

"Copy," I added lamely while looking back and forth between my fire team.

Depweg went through the hole and we followed suit. Once Joey was through, Depweg took off toward the castle at a moderate run, keeping his rifle muzzle down rather than attempting to try and sight anything at that pace.

I did my best to prevent my labored breathing from turning into loud wheezes that might as well have been cowbells attached to my boots. Lilith, I really needed to drop some el-bee's. Oh, wait, I can't change my body as a vampire. Maybe I'd get lucky and burn twenty or thirty pounds of fat while still a mortal. And what the hell was this? My lower back felt warm and tight all of a sudden.

Depweg cleared the entrance and began clearing adjacent rooms down the stone hallway that led to the throne room.

"Look for stairs," Depweg whispered over his shoulder.

"Copy," I said quickly between labored breaths while Joey and Locke said nothing. I sighed and brought my rifle up, trying my best to take deep, controlled breaths before I threw up. Sweat stung my eyes, and I was alarmed to discover that I must have forgotten to put my underwear in the dryer before putting it on. All I knew was that these boxer briefs were going in the trash later, if they didn't dissolve in the next few hours, that is.

Depweg came out of a cleared room and saw me take an obvious adjustment step to the side. He smiled before whispering, "Compression shorts."

"Here," Locke called out, coming out of a thin stairwell down an adjacent hallway. We beelined over to where he stood and filed down the spiral staircase with our rifles up and left hand on the right shoulder of the person in front of us.

As we stepped onto the landing at the base of the stairs, we spread out in a half circle, with Joey watching the stairwell behind us. In front of us was the typical dungeon that you would expect to see in any medieval movie. An assortment of torture devices littered the room, vying for dominance. I recognized about three quarters of the machines in the dungeon. It was like I was in a 24 Hour Fitness; but for torture.

Depweg began clearing the cells that lined the left wall while Locke repeated the process on the opposite side. Joey stayed crouched at the stairwell, his rifle covering the only entrance to the floor.

Something tugged at my attention, and I began a fast walk to the backmost cell against the far wall. It was the only cell there, and it connected the left- and right-side cells in a perfect U shape.

Locke and Depweg looked up as I strode past them, heedless of the standard clearing protocol. Locke motioned at me to get back into formation, but I ignored him.

I began jogging until I reached the back cell, grabbing the thick iron bars that I was vacantly surprised weren't making my hands tingle. The fact that I was a mortal became the least important thing in the world as I peered through the bars to see something that took my breath away.

A human-sized Da stood chained against the far wall, naked and bloody. His arms were out and above his head, while his legs slumped to the side. Da was unconscious, and his weight was being borne solely by his wrists. Dried blood caked from his shackled arms down to his armpits and then to his waist. Even his legs had black crust from the mass exodus of blood from his densely scabbed wrists.

"Da," I whispered. He didn't respond, though his chest heaved slightly. I was relieved to see he was breathing. But relief was eroded to be replaced by worry once I realized his breaths were coming in shallow, with several seconds of pause in between.

"Da," I said louder.

"John!" Depweg whispered harshly as he approached. Then his eyes locked onto our friend, and his demeanor stiffened. Depweg had the experience and mind of a marine, so had been mentally prepared to find the most horrific of scenes. So for him to stiffen was the equivalent of a normal person collapsing to their knees and screaming.

"Find Ludvig and Magni," I told him, breaking Depweg from his stunned state and taking command of the situation.

Depweg didn't say anything as he stared at Da and lifted his hand to reveal an iron skeleton key.

"Found this on the wall back there," Depweg said weakly as he inserted the key into the lock and turned it. His eyes never left the cell. A clang sounded before he retrieved the key and broke away to walk to Locke, who was motioning toward him. Locke gave a thumbs-up as he pointed with his other hand to two cells on the wall. A small semblance of peace entered my mind to know they had found the hunters; but that wasn't my main concern right now.

With numb hands, I pulled on the iron cell door and entered on weak legs. I began taking in ragged breaths as I walked in what felt like slow motion. My vision began to blur as the full impact of what had happened to my friend of several decades became clearer. I wiped at the tears that were forming and called again with a voice that trembled, "D-Da?"

My hand gently touched his cheek and he snorted awake, terror in his eyes. His lips were cracked and began to bleed as his mouth tried to work, mouthing the word "no" over and over as he squirmed. Every rib could be counted through thin, dirt-covered skin. Even his thighbones were evident. Da's eyes were sunken and bloodshot, accented by sockets that looked like horror movie prosthetics. A deep and dark feeling emanated from my chest as I realized in an instant how much he had suffered; and for so long.

"Da...Da, it's me. It's John," I said as reassuringly as I could. My bottom lip and brows quivered in sync with each other. "It's okay, man. I'm here, now. I'm here." Da stared with trembling, disbelieving eyes. Then they stopped shaking and squinted as if he were seeing me for the first time. Recognition smoothed his features.

"J-John?" Da said with a hoarse voice that sounded scarred from years of screaming.

I turned and saw a bucket of water by the door with a wooden ladle sticking out of it. I gagged as I walked to it, seeing unknown debris floating throughout. Having no other option, I brought the water-filled bucket over to Da, who responded by squirming and staring wide-eyed at the water like a dying man in a sweltering desert. I had never seen my friend so demeaned and broken, and furious anger began to crawl under my skin as I spoon-fed him the foul-smelling water. I stirred the surface, trying to move the debris sitting on top out of the way to allow access to as much clean water as possible. It was a hopeless battle.

As I brought the water up to Da's eager mouth, I could hear Depweg call out behind me, "Objective complete. Time to go."

"John," Da said with a voice that sounded reminiscent of his former self. "There's something I need to tell you."

"Take it easy, brother. Let's get you out of here, then we can talk and talk and talk. We'll jab like a couple of high school girls," I said as I began to unclasp his shackles. The blood had dried over the leather, and I had to coat both his hands in water and scrape at the gangrenous scabs with my fingernails. I fought to swallow the lump in my throat as my body warred between fury and sorrow. I was a churning ocean of emotions that rose and fell.

"No. NO!" Da said behind his own wave of emotion that threatened to break on the shore of his sanity. "You need to know."

I freed his first hand, and it dropped like a stone to his side. I placed my shoulder under his armpit and used both my hands to free his other one. He smelled like a corpse that had been left in a sewer to rot. I wanted to vomit, but I kept my shit together for him…for Da.

I gritted my teeth in building rage as I let him slowly slide down the wall. From the back of my mind came the thought that he was smaller than the Archangel Gabriel or Valenta had been.

"John, you…are…you are…" Da began, fighting the wave of unconsciousness that steadily approached like the tide. He clearly hadn't been fed in a long time and barely had the energy to speak.

"Contact!" Joey cried out as his Springfield began barking a steady staccato up the stairs. I whirled with my shotty at the ready and watched as Joey sent eight rounds into the darkness before the firing ceased and we were left in a tense silence.

My heart thudded, and I could feel it impacting my breathing. I tried to take steadying breaths now that it was game time. But as I sucked in a count of three, my heart would slam against my chest, making my breath catch for a millisecond as if someone were jabbing my stomach at quick intervals.

A shriek pierced the thick silence, followed by another, then another. After a few seconds, there was a cacophony of high-pitched screams threatening to burst my eardrums.

"Contact, left flank!" Depweg cried out as he began sending three-round bursts into the darkness behind the stairwell in the middle of the long room.

"Right flank!" Joey yelled as he pulled back from the stairs and began firing steadily down the right side. This cleared my line of sight for the stairwell just in time to see a flood of featureless creatures with glowing amethyst eyes spilling down toward us.

I pulled the trigger and was surprised at how much the shotgun kicked. It freaking hurt! Though I wouldn't admit that to anyone.

A silver slug went straight through the first wave of Shadow faeries, dissolving them like a hand through a cloud of smoke.

From in front of me and to my left, I was aware that Locke had begun firing his .22 on single-fire option rather than the spray-and-pray of full auto. Magni was supporting the injured Ludvig, who tried to lunge forward and fight. The boy was stronger than he was at that moment and kept him in check.

I took a step forward, trying to keep myself between Da and the door as I squeezed off two more rounds. The floodgates opened, and more faeries began to swarm the dungeon.

"Joey!" I cried out, realizing the direness of the situation. He glanced to the left and started firing into the building mass. I saw Depweg do the same, opting to focus on the immediate threat.

I squeezed the trigger again, and a cloud of iron rocketed out, slamming through multiple enemies in a much larger area than the slugs.

I shot the weapon one more time before the horde began to react and spread out.

"Shit," I barked through my teeth as a wave collected and then slammed into Joey, swallowing him in writhing blackness.

"NO!" Depweg bellowed. We were helpless to act. Our ammunition would go through the incorporeal Shadow faeries and hit our flesh-and-blood ally.

All firing ceased as the wave stopped progressing and calmed like a body of water after a violent windstorm.

"You see, I told you they'd come to us," a familiar authoritative voice proclaimed from the darkness. The wave dissipated to reveal Oberon in his perfectly tailored black suit. He was holding Joey by the throat as he walked into view. A featureless black cat with glowing purple eyes was sauntering behind him, twitching its tail as it walked. The Shadow army circled the air like a picture frame around their masters.

Joey pulled his KA-BAR and tried to stab Oberon in the neck, but couldn't reach with how long the Shadow King's arms were. Oberon smiled at him and effortlessly hurled Joey to where Depweg and Locke had backed up to the cell doors. Joey bounced off the metal with a bone-crunching *clang* before collapsing to the ground. The tough son of a bitch (no pun intended...well, a little) slowly lifted himself to his feet and brought his gun up. As if he were starring in an action movie, he spit blood to the ground before returning to business as usual. With dread, I noticed he had several cuts covering his exposed skin. The puckered edges were already turning black.

Depweg ejected his nearly spent magazine and replaced it with a fresh one. Locke and Joey took their cue and did the same.

My fingers fumbled at the bandolier, and I removed a single shell and tried to load it into the breach. As I did, I took a protective step backward to my friend and accidentally kicked his foot with my boot. I dared a glance at Da and saw him struggling to keep his eyes open as he gasped in lungfuls of air. My hands let go of the weapon, which bounced against my chest on its sling. The shell clattered to the ground in seemingly slow motion.

Blinding rage turned everything a tinge of red as I turned to face the person responsible for torturing my friend, my mentor. My fists clenched so tight that my knuckles popped and blood began to trickle from where my nails dug into the flesh of my palm. My jaw hurt from how hard I was clenching it. Spittle flew from between bared teeth as my breathing became heavy. Every breath filled my body with oxygen that fueled the fire of hatred which threatened to ignite my entire being. I was wrath incarnate.

Depweg, Locke, and Joey began firing their weapons at Oberon, who held up his hand, palm open. Oberon shifted his eyes to me and fucking smiled as the bullets stopped in midair just in front of his hand. With his other hand, he reached forward and then yanked backward. The weapons that were being held flew out of my friends' hands and clattered to the ground in front of Oberon, the slings ripping apart. Oberon began a slow, throaty chuckle before he said, "You're in my world, children. I make the rules here."

My squad stood frozen in confusion, even Depweg. No military in the world had a training protocol for this kind of enigmatic enemy.

"Depweg, key!" I yelled. Depweg didn't even hesitate. He threw the key underhanded toward me, which I caught without looking. With my other hand, I pulled out a white pebble from my coat and threw it at the clustered group while screaming at the top of my lungs, "HOME HOME HOME!"

"NO!" Depweg cried before there was a brilliant white flash. Oberon shielded his eyes from the flash while the shadow creatures shrieked in pain. In the brief reprieve, I slammed the door to the cell shut with a reverberating *clang*. Dust and dirt rained down around me from the impact as I reached through the bars. I inserted the skeleton key into the lock and secured the door before trying to break it by yanking it sideways. Well, the movies lied—as usual—and the iron key did not break. Instead, I pulled it out and pocketed it.

Oberon recovered and bellowed in rage before pointing at me and yelling, "Lolth!"

The cat leaped toward me while transforming into a vicious reptilian beast in midair. It filled the entire height of the dungeon, knocking over the torture machines as it charged forward. Saliva dripped from a mouth full of gleaming, jagged teeth while amethyst eyes blazed, lighting the room in a bright purple light.

Reaching my hand into my coat, I smiled, knowing how much this was about to hurt. I pulled out my military-grade flashlight, pointed it at the charging monster, and pressed the button. Light that was so bright as to be banned from civilian use due to the risk of blinding airline pilots slammed into an unprepared Lolth. The reptilian shriek that pierced the air and ricocheted off the stone walls stabbed my eardrums like an ice pick; I didn't fucking care. I began screaming back at the monster that recoiled from the brilliant beam before setting the flashlight on the ground and forcing myself to turn back to Da.

I kneeled next to him, looking back over my shoulder, as Lolth disappeared back up the stairs in a blur of pitch-black mist, the volume of her cries diminishing as she fled.

I turned back to Da, who had the smallest crease of a smile touching his eyes and the corner of his cracked and bleeding lips. I could hear Oberon's boots slamming against the stone floors behind me as he charged forward while screaming in rage. Though the light wasn't as affective against him as the pure shadow goddess, it was still uncomfortable as hell. I was also banking on it stunting his adopted shadow abilities.

He slammed into the iron cell and tried to tear it free, prompting me to begin laughing. He froze in indignation before I turned to regard him and said, "Nuh-uh-uh. Iron doors, King Fuckface. The irony that they are used to keep people in shouldn't be lost on you, huh, fairy boy?"

"I will tear your world asunder. You will watch as every mortal on your precious Earth withers and dies. I WILL SIT ON A THRONE OF BONES AND WATCH YOU SHRIVEL AS YOU STARVE!"

"Gonna take a while, big guy," I said while extending my ample belly and slapping it before rubbing my hand all over my stomach and chest. I made completely inappropriate moaning noises while licking my lips suggestively. "You like that, don't you? Yeah. Mm-hmm." The confused rage in his eyes was almost palatable on my tongue, like a rich and tasty delicacy.

My brow furrowed in an instant and I stuck my roaming hand toward Oberon, giving him the universal salute as if he had just cut me off in traffic. His dark face turned burgundy, or maybe it was maroon, while he yanked on the cell door with renewed vigor. His screams became unintelligible at the insults I threw his way, which I was confident he had never experienced in his entire existence.

I turned back to Da with a beaming smile. While Oberon reacted exactly as intended and bellowed while rattling the iron cell, I winked at Da. I charged the handle on the Benelli semi-auto shotgun that hung across my chest until I saw the first red shell enter the breach.

"Hey, Oberon," I called out as I turned to face the front of the jail cell before bringing the stock of the weapon to my shoulder. "Say 'cheese,'" I said before squeezing the trigger and sending a white phosphorous cloud from the dragon's breath to coat Oberon from head to waist. In his hubris of being on his home turf, he hadn't manifested his celestial armor, leaving behind flesh that was ripe for incinerating.

Oberon's cry of surprise and pain was music to my ears. I wanted to record it and make a remix to listen to while trying to go to sleep.

I squeezed the trigger again and coated from his midsection down to his knees to help even things out. I had to shield my eyes from the burning man as he turned and raced to follow Lolth. The iron bars on the cell had also been coated and had begun to morph as they melted.

I kneeled back down next to Da while chambering more red shells until no more would fit.

"We don't have a lot of time," I said to Da as I tried to help him to his feet. He pulled his arm from my grasp while shaking his head.

"I-I'm not going anywhere. I'll just...slow you down," he said between weak breaths. I could tell he was fighting to stay conscious. "John, I have to tell you..." a chorus of screeches sounded from the stairwell as what I could only assume was an entire army of Shadow Fae began rushing to us. The first pair down instantly evaporated from the light, but not before allowing the pair behind them to inch forward before meeting the same fate. With each shadow that died, its disappearing body allowed enough cover for the one behind it to move closer and closer. Then they spilled into the room, with wave after wave meeting their fate before the ones behind made it ever nearer.

"John, ta-take my blood. Take...all of it. But you must hold on to it. Don't-don't let your body process it," Da babbled near incoherently.

"What? No! Besides, I can't. I don't have Baleius with me. I-I'm a mortal," I explained as I dropped to a crouch in front of my friend. For once, I was relieved I didn't have my abilities. It was the perfect excuse to not follow through with his wish.

Da shook his head weakly before he reached up with heavy hands and placed them on my shoulders. He closed his eyes and my body began to shimmer like the air above the asphalt in a Texas summer.

"What the…" I started before I noticed I was covered in a white armor etched in gold. It fit like it had been custom-made for me, including the helmet that hugged my face comfortably. Power rushed into me and I stood straight up, feeling my preternatural power flooding into my body as if every storm cloud on Earth had unleashed their pent-up lightning all at once.

I yelled with delighted power before looking inward and seeing a very confused Baleius. *Grab the fucking wheel!* I commanded before returning to Da.

"Take…this," Da said on the verge of passing out. In his hand was his celestial gladius. He tried to lift his arm but couldn't bear the weight. I reached down and grabbed it, worry growing in my chest like a wildfire.

"Drink. Drink it all," Da said, turning his head to expose his neck. I could see the artery pulsing just beneath the paper-thin skin.

From behind, I heard the screams of the Shadow Fae growing closer. They were right outside the door to the cell now, which was almost completely melted.

"No!" I cried out, mortified.

"You-you must. It will allow you to control the gladius. Drink…drink and keep my blood in you."

"I can't! Da…no, please!" I began to sob uncontrollably, knowing it was either one of us, or both of us.

"Do it," Da commanded with the last of his strength.

The Shadow Fae were almost inside the cell as I kneeled and placed my mouth against his thin neck.

In my mind, Baleius placed his hand on my shoulder and said, *Let me do it. We don't have time.*

No! I cried in defiance. *He-he's my friend. I need to do it.*

Hurry, or we all die! he urged.

I opened my mouth, letting my fangs elongate until the tips pushed into his flesh to the point just before breaking the skin. I froze, knowing I was about to kill one of my dearest friends who had watched out and guided me for decades. Tears streamed down my face. I could taste the salt as they fell to his skin.

It's 1990 and I am waking up in my room the night Father Thomes and I agreed to become partners.

"You have such potential to help this world," Da says, brimming with pride. "And here, I made you a small gift to commemorate the occasion." Da extends a gray beanie he knit during the day.

A whine escaped my throat as I began to pull back, unable to do it. Da grabbed the back of my neck with the last of his incredible strength and pulled my head down until my fangs pierced his skin and the pulsing vein underneath.

Angelic blood, older than time itself, erupted into my mouth and down my throat. Once it hit my stomach, energy shot out from my core in all directions like a nuclear explosion. My fingertips, toes, and nose began to tingle as I drank deeply. I closed my eyes and squeezed out enough tears to fill a swimming pool.

"He chose wisely," Da said to the air in a whisper. I barely heard him over the din of shadow screams as I continued to drink. The power was tremendous. Like standing on a mountain in Sweden while the northern lights danced in the sky, it took my breath away as I basked in its wonder. The dark parts of the dungeon not being bathed in the luminous flashlight became as bright as day. I was fully aware of every being struggling to rush the cell where I was ending my friend's life.

The blood flow stopped, and I stood with my eyes still closed, focusing on making the blood a part of my very essence rather than just processing it like normal. Da's angelic blood became one with my flesh—infusing with my DNA—and I felt my sword hand tingle.

I opened my eyes and Da's gladius—*my* gladius—was aflame with brilliant heavenfire.

Looking down at my lifeless friend, I saw there was the hint of a smile permanently etched on his face. I returned the grin while wiping my eyes with my free hand, and nodded before I said, "Thank you, Raziel. I won't let you down. I promise." Then I turned and unleashed the fucking fury that had been itching to escape, like a supervolcano exploding through the Earth's crust.

My eyes blazed red mixed with plumes of white that snaked up my forehead at the edge of my vision. I bared crimson-coated fangs as I lifted the gladius to the first wave of Shadow Fae that had made it to, and destroyed, the flashlight.

I channeled all my rage, all my sorrow, and unleashed a violent scream that stopped the approaching army dead in their tracks. A biblical torrent of white-blue fire rocketed forward, incinerating every being it smashed into in an instant, like a soap bubble against a speeding freight train. The entire dungeon was lit up in blinding light, turning the remaining shadow monsters into wailing puffs of smoke that dissipated within seconds. The flames swirled throughout the entire dungeon, melting the iron of every fucking cell as the destroyed torture machines were reduced to embers in the blink of an eye.

The flames went full circle and splashed into me; but I knew they wouldn't burn my flesh. Da, however, was cremated in a flash of heavenfire. I let it happen because it felt proper.

My scream petered out, and I slowly lowered the gladius as the flame tsunami was halted. Silence and darkness rushed to fill the void, the only modest light being provided by the glowing pools of melted iron and dying embers.

I turned to where Da's ashes lay in a pile, and kneeled while lowering my head. With no discernible reason as to why, I put two fingers in my mouth and pulled them out covered in Da's blood. I reached down and placed them into the ash pile, mixing what was left of my friend. Without knowing why, I pulled my fingers out and pressed them to my chest, where I made two strokes on my armor, forming a cross. The armor pulled the blood and ash into itself, but left the image of the painted cross on my chest.

"You'll always be with me," I said in reverence as I stood and faced the stairway.

Closing my eyes, I took in a massive, slow breath before I bellowed into the darkness, "OBEROOOOOOOON!"

Dirt fell from the ceiling from the power of my voice, and I was sure that every being in Faerie had heard my call.

I strode forward and up the stairs, my armor clacking with every step. I was aware that my trench coat was still on under the celestial armor that covered me from head to toe. It made it slightly awkward to move, but only slightly.

At the top of the stairs, I turned and stomped toward the throne room. Oberon was nowhere to be seen, but I could smell charred flesh in the air. As I stalked forward, a column of Shadow faeries rushed out of a side room. Smiling, I tossed the gladius from one hand to the other and reached to my side in pure instinct. Lifting my right arm, I thumbed the safety to full auto and began spraying silver-tipped rounds down the hallway.

When the magazine ran dry, I dropped the Sig and reached for the fully loaded semi-auto shotty sitting atop my chest. Without even aiming properly, I sent round after round of phosphorus into the advancing column of Shadow Fae. They screamed as they died. I grinned maliciously.

The remaining Shadow faeries fled into the darkness, unwilling to continue the fruitless barrage. Then I stepped, unmolested, into the throne room.

"OBERON!" I screamed with enough ferocity to send spittle laced with blood flying from my mouth. There was no answer in return, and I stepped to the imposing throne. I looked up to see it was powering a churning cloud at the ceiling of the throne room. Black and purple tendrils lanced out, mingling with the dark swirl cloud. I could see the Earth at the center, and realized I was looking through the black hole that was swallowing the sunlight.

I ignited the angelic gladius again, feeling the unimaginable power in my hand. With a rage-filled yell, I swiped my flaming sword at the base of the thick throne, sending a hailstorm of black stone crashing into the wall. A huge chunk had been cut free, and the throne leaned precariously before gravity took hold and pulled it the rest of the way to the ground. It exploded into rubble that tumbled in all directions.

Looking up, I noticed the churning storm above remained even though its source of power had been cut down like a rotted tree.

A pained laugh came from behind, and I whirled to see King Oberon fully decked out in his own angelic armor. The black armor with red etching stood in direct contrast to my white and gold. His gladius was out and had a black flame running down its length, with wafts of amethyst fire intermixed. I wondered if it glowed purple due to him being in his bailiwick.

"You're too late, vampire," King Oberon said from bleeding lips. His skin was still smoking and had bubbled where the phosphorus had eaten away at his flesh. "The black hole is self-sufficient now. Your world will never again see the light of day, and the shadows will rise from the darkne—"

I blurred forward with blinding speed and decked him in his bitch mouth where the helmet offered no protection. Oberon flew back to crash into the stone wall behind, leaving a crater that rained down rock. To his credit, Oberon recovered almost instantly and glared at me with surprised eyes.

"Oh yeah, got my powers back, bitch," I mocked as I rushed forward, blade in hand and ready to take his smoldering head.

Oberon pushed off the wall, cracking it further, and rushed to meet my blade with his. We stood there, locked with our blades and almost nose to nose. My white-and-blue flames dancing wildly with his black-and-purple ones.

Filled with angelic blood that was now a part of my very soul, I began to push Oberon back inch by inch.

"My demon-infused soul now has an angel added to it, you weak, pathetic fairy," I spit out as my blade grew nearer and nearer to his straining face. "I...am going...to fucking kill you."

Anger gave way to fear as my heavenfire began licking at the already charred skin at his neck. I smiled as the blade touched his flesh, drawing blood that immediately sizzled away from the flame.

Something grabbed me by the helmet and ripped it off my head with enough force to almost snap my neck. My gladius went out and Oberon shoved me back a few feet before slicing his still flaming sword in the air, creating a hole in space.

"Lolth!" Oberon yelled as something hit me hard from behind and sent me flying toward the rift.

"No!" was all I could manage before disappearing into the abyss.

Chapter 19

I tumbled through the darkness, the only light coming from the hole in space that seemed to fly in a circular path all around me. With each revolution, I was alarmed to see the hole cinching itself up, getting smaller and smaller as I toppled through the nothing. I handled it pretty well, though.

"Oh fuck, oh fuck, oh fuck, oh fuuuuuuuuuck!" I said calmly without even a trace of panic.

Then a hand was on my chest, and the rift stopped flying around me to settle in one position in space. I followed the hand to look into familiar eyes that were bigger than I was used to. The healthy man was beaming a warm, knowing smile.

"Da?" I asked dumbly.

"What are you doing, John?" he asked, amused.

"Making a sandwich. The fuck does it look like?"

"It looks to me that you are floating in a void between planes."

"Right. That's what I said," I mocked. Panic really brought out my snark.

"Why don't you get yourself out of it?" Da asked as if the answer were as obvious as flipping a switch.

"I'm all for suggestions, buddy! But I don't have the helmet, and I lost my powers."

"Can you feel the armor through the closing rift?" Da said, glancing at the shrinking hole.

Knowing there wasn't a lot of time left before the door was closed forever, I went with what Da was saying and closed my eyes. I reached out with my senses and landed on the helmet that was sitting in the throne room near the rift hole.

"I can," I said through my concentration.

"Well, bring it here," Da suggested.

I reached out again and thought about picking the helmet up. To my surprise, it lifted off the ground and flew into the rift right as the hole was closed. The darkness was blinding. The silence was deafening. Da was gone.

"Da?" I called into the abyss. "Da?!" I cried out again. Then the helmet smacked me in my head, and I grabbed at it like a drowning man grasping at a life preserver. I slammed it on my head, a little harder than I had intended, and felt my power rush back into me.

"Now what?" I yelled into the empty void of space.

Use the gladius, John, Baleius instructed with slight annoyance in his voice.

"Oh, right," I said out loud as I willed the sword to life, flames growing down its length in a whoosh.

I cut at the space in front of me, and nothing happened. I tried again at a different angle and was met with the same result. Then I did the video game equivalent of bashing all the buttons randomly and began frantically slicing the space all around me.

Think about where you want to go, Baleius said. I could almost hear his face resting in the palm of his hand as he shook his head in embarrassment. Almost.

Ah, makes sense, I said sheepishly before closing my eyes and picturing Valenta's Saloon. As I held the image, I sliced the air in front of me and was sucked through the hole I created, like opening the door on an airplane forty thousand feet in the air.

Close it! Baleius instructed as I rolled in a heap on the familiar wood floor of Val's bar. I quickly got to my feet and turned the sword in my hand and slashed at the rift with the flat side of the blade. I imagined I was erasing it as I swiped, and the hole closed with a pop. My head shot around searching for the flying debris that had to be rocketing toward where I stood. The room was still, as if I had been the only thing affected by the hole in space and time.

"Jesus Christ!" Depweg cried out as he ran to where I stood, my chest heaving up and down under my armor. I turned to face him and the rest of the group, and without thinking, let go of the blade to embrace my friend. As I did, it vanished into thin air, though I was acutely aware that I could still feel its presence.

"Thank Lilith you guys made it," I called out, my eyes darting over my friends. Ludvig was laid out on the bar, with Valenta operating on him.

I broke the embrace and rushed to stand by where he lay cringing in pain.

"What happened? Why can't he heal himself?"

"Iron," Ludvig forced through bloody teeth.

"They filled him with dull iron rods," Depweg said, sickened, as he came to stand by me.

It wasn't until I saw Magni just off to the side with red-rimmed eyes that I realized the severity of the situation.

"Is he going to make it?" I asked Valenta.

"Shut up, boy. Concentrate'n," Val responded sharply as he pulled a six-inch rod of gore-coated iron from Ludvig's thigh. Joey covered the wound in gauze before taping it shut. I looked up Ludvig's body and saw several leaking bandages in seemingly random intervals.

"Why did they do that?" I asked, the formation of an educated guess constructing itself at the back of my mind as if it were being created by Legos. Lolth had been waiting for us at the cabin.

"Dey made me tell where Depweg was. I held out until Oberon decided dat I wasn't going to talk and den moved to Magni's cell. I-I'm sorry, Depweg. I didn't have a choice." Tears flowed down his dirt-covered and bruised face.

"I understand," Depweg breathed out as his head hung low.

"Well, I fucking don't!" Joey cried out as he strode to the front doors and slammed them open with a kick. They bounced back and he stopped them with his elbows and a scream of frustration as he made his way outside.

"That Shadow bitch killed Dawson," I informed Ludvig. He raised his head to regard me and began nodding his head slowly at first, and then vigorously. He had known what the consequences would be when he had revealed the location of where I had been heading. Now, what he had suspected might happen had been confirmed, and he would have to carry that guilt.

"How did you appear out of thin air?" Depweg asked, searching the room behind me like trying to find the hidden door the magician had used.

"I, ah..." I started, unsure of where to begin about Da.

Valenta barked a cry of surprise, and my eyes shot to meet his gaze. He was looking me up and down with mouth hung agape and eyes mixed with fury and sorrow.

"What?" I asked as I looked down to see Da's angelic armor. My gaze shot back to Valenta in an expression of "I can explain," but he turned his head and shook it twice before returning to Ludvig. At that moment, I really didn't want to have the armor on and was surprised when it disappeared in an instant at my wish. As with the gladius, I could still feel it as a part of me and awaiting my command to reemerge. My black trench coat flowed free, and my hands went up to feel my gray beanie still atop my head.

Magni stopped sniffling as I performed my magic trick and looked at me with an expression of awe on his face.

I turned back to Valenta, stepped closer, and whispered, "Val..." before he shot me a look filled with daggers and said, "Not now, abomination." His Southern drawl was gone, leaving only his powerful angelic voice. In his anger, his words pierced into my mind like the guardian's had when I had first been made. I flinched slightly before returning his cold gaze. Da was *my* friend and had saved my life in his sacrifice.

"No, NOW!" I bellowed in return, my own voice permeating the fabric of space all around. Ludvig, Magni, and Depweg all cried out as Magni and Depweg rushed to cover their ears. Ludvig was too weak to move his arms.

Valenta's eyes began glowing a fierce white as he dropped his medical instruments and squared off with me from across the bar. His body began growing to full angel height. Once again, I noticed how small Da was compared to the other angels I'd encountered. A flash of light, as if being bounced off a highly reflective surface, shimmered over his entire body, and Varhmiel stood coated in ivory armor etched in gold. Beautiful white feathered wings extended to the sides in warning as a flaming gladius grew from his hand.

Depweg stumbled backward, startled by the events unfolding, while Magni just watched in horrid fascination.

In reflex to Varhmiel's actions, my own armor shimmered into existence along with my matching sword coated in heavenfire.

"You have killed two of my brothers, abomination," Varhmiel's voice rumbled the very ground I stood on. "Raziel was one of the best of us, and you stand wearing his armor and wielding his blade." Varhmiel exuded fervent anger with his words.

"I had no choice, Varhmiel," I responded feverishly, calling him by his angelic name so as not to piss him off any further. Respect seemed apropos, mostly because he was right. "Da made me drink from him."

"Raziel! His name was Raziel," Varhmiel asserted.

"Raziel put the armor on me and placed the sword in my hand as we were being overrun with Shadow Fae. He was near death and sacrificed himself to save me—to save all of creation, Varhmiel."

Varhmiel stood glaring, but didn't combat my words. I continued.

"Because of him, I was able to destroy hundreds, maybe *thousands* of those fuckers. I even hurt Oberon and was about to cut him down when that bitch, Lolth, attacked me from behind. Raziel saved me as I was thrown into the abyss," I said aggressively, pissed I was having to justify myself as if I had killed one of my dearest friends wantonly.

Varhmiel's wings folded in slightly, and the gladius he had been pointing at me lowered as he said, "What do you mean he saved you."

"I was tumbling through the nothingness when Da appeared and told me how to get out. He was the fucking Obi-Wan to my Luke." I took a risk by calling him Da, but it was how I knew him. It felt...odd, to call him by any other name. I supposed I could say the same thing about how I called Depweg by his last name instead of by Jonathan. It was weird to call him by anything else.

Varhmiel's wings folded completely as the flames extinguished along his blade. "How is this possible?" he asked himself.

"Da told me to make his blood a part of my essence. I could feel him becoming one with my flesh. Once I had, the gladius burst into life," I said as I turned my blade over in my hand and looked into the hypnotic flames. They didn't crackle like a normal fire, and though there was heat I could feel, I knew it would never burn me.

Varhmiel began to shrink as his armor and gladius shimmered and disappeared. A look of consternation was on his face as he regarded me, unsure of what to do or say.

"Raziel was my oldest friend," Varhmiel said as he shrunk to become Valenta again.

"I understand," I said empathetically as I shot a quick glance at Depweg before returning my gaze to Valenta. Depweg caught the look, and from the corner of my vision, I noticed him shifting where he stood, his chest puffing out ever so slightly in what I took for pride. I was going to have to punch him in the arm or something later, though I wasn't sure why I felt the need to do so.

"Of all my siblings, he was one of the few that stayed behind after the revolt and who remained in contact with me, uncaring of my desire to remain absent from the senseless politics and entitlements." Valenta looked up at the ceiling, then, and I wasn't sure if it was to stanch the flow of tears or to regard Heaven. "I honestly believe he, alone, helped to keep my mind intact in the overwhelming loneliness of eternity." His face twitched in thought as he looked back down at me with a gaping mouth. "You were a mortal who had a demon infuse with his soul and body to become vampire. Now Raziel, an angel, has become a part of you, too. You," he said, pointing a trembling finger at me, "are truly an abomination that has never before existed in all of time."

"Th-thanks?" I stammered, confused as to the appropriate response.

"The prophecy..." Valenta whispered as his eyes went unfocused and a look of worry spread across his features. "She was right."

"Who?" I asked, taking a step closer to the bar. Valenta ignored my question as his eyes shifted around as if searching for an answer that eluded him. Then he snapped back to reality while shaking his head to clear his mind. He returned to Ludvig and began packing up his instruments.

"Hey, where's Locke?" I asked, looking around the bar, deciding to let Valenta's comment slide.

"Downstairs," Valenta said heavily, still with his angelic voice, though at a normal volume. He spoke as if extremely tired all of a sudden. "He asked to view my collection to see if there was anything he could use to summon you back to this plane."

My eyebrows jumped up my face as I realized that he had let Locke, of all people, rummage through his holy relics.

As if on cue, Locke burst through the kitchen door holding an armful of various items. "Alright, one of these might work. And what was that yelling?" Locke said before lifting his gaze from his armful of goodies to spot me, still in full angelic armor. "Oh," he said with a mixture of relief followed by sudden sadness. His eyes inspected every inch of me as his brow furrowed. "Da?"

My lips tightened into a thin line, and I shook my head with sorrow in my eyes. Valenta unconsciously turned his body away from me to stare at the back wall. I could see through the mirror that his bottom lip was quivering.

Valenta had never been one to show much emotion or reveal his feelings below the surface, but I could appreciate how losing a brother who had also been a friend since the beginning of time might be difficult to process. Hell, I had almost lost Depweg a few times after knowing him less than a century, and could remember how impossibly hard that had been on me. I couldn't imagine, you know, the *beginning of time* itself. It made me dizzy to try and fathom eternity.

Locke didn't say anything else as he gently set the armful of artifacts on the edge of the bar, as if he were handling priceless china.

"How's the Swede?" Locke asked, breaking the tension and changing the subject. He nodded to the now unconscious paladin that had begun breathing in a deep, slow pattern. There was a pile of dull iron rods that were coated in blood and even some flesh. It made me shudder to imagine Oberon slowly sliding *dull* rods into Ludvig's flesh to get answers.

I admired the Hunter as I admitted to myself that I wouldn't have made it to half the stack had our situations been reversed. I would have been singing like Whitney Houston.

"Asleep. He's going to make it," Val said as he turned to face where Ludvig rested. A single tear had run down his cheek, and he wiped it away quickly. "All the rods have been removed, so now all we need to do is give him a blood transfusion and let him heal."

"I know just the place!" I said excitedly. I looked to Depweg, who caught my meaning, and we began to move.

Depweg grabbed the huge, unconscious Ludvig under his knees and just below his neck as everyone made their way outside. I turned to regard Valenta, who watched me with crossed arms and a look of sorrow across his face. I went to open my mouth, thought better of it, and turned to join the others.

As I pushed open the doors, Val called from behind, "John."

I turned while keeping a hand on the door.

"Yeah?"

"Do 'em proud. Ya hear?" he said, his Southern drawl returning.

I tried to smile while nodding, but could tell it was only a mere stretching of my lips. My eyes remained unaffected, heavy with the burden Val had just laid at my feet.

Once in the parking lot, everyone removed their rifles, shottys, and all other long-barreled weapons and placed them in the back near the turret. It would have been uncomfortable to have them strapped on while seated. We loaded the unconscious giant of a man into the passenger seat of Depweg's Hummer and piled in. Once again, I sat at the turret while Depweg drove. Magni sat behind Depweg so he could keep watch over his master. Locke sat just behind the Swede.

"Joey coming?" I asked.

"Better to give him some time," Depweg said as he pushed the button, bringing the Hummer to life.

"I don't think he should be alone," I responded.

"I don't either," Depweg confided. Something about Joey whispered in my mind, something I was supposed to remember, but Depweg broke my train of thought as he said, "I also know he shouldn't be in a vehicle with the person he deems responsible for his brother's death."

A dark feeling crept over me that made me momentarily dizzy. "You mean...me?" I asked, terrified of the response.

Depweg thumbed toward the unconscious Lude, whose bandages were starting to soak through. I could smell them from the back of the Hummer. At the realization of who Depweg had meant, relief washed over me, and I let out a breath I had been holding. In my reprieve, I let my thoughts wander the wastelands of my mind to find what I needed to remember about Joey.

"John," Depweg started somberly as he looked into the rearview mirror. "I can't say whether or not Joey blames you, too."

A dagger pierced my heart at the thought I was to blame for the incalculable anguish Joey was experiencing at this very moment. I knew his pain all too well, and to be responsible for someone else to feel that was nearly more than I could bear right now.

As Depweg pulled the beast of a ride onto the road, I looked at the back of Magni's head, feeling the weight of Joey's pain stack on top of what I had done to this kid in front of me. My chest felt dark and cold where my heart was, and I promised myself I would make things right with both of them.

"John," Locke said, turning in his seat to better face me. "It's not your fault what happened to him. Don't blame yourself."

"What makes you think I blame myself?" I asked, faking normality. My voice betrayed me as it cracked a little.

"Your silence," Locke responded, staring right into my eyes. I felt as if he were reading my soul. "It wasn't your fault. Joey will be fine, with time. All you can do is be there for him and endure his anger."

The dagger that had been in my heart retracted slightly as Locke spoke.

"He's right, John," Depweg added as he turned onto the highway, glancing into the rearview mirror periodically as he spoke. "I only told you the truth that, in his pain, Joey might blame more than just Ludvig for what happened. It's normal."

"What if he's right?" I asked, defeat in my voice.

"Cut that shit out, right now," Depweg said, stern eyes piercing my soul from the rearview mirror. "Get your head on straight. We have an entire fucking world to save."

I let his words seep into my brain and marinate.

"You're right," I said, wiping snot from my nose from the tears that I had refused to let out of my eyes. Instead, they had opted for the back exit to the outside world.

"And don't pull that kind of shit again, like with the pebble portal," he added.

"Didn't have much of a choice," I said.

"Explain what happened, then," Depweg demanded through building agitation.

I recounted the events after I had thrown the pebble, starting with Lolth turning into the giant lizard thing and then the wave of self-sacrificing Shadow Fae that had been determined to tear us apart. They had almost won until...

"So, ah, thanks for throwing the portal at us," Locke said, breaking my pitfall of a thought. Depweg didn't say anything, and I knew *he knew* I had done the right thing.

I continued, leading up to destroying the throne that had powered the black hole. Then being tossed into the abyss.

"So the black hole can't grow stronger," Depweg said to himself. "That's a positive, at least."

"Except for the fact that we have no way of shutting it down now that it is self-sustained," Locke added in annoyance. Glass half full, meet glass half empty.

"We will figure something out," I threw out, completely at a loss of what we could do to stop a fucking black hole from swallowing all the light from the sun that was destined for Earth.

"I'm all ears," Locke said facetiously.

"You're about to be missing those ears if you keep talking back, young man," I said while lightly flicking the back of one ear.

He smacked my finger away as I did and turned to glare at me. His adult head on a ten-year-old body was morbidly funny to me. It was like a really good CGI effect from a movie.

We rode in silence as we drove closer to Doc Hunt's clinic. I could hear the gears in our collective brains straining to figure out a solution to the impossible problem.

Depweg slammed on the brakes in a squeal of rubber on asphalt. The Hummer pulled to one side as it lurched to a stop. Luckily, everyone was wearing their seat belts—Oh, right. There wasn't a seat belt in the turret, and my face raced to kiss the back of the minigun. My angelic helmet sprang into existence, stopping most of the force against my skull. I was both impressed and confused at how something that was so tightly fitted to my head could mitigate the impact. It wasn't like it was full of padding like a motorcycle helmet.

"What in Lilith's name was that?" I called out, gripping both sides of my head.

"We have company," Depweg fretted quietly.

I squinted to see past the turret and out the windshield. What I saw would have made a lesser man pee his pants.

As the warmth spread down my leg, I popped the hatch, and the turret platform sprang through the top of the Hummer. The roof that had separated cleanly at the middle acted as a bullet-resistant armor on either side of the turret.

Purple eyes shifted to crimson as my fangs grew. The scene around me lightened with the change, as if illuminated by daylight, and I could see everything clearly.

I turned the minigun to face the wall of Shadow faeries in front of us. Mixed with them were the drow—dark-skinned elves that were very much corporeal compared to their Shadow buddies. And oh, goodie! Behind the army of Fae were monstrous demons ranging in size from very small houses to very large houses.

The rest of my angelic armor shimmered into life as I sighted a swirling mass of shadow on the ground at the front of the line. Lolth dramatically climbed from the abyss—bulky arms shooting up before slamming onto the ground—to stand at the head of her army. I rolled my eyes at her showmanship.

"Come on, then. Ol' Painless is ready," I whispered as I released the safety on the minigun. The electric barrel started spinning with a high-pitched whine, ready to send silver-tipped freedom seeds to the enemy. God bless America.

Lolth smiled her Cheshire grin—stunning me in her confidence—as waves of darkness on either side of the road rushed to the center and toward the Hummer. They were as long as the eye could see and closing in. Streetlights exploded from behind where the wave demolished the poles like an out of control train derailing at Mach speeds. Bursts of black mist wafted into the air where the wave—made of countless shadow bodies—was bathed in the streetlights before their brothers and sisters took out the poles. Just like in the Faerie prison, the Shadow zealots didn't seem phased by sacrificing their own existence for their mission.

Without further invitation, Depweg threw the Hummer into reverse and began speeding backward. The electric engine provided immediate torque that got us up to an impressive speed quickly.

Smoothly pivoting the turret to face the road behind us, I let loose a volley of 7.62mm gunfire at over five-thousand rounds a minute. Every fourth round was a tracer so that I could see where I was shooting, the ammo creating a streak of orange into the darkness that looked like a sci-fi movie laser blast. My hands began to tingle from the vibration of the weapon as I bared teeth and fangs in concentration. The distinct smell of the rounds' propellant quickly permeated the air around me, morphing my clenching jaw into a delirious smile. I had always enjoyed the smell of gunpowder and cleaning oils; I assumed it was like how women at the mall must feel at one of those candle stores.

As I focused on the crashing shadow wave directly behind us, I let loose a maniacal laughter that could only come from behind a military-grade death machine. I cleared out huge chunks that went straight through before pivoting the Gatling-style turret to another portion of the oncoming wave. Lucky for me, one round could pierce through the wave from head to tail, as the Shadow Fae had incorporeal bodies that didn't slow the projectiles. So, effectively, one bullet could take out hundreds of enemies standing in a line, and I had thousands to spare. Tee-fucking-hee.

The shadow wave approaching from behind realized this and spread out to join the waves on either side of the road. I had effectively cleared a path for us.

I followed one of the flanking waves and kept firing until I was perpendicular to the Hummer. I could almost hear the shrieks over the constant *brrp* of the minigun; it made me smile.

From the corner of my eye, I saw the drow, who had been standing in several rows, begin rushing forward at supernatural speeds that caught me completely off guard. I pivoted the turret with a curse as my smile melted and sighted the chain gun on their rushing position. I pressed the firing buttons with my thumbs, and the weapon burped out enough rounds to cut down a small forest. But the drow continued to bear down on us, gaining ground. Not a one of them fell or exploded into mist.

"The fuck..." I said as I glanced down at my weapon and back to the approaching drow. At this point, Depweg saw we were losing the race and swung the Hummer around like he was the star of Speedy and Superfluous—or whatever that movie series was called starring that Riddick guy. Cars were never really my thing.

As he swung us around in a full one-eighty, I was impressed to see the turret kept me pointed toward where I had positioned it.

We lost some speed in our turn, allowing the drow to get uncomfortably closer, but once again, electric Hummer with megatorque. Depweg slammed on the gas and we rocketed forward. I sighted the gun again and began sending test bursts down the lane. A tracer passed right through one of the sprinting drow, who responded by manifesting a bow and launching an arrow straight at me. It struck my armor center mass and I inhaled sharply in surprise at the force of the impact. I knew what the darkness could do if it got under my skin.

I was relieved to see my angelic armor had destroyed the arrow on contact.

"Thank you, Da," I whispered before focusing my attention on the same drow again. He was notching another arrow as I fired. This time, I held the thumb triggers and kept the gun trained on him and only him.

We passed where I assumed the wave had first formed, and a bright LED streetlight passed overhead before washing over the drow. At that moment, the silver rounds did their job and shredded the bow fucker into pieces of flesh that flew everywhere like a firecracker inside a meat patty.

"Light!" I called down into the Hummer. "I can't attack the dark elves without light!"

"Got it!" Locke cried out as he climbed over the back seat and into the turret. It was a tight fit, but his tiny body could squeeze into compact spaces.

He stood in front of me between my chest and the gun, and took out a flashlight from the tactical vest he was still wearing. An almost comically bright beam of light bathed everything in front of the minigun in the blueish tint of the LED flashlight. Without hesitation, I pressed on the thumb triggers and began ripping the drow to itty-bitty dark elf pieces.

As soon as they realized what was happening, the drow fell back without a word between them. Even their dark faces seemed steady and emotionless. It unnerved me.

We rode in silence before Depweg slammed on his brakes again. I gripped the minigun to steady myself as Locke flew into me, the flashlight tumbling to the ground below.

"Son of a..." I said as it rolled into the concrete barrier along the side of the highway, the light flickering before blinking out forever as it shattered into little black plastic pieces.

I pivoted the turret and saw what had caused the emergency stop. We must have been in an episode of *The Twilight Zone* because an army of Shadow Fae, drow, and demons was smack dab in front of us, identical to the first.

I didn't wait for them to rush. Pressing the trigger, I sent hundreds of rounds in an arc, aiming for the knees of the formidable demons this time. My strategy worked as the heads of Shadow Fae evaporated in a puff and the house-sized demons began bellowing in pain before falling to the ground, clutching at their knees. Another pass, and the rounds tore through their flesh, ending their visit to Earth in the largest pools of melting ectoplasm I had ever seen.

Drow rushed forward and Depweg turned on the Hummer's high beams. I mowed down the dark elves who were in front of the vehicle with extreme prejudice. Horror struck as the remaining drow shifted directions and quickly began making their way to the edge of the Hummer's headlights and then forward, trying to flank us. A small group that had already been near the front of the line made it to the Hummer and began tearing chunks of metal off the vehicle like it was made of popsicle sticks.

"Locke, take over!" I shouted at him as I leaped from the turret and to the nearest drow. I manifested my flaming gladius and tore through him as if he were made of paper before multiple hands latched onto both of my arms. I struggled and was horrified to see how strong these emotionless dark elves were. Shadows grew from under the Hummer, and featureless monsters grabbed my legs.

"Fuck!" I cried out as my sanity began to give way to panic. "Someone help!" Even as I said it, I knew no one in that vehicle could do anything to stop what was happening.

Drow and Shadow Fae alike tried to stab me—with a plethora of different style blades—only to find that my angelic armor was impregnable. It wasn't going to be long before one tried my exposed mouth or found a space between the plates.

One of the shadow monsters at my feet morphed into three basketball-sized spiders that scurried up and around my torso. I cried out in wide-eyed horror as clicking mandibles searched for weaknesses between the armor. I did my best to keep my body rigid to prevent them from sinking their dripping fangs into my flesh.

"Why is it always spiders!" I cried out.

I became aware that the chain gun was not spitting silver-tipped rounds downrange and anger started to replace my panic. Then I heard Locke chanting over the chattering of spider fangs and drow blades against armor.

A ball of light the size of a baseball appeared over the Hummer and began levitating into the air, growing in size as it did. The bigger the sphere became, the more light was spilled over the landscape. The spiders hissed and retreated into the shadow under the Hummer, as did the Fae at my feet. The drow, on the other hand, kept up their goal of piercing my flesh with their hungry blades.

With my legs freed, I did a wide backflip, yanking the drow attached to my arms with me. As I landed, I tossed them back and brought my blade up to the remaining elves. It sliced through their flesh with ease as I danced in an offensive attack meant for multiple attackers. Heads rolled, limbs fell to the ground, and insides became outsides as my sword struck with unparalleled expertise.

As the shadows and drow began to move away from the light of Locke's growing death star, the remaining demons charged forward. Some wielded obsidian weapons while others had claws made out of the Hell stone. I would have to be careful because I knew those would effectively counter my angelic blade. Oh shit, could they pierce my armor?

I was determined not to find out as I rushed forward. As I did, a muscle-laden werewolf, eight foot long and weighing over five-hundred pounds, ran alongside me. The demons who had been left standing from my initial volley of rounds charged and tried to encircle us.

Depweg leaped at the first one that strayed too far from his buddies. The demon swung its fat fists as Depweg's powerful jaws closed around a thick throat and his momentum and weight brought the creature down on its back. It was practically dead before it landed as it gurgled its last breath. Black bubbles formed where the missing flesh from its throat had been while a leg twitched sporadically.

I rushed the center demon, increasing my speed from pretty darn fast to inconceivable preternatural speed at the last second, throwing the demon off. My blade sliced cleanly through its torso while its own sword remained poised above its head, ready to strike. As I passed through the spine, the impact traveled up my arm before my sword finished its trajectory and bisected the demon.

The minigun began burping again in short bursts and I turned to see Magni expertly taking out the enemy like it was some sort of video game. I smiled proudly as scores of enemies were reduced to clouds of black mist or ectoplasm.

An obsidian-clawed hand slashed at my arm, deeply scratching my armor—Da's armor. Time froze as I stared at the cuts in the once pristine armor I had been entrusted with only an hour ago. A nuclear bomb of wild and violent anger exploded into a mushroom cloud of rage. Every nerve ending cried out in indignation, and my skin began to heat up and crawl at the same time. My muscles tensed like an armed bear trap, and I sucked in a breath before erupting in a battle cry that sent spittle flying from my mouth.

White interlaced with red plumed from my eyes as my gladius became a solid mass of rampant heavenfire. The ground on which I stood started to ignite, melting the asphalt into bubbling sludge while energy flowed around me in waves like a helicopter above a wheat field. The road split apart and cracked where the fire hadn't yet consumed it from the coursing, raw power.

The demon who had clawed my armor stumbled backward in response. Eyes made of raging white-and-red fire locked onto the hunchbacked demon as I lifted the blinding blade to the sky and brought it down with all my might. A line of energy infused with heavenfire lanced out, cutting the beast's head off while splitting the highway in a straight line for eighty feet. My sword became lodged in the ground to the hilt, followed by a shock wave from breaking the sound barrier. I was vaguely aware of the sound of clattering glass striking the road coming from behind, and the simple action brought me out of my battle rage. The plumes stopped wafting from my eyes, and though I couldn't see the flames from where the blade had lodged deep into the ground, I knew they had diminished as I regained control.

An obsidian blade came down at me while my sword was still wedged into the ground, and I lifted my left hand while manifesting a bloodshield out of pure instinct. I knew the demon blade would slice right through my shield. All I could hope for was that it slowed it down enough to allow the celestial armor to stop it.

I shut my eyes tight as I hoisted the shield into place. There was a clang of metal on metal, and I opened one eye to see my normally red manifestation replaced with a full ivory white shield with gold lining at the edges.

The demon had been thrown off balance from his weapon bouncing back, and when I lowered the celestial shield, I saw the obsidian sword had embedded itself into its owner's face. One of the demon's eyes was searching from left to right like he was trying to figure out what had happened. His other eye stared straight forward, unmoving.

I willed the shield to morph into my gladius and then grabbed the hilt of the demon's sword with my other hand, pulling it free as he fell backward before melting into ectoplasm.

A hellhound tackled me and began ferociously chewing at the pauldron protecting my neck and shoulder. I struggled to bring one of my swords around to strike at the beast, but only succeeded in lightly cutting it in my attempts. I tried rolling on my back, but the hellhound kept the bulk of its weight squarely on my back, pinning me to the ground as it ferociously gnawed at my armor like I was its favorite chew toy and my flesh was the peanut butter–filled center.

The hound, in its frantic attacks, moved its massive paw off my back, allowing me to scuttle forward on hands and knees. Powerful jaws closed around my ankle before I was violently yanked back into position, my gauntlet-covered fingers ripping chunks from the shattered road.

I was pulled into the still bubbling pool of asphalt I had melted, and the hellhound placed a paw on the back of my head, pushing my head into the boiling slush. I screamed as my beard and eyebrows burned up like I had glued thousands of firecrackers to my face. My exposed skin began to scar like meat on the grill. My flesh bounced bullets almost as effectively as a red-underwear-on-the-outside-of-your-pants superhero, but introduce a little tiny thing like fire or any of its extended family, and all bets were off.

In a panic, I pushed off the ground with one hand in an explosive move and was thrown in an arc into the air. The hellhound, quick to react, latched onto my throat while I was in midair and slammed me to the ground on my back before climbing on top of me, his teeth piercing the flesh around my neck. Thank Lilith half his jaw was trying to close on the base of my celestial helmet.

Copious amounts of drool mixed with the boiling asphalt still coating my face and began to add volume and liquidity. One of my wide eyes was covered in a puddle of melting sludge, prompting me to slam both eyes closed with a yelp. I could feel the damn orb melting precipitously in my socket.

As I struggled on the ground, I heard thunderous footsteps and felt the ground rumble. I dared to open my remaining eye and was rewarded with the sight of a giant demon lumbering toward me with fists the size of smart cars raised to crash down.

While keeping my mouth closed in an effort to keep the boiling drool sludge from entering it, I screamed through my nostrils, my cheeks puffed against my helmet.

A blur smashed into the hellhound on top of me, and Depweg and the beast went tumbling, allowing me to scurry backward several feet. After they recovered, both canines squared off, growling their warning. The hellhound leaped at Depweg, who feigned his own charge before standing on hind legs and swiping upward—with claws that belonged on a bear rather than a wolf—as the hellhound flew through the air, helpless. It landed and began to stumble as black blood gushed from the four gashes on its throat. Depweg didn't even wait for the thing to finish dying before moving on to his next target.

"Oh shit..." was all I could manage in admiration. I wiped at my melted eye and bubbling face with my forearm before I remembered Captain Ham-Hock-Hands, who was slamming his fists downward. At the last second, I brought both of my blades up in a powerful strike that removed his hands at the wrist. But they still fucking continued their path and pounded me into the ground like a pair of asteroids. I saw stars as my body crashed through structurally sound asphalt that was neither melted nor cracked, and even compacted the earth underneath.

In my haze, I heard the distant roar of a train somewhere in the distance. It was growing louder as my swirling vision attempted to coalesce, my melted eye healing only to burn again from the sludge that had seeped into my socket. Relying on my remaining eye, I looked up to see the house monster was screaming its indignation and pain while stubs at the end of its wrists gushed viscous black blood. I let go of the obsidian blade, which I noticed had shattered just above the crude hilt, and stuck a finger inside my eye socket. I scooped out as much of the solidifying sludge as I could so I could freaking see. I started wiping the asphalt on my armor when I realized what I was doing and shifted to rubbing the goo on the detached demon hands instead.

My depth perception slowly returned, and I could see that my body had become one with the ground, the giant hands on top of me like bride and groom figurines decorating the top of a wedding cake.

Dizzy, I looked around and noticed I was at least three or four feet beneath the road.

"Oh, shit..." I struggled to repeat, but in a different context this time.

Regaining my senses, I attempted to lift the demon hands off of me, but couldn't move. That meant lots of things were broken and needed to heal. I closed my eyes and focused on healing as the monster recovered and began stomping back to where I lay, helpless.

The demon lifted a foot that was even bigger than his hands and started to bring it down in a crushing blow that would no doubt squish my flesh out of my armor like a tube of toothpaste under a monster truck's tire. All I could do was lift my gladius straight up and hope for the best.

The demon saw the flaming blade and tried to reverse his attack, but it was too late—for both of us. The blade pierced his flesh before his foot crashed down on top of his hands and my body. Luckily for me, his foot was bigger than the crater I had created, and the road slowed his attack. But his hands had been sticking well clear of the road, and his foot crushed them further into me. I heard more than felt the crunching of my bones and knew that wasn't good. Then I got mad...again. Did I have an anger issue? Nah. Probably. Yes.

"I'm...not...fucking...dying...here!" I screamed between heaving breaths and with increasing intensity as I willed my blade to blaze aggressively with heavenfire. The gladius, still inside the demon, began to surge with flames that ate at the innards of the beast. In a few moments, he was burning from the inside out, all while screaming in agony. He began to fall on top of me, and I could see the flames coming out of his eyes, nose, mouth, and even ears as he fell. Then he began turning translucent and melting into ectoplasm as his bulk landed on the John-sized hole I had delicately crafted with love. The weight that had been crushing me began to lighten before the fists fully melted. The body followed after and filled the hole with warm demon leftovers, leaving me in an ectoplasm-filled crater. I took a moment to soak in the tub while keeping my eyes and mouth closed as tight as possible while I let my body heal—again. Part of me wondered what ectoplasm tasted like before my brain caught on to the question and yelled a command to keep my mouth closed.

I was surprised to feel that it didn't take as much energy to recover from my wounds in the angelic armor. I would have to do some research on whatever magnificent magic this was. It was like it amplified my own abilities, which was just fine and dandy by me.

After my bones cracked and popped back into place, I reached up and grabbed the ledge of the hole and pulled myself out of the slimy muck. I took a deep breath, placed my hands on my knees, and began spitting intermittently like a college kid on a bender who had just thrown up and wanted to get the last of the vomit out of their mouth.

"Yuck!" I cried out as I flung ectoplasm off my limbs and rubbed at my face. At least the asphalt sludge had stopped burning and had washed off with the demon juice. Oh Lilith! It had soaked through my brand-new, freshly regrown beard! I sniffed through my nose and the wafting aroma from my epic facial hair made me gag. I grabbed at my impressive and full beard, and ripped it off my fucking face with a tearing sound. The flesh came with it, and I held up what looked like a Native American trophy taken from their enemy. Within seconds, my skin and beard had regrown sans the slimy ectoplasm of the demon. I tossed the beard to the ground and regarded the battlefield, spitting one more time for good measure.

Depweg was tearing through demons with an unhinged brutality that made me kind of cringe as I gawked. I could sense his insatiable hunger for violence and frowned at the thought of Dawson being in the wrong place at the wrong time.

Depweg was working through his hurt, and right now, I was just fine with—A small squad of drow tackled me from the side and held down my hands and legs while I struggled on my back. One began lining up a dagger strike above my head. I screamed and shook my head back and forth as hard as I could, not wanting to get the darkness inside me, before one of the drow slammed his knees into the ground on either side of my face. My head was caught in a vise I could not escape from. It was unnerving to feel how absolutely strong these elves were.

As the drow pulled his dagger back for the killing blow, I saw past him to the giant death star that was flying downward at an alarming speed.

"Oh shit," I said once again as the drow stabbed his blade into my face. The supernaturally sharp dagger pierced through my cheek and lodged itself at the base of my skull. It burned, and I knew I was fucked. I didn't scream or even gasp; I just lay still, staring in disbelief at the drow who had just stabbed me in the Lilith-damned face.

The drow attempted to pull the dagger from my skull as the death star continued to careen toward the ground near where we were.

Unable to use momentum, I realized my sword was useless, so I retracted the gladius and reached with all my might for the holster strapped to my leg. I poured my energy into my arm, moving it at an agonizingly slow pace toward my gun while the multiple drow struggled to hold me in place. My leg armor disappeared as I reached for the Glock—how the hell had the protruding gun stayed on with my celestial armor? Thoughts for later.

My hand finally wrapped around the sidearm and I pulled on it before becoming alarmed to feel it resisting me. I tugged again, harder this time, and knew it wasn't going to budge.

The drow yanked the blade from my face with a sickening pop as metal was freed from bone before he raised his dagger again. I saw the fission ball was almost on top of us.

With a moment of clarity, I thumbed the release on the Glock, slipped it out while turning my wrist, and put several rounds into the drow on top of me. His arm dropped and I set my jaw to prepare for another knife to my face when his hand landed gently on my chest before he slumped to the side and off of me.

I laughed once in surprise and let loose with my firearm, aiming for center mass at point-blank range. Each dark elf holding me down received two silver-tipped rounds to the chest. It was ironic that the ball of fission that was about to consume me provided enough light to make the drow vulnerable.

"John! Run!" I heard Locke cry. It sounded like he was struggling to get the words out and I risked a glance to see Lolth had him in her massive hands. The turret was empty and Magni was nowhere to be seen.

A pair of skinny demons stood on either side of the Hummer, waving their hands while chanting in hellion. As they did, a bubble appeared over them that not only shielded Lolth from the light, but I felt it safe to assume would protect them from the blast. Lolth was staring at me with malicious glee in her purple eyes as my death approached with exponentially increasing heat. I seriously doubted the angelic armor would be able to save my flesh from becoming reduced to ashes.

I heard paws on asphalt and saw Depweg hauling ass toward the Hummer. Lilith, I hoped he made it through the bubble. He didn't. Depweg leaped through the air and landed on the bubble as if it were solid ground. Then he climbed over it and began digging at the top, his claws doing no damage to the protection spell.

"Get behind it!" I called out as I searched for a way out of this mess. He looked up at me with ears that pointed in my direction before they flattened against his skull. With a quick jump, he placed himself behind the bubble and crouched while keeping his yellow eyes locked on Lolth and growling.

With Depweg as safe as he could be, it was time to focus on my favorite person ever: me.

Out of pure instinct, I looked at the ground in front of me while I moaned out loud, "Oh, man, gross," before holstering the Glock and jumping into the ectoplasm-filled crater. I was aware that my leg armor had shimmered back into existence once I had no more use for the firearm.

As I became submerged in the evaporating remains of the huge demon, the explosion rocked the ground around me. It felt like I was on top of a pile of wooden pallets during an earthquake. The shock wave that rocketed outward from the explosion was enough to level trees for tens of city blocks all around the impact site. The asphalt of the road melted, while the concrete of the barrier between the highways crumbled to dust.

The heat sped up the evaporation of the pool I was in, and within a few seconds, the exposed skin of my face was poking out into the superheated air. I felt the tip of my nose sizzle before I flinched downward and tried to flatten myself against the floor of the crater. I felt the ooze seep into the gaping drow dagger wound on my beautiful face and started to dry heave. I opened my eyes under the almost clear ectoplasm and immediately regretted it. The blinding light caused by the controlled fission explosion ate at my retinas with vigor. I shut my eyes so tight I thought the bones of my sockets were going to collapse in on themselves.

The ectoplasm dissipated to the point where the front of my body began to meet the air. I screamed as I shot my hands out in a vain effort to protect my body. As I did, my arms began to violently shake, and I opened my healing eyes to see a blurry rush of fire racing into my opened hands.

My irises finished repairing and I saw the mushroom cloud of fire getting sucked into my outstretched palms. For some reason, I thought about the movies where a large hole breaks in an aquarium and water shoots out like a supercharged fire hose—only it was flowing *into* my hands.

The gold that lined my armor began to glow as if reflecting the brightest sunlight, starting at my hands and working its way up my arms. My reeling mind equated it to a battery charge, at least visually.

I stood, feeling the rush of power flow into my angelic armor, and then into me. I shouted again, but this time in overjoyed excitement at what was happening. The fission bomb was becoming a part of me in sci-fi contrast to how I siphoned energy from blood. From the gash in my face to the base of my skull, I felt warm tingling for a few seconds before the feeling faded into the storm of euphoria that flowed throughout my entire body.

The wind howled as what sounded like a tornado was sucked into my hands. I could feel my eyes giving off white plumes of heavenfire that crawled up my helmet, and I turned to see that Lolth's face had dropped into a confused frown. Locke, on the other hand, was smiling from ear to ear with eyes bathed in awe and wonder.

I kept my right hand up while moving my left hand toward the Hummer. Smiling, I closed my fist while I left my index finger pointed at Lolth like a gun, cocked my thumb, and said, "Bang," while my thumb mirrored the hammer on a gun.

A beam of fission-formed plasma rocketed out at relativistic speed, crashing into the bubble surrounding the Hummer. The protective spell glowed brightly before reaching its threshold and shattering like glass. The two magic-wielding demons shrieked in agony as they crumbled into smoldering embers. Sons of bitches had redirected my attack unto themselves to protect Lolth—which wasn't at all concerning. Nope. Not even a little bit...FUCK. Demons were protecting the Shadow Court now? Neat. Super neat.

Bubble broken, I cocked my thumb again and smiled at Lolth, whose eyes went wide in recognition.

"Bang," I said as the last of the fission bomb was sucked into my right hand. The beam hit air as Lolth shrank into the shadows. Locke screamed as he was being dragged into the darkness, prompting Depweg to leap at Lolth now that the protective spell was broken. There was a moment of hope as the large werewolf soared toward the shadow bitch's back before being erased as he passed right through her. As he did, Lolth grabbed the scruff of his neck and continued her descent into the shadows.

I blurred forward at speeds that were impossible—even for me—as I brought my flaming gladius out to swipe at Lolth's arms. Locke and Depweg toppled to the ground as the hands holding them evaporated into mist. Lolth's shrill cry pierced the night before it became muffled behind the veil between planes. Then she was gone, leaving the three of us to warily look at the ground at our feet. Locke had rolled away from where the Shadow goddess had disappeared and clambered to hit feet in an offensive stance, his hands glowing purple and green with runes floating in the air. Depweg lifted a leg to accentuate his feelings of what he thought of the shadow coward.

Once Locke realized the danger was over, he turned to face me, letting his hands grow dim, and said in disbelief, "How did you do that? She-she grabbed my arms and made me drop the attack. There's no way you could have survived."

Looking down at my hands, I said, "I don't know, man. This angel armor didn't exactly come with an instruction manual. But neat, huh?"

"Yeah, that's one way to put it," Locke said slowly, almost wary of me, as if my hands were now a nuclear weapon.

I turned and took stock of the damage around us. Any remaining demons had been liquefied in the blast, while the Shadow Fae had either evaporated or fled. I wondered if the drow had the same abilities to shadow walk as their incorporeal brethren; though I was sure of the answer.

White smoke from the burning grass rushed to mix with the brownish smoke from the trees that were ablaze, the resulting clouds blotting out the stars as they drifted with the cool breeze.

There was a crater in the ground spanning the entire width of the four lanes and then some. The concrete barrier running down the center of the four lanes abruptly stopped before continuing eighty or ninety feet away. Scorch marks marred the remaining gray concrete median for as far as the eye could see in either direction, while melted asphalt began slowly oozing into the spherical depression where the ball had initially struck.

"Oh...sh-shit," I stammered, beginning to realize the full scope of what the fuck had just happened. A quarter of a mile down the road, there was another fire raging. I was confused for a moment until I remembered that the second fission shot had missed Lolth entirely and had had to hit something eventually. I let out a long whistle as I gawked at the raging flames down the road. It looked like a bus made of fire had slammed into the tree line and hadn't stopped for as far as I could see.

"Did...did you draw an entire fission bomb into you? And then used the energy as a weapon?" Locke asked in complete and utter disbelief.

"I, ah, think...so?" I answered in my own world of doubt. My eyes followed the still glowing gold edges of my armor, which seemed to pulse with power.

"And how many times," Depweg struggled to get out as he finished transforming back into his man-suit, "are you going to say 'oh shit'?"

Ignoring his question, I walked over to the passenger door to inspect Ludvig. He was paler than before and his breathing had gone shallow.

I placed my hand on his chest and was about to will some of my energy into him when Locke came up beside me, grabbed my wrist, and gently pulled it away.

"Don't," Locke said. "You don't know this power yet, and you might do more harm than good. Our best shot is to get him to the doc."

I lowered my hand and looked back and forth between the dying paladin and Locke before relenting to his point. I needed to practice what this armor could do, and not on someone on the brink of death.

My brain signaled something was missing from this equation. "Where's Magni?" I asked in alarm.

"He-here," Magni said from between the front and back seats. He had curled into a ball on the floorboard. There was a look of shame as he pulled himself up onto the seat.

"Hey, you did the right thing, kid," I said reassuringly. "Great job with the minigun, by the way. You kicked some major ass!" With that, his face lit up before he tried to hide it by turning to look out his window.

As Depweg replaced the clothing he had had the presence of mind to toss into the Hummer before transforming, I climbed back into the turret, checking the remaining ammunition. A frown etched itself on my face when I saw it was almost depleted. Locke climbed into the seat behind Ludvig while Depweg scooped up his wolf teeth from the ground. He walked around to the driver's side, slid in, and dropped his were-teeth into the cup holder.

"When did you start doing that?" I asked, crouching to peer into the cabin from the turret.

"It's a habit I should have developed decades ago. It'd never been a problem...until now."

"What hadn't?" Locke asked.

"It's not a coincidence that these fuckers keep finding us," Depweg said with anger in his voice. "I-I think they used my fangs to track us. They probably have several left to cast tracking spells, but I don't want to give them any more ammo."

Nodding my head, I said, "Makes sense. But not to worry. They now know who they are fucking with." As I finished, I held my gauntleted hands out in front of me and began squeezing them into fists before relaxing again in a show of power.

"Now they will increase their efforts," Depweg said coldly. "With each counter we complete successfully, they double down on their attacks. This time, they brought demons who aren't affected by light. What will Oberon and Lolth have with them next time?"

The words he spoke created seeds of doubt that planted in my mind as my worry watered them into blooming flowers of anxiety. I was going to have to nip them in the bud.

"We will handle whatever they throw at us, brother. Now, let's get Ludvig to the clinic before we lose another ally," I said, leaving no room for debate and forcing myself to overcome my growing emotions.

Depweg threw the Hummer into reverse and did a three-point turn to take us back toward our destination. Luckily, the military-style vehicle was more than capable of traversing the destroyed battlefield. I stood on the turret with the gun facing forward, fully expecting to see another army waiting for us; but there was none. The wind dragged smoke across the road, forcing me to squint with the sheer volume of it in the air. The warm smoke was in direct contrast to the cool air.

Once clear of the danger, I lowered the turret and closed the hatch on the roof so as not to arouse mortal suspicion and concern. I could see the phone call now: "Yes, police? There is a military assault vehicle with a long scary gun sticking out of the top with a dashingly handsome man behind it. He looks like that main guy from that one movie, *300*, but with better abs." I chuckled to myself while Depweg took the turnoff to the clinic. My armor wavered and disappeared, allowing me to sit more comfortably in the confined space.

Within three minutes of driving, we passed a speeding police cruiser with its lights flashing and siren blaring. Another minute and two more blurred by, along with a firetruck. Then there was a whole cavalcade of varying vehicles rushing by with flashing lights.

"Wonder what they're looking for," I said.

Depweg's eyes shot to the rearview mirror as Magni and Locke slowly turned to look at me.

"Dude, either my sarcasm is on another level or you guys are just idiots."

Depweg's eyes returned to the road as Magni turned forward again in his seat, leaving just Locke to stare at me while his head bobbed with the movement of the Hummer.

"How are you okay after what just happened?" he asked.

"No choice but to be okay," I answered with complete honesty. "I worry about the things that I can control and say *fuck it* to the things that I can't."

"I don't know how true that is, but I can appreciate the message," Locke said, turning to face forward again. I could sense the rattled nerves emanating from everyone in the vehicle.

Within a few more minutes, we arrived at the clinic, and all of us piled out. I cradled Ludvig under his knees and upper back—just as Depweg had done—as we made our way to the door. Locke tried the handle, and when the door refused to budge, pressed the doorbell and we waited. Magni stood off to the side, away from the group. I took it he was still embarrassed about hiding during the battle, though not a one of us would blame a kid for trying to survive.

Ten seconds into waiting, I asked Locke, "So, are there any new Avengers movies?"

"Hmm? Oh, I wouldn't know. Movies were more of yours and Da's...thing." As he mentioned his name, the realization that he was gone became that much more solid and real.

Feeling the pain in the air, Locke quickly added, "But there's been, like, six more seasons of *Stranger Things* on Hu-flix."

"The fuck is Hu-flix?" I asked. I *hated* Hulu. You paid a monthly fee and they STILL HAD COMMERCIALS. Made it really hard to enjoy *Brooklyn Nine-Nine*.

"Hulu and Netflix merged once Disney started its own streaming service and took all its programming off other company's platforms."

"Ah, makes sense," I said, still not happy about the situation. "They must have been desperate if they merged their names. I thought for sure Netflix was powerful enough to swallow the other guys whole."

"Well, they were before Disney," Locke said as he pressed the doorbell again. "They had all the biggest brands to play with: Marvel, Star Wars, Pixar, and of course, the classic Disney content."

Depweg came up next to us, opting to only carry his holstered sidearm into the clinic, leaving everything else in the Hummer.

"Hey, what ever happened with *The Little Mermaid* being black? Last I remember, people weren't happy about that," I asked.

"It made money but wasn't critically successful. Even fans lambasted the movie, but not because she was a different race. She wasn't a bright redhead like the hugely popular animated movie, and fans knew it was all a PC move. Don't get me wrong, I saw the movie and the actress did a great job, but it didn't *feel* right," Depweg said nonchalantly.

"Bah haha! *You* saw *The Little Mermaid?*" I shot at the massively muscled, military-minded Depweg.

"Saw it with Da," Depweg said flatly without looking at me. He was looking through the door to see a light come on in the back. My smile was wiped off my face in an instant—as if taken off with a shotgun blast—as he mentioned Da. Numb, I looked forward as a disheveled Doc Jim came into view. He was rubbing his eyes as he approached the door.

A quick glance at us and I could see him visibly sigh before unlocking and then opening the door. We entered and wordlessly followed him to the familiar operating room.

"Set him there," Doc said as he went to pull an instrument table to the side of the gurney where I was placing the eerily pale Ludvig on.

"He needs blood," I informed Doc Jim.

"Yes, yes, I can see that," Doc said as he approached a large, double-door freezer. "Don't suppose you know his blood type?"

We looked at Magni, who shook his head.

"O-negative it is, then," Doc said, pulling out a bag before closing the doors and walking to hang it on the IV stand next to Ludvig. He stuck the IV into the normally huge veins on Ludvig's hands that blood loss had shrunken down. That wasn't even a minor inconvenience for the vet who could run a PICC line on a kitten, though. A quick motion, and the line was delivering precious blood to the nearly dead Swede. Doc checked his other vitals.

"No head trauma. There doesn't seem to be bleeding in his abdominal cavity. It'll take some time, but I think he will be fine," Doc said as he went to a locked cabinet that required his fingerprint to open. He pulled out a glowing yellow compound and extracted a few milliliters of fluid with a syringe. Then he replaced the vial, closed the cabinet that locked once the door was in place, and walked to Lude's IV line. Sticking the needle in, he delivered the compound, which mixed with the crimson in the line to create an orange liquid.

The doctor removed one of the bandages with a quick tearing sound as the tape protested, and inspected the wound. It began to ooze again, and I was about to ask him what the hell he was doing when the blood flow stopped and the wound began to close in on itself. Doc Jim repeated the process on the other bandages until he was happy that all the wounds were closed.

"You have something for everything, don't ya?"

"Always be prepared," he answered absently as he worked, spouting the Boy Scout motto.

"Hello, Jonathan," the voice of the Archangel Gabriel came from behind me.

"It's just John," I responded with dramatic annoyance as I leaned my head back and slowly turned on stomping feet to regard our new guest.

"I know. It's just entertaining to see your reaction," Gabriel informed me before turning to Depweg. "Hello, Jonathan," he said with full sincerity.

"Hello, Gabriel," Depweg responded respectfully.

"So confusing," Locke complained, shaking his head and crossing his arms.

"Locke," the angel said, giving Locke a slight nod of the head. Locke responded by lifting one hand in a half-assed gesture and rolling his eyes. I supposed it made sense that a warlock who got his power from Hell itself might not enjoy the company of an angel.

"You two know each other or somethen?" I asked, pointing a finger and drifting it between Gabriel and Locke.

"We've met," Gabriel said with a wry smile, deflecting my question. "John, I'm here to give you a warning."

"A warning? The hell did I do now?" I asked, crossing my arms to unwittingly mirror Locke.

"Not like that," Gabriel said, backtracking his words. "I meant, to provide you with pertinent information regarding the end of all life on Earth."

"Oh, 'cause that's better," I complained melodramatically. "Go ahead, then."

"The Earth, and all life on it, will be snuffed out in twenty-four hours unless you can close the black hole."

"Wait, wait, wait," Depweg interjected, stepping forward to join the conversation. "It'll take weeks for plant life to die. Then the animals, and finally man. The whole process should take, at the very least, months. Where is this twenty-four-hour number coming from?"

"The black hole was created perfectly halfway between the Earth and the sun," Gabriel began.

"Forty-six million miles away," I added excitedly. "Not sure why I remembered that off the top of my head."

"Correct. Very good, John," the angel said. I put my sarcasm Geiger counter to full power and the results came back inconclusive on if I had just been burned or not. Damn crafty angel. "The Earth is hurdling toward the black hole, which, in turn, is rushing to meet us."

"The Earth travels at, what, sixty thousand miles an hour through space?" Depweg asked.

"Sixty-seven thousand," I corrected. Where the heck was this random information coming from? Normally I had to dig through the city in my mind to locate obscure information.

Both Gabriel and Depweg looked at me then. I could even see the doc lifting up his head from where he was tending Ludvig to stare at me.

"Curiouser and curiouser," Gabriel mused. Then he began alternating his gaze between Depweg and myself as he said, "Considering the speed of the Earth and the self-powered black hole rocketing toward the planet, we have precisely twenty-four hours before…well, you can guess."

"This doesn't make sense," I said. "Why would Oberon try to destroy the Earth when all he has to do is create a black hole that travels at the same speed as us. The world would be perpetually coated in darkness, and his Shadow assholes could roam freely."

"Management has concurred that Samael has a hand in the events that are unfolding."

"What makes you think that?" Depweg asked, stroking his chin.

"The black hole is traveling at sixty-seven thousand miles an hour toward Earth," Gabriel informed us as he clasped his hands behind his back. Damn, I was jealous of his nice suit.

"That's more than coincidence," Locke chimed in.

"Precisely our thoughts," Gabriel said, glancing toward Locke. "We think that Oberon, powerful as he may be on his plane, couldn't possibly have the knowledge or energy required to create a black hole on his own."

"You're saying that Satan helped Oberon create the anomaly and then, what, gave him the wrong formula so the thing would fly toward Earth instead of with it?" Depweg asked, dropping his hands to his sides and scrunching his face in concern.

"It would certainly appear that is the case," Gabriel said. "In so doing, Samael knows Father will have to step in, breaking the covenant."

Doc Jim stepped forward and asked, "Forgive me, sir, but I've always wondered: why would God need to make a pact with the Devil to not interfere with mortal affairs?"

"Especially when Satan is clearly breaking the rules by gambling with everyone's life on Earth," I added.

It was Depweg's turn. "You're saying that God won't stop the black hole because if he does, Satan will win a wager?"

"I'm willing to bet that if Earth is destroyed, then the fucking Devil will also have a laugh that he knew God's pride would keep him from saving us," Locke threw out just above a whisper as he looked at the angel's feet.

"You call it pride," Gabriel said with the slightest hint of annoyance in his voice, as if he were having to explain to a group of rowdy kids why they couldn't throw rocks at the abandoned building's windows. "I call it His word. Father created the entire universe with His word. Remember that fact the next time judgment is thrown around about the pact and anything else you might not comprehend."

"Let's focus on what's important here," Depweg said, stepping closer to almost stand between Gabriel and Locke. "You are here now, Gabriel, which means we have a chance, right?"

"I'm pleased that you see it that way."

"Wait a second," I interrupted. Both Depweg and Gabriel turned to look at me as I finished thinking before I said, "We should have just under fourteen and a half days. The black hole only just started, like, a day ago. Right?" I lifted my hands palms up as I turned to address the room, searching for confirmation.

"You were in Faerie for nearly two weeks," Gabriel stated matter-of-factly. The bottom dropped from my stomach and I wavered where I stood.

"Lilith-damned Faerie, man," I said with a long exhale. I felt light-headed.

"What do you think happens when you travel between dimensions?" Gabriel asked.

"Ha! I knew it! Which one is it? Seventh dimension? Eight?" I asked eagerly.

"Perhaps we should focus on what's important?" Gabriel replied.

A desperate idea leaped to the front of the line. "Wait, are you saying Lily *didn't* screw me over?" I asked, drawing a swift, fierce look from both Depweg and Locke.

"I cannot speak to the actions or desires of the one you call Lily. What I can confirm is that time dilation for those traveling between planes is simply physics. The doorway Varhmiel allowed you to use was of impeccable design and construction; but our universe is tied to the laws of physics, John," Gabriel explained. I took note that he had tilted his head down slightly as he spoke that last part while staring right at me.

"Well then, I must be off," Gabriel said as he began to make his way through the OR doors and toward the lobby.

"Wait!" I called out. Gabriel stopped and turned patiently to await what I would say next. "What can you tell me about the armor?"

Gabriel smiled and then replied, "Be mindful of your abilities, John, for if you leapt toward the moon, you might land amongst the sun and be unable to erase your mistakes." Then he tipped his head and gracefully strode into the lobby. As the swinging metal door flapped in on itself, Gabriel disappeared. He was just...gone. Of course, *now* I knew angels could shift planes, just like Da had always told me.

"The hell did that mean," Locke asked, frustration in his tone.

"He turned the 'leap for the moon, land amongst the stars' phrase around on purpose, but why?" I asked myself. Then something else bothered me. "He knows about Valenta."

"I think he mentioned the moon and sun on purpose," Depweg added, ignoring my comment about Val.

"Yeah..." I let out slowly, remembering how he had looked at me when talking about physics.

"Maybe he meant you can survive in space?" Locke suggested, shrugging his shoulders as he let his arms drop.

"I doubt that. What need would angels have for space when humankind is firmly on Earth? And what's with you and Gabriel?" As I finished, I turned toward Locke with a cocked eyebrow.

"He made me an offer I couldn't refuse," Locke answered.

"Which was?" I asked, shifting my weight from one leg to the other.

Locke hesitated before he said, "Gabriel stopped my soul from leaving my head when we...when you..."

"Killed you," I finished for him.

"Right. Killed me. He gave me the chance, as he called it, to redeem my soul if I agreed to work with you to fight Satan."

"I thought you said you did it because you didn't want to go back to Hell?!" I asked, frustration growing on my already thin patience.

"Exactly! I tried to tell *him* that, but he insisted on drilling the consequences into my head. John, I-I'm going to tell you something, okay, that you aren't going to like. But please, let me fully explain," Locke said hesitantly.

"Oh, man, this is going to be good, isn't it?" I asked while rolling my eyes and crossing my arms tight across my chest.

"It-it was actually Gabriel who made me endure your mother's and father's—passings—over and over again. The angel placed his hand on my forehead and cleansed my soul in the fire of redemption, as he called it. A sort of deliverance." Locke began crying before blurting out, "I was already going to be on your side! He didn't need to make me suffer that much. Not *that* much. I regretted what I had done after the first experience—the very first death, John! But he made me endure for what felt like an eternity, and I hate him for it! I HATE HIM!" He collapsed slowly to his knees as his emotions took hold and his body was wracked with sorrow. "I'm so sorry, John! Oh, God. I'm so sorry I lied to you!"

I stood, frozen, as I looked at him. He looked up at me and I crossed the room in a blur and smashed my fist into his face hard enough to send blood squirting out. He cried out in surprise as he went sprawling backward to the floor.

"That's not for my parents. I told you I had already punished you when I ripped your fucking head off for what you did to them," I said with much more anger and aggression than I had meant to. "That was for *lying* to me. You told me Satan had punished you, and I don't appreciate being lied to, Locke."

Depweg took a step forward, concern on his face, before deciding to let the scene play out.

Locke had stopped crying and was grabbing his gushing nose to stanch the blood. I felt the warmth from his blood on my fist and resisted the urge to lick it off. This wasn't about punishing Locke like he was my enemy. This was about setting a clear expectation. He needed to be reminded that the grace Depweg and I had afforded him was not to be taken for granted.

"Gabriel said it was best to not tell you until, well, *now*," he said in a nasally voice as he held his nose closed.

"Now? Like he mentioned right now?" I demanded incredulously.

"He didn't mention right now specifically, but he said I would know when the time was right." Blood spilled into his mouth, staining his teeth bright red, before continuing down his chin.

"Anything else you want to tell us," Depweg added in calm contrast to my agitation.

"No! I swear!" Locke said as he looked back and forth between Depweg and myself. My brow remained furrowed as I glared at him. "Dude!" Locke cried out in frustration, "The

Archangel Gabriel told me to keep my mouth quiet, and I did just that! Much like you, John, I want to go to Heaven when I die. What would you have done? Huh?"

His words forced themselves past my defenses, and my brow relaxed as I realized he was right.

"Ironic that a warlock wants to go to Heaven," I mused like an asshole. As soon as the words left my mouth, I realized the *real* irony of me having been the one to say it. Both Depweg and Locke let it slide.

"Doesn't make sense why Gabriel didn't want him to tell you, John," Depweg added, still unsure of the situation.

"Does anything make sense with Gabe? That dude's an enema, wrapped in bacon, in a riddle."

"Swing and a miss," Doc Jim said under his breath from where he stood, filling in a chart.

"Here's the truth about what happened when I died: I went to Hell and it was all chaos and random attacks from bored demons. I fought them off as best as I could, which is what caused Satan to eventually take notice of me."

"How did you have powers while in Hell?" I asked, super curious about this revelation.

"The powers of a warlock come from Hell, technically speaking. I infused the power into my very soul once I was shown how."

"Who showed you?" I asked as I thought about Ulric teaching me about vampirism.

"Before Satan himself, it was my master, Hecate."

"Weird name for a dude," I said.

"My master was a woman."

"Weird name for a dudette," I said lamely as I looked to the ground and scuffed at the clean tile with my boot.

"None of this is important right now," Depweg exclaimed, course correcting the conversation.

"Oh shit," Locke said to himself. I looked up as he realized something and said, "Gabriel mentioned I had created a hole in your heart that had sucked all the light of the world into it, and it was my job to help return that light."

"See, this is what I mean," I fumed as I threw my hands up in surrender and began pacing. "That holy dude could have just told us what we needed to do to save the world. Instead, he-he-he makes a game of it. Are we his entertainment or something?" I asked, struggling to find the words in my exasperation.

I went to where Locke sat on the ground and extended a hand out to him. He looked at it then grabbed it, accepting my wordless apology.

"Aren't you going to apologize?" Locke asked, hurt in his eyes. Aw, damn it.

"Locke, I'm sorry I brokeded your nose," I said, throwing in a funny word because I had to inject levity into awkward or stressful situations. I thought of it as a positive attribute.

I grabbed his nose, twisting it back into place, before sending my blood out to repair the damage. He closed his eyes and lightly held onto my wrist as I worked.

"I feel like we've been here before," I joked while retracting my blood back into my hand. Locke rolled his eyes in answer.

"Let's recap," Depweg started. "Gabriel mentioned John jumping to the sun, right? And then Locke mentioned Gabriel telling him to help return the light of the world...surely he isn't suggesting John fly into space and—I don't know—use some of Locke's magic or something to destroy the black hole."

"Dude, this is urban fantasy, not sci-fi," I said, winking at the camera.

"What's that supposed to mean?" Depweg demanded through a fatigued sigh at my jesting. "And who are you winking at? Are you having a stroke? Can vampires *have* strokes?"

"Never mind," I said, ignoring his question. "We can assume that Gabriel isn't being literal. I'm not flying into space, no matter how fucking cool that would be." I raised my hands and scrolled them across the air as if revealing a name as I said in a dramatic movie voice, "Sexy Vampire in Space, coming this summer..."

"John..." Depweg started before I continued.

"Rated R."

Depweg looked at me in silence, waiting for me to finish my tomfoolery.

I looked back at him.

Locke looked back and forth between us.

I continued to stare at Depweg, whose eyes dared me to keep talking.

I did not.

"So, if it is a metaphor, what could it mean?" Locke interjected, breaking the silence.

"I mean, sounds better than 'Werewolf in Space,'" I said under my breath.

"John!" Locke and Depweg called out in unison.

"I don't have a hole in my heart. At least I don't think I do. So how do I return the light to Earth?" I looked up as I spoke, staring at a portion of the ceiling I thought the black hole might be behind, albeit about three million miles away.

"We have twenty-four hours to figure that out," Depweg said as he pinched the bridge of his nose between thumb and forefinger.

Ludvig moaned and began squirming on the stainless-steel operating table.

"Ludvig!" Magni cried out as he ran to his master's side, taking one massive hand into both of his.

"By Odin's beard!" Ludvig said, sitting up.

"How are ya feel—" I started to ask before the sound of breaking glass interrupted me. We all froze in place and slowly turned to watch the OR doors that led to the lobby. There was the sound of slapping flesh on the tile floor, followed by a sloshing drag. Then another slap, drag. Slap, drag.

Nervous glances were exchanged as Depweg, Locke, and I spaced out evenly around the OR entrance, preparing for whatever was about to come through those doors.

A thud sounded as one of the metal doors slowly inched open with an agonizingly long creak. We all stared, with Doc Jim taking several steps backward, as a familiar face fell into view about two feet off the ground.

"Oh God," Doc Jim said as his hand covered his mouth in shock. Depweg's bug-eyed expression matched my own as we looked at an impossibility.

His eyes were now purple, while white skin had darkened to charcoal. He smiled, shredded cheeks revealing teeth caked in dirt, pale gums, and jawbone.

"Da-Da-Dawson?" I stammered as my eyebrows raced up to my hairline.

"Ye-ye-yeah, dumbass," Dawson responded with a voice that sounded two-toned. It was like someone with a different octave voice was speaking the words with him.

I took a step back while exhaling, "No. Oh no, no, no."

Dawson pushed the door the rest of the way open and slapped a hand on the floor before pulling his torso into the OR. His intestines left behind him a trail of blood and dirt extending all the way to the door whose glass had been shattered.

"Glad to see everyone's here. But wait—where's Joey?" Dawson asked, making a show of looking around, even to the point of lifting up his flapping pieces of skin gliding across the floor. "You-you didn't lose him, did you?" As he asked the question, he turned to me and tilted his head.

I nearly fainted as I remembered what I had wanted to focus on earlier. I had seen Joey's multiple scratches from the shadow wave that had enveloped him back at the Faerie prison that had begun to turn black around the puckering edges even then.

Depweg took a step forward and screamed, "What have you done with him?!"

"We turned him to the dark side," Dawson said with a haunting smile while he kept his gaze on me. "Did you like that? Made a *Star Wars* reference for ya. I know how you loooooove your movies." As he said love with its extra letters, he let his head roll in a dramatic circle.

"What do you want?" Locke asked calmly but with an audible gulp.

Dawson's head snapped to face Locke in a quick gesture that sounded like snapping twigs before letting his smile fade. In the quick gesture, dirt from his grave flew out of his shaggy hair.

"From you, warlock? Only your soul." His head snapped back to me with that same sickening, bone-grinding-on-bone sound. His voice went deeper and his amethyst eyes began to glow. "But from you, vampire, all we want…is your life."

"Lolth," I said authoritatively, "Satan tricked Oberon. The black hole is rushing *toward* Earth, not with it."

"I know," Lolth said through Dawson's decimated face, the smile never wavering.

Something tugged at my attention. My eyes flicked to the lights above and then back to Dawson's animated corpse. I took note that the bright light of the OR was not affecting him.

"Why? I thought you wanted this plane for yourselves," Locke asked, fear stealing the power from his words.

"I'll stop it, vampire. All you must do…is die. Hehehehehceeeeee."

"How about no, Scott?" I responded in my Dr. Evil voice.

"I knew you'd say that," Dawson said, his voice going back to the original two-toned one from when he first arrived. His eyes dimmed, signaling the end of our conversation. "Doesn't matter either way. By this time tomorrow, you'll be dead, and I will have won."

"Okay, well, thanks for dropping by!" I said as I willed my flaming gladius into my hand.

"Wait!" Doc Jim said, "We can study him."

I thought for a moment and then let my celestial sword begin to go out before it faded into thin air.

At that, Dawson's smile dropped to a frown as he looked around, confused. "Y-you're not going to kill me?"

"Why would I strike you down? So you can become more powerful than I could possibly imagine?" I inquired, tossing the *Star Wars* reference back into his creepy face.

Dawson began to look worried and shifted back and forth on his hands.

"What is it? I thought you liked movie references," I said as I willed a bloodwhip out of my palm.

Dawson, who had painstakingly dragged himself in, sprang backward and began a full-on sprint to the door. Using only his hands, he moved with a horrifying speed that surprised and disgusted me. I lashed out with my whip and was surprised to see it was a real whip and not just a bloodwhip.

"The fuck…?" I drawled as my eyes ran up and down the length of the ivory with gold sigils etched down its length that started at my palm and ended around Dawson's neck. Forcing myself back to reality, I yanked Dawson back into the OR, letting my rope swarm over him like a snake about to squeeze its prey.

"Where do ya want him, Doc?" I asked, reeling in the excess rope and lifting Dawson up like a freshly caught fish. Then I leaned in and whispered, "I know you aren't him, Lolth. Dawson is dead, and soon you are going to join him." I feigned looking at the watch I didn't have on my bare wrist and said, "Actually, in less than twenty-four hours. So get comfortable."

"In here, please," Doc Jim said as he punched in a code on a digital screen. A wall on the back hissed open to reveal a path leading below ground level.

"Okay, seriously. When did everyone in Houston get freaking basements?" I asked with my free hand out to my side, palm up.

"Where is your home located?" Doc Jim asked with a knowing smile as we walked down the metal stairs.

"Firstly, it's a lair. Second, how the heck did you know about that? Does anyone *not* know where the hell I live? And lastly, touché, good sir. I do suppose most people wouldn't search for an underground structure in Houston."

"In Texas, it is either the clay or being below sea level, especially so close to the coast, that renders basements obsolete," Doc Jim said as he approached a clear plastic cell. It looked like Hannibal Lecter's prison, but much, much smaller.

I noticed Depweg hadn't followed us down and I raised a single brow as I looked over my shoulder to the empty staircase.

Doc Jim pressed some more buttons on another pad and the cell door slid open. I tossed Dawson in, who landed surprisingly gracefully on his hands before he turned and lunged at the closing door.

"Turn up the lights," I instructed Doc Jim. Still at the panel, he made some quick movements and the lights increased not only in the cell, but the hallway as well. "I'm willing to bet they can't find—um...*it* when it's exposed to this much light. No shadows at all," I said as I looked around, verifying what I had just said. "Also means it can't escape."

I leaned close to the industrial-grade plastic that was several inches thick, rapped on it with a knuckle, smiled, and said to the shadow vessel, "You still with us, Lolth? That OR is pretty bright, and so is the lobby. Don't you fucking love LEDs?" I goaded.

Lolth glared at me with a ferocity that would wilt flowers.

"Yeah, you're still in there. At least part of you is, and that part is going to die tomorrow. But don't worry," I said as I turned to make my way up the stairs, "I'll make sure the rest of you is dead before I come back."

Lolth began to shriek using Dawson's decimated face, and it reminded me of a velociraptor from the *Jurassic Park* movies.

"Pfft, some goddess you are. Hope you enjoy your stay! Make sure to rate us five stars on Yelp!"

Doc Jim closed the door behind us and it locked with a pressurized hiss.

"Is Yelp still a thing?" I asked him.

"I'm afraid it is," Doc said as he formed an L with his left thumb and index finger, bringing up a screen. He typed into the air and brought up the Yelp app within seconds. I watched as he typed in "vet" in a five-mile radius and hit search. The first page of results were all labeled with "ad" on them and did not reflect the intended query. There, on page two, was Doc Jim's listing: Super Vet Clinic.

"Clever. I've never really paid attention; do most businesses that have 'super' in them tailor toward supes?" I asked with air quotes on super.

"Probably about eighty percent," Doc Jim answered as he put his phone away by letting his fingers relax.

"Oh shit, I feel bad for the other twenty!" I spit out through a hearty chuckle.

Doc stretched his lips in an awkward smile while his eyes remained heavy, unsure of what to say.

"I'm doing it again, aren't I?" I asked quietly.

"For some, humor is a completely normal reaction to stress, John," Doc Jim responded.

"I must be one stressed out mofo, then."

Everyone looked around, waiting for someone to take the lead. I could safely guess that, in my absence, Depweg had become the leader; but I was back now, creating a peculiar predicament of power placement. Shit, I was doing it again, wasn't I?

I glanced at my were friend, who seemed to be gazing at a far wall as if it were playing a captivating movie. His face twitched periodically as he stared.

"So, what's the plan?" I asked, breaking the tense silence.

"Well, I'm going to study the, uh, creature downstairs, and see if I can come up with something helpful," Doc Jim explained, careful about his chosen label for the puppet that had once been Dawson.

"Excellent," I said, clapping my hands once. Turning to Depweg, I asked, "Well, Deppyweg?"

Shifting his stare from the wall, he glared at me with red-rimmed eyes that had a tinge of yellow to them.

I froze, knowing I had done something wrong and afraid to make things worse. Locke grabbed my arm and escorted me to where Doc had a small room with an attached bathroom in the back.

Once Locke had shut the door behind him, he turned to me and said, "John, he lost a damn packmate *and then* found out his other one has been taken. Cool it with the jokes."

My head hung low in grief for my friend.

"I'm honestly surprised he isn't exploding in rage. I feel like that's what I would do," I admitted.

"That *is* what you would do; but Jonathan isn't like that. He's..." Locke trailed off, searching for the best word.

"Stronger than that," I finished for him.

"Yes," Locke said slowly. He had meant to use that word but had had enough political sense to not boast Depweg up by putting me down.

"What can we do for him?" I asked, lifting my head to look at Locke.

"Be there for him. Realize what he's going through and how hard it must be," Locke suggested in a sincere way that—for some reason—pissed me off. Depweg was *my* bromego.

"We have less than twenty-four hours until the world is swallowed by a Lilith-damned black hole. Should I ask him about his feelings? Hmm? Or can we have a little chitchat about saving the fucking world." My words came from a place of senseless pride, and I was immediately ashamed.

"One is not exclusive of the other, John. Come up with a plan to save the world while still being considerate of Jonathan's fragile state of mind." My verbal barrage hadn't fazed Locke, and that made me even more angry. However, the little bastard was right. I needed to squish the monster that was pride and realize it only wanted to destroy under the guise of self-preservation. Proud people bred sorrow unto themselves.

I decided to pick my random assortment of emotions off the ground and take control. Though it was hard, I accentuated my placation with my usual one-size-fits-all tool: levity.

"Ha! You said *plan*." He shoots; he scores.

Locke's face scrunched in brief confusion before realization set in and his features went lax again. I'd give it to the lil' guy; he was able to read a room pretty well and grasp subtle nuances.

"John," Locke started with a soft, conversational voice that threw me off. "I'm not trying to steal your friend from you; it is important that you know that. You've been gone for a long time, and Jonathan and I have been working together. Same with the twins, okay? That's why I get where he is coming from, because they were my friends too. We've had time to build a friendship because Jonathan forgave me. I've spent the last ten years trying to make it up to him." He placed his hand on my forearm, drawing a cocked eyebrow from me. "He needs you right now, John. You can save the world *and* your friend."

The emotions I clutched onto toppled to the ground, leaving only anger prevailing in my arms as he spoke to me like a child about my best friend of almost a century. I slowly pulled my arm away while staring him in the eyes. "I would die for my brother out there, so don't fucking question what I would be willing to do for him," I said in a low, stern tone that dared defiance. "But know this, Godwin: I haven't had the same time to forgive you fully for what you fucking did, unlike the golden-hearted man standing on the other side of that door. There's still a fire that *burns* in my chest and hungers for your blood." Without telling my feet to do so, they began taking slow, deliberate steps toward the small man while my shoulders squared up. "Did you know, warlock, that a vampire's memory doesn't fade with time? That I can perfectly recall any moment in my existence with complete clarity, as if reliving it all over again? I still see my dead parents when I close my fucking eyes, you little shit. I buried them, in an unmarked grave, with my bare hands." I could feel my eyes beginning to shift and glow red while my fangs elongated from bared teeth. My chest began heaving with massive breaths as I lost the battle for control and my anger grew into hatred. "I'm trying, real hard, to do the right thing. Don't. Make it. Hard. For me." My words were venom that had been lit on fire and electrified.

Locke lifted his hands, palms out, as he matched each of my steps in reverse. His back had become flat against the wall by the time I was done lambasting him…for caring about Depweg. There was fear in his eyes, and I immediately felt like a monster for bullying an ally against Lucifer and the apocalypse. I was aware of a light pressure that rested on my shoulder that was almost imperceptible.

"What's going on?" Depweg's authoritative voice came from behind. I felt like a kid whose hand had been caught in the cookie jar. My eyes bulged as my fangs retracted and pupils faded back to purple.

"I-I'm sorry," I said to Locke.

"What the hell are you doing, John?" Depweg demanded as I turned to face him. He wasn't in arm's reach of where I stood. The feeling on my shoulder had vanished as quickly as it had arrived, leaving me perplexed.

"It's okay, Jonathan," Locke said, holding a hand up to Depweg. "I think John and I just had some much-needed closure."

"Yeah…I, ah…guess so," I said, trying to wrap my head around what had just happened. I wanted to look inward to see if Baleius had grabbed the wheel when I wasn't paying attention, but I knew what I would find. My demons were my own.

"Well, if you two are done pussyfooting around, I'd like to discuss how we are getting Joey back from those Shadow fucks," Depweg asserted with a tone that wasn't quite yelling but sure as shit wasn't pleasant either.

Locke and I shot glances at one another before settling back on our friend, who was blinded by grief. His eyes still pulsated with a yellow tinge as if he were losing the battle for control.

"Hey, man," I started, approaching my werewolf best friend to place a hand on his boulder of a shoulder. He appeared much more imposing than normal. "We are going to get Joey back, I promise. But first, we need to stop that black hole." As I finished, he poignantly shrugged back, forcing my hand off of him. A part of my mind pointed out the irony of Depweg doing to me what I had just done to Locke, and I knew I deserved it.

"How the hell do you expect to stop a Goddamned black hole, John? Are you going to ask it nicely to not swallow the Earth? Hmm? Gonna reach up into the fucking sky and squish it between thumb and forefinger? Are you? Tell me—I'm all ears, man—how are you going to stop it?" Depweg snarled. He was shaking as his rage escaped through rupturing fault lines in his usually stoic demeanor.

My head rocked back in surprise, as if his words were a blast of skin-melting steam.

"Jonathan!" Locke cried out in my defense. "I understand your frustrations—"

"Do you? Do you understand what it's like to see a dead packmate being used as a puppet? Do you get it, boys? Do you also get having the puppet master use my packmate's mouth to tell me his brother has been taken? My *whole* pack—and I couldn't save either one of them," he trailed off, fighting back sobs that had begun shocking his body like a cattle prod.

Locke stood frozen, unsure of what to say.

I stepped up to bat and did for Depweg what he had done for me in the past; I told him the truth while withstanding his verbal barrage.

"This time tomorrow, he'll be dead. But so will you, me, this short little fuck right here—oh, and every mortal on this rock. All seven billion of them," I scolded.

"Eight and a half," Locke corrected.

"Right," I acknowledged with a quick nod, appreciating the support right now. Turning back to face the distraught werewolf on the verge of snapping, I continued, "Here's what we are going to do, fellas: First, Doc in there is going to study the thing downstairs that is *not* Dawson. Maybe he can provide some insight on how to stop the darkness, or even reverse it. Second, we are going to save the Lilith-damned universe, because let's not forget, if I die, the freaking gates of Hell will open and the final battle will take place. So it's not just eight and a half billion lives, gentlemen. I gently remind you that it is every soul that has *ever* existed since the beginning of time."

Depweg's red and yellow eyes stared into my soul. "If the world is destroyed, there will be no Earth left for the last vampire to walk. No apocalypse," Depweg said coldly. It worried me how far down the rabbit hole my friend was falling.

"Get control of yourself now, marine," I demanded loudly as I moved to stand almost nose to nose with the unflinching man. "That isn't a risk I am willing to take. Do you understand?" My finger aggressively pointed at his face while my head slightly bobbed in all directions. I was uncomfortable with having our roles reversed, and let my anger be the controlling emotion to combat my building anxiety. I knew I had to win this battle of wills.

Depweg—my best friend and nonblood brother—flashed fully yellow eyes at me as a cavernous growl built in his thick chest.

"Don't," I warned in a low whisper as I tilted my chin closer to my chest in a defensive stance to protect my exposed neck. My eyes never left his as my face shifted to the ground to the point where I was almost staring through my own eyebrows at the yellow orbs of a pissed off werewolf. I fought with everything I had to not summon my gladius. My pride had returned and was siphoning energy from the discord flowing around the room like a maelstrom, growing stronger. I knew that pulling my weapon out against Depweg would create a permanent rift in the foundation of our trust. My hand twitched and tingled while at the precipice of willing the angelic weapon to life. I repeated what I had said in a softer tone, but this time to me as well as him, "Don't...please..."

Depweg blinked twice while his face scrunched when I said please, his eyes returning to somewhere between were-yellow and Depweg-brown. He grunted in frustration and turned to storm out of the room, leaving me and Locke in stunned silence. We looked at each other before Locke spoke up.

"I've never seen him like this."

"Me neither. At least, not this bad. But I know he just needs some time to cool off," I said as I removed my gray beanie and ran a hand through my hair while letting out a gust of air. I noticed my fingers tingled slightly in my right hand.

"That is the one thing we don't have," Locke reminded me as he stared past me and to the door Depweg had burst through as he left.

"What are we going to do, man?" I asked, regarding the beanie still in my hand. Da had made it for me in 1990, and next to my WWII trench coat, was my favorite article of clothing. I didn't think I'd ever admitted to Da how much it had meant to me and how I valued the gray cloth. That sent a pang of regret through my heart.

I replaced the beanie and flexed my fist open and closed, trying to diminish the feeling of almost summoning my gladius. My mind dripped with soul-wrenching sadness at the thought of Da, Dawson, and Joey being taken from me...from *us*.

Luckily, Locke interrupted my self-pity by saying, "I think I have an idea."

"Good, 'cause my mind is a freaking stadium with every seat filled with different aggressive emotions all fighting to be heard."

"Okay...come again?"

"Lilith help me," I said while rubbing my eyes, "I mean I'm having trouble maintaining my emotional equilibrium. I don't know if you noticed or not. It's like a roller coaster inside my mind, and I can't get off."

"Hadn't noticed," Locke said sarcastically. "But that honestly isn't important right now."

A muffled howl interrupted our conversation, prompting Locke and I to freeze, look at each other, and then storm into the OR where a frazzled Doc Jim stood by the back door. There was a trail of clothes that had been ripped off and discarded as Depweg had transformed into his were form.

I rushed to the back door, which had four deep gashes in the metal, and looked out to see a bulky blur disappearing behind some warehouses in the distance.

"Shit!" I called out as I prepared to sprint after him.

Locke grabbed my arm and shouted, "John! We don't have time for this!"

My head shifted between Locke and where Depweg had just been, and I felt an overwhelming sense that I was watching my brother run to his death. My brain screamed that if I didn't catch him now, I would never see him again, and it would be all my fault. Bugs of anxiety shuffled under my skin, and I began to hyperventilate.

"John, he needs time. I also have a feeling he wouldn't be as helpful as usual for coming up with a plan right now."

"But-but what if they get him, like Joey?" I blurted out near panic. "I can't lose him, man."

"Neither can I, but we don't have much of a choice right now. Come inside. I have something to run by you."

I looked one last time at where Depweg had been and let loose a yell of electrified frustration into the eternal night. Once it was out of my system, I turned and dragged my feet back into the OR to hear what Locke had to say.

Chapter 20

"I know a woman—a seer—who we can visit to attempt to gain insight from," Locke started to explain.

"What kind of seer?" I interjected.

"She has the ability to see things that we would never be able to, and might be able to point us in the right direction."

"Why have I never heard of her? What's her name?"

"No offense, but you've existed inside your own bubble for most of your unlife, wouldn't you say?"

"Fair enough," I admitted.

"Know this: Lachesis requires a payment," Locke warned.

"And how much does she charge?"

"It's different for everyone. It might be a pound of flesh or a penny from your pocket. You don't know until you are there."

Without direct command from my brain, my hand began patting my pockets, searching for change that I didn't have.

"How did you meet her? Is there, like, a Tinder for magic users or something?"

"She would say I know her because I must know her," Locke said with admiration.

"Well, alrighty then. No time to waste. Can't wait!" I facetiously commented as we started making our way to the lobby.

"Where are you two going?" Ludvig asked, struggling to sit up on the table he was resting on.

"We need to do this alone," Locke said, holding a hand up to Ludvig.

"Why's that?" I asked, stopping at the OR doors.

"It will tangle the skein if too many threads are pulled at once." I eyed him dubiously. "Just-just trust me on this one, alright? You'll see when we get there."

"You still need to rest," Doc Jim said as he laid a hand on Ludvig's shoulder. "I could also use some help studying the specimen below."

"I have to agree with the doc on that one, guys," I said. "I would like as many minds on the problem of the darkness plague as possible." Ludvig nodded a few times as a thought came to mind. "Oh, I was stabbed in the face by one of those dark elf bastards, and I could feel the darkness spreading in my skull. Then I—how do I say this—siphoned a fission bomb into myself, and it kind of...cured me, I guess. Don't know if that helps or not, but that's what happened."

"Yes, that is very good information. Thank you, John," Doc Jim said as he picked up a black handle that looked to me like a knife hilt, and a digital screen came to life, much like a wrist-phone. He began typing with incredible ease, destroying all myths about old people and technology. Then I wondered how old he really was, considering the vial of life-extending juice he had given to me for Father Thomes.

"Ah, shit. Father Thomes," I said as if remembering I had left the oven on.

"What about him?" Locke asked.

"We need to see him after Lackylass."

"Lachesis," Locke corrected.

"Right, that's what I said. After we visit Lockness, I want to stop by the church and see how he's doing. Carry on, good doctor!" Doc Jim didn't even register my farewell, being so engrossed in the information about the fission siphoning.

With a shrug and a "Meh," I made my way through the glass-covered lobby and into the parking lot with Locke in tow. We stopped in unison and gawked at the Hummer. The drow had done a serious amount of damage in the few seconds they had had before I had whooped the shit out of all of them with no problems at all.

The entire front bumper was gone, along with both quarter panels. Even the metal hood had indentations and holes from where powerful elven hands had almost gotten to the engine itself.

I let out a long whistle as I called out, "Shotgun," and jogged to the passenger side. It was locked.

Locke hadn't moved, anticipating the problem using something called, "thinking ahead" or some such bullshit. Maybe it was "common sense." Either way, we didn't have the keys.

"Hey!" I called out as a light bulb sprung to life over my head. "Depweg ripped all of his clothes off. I bet the key is back in there."

"I'm willing to bet you are right. But are we really wanting to drive around Houston in *that*?" Locke waved a finger over the very noticeable damage. "The thing already stuck out like a sore thumb. And now..."

"Yeah, yeah, yeah. I get ya. And who came up with the sore thumb saying? I bet it was a carpenter who sucked with a hammer or something."

Locke ignored the question before suggesting, "We might need the guys to help summon a doorway."

"Wait! I have another suggestion."

"Oh? Well, let's hear it, smarty-pants." As Locke insulted me, I felt closer to him, as if doing so meant we had transcended to the next level in our relationship.

"How about I show you instead," I said with an excited smile as massive, reptilian wings sprang from my back with a whoosh. I stood, chest puffed out and fists on hips as I turned my head in a classic superhero pose, trying to look out of the corner of my eye to see Locke's reaction.

"Holy shit!" he cried out as his hands flew up in surprise.

"Damn right. Now come 'ere. Show me where we are going."

As he approached, I noticed my bloodwings were real now. I folded one in front of my body and ran my hands over the thick leather, noticing a few small white puffs that I picked off with ease.

"Neat," I said while letting the wing rest behind me again. "I freaking love this armor!"

"Don't suppose I could try it o—" Locke began as he approached.

"HA! Nope," I interrupted as I pushed on one of his shoulders, turning him around. I stuck my arms around him just under his armpits and clasped my hands around his chest before I whispered into his ear, "No homo," before giving his neck a tender little kiss and then launching into the air.

I might have thrown a little too much force behind my initial launch because Locke began screaming at a pitch that was so high I thought Depweg and the neighborhood dogs might be the only ones able to hear him within five miles.

The clouds rushed to meet us, and I stopped just under their cover while Locke trembled in my arms. I probably could have taken it easier on him and flown at a more reasonable pace, but what fun would that have been.

"Where we going?" I asked loudly so Locke could hear me over the whipping wind.

"O-o-over that way," Locke said, pointing to the northern horizon while shaking.

"What's wrong, scaredy-cat?"

"Co-co-cold." Steam billowed from his mouth before being carried off by the strong wind.

Oh, right. High in the air, in a constant wind, while the Seelie Court is out of commission.

I focused on where he had pointed and began flying while pulling him a little closer for warmth.

In short order, Locke pointed down to a small shack with decaying wood paneling that had once been coated in yellow paint. A sign sat by the road that read, "Psychic: Tarot, Palm, Aura Readings."

We landed—super gently, I might add—at the end of the dirt driveway. Locke picked himself up off the ground from where he had lost his footing or something and glared at me.

"What?" I asked innocently.

"Couldn't you have just crashed directly into the ground? It would have been a softer landing!" he scolded angrily as he patted his clothing, sending puffs of dirt into the air.

"I'm fine," I countered, signaling up and down my body with one hand dramatically.

"You also have a stronger physical constitution than I do."

"Yeah, I did put all my points into strength and charisma."

"Too bad you didn't save any for intelligence," Locke whispered as he turned to regard the house.

"What was that?"

"Hmm? Oh, nothing. Shall we, then?" Locke said dismissively as he approached the house.

"You have got to be kidding me," I said as I looked around at the ramshackle of a house that looked like it had been built when people bought everything from the Sears catalog—the Amazon of its day.

"It's not like she's a wizard advertising in the newspaper or anything," Locke epically commented.

"I see someone found my book collection in my absence." A thought struck then. "You, ah, didn't go through my drawers, did ya?"

Locke didn't answer or look at me as we approached the front door.

"They were Lily's," I said lamely, like telling the cop that the pants you were wearing weren't actually yours and you had no idea where those drugs had come from.

"Oh, I'm sure the strap-on was indeed hers," Locke said awkwardly.

"One time, jeez," I let out just above a whisper.

A quick chuckle escaped Locke's mouth before we stood on the rickety landing. I retracted my wings as I realized they might be an odd sight when meeting someone for the first time.

After a few moments of silence, I asked, "Are we going to knoc—" before the door opened.

A small, lean black woman the color of midnight stood in the doorway. Dreadlocks decorated with gold rings hung down just past her shoulders, while milky eyes that were pure white ran up and down my body. She clasped arthritic hands—that reminded me of Father Thomes—on a cane that supported her lightly hunched frame.

She spoke with a thick African accent as she said, "You stink of doubt."

"It's Old Spice, actually," I retorted with perfect comedic timing.

"Locke," she drawled out, putting emphasis on the "k" sound with a click as if the word had spoiled in her mouth.

"It's a pleasure to see you again, Lachesis," Locke greeted sincerely with a slight bow.

"In wit you, den." Lachesis turned and disappeared into the darkness of her home. I could hear the cane thwacking the ground with every other step. Locke followed confidently, leaving me alone on the stoop, confused.

"John, come on," Locke instructed without turning around.

With a grumble, I stepped into the home and traversed the tight, dim corridors that smelled of incense. I came to a section of the house I assumed was the dining room, where Lachesis was already sitting and Locke was pulling out a chair.

"No. Only him," Lachesis said with a pruney, sinewy finger pointing directly at me. What bothered me was she had done it without moving her milky eyes.

Being the smartass that I was, and finding myself in a situation that was definitely out of my comfort zone, I did what a John must do; I sat down, leaned forward, and waved my hand in front of her face.

Locke, without further explanation needed, made his way down the hallway and outside. The door clicked shut behind him.

"Why just me?"

"Payment is required from all who hear. Right now, he cannot afford to pay my price."

"What is your price for me?" I asked, surprised to hear how unsure I was at that moment.

"Dat," Lachesis answered, pointing at my chest.

"What?" I asked in confusion as I looked down while my hands patted my chest. One landed on the silver crucifix around my neck, and I looked up in shock. "My silver cross? You can't be serious."

"Dead serious," she responded flatly while holding her hand out. I sat frozen for a few breaths before lifting the chain above my neck and dropping the pendant in her awaiting hand. I supposed Father Thomes could just make me another one so I could get past his defenses.

Without a word of thanks, she pulled her hand back, where it disappeared under the table before reappearing again, empty.

"What now? Don't you need a crystal ball or somethen?" I asked, a tad less politely than intended. Or maybe it was the perfect amount of rude. I didn't like giving up things that belonged to me, especially to people who seemed entitled instead of appreciative.

"Give me your hands, child."

"Okay, Mom," I answered with a roll of my eyes as I placed my hands on hers. They were cold, and her skin felt like old leather that had been moisturized and taken care of, but was still ravaged with unforgiving age.

Her face scrunched as she concentrated, running her thumbs over the backs of my hands.

"I cannot see your future. Hmm, but I can see your past. Yes, der it tis. Oh!" she cried out in surprise as if stung by a bee.

"What?!" I asked, now incredibly interested in what she had to say.

"You have killed the ones that you loved." Tears began to build in the corners of her eyes as she spoke. "Da gave you the gift of life and protection. He loved you like a son, John. He was very proud of you." I was having trouble believing what she was saying, even though she knew my friend's name and what he had done. "Yes, he was proud, though you annoyed him so greatly." Never mind; this was real.

"It is dis gift he has given you that is preventing me from seeing your now and your future, child."

Something tickled the back of my forehead and I said, "I can remove it, I think." As I finished, I pulled my hands back while willing my gauntlets into existence. One after the other, I slowly, purposefully, removed them, setting them on the edge of the table close to my chest. I felt something give way inside me that I couldn't explain, and I felt…at peace.

I placed my hands back into hers, resuming the session now that I had removed my protection.

"Let us start at the now," she said, resuming her rubbing over my hands. "Hmm, the angel spoke true."

"About what? The black hole?"

"Yes, child."

"So how do I stop it? He didn't exactly give me a clear answer," I said, inching forward to the edge of my seat. I could feel how intensely I was scowling from concentration, as if in doing so I would absorb the answer more readily.

"You must believe in yourself."

"What the hell does that mean?"

"Our doubts are traitors, and make us lose the good we oft might win, by fearing to attempt."

"Wha—"

"Dere's more. Your greatest strength is also your greatest weakness, John. To grow stronger, you must make yourself weak." As she spoke this part, I was aware that her pupilless eyes were staring directly into mine.

This took me aback as I realized, with complete clarity, what she meant.

Changing the subject, I asked, "And the darkness? Can Joey and Dawson be saved?"

She looked into the air between us, squinted, then shook her head. "No, child, not both. But the darkness can be taken as well as given."

"How?"

Her face burst into an expression of horror as her white eyes shot all around the room. Gaping mouth let wordless syllables fall from it, coming out as incoherent squeaks. A violent wind birthed from nothing and began swirling in the room like an eager tornado. Cabinet doors flapped open and closed like a school of piranhas' jaws on a slab of beef. Dim lights began flashing like it was a rave party. Cracks formed up the walls as if watching a bolt of lightning in slow motion.

"NO! Please, no!" she croaked loudly as if in indescribable pain.

"WHAT?!" What do you see?!" I cried out over the din.

Her accent dropped and her voice changed, not matching her animated expressions at all, as if someone else were speaking through her. "You kill more of the ones you love," said the eerily calm, dreamlike voice that pierced the howl of the wind as if it were a gentle breeze. Her head rocked to the side as if she were trying to see behind her, dreadlocks floating in the air as if they were underwater. "Countless will die by your hands. Men, women, even children will be punished." Her face shot skyward with flickering eyes. "You are being kept in the dark by those you trust."

She shrieked then, as if being electrified, before crying out in a voice that shook the walls and table, "The gates of Hell will open, abomination, and you will descend to Hell for all eternity!"

"What happens to Earth?" I screamed, "My friends?"

Lachesis screamed at the top of her lungs, ripping her hands back away from mine and falling out of her chair to land in a panting heap on the ground. The wind died, leaving a piece of paper to flutter to the ground.

I stood and rushed to her side, trying to help her up.

"No! Do not touch me!" she cried out in her African accent, batting my hands away while trying to catch her breath. She was shaking as tears poured down her face.

Locke burst through the door and ran to find me standing over the collapsed Lachesis.

"What did you do, John?!" Locke demanded furiously.

"N-nothing!" I said defensively as I held my hands up to proclaim innocence. I noticed I hadn't put my gauntlets back on, and I picked them up as I slid my hands into them, feeling the power resume. They vanished once back in place, and I could feel that something in my mind was...wrong.

Locke rushed to her side, and she took his hands as he helped her up. Once on her feet, and still holding his hands, she looked up at him as if nothing had happened, and whispered, "You have the choice."

Locke stopped frantically looking her over to make sure she was alright and froze as he stared into her face. He pulled his hands back as if touching something hot, and Lachesis ended her episode.

Placing a gnarled hand on the table to support herself, she used her other hand to point to the front of the house and demanded, "Go. Both of you, now."

Locke and I looked at each other before he took the lead and went outside. I stopped in the hallway just outside the dining room and asked Lachesis, "Who do I kill that I love?"

A knowing smile formed on her lips as she whispered, "Are you sure you want to know, child?"

My head felt numb as I nodded once.

"I will only give you one answer, and only one answer, to the question you have not paid for."

I held my breath in anticipation of the seer's answer as I shifted my weight where I stood, nervous to the words she was about to speak...

"The boy."

I became dizzy as what she said struck my head like a semitruck. My knees turned to jelly as my hands slid on the wall, looking for purchase. "No. No! Not Magni! Not after…"

Lachesis began to cackle from the dining room as I stumbled to the front door, feeling my stomach roll in knots as the world swam around me.

I barely made it through the front door before turning to slam it closed and resting heavily on it, panting and trying to let my mind settle.

Locke seemed no better than me as he paced back and forth in front of the porch.

"Let's get the hell out of here," I said as my wings sprang to life. Without waiting for his acquiescence, I grabbed him and exploded into the night sky, ready to get as far away from there as possible.

Chapter 21

We flew in silence back to Doc Jim's. My mind bounced back and forth between everything she had said like a chew-happy puppy in a room full of toys.

Believe in myself? Shit, if anything, I believed too much in myself. What did she mean I was going to Hell for all eternity? And…and that I was going to kill Magni. That wasn't possible. There's nothing in this world that would make me hurt him after what I'd done already. Lilith, I was going to let him blow my head off because that's what I deserved, damn the consequences!

Locke seemed to be having his own internal battle as we traveled because he didn't say a word, not even about the bone-chilling cold.

We landed in the parking lot and I retracted my wings. My real wings. My wings that were real because of my celestial armor.

I stopped and looked down at my body, my armor shimmering into life at my thoughts. My hand gingerly ran over the crimson cross permanently etched into the breastplate.

"My greatest strength…is my greatest weakness," I said just below a whisper as I turned my hands over as my eyes traveled up the glowing gold lining. My wandering gaze stopped on the claw marks on my arm, and without thinking, I placed my hand over the marks and willed some of the stored energy to heal the ivory. Bright light escaped through my fingers, making me squint as I watched. As I pulled my hand away, pristine, smooth armor greeted me.

Locke turned as he pulled on the door, looked at me for a second with conflicted eyes, and stepped into the clinic without a word. I stood alone and let my armor shimmer away, leaving me in my usual garb, albeit with some holes in my new shirt.

"At least I'm not the only one," I said to the empty parking lot. As I walked to the door, I glanced skyward, trying to see if I could spot the black hole. Of course, I couldn't, and felt stupid for even trying. But it was a compulsion I couldn't help.

Passing through the lobby, I noticed the glass had been all swept up. I shouldered my way into the OR and saw as the door that led to the back room where the bathroom was swung shut. Locke needed some alone time. Lilith, so did I.

Ludvig, who was looking at the same door I was, turned his gaze to me and asked, "What's wit him?"

"We had a tough visit with a seer."

"What did she say?" Ludvig asked. It took everything in me to keep my eyes from drifting to Magni out of reflex.

"A lot. And nothing at all," I said as I ran a hand over my face. Only that my worst fear of going to Hell for all eternity was going to happen. No biggie, right?

"How do we stop the black hole?" Magni asked. I looked at the ground, still unable to meet his gaze.

"I don't know. Believe in myself and reach for the stars or some crap."

Ludvig and Magni remained silent, waiting for more information. But just as I had to bathe in the shower of ignorance, so must they.

Doc Jim appeared from the stairway that led downstairs. He was holding his tablet and staring at it intently as he walked, tripping on the last step at the top. He caught himself before looking up at me.

"What did ya find out, Doc? Anything yet?" I asked.

"His physiology is…fascinating. Dead, but alive like a vessel."

"Yeah, that's neat and all, but did you find out anything about how we can stop, or even reverse, it?"

"Not yet. Silver and iron work, of course, but I suspect only while under the light. At least from what your friends have told me," Doc said, looking between Ludvig and Magni.

"It's important that you do not let Dawson get into the darkness. Lolth could escape." I looked around and noticed Depweg's clothes in a neat pile on a counter near the back door. "He still not back?" I asked, hope leaving my voice.

"No, I'm afraid not," Doc responded.

"We will go and get him," Ludvig declared, standing strongly on his own two feet.

"Well, glad to see you back with us, big guy," I said with a smile that I tried really hard to make convincing. I just had too much damn weight on my shoulders right now and was starting to buckle from the pressure.

Locke came into the OR from the back room with some water in his hair and on his black tactical shirt. He seemed to have gotten his shit together while splashing his face because there was a calmness about him.

He set the body armor he had apparently taken off on a counter and walked to stand next to Ludvig and Magni. As if to accentuate his return to mental stability, he looked at me with steady eyes and nodded once slowly. I returned the nod before looking around at the ragtag group we had to save the world with.

Ludvig stood with chest puffed and arms crossed, ready for battle. Magni seemed to stand a little straighter in direct reflection to his master. Locke remained where he was, cool as stone now.

I clapped my hands before rubbing them together and said, "Well, boys, it's time to save the world."

Chapter 22

"Right. Save da world. Um, how do we do dat?" Ludvig asked. All eyes fixated on me, prompting me to unveil my master plan that would make Sherlock blush.

"Oh, I have no fucking idea," I answered. "I was hoping you guys had thought of something."

"Well, you have approximately twenty-one hours to figure it out," Doc said, glancing at his phone.

"Doctor Jim, did you find out anything else from Lolth? Did she say anything?" Locke asked.

"My apologies, but she won't speak to me."

"Let me try," Locke said with a coldness that made my hairs want to stand on end. Warlocks had the ability to steal souls from their victims, and Dawson was but a vehicle to transverse this mortal realm. Lolth was the driver.

"Um…" Doc started.

"No, it's okay," I said, "Locke can try to get some information out of her. I'll work with Ludvig on some elemental magic." I remembered the static between Locke's fingers while in Faerie.

"Uh, okay," Ludvig said, shifting on his feet. "Not sure how much I can teach in only a few hours, broder."

"I'm a quick study," I said, winking.

Locke disappeared down the stairs as the wall closed behind him while Ludvig, Magni, and I made our way out back.

"What would you like to attempt to learn first?"

Thinking back to our fight with Lolth and how Magni had almost gained the upper hand, I said, "Lightning. I want to be able to surprise Lolth when I see her again."

"Okay. Are you able to conjure any elemental magic right now?"

"No. Wait! Yes! I can make fire. That's elemental, right?" I said excitedly.

"Yes, exactly. How do you do it?"

"I just ask the molecules to excite in an area, and bam, fire." I held out my hand and ignited the air, creating a small ball of fire.

"Good, you have a basic understanding. Now we need to expand on dat. Here," Ludvig said, holding out a smooth wand.

"Hey, where are all the swirls and stuff?" I asked, looking it over.

"De runes enhance de wielder's abilities. You are not ready for dat just yet."

"Bah, fine," I said, holding the wand to my side. "You just walk around with noob wands in your back pocket?"

"It's mine," Magni said.

"It was yours. You did so well last time dat I am giving you dis one," Ludvig said proudly, holding out a wand with runes etched sporadically down its length.

"Okay, so you just walk around with intermediate wands in your back pocket?" I asked, crossing my arms.

"It is my backup. Don't you have a backup weapon at de small of your back, John?" Ludvig asked with a smile.

A hand reflexively wandered to my lower back where the silver kukri was, primed for action.

"Fine. Point, match, Lude," I said as I looked at Magni's wand. "Why not have a full backup? You know, like an exact copy of your main weapon?"

"It takes many years to properly create a wand. Each rune is etched with a skilled and delicate hand while de maker meditates on de power it enhances. You must pour a lot of your own energy into making such an important and effective weapon."

I looked at my own wand with a renewed respect and desire to see its full length etched in runes of power.

"To create a bolt of lightning," Ludvig started as he pointed his own powerful wand into the sky, "you must excite de molecules so dey bump and grind into each odder to create de charge. Den, you connect de dots, and bam!" As he finished, an impressive bolt of raw electrical energy shot into the clouds, forking over and over from his wand. He stopped it shortly after beginning, looking at me with a shit-eating grin.

"Holy neat! That was shit! I mean...eh, never mind. You know what I meant. Now watch and behold my mighty power!" I said as I held up my own wand and focused on exciting the molecules around it. I released them, and the biggest torrent of lightning ever conceived launched into the sky, catching the very air on fire—OR the smallest fizzle of static popped like one of those little white popper things you gave kids on the Fourth of July. You know the ones, they run around throwing them on the ground while giggling. So, between the two options, I'll let you decide which one actually happened—kind of like a Choose Your Own Adventure story.

Magni fell on the ground laughing, clutching his stomach as he tried to catch his breath. Tears welled at his eyes from mirth and I thought to myself, "This is it. This is how you kill him."

"Try again," Ludvig said, having fully expected that result.

"Bump and grind the molecules," I whispered to myself, hating the Swede's analogy. Or was it a metaphor? I did as instructed, but instead of just asking the molecules to move at a ludicrous pace, I focused on them rubbing on each other like a balloon on someone's head. As they did, I made them go faster and faster, grinning with glee as I felt the charge build up.

"Be careful, John," Ludvig warned as he took a step back. Magni had gotten back to his feet, face serious now that he felt the air charging around us.

"I got this," I proclaimed as the air around me began to waver before catching on fire. I yelped, releasing my focus, and a bolt of lightning erupted into the sky with an earth-shattering crack. I said "bolt," but it had been more like a "skyscraper" of energy being launched into the clouds. Ludvig and Magni fell to their backs, holding their ears, as power transformers burst in an explosion of sparks. Lights flickered as far as the eye could see before going out, including the ones at the clinic.

"Oh. Em. Gee," I enunciated slowly as I looked at my wand like it was actually a primed nuclear warhead. Glancing upward, I saw a massive hole in the clouds directly above me.

"John!" came a muffled cry from inside the dark clinic.

"Oh shit!" I cried out before running back inside. I made it to the stairs in two bounds before gracefully descending the steps to the basement. Of course, by gracefully descending I did not mean tumbled toes over nose to the basement floor.

Getting to my feet, I used my preternatural sight to spot Locke, who was summoning a tiny ball of light.

I ran over to him and looked inside the prison to see a lifeless torso lying on the floor, unmoving.

"Fuck!" I cried out.

"What just happened outside? What was that?" Locke asked, panting in frustration laced with confusion.

"Um...Ludvig did it."

"Forget it," Locke said, holding his tiny ball of light up to see before walking toward the stairs.

"Did you at least learn anything?" I asked, hoping for some good news.

"Yes," Locke said as he disappeared into the OR. I followed closely behind to find Ludvig holding his hands over Magni's ears and chanting in a whisper. His hands glowed for a moment before he removed them and repeated the healing process on his own bleeding ears. A pang of guilt passed through my gut.

Locke lifted his hand in the center of the room and left the ball of light hovering so we could see each other.

Once healed, Ludvig looked at me and said, "Dat's why you don't get de rune wand."

"Fair enough," I answered before turning to Locke. "What did Lolth say?"

"In her weakened state, I was able to put a spell on her that made her reveal the truth. She told me that if she were to die, all the darkness would die with her."

"Well, neat! That's really good information. Good job, dude!" I said, patting Locke on the back a little harder than intended.

"There's more," Locke interjected heavily as he straightened his back after my pat-attack.

"Of course there is," I said, rubbing my temples in little circles. "What is it?"

"Lolth has infected the world tree."

"Yggdrasil?!" Ludvig called out, taking a step forward and looking between Locke and myself in repeated succession. "She's poisoned Yggdrasil? Are you sure?"

"Yes," Locke said, crossing his hands in front of him and looking at the ground. "If we don't kill Lolth, Yggdrasil will die, leaving all the planes that are attached to be consumed by the darkness."

"Let me guess. Earth and Heaven are part of the tree, aren't they?" I asked, looking toward Ludvig for answers.

"I honestly do not know if de afterlife is part of de tree or not, but I can confidently confirm dat Midgard is," Ludvig answered, using the Nordic term. I could tell there was a hint of shame in his voice at not having all the answers when we needed them. It made him...endearing, somehow.

"Doesn't matter," I said, setting my jaw and assuming control of the conversation. "We know for sure that the Earth is in jeopardy—again—and that's all we need to know. Everything else is inconsequential to the mission."

"I don't know if I would say that," Locke started.

"Would it change our plan? We already have all the motivation we need to kill the bitch," I said authoritatively. "Locke, where do we think Lolth is?"

"I don't know, John. I was getting to that part when the damn lights went out," Locke challenged.

I waved off his sassy comment and said, "Then we go to Faerie. Lolth's there somewhere. I just wish we had someone who could help us on the other side."

"You don't mean..." Locke started; his mouth hung open in disbelief.

"I'll take whoever's help I can get right now," I answered.

"What about Taylor?" Doc asked from the corner of the room where he had been watching the back and forth.

"Taylor's in Vegas, I think. Plus, I don't have a phone anymore."

"I do," Doc said, holding up his hand in a L shape and bringing up his contacts list. I could see from beneath the screen Taylor's name spelled backward from this angle.

"Call him," I instructed. My heart sunk a little as my excuse to see Lily—who might *not* have screwed me over by ten years—was overruled.

Doc hit the name and I watched as he brought his thumb up to his ear and positioned his index finger in front of his mouth.

After a few moments, Doc said, "Taylor, it's Doc. Yes. Yes, I'm doing well, thank you. How are you?" I moved my hand in a circle, in a gesture that said, "Could you pretty please hurry up and maybe get to the point?" Doc held a hand up, signaling that he understood and he would get to that momentarily.

"Listen, the reason I'm calling is because the boys need a guide in Faerie. Hmm? Yes, a guide. Seems they need to locate Lolth or the world tree will die." At that, he pulled the phone away from his ear quickly as if it had burned his face. I could hear Taylor freaking out on the other side.

Placing the phone back to his ear—or should I say fingers? Damn kids and their eight-track cassette players—he said, "So you'll come? That's excellent! When can you be here?"

There was a small pop and I turned to see Taylor standing in the OR as he pulled his fingers from his ears and pressed End on the floating screen.

"Now," Taylor said without levity. He walked to where Doc was standing and extended a hand. Doc shook it with a smile of one who was greeting an old friend.

"Why is it dark in here?" Taylor asked, looking up at the dark ceiling and then the glowing ball hovering in the middle of the room.

"John learned some magic," Locke said sarcastically.

"Did he, now?" Taylor asked, impressed.

"I only gave him a basic wand, showed him how to channel de elements, and he nearly killed us all wit lightning," Ludvig said.

Taylor turned and regarded the hunters with a nod and an articulated, "Oh, hello there," before making his way to me.

Ludvig nodded in return while Magni lifted a hand awkwardly in greeting.

Taylor and I stood facing one another for a moment before we both went in for a hug at the same time. Where Doc and Taylor might have a business relationship, Taylor and I had experienced too much together at this point for a mere professional handshake.

"So, you know elemental magic now, do you?"

"Dude, I have so much to tell you," I told him as we broke the embrace.

"You can tell me on the way," he said before turning to address the room. "Before we depart, there is something you must know." Everyone in the room looked nervously at each other, knowing he wasn't going to tell us he had ordered pizza for the group. "Queen Mab is dead, and with her death, her castle has fallen."

"Yeah, Oberon told me that personally," I said, feeling relieved that the situation hadn't gotten worse.

"Did he tell you that Mab hadn't killed all the supernatural refugees? She was planning on enslaving them, forcing them into things like menial public service jobs for her court nobles, at least the weaker of them. For the more dangerous, she was planning to add them to her army for when she invaded Midworld."

"What are you saying?" Locke asked. "That we still have supes that might be able to defend the Earth from Satan?"

"What I'm saying is that Lolth has infected them with darkness," Taylor informed us, making my blood run colder than normal.

"Which ones? The army?" I asked, fearing the answer.

"All of them," he said, and I could swear the room felt like it had elongated around Taylor like in a horror movie. "Rest assured that even the smallest of the infected can transmit the darkness unto you."

"Then I should go alone," I appealed to the room.

"No," Ludvig asserted. I noticed Magni looked back and forth between us, unsure of himself.

"You don't get it," I said, turning to the big man. "Only Taylor and I will have our abilities in Faerie. You'll be completely human."

"I can still fight," he said, touching the hilt of his sword.

"That, I don't doubt. I'm simply afraid you'll be a liability."

Taylor spoke up then, "If I may ask, how is it you think you'll also have your abilities while in Faerie?"

With the simplest of thoughts, the celestial armor shimmered into existence, complete with flaming gladius. The light from the sword created wavering shadows against the walls. Locke raised his hand and twisted it, like turning on a faucet, and the ball of light in the center of the room brightened, making the shadows fade. I didn't know if it was a show of power born out of jealousy or if he was simply being helpful.

"Ah, I see," Taylor said, breaking my thought. "Then I agree with your thought process. You and I will go to Faerie alone."

"What would you have us do?" Ludvig asked, defeat at losing the chance for glory in battle evident in his voice.

"Find Depweg. You hunted him once; do it again. We need him with us for when the gates of Hell open," I said somberly.

"What makes you think they will open?" Doc asked nervously.

"Lachesis..." Locke whispered while shutting his eyes tight as if he was fighting a massive headache.

"Curious," Taylor said while crossing his arms and placing his index finger on his chin in thought. "If the seer saw the gates open, could that mean that you die in Faerie tonight?"

"If we don't go face Oberon and Lolth, then the black hole will destroy the Earth. We aren't sure how exact the prophecy is or what would happen if Ulric and I die at the exact same time and if there is no Earth left. For all we know, Hell and Heaven can battle in the space Earth used to inhabit like a freaking straight-to-VHS movie." I shook my head to erase the derailing train of thought like it was an Etch-A-Sketch. "Look, it doesn't matter.

What we do know is that we have no choice but to go to Faerie, and now. With the time dilation, I might be there for a few hours and come back to find Earth swallowed up. So we go right this moment. Taylor, ready?" I asked sternly. He nodded once and we began to make our way outside.

As I pushed on the OR doors, I turned to Ludvig and repeated, "Find Depweg," before disappearing into the lobby and out the front door.

"If I may," Taylor began when we were alone, "why did you tell the big one that his abilities won't work? I assume he has access to elemental magic if he showed you how to channel it, yes?"

I chewed on my answer for a moment before I said, "Two reasons: he and the boy would be a liability against an army."

"And the other?"

"Depweg...Depweg has gone rogue, and I want the hunters to find him before he does something stupid."

"May I ask what caused his distress?"

"Lolth took both of his packmates away from him. He's not handling it well."

"I think I understand," Taylor said respectfully. "Losing the ones you are responsible for can be a heavy burden to bear." As he spoke, his eyes went unfocused for a moment as he took in a deep breath. Then, as quickly as he had wandered off into Sorrowville, he returned, ready to complete the mission. "Very well. What would you have me do now?"

"Meet me at Val's. Explain to him what we are doing and take any weapons he can offer. I'll be there momentarily." As I finished issuing my orders, my leather wings sprouted. There were several puffs of a cottonlike substance on them now, and I chose to ignore them.

"See you in a moment," Taylor said as he winked out of sight. I really needed to learn how he and Lily shifted locations on the plane they were on. It was a super neat trick.

I exploded into the air, sending dirt that had collected on the parking lot out in a circular wave.

As I made it to just below the cloud cover, I noticed a few small snowflakes that had squeezed out the bottom of the dark gray clouds, like a teenager sneaking out of their bedroom window after curfew. The lack of balance in the Fae Courts coupled with a few weeks of not having sun was beginning to bear worrisome fruit. Snow in Houston was exceedingly rare.

After a few minutes of flying, I landed in front of Valenta's Saloon and made my way inside. Taylor and Val were nowhere to be seen, and a dawn of doubt birthed in my mind.

"Shit, shit, shit," I whispered as I hurried into the kitchen. Relief crashed over me as I saw the doors to the basement were open. My nerves were placed precariously on the edge.

I rushed downstairs, taking two steps at a time, eager to lay eyes on my friends and confirm my worries were fabricated. There, standing in front of a bay of storage boxes, were Valenta and Taylor.

They stopped talking as I came into view, watching as I approached at a faster than what was socially acceptable pace.

"Everything alright?" Taylor asked with a cocked eyebrow.

"Hmm? Oh yes. Fine and dandy," I said while crossing and uncrossing my arms, unsure of what to do with my hands. "What did we decide for weapons?"

"See'n as how failure means tha end of existence, I'm will'n ta lend ya tha big guns," Valenta said. I took note that he kept his thick Southern accent up in front of Taylor.

Val grabbed a sealed box off the shelf and gently set it down on the ground. He removed the lid to reveal a few Nordic-looking artifacts, including a hammer-looking item. It was covered in sigils and runes, but didn't look like a normal hammer or mallet. The top was curved, almost like a banana, with flat ends on either side. What was truly impressive was that the whole thing looked like a single forged piece of metal.

"Neat. What's that? An anchor or somethen?" I asked, pointing.

"Mjolnir," Valenta and Taylor both said in unison. Val glanced up at Taylor, who remained fixated on the hammer.

"Who are you?" Valenta asked Taylor through narrowed eyes.

"The same question could be addressed to you," Taylor responded nonconfrontationally.

"I trust both of you, and that's what matters. Now cut the crap and let's focus back on the part where you said this was freaking *Thor's* hammer! What?!" I let out some excited giggles as I clapped my hands while gazing upon the weapon of the Norse god. "Hey, it doesn't look like Thor's hammer."

"Please, do not tell me you are referring to the movie version..." Taylor let out with the hint of a smile.

"Boy, this is the *real* weapon," Val said, reaching down to pick up the hammer. His fingers wrapped around Mjolnir before lifting it easily from the box.

"Holy shit! You are worthy!" I proclaimed with a hand over my mouth.

"Damn it, John. Get those movies out yer head," Val said, extending the hammer out to me.

My breath caught in my throat as the implications of what he was offering ricocheted throughout my mind.

"Me?" I mouthed, unable to press air out to form the words.

"I do apologize for shortening this, no doubt, *epic* moment for you," Taylor started, using a colloquialism I would have used. "But time is a priceless commodity, and we are simply running out of it."

That snapped me back.

"You're right," I said without my usual snarky humor. I reached out and grabbed Mjolnir from Valenta. I hefted it in front of me, feeling its weight and balance. "What do the runes mean?" I asked.

"A multitude of things," Taylor answered before Val could finish drawing a breath for his reply. "Since you have become adept at using elemental magic, it is best you use this to focus, and even enhance, your attacks."

"What he said," Val concurred while hooking a thumb at Taylor, though I could tell he was irritated. "Try not ta crack Faerie in two with a lightning bolt, would ya?"

"Ah, I see you and Taylor had some time to chitchat before I arrived."

"That we did," Taylor agreed.

"Alright, chatty Cathys—what's the plan?" I asked while awkwardly crossing my arms with the hammer sticking out and pressing against my cheek. With a sigh, I uncrossed my arms and let them fall to my side.

"To save Yggdrasil, we must destroy Lolth. She, and only she, is the reason for all of this," Taylor said.

"What about Oberon? I thought he was the mastermind?" I asked, perplexed. "Lolth has been Oberon's servant this whole time. I watched him issue her orders."

"I've known Lolth for countless centuries," Taylor said. "She wanted you to think Oberon was in control so any attack would be focused on him."

"Classic misdirection," I said, bringing my free hand up to rub my forehead in frustration.

"Hindsight is twenty-twenty, John," Taylor said. "She has fooled more than her fair share of creatures in her existence. Even me. I should have known she was the cat from legend that you described."

"So she's like Faerie's version of the Devil?"

"That is one way of putting it," Taylor responded, nodding his head slightly. As I looked at the Fae, I saw Val shift uncomfortably at the comparison, but he didn't argue on whose nefarious bad guy was worse.

"Man, I'm glad Doc called you. Otherwise, I would have gone in guns blazing for Oberon."

"Things happen for a reason," Valenta stated confidently and without his drawl. Now it was Taylor's turn to shift where he stood.

"I hope you are right, Val," I said, going over the events of the past several hours in an instant.

"Shall we, then?" Taylor prompted, bending at the waist and motioning down the hall with a hand.

"Lilith, how long did it take me to get here? You told him about the portals already, too?"

"No," Val said with narrowing eyes.

"It behooves me to know any and all portals being used to smuggle enchanted items to and from my queen's lands," Taylor said as if it were pure business. Then his shoulders slumped ever so slightly, and he corrected himself, "*My* lands."

"Hmph," Val responded as he led the way deeper down the hall.

We stopped at the doorway to Faerie and I turned to address Taylor.

"Ready?"

"I am."

I looked him up and down before asking, "Don't you need any weapons?"

"Not in Faerie."

"You're just full of surprises, aren't you?"

"Mayhap," he replied with a grin.

"Good luck," Valenta said as he placed a hand on the aperture and willed it to open. The space between shimmered before opening on a now familiar dark room. Taylor and I walked through the portal into the darkness that was Faerie.

Chapter 23

I walked through first, anticipating the loss of power and unwelcomed return to mortality, but it never came.

"I love this armor!" I said, moving my free hand over the plates that shimmered to life at my thought. I lifted Mjolnir with the other hand, unsure of where to place it when not needed. Taylor must have seen me inspecting the weapon.

"Touch it to your hip," he said.

I did as he suggested and felt it adhere as if fastened by an invisible harness. I tentatively let go of the hammer, keeping my hand close just in case, and was impressed to see it remain floating about half an inch off my waist.

"Neat!" I exclaimed as I looked at Taylor, who was adorned in epic (damn it, he had been right to use that word earlier) elven armor. It was made of thin, moss green metal etched in brown markings. In the center of his chest piece was a line design of a large tree with flowers blooming in the leaves. Though it wasn't thick, I would be willing to bet it would stop a shot from one of Depweg's high-caliber rifles. He was a noble of the Seelie Court after all. Only the finest of armor and weaponry would be permitted.

The armor covered him completely from neck to toes with no apparent breaks in the plates, leaving me to wonder how he could move. After taking a few steps toward me, I was amazed to see the armor act like it was made of cloth instead of metal. His helmet looked like it had been modeled after a fierce bird, wrapping all the way around his head, minus an adequate opening for his eyes. The wings of the bird interlaced just below his chin and all the way up to his nose. Above the eye opening sat the face of a predatory bird whose beak came down to the bridge of Taylor's nose.

"Dude, you look like you belong in *Lord of the Rings*," I said excitedly while pointing at him.

"Mr. Tolkien was a friend to the Fae," Taylor said, leaving *so* many questions to be asked later. "Now, be vigilant." As he spoke, a bow that perfectly matched his armor grew from his hand while a quiver full of wooden arrows materialized on his back. A golden sword sheathed in wood shimmered to life on his hip.

I began to comment on how awesome that had been when Taylor looked at me and shook his head once. Point taken. Enemy territory and all that. Roger 10-4 copy.

After a while of walking, we came to the toll bridge, and I snickered to myself. That is, until Taylor stopped dead in his tracks and stood upright.

"What is it?" I whispered while Taylor's head pivoted around, searching.

"Well, well, well," a two-toned voice pierced the silence as a familiar troll pulled himself onto the bridge. His bullet hole remained prominent in the center of his forehead, but now his eyes were purple and his skin had darkened.

"Oh, good! I get to kill you again," I said as I willed my gladius to life.

"John," Taylor urgently whispered as his eyes landed on the tree line. I stopped where I was on the bridge and turned to look at him before my eyes followed the direction he indicated with a quick nod.

From the tree line came hundreds of purple eyes of varying heights.

"Oh...good..." I said, a tad less confidently now.

"You have come to face your death, abomination," said the troll zombie. Fear clutched at my guts and made my feet as heavy as stone, rendering me unable to move.

Move aside, coward, Baleius demanded inside my head. Keeping my consciousness on the scene outside, I let go of the wheel without looking. Baleius took full control, and I could feel the shift in my eyes and fangs. With my Predatory Self in control, I blurred forward, grabbing the troll by the throat before pulling him up to my face.

"Wrong, bitch. I've come to rip your fucking heart out and swallow your soul."

The troll's face went from surprised to horrified as I shoved the flaming gladius down its throat, willing the flames to rage while deep inside the zombie creature. It bucked and thrashed while in my grip with eyes that searched desperately around for a way out. Then the eyes dimmed from purple to black before the creature began to turn to dust.

Turning to the tree line, I let out a battle cry that sent waves along the water under the bridge, and rushed forward.

"Wait!" Taylor cried out, but it was no use. Baleius was single-minded when it came to battle.

Leather wings sprouted, and I noticed they were clear of the fuzz from when I had flown earlier. I continued to rush forward before letting the momentum give my wings lift as I approached the tree line.

Countless zombie faeries burst from the trees, eager to do their master's bidding and kill me.

A few yards away, I tilted my wings and lifted higher off the ground while bringing my flaming gladius up in an arc. Hellfire erupted from the gladius and soared through the air like napalm, landing on the awaiting flesh of my enemy. Shrieks rang into the night like wolves howling at the moon as the insatiable flames ate everything around them. The hungry fire spread with a fierce speed and intensity, as if the ground had been soaked in accelerant and the flames were being carried by a strong wind.

Wooden arrows tipped in gold pierced chests dead center, cutting off the cries of the burning masses.

Cackling with maniac eyes, I unleashed another torrent of flames at the creatures that attempted to run. The forest began burning with green and red flames.

"John, stop!" I could hear Taylor call out.

A cloud of arrows rocketed from somewhere in the forest, smashing into me. My wings were shredded to pieces while I shielded my exposed face from the darkness-infused weapons.

As I fell toward the ground, I willed my wings to disconnect before the disease spread into my body. I didn't have another fission bomb to suck up and burn out the darkness. The loss of energy stole my breath, stunning me, as the ground rushed up to embrace me.

I crashed into the soft forest floor and attempted to regain my senses as several footsteps closed in from all around.

"Get the weapon," a hoarse voice croaked, followed by several hands grabbing my gladius arm and pinning it down.

Everything snapped back into place, and I released my gladius, letting it fade from existence and willing it back to life in my other hand.

I lifted my sword, letting it rest on my palm, and willed the weapon to rotate like a helicopter blade. Cries of surprise mixed with gasps of pain as I focused on making the whirling sword leave my hand and hover over my body. I sent the blade from head to toe, severing limbs and heads from torsos before having it rocket back to my right hand as I stood up.

The forest was empty around me except for the writhing bodies of the dying.

"John!" Taylor cried out as he made his way to where I stood, searching for the rest of the enemies.

He latched onto my shoulder, and I reflexively smacked him away, hard. He flew through the air, dropping his bow, and crashed into a tree, where he rebounded with amazing ease. His sword was at the ready as he crouched down where he had landed.

While keeping my eyes on Taylor, who I assumed quite confidently could be a deadly foe, I grabbed the steering wheel with one hand. Baleius didn't protest now that all our enemies had been brutally slaughtered.

"Taylor! Sorry about that! When I let go of the wheel, I can go a little crazy sometimes," I explained.

Taylor lowered his sword slightly as he straightened up, but his expression did not change as he glared at me.

"Look, I'll explain later. Let's finish this."

"Be more careful, John," Taylor said through dagger-filled eyes. "You coated the forest in hellfire. Kill the creatures of darkness, but leave Faerie unscathed."

I looked past him to see the green and red flames consuming the wilderness where we had been. My eyebrows raced to my hairline as I understood that I had created the hellfire by releasing my inner demon. A feeling of guilt and shame flushed my cheeks, and my heart felt heavy.

"I-I'm sorry," I said slowly, having trouble with the words. I knew better than to let Baleius take full control.

I looked down at my gladius, which had heavenfire dancing up its length, and noticed here and there a bit of green reaching up through the flames.

"Let's go. We are running out of time," Taylor instructed as he bent to retrieve his bow and continued toward the castle.

"Where did they all go?" I asked, searching the trees around where I stood.

"Back to Lolth. They will be expecting your attack next time. Of that, you can be sure." There was anger in Taylor's voice, as if I had used a nuke on a small squad of insurgents rather than saving it for the capital stronghold. Now, our hand had been exposed and Lolth had more information to use against us.

I followed Taylor, careful to keep one hand firmly on the wheel, and we eventually made it to the castle. The tree looked even worse than last time, and it made me worry that we might already be too late.

"Get us over the wall and to the throne room," Taylor whispered as I stopped to stand next to him.

I nodded, and new leather wings sprang forth. I was annoyed to see some of the fuzz had come back; but I'd worry about that later.

Taylor stuck one hand up into the air and I lifted off the ground, grabbing his wrist as I soared into the sky. I was careful not to beat my wings too hard, lest I gave away our position. They already knew we were coming, but I didn't want them to know exactly where we were.

In less than a minute, we had made it high enough to be level with the castle. It amazed me that the castle seemed to be closer to the front gate when walking than when flying. I chalked it up to Fae magic.

We landed at the front entranceway and began making our way inside. Taylor slung the bow over his shoulder and opted instead for the sword for close-quarter combat.

I willed my gladius to life, but focused on keeping the flames as low as possible. I could have extinguished them, but I didn't know if that affected the power of the blade or not, and now was not a time for trial and error.

We made our way to the throne room where, sitting on top of a pile of rubble that had once been the throne, sat Oberon. He rested his hands on top of the gladius, the point of the sword resting on the ground. Oberon looked up to see us and smiled, letting his hands move around in a circle while the tip of the blade pivoted on the stone floor. He was covered from head to toe in his black celestial armor etched in red. The skin I could see was healed but scarred from our last encounter. Oberon stood straight up, making a show out of stretching, before squaring his body to us.

Taylor and I entered the room, spreading out to either side of the imposing nine-foot-tall King of Faerie. I was confident I could beat him again, but a part of me knew that last time he hadn't been expecting my attack, and he had been injured from the dragon's breath.

"Keep an eye out for Lolth," I whispered to Taylor. He didn't respond, but I knew he had gotten the message.

"No need," Oberon said. "It's just us."

"You know Lolth betrayed you, right?" I asked Oberon. "She knew the black hole would rush toward Earth instead of with it."

"Yes, yes, I know," Oberon sighed, letting his shoulders slump slightly. "Then again, since TalGoid is with you, I assume you already know that I do not have a choice. I was tricked by the darkness and now must abide by its laws."

"That sucks," I spoke flatly while keeping my sword up in a defensive stance.

"Truly," Oberon said. "But not as much as this." He turned and looked down one of the passageways where two tiny purple eyes shone from the darkness. They were only about six inches off the ground, so I assumed they posed no threat. Oh, Lilith, how wrong I was.

The sound of squeaking wheels reverberated in the silence, and my throat constricted at the recognition of the sound. I watched in pure horror as the glowing eyes moved slowly through the darkness and into the dimly lit throne room.

"Here, let me help you see," Oberon said, waving a hand toward the ceiling. The visage of a full moon appeared, bathing the room in a bluish-white light.

A high-pitched moan of heartbreak escaped my mouth like the air from a leaking balloon as I dropped to my knees, lowering my weapon.

"John, get up," Taylor whispered from somewhere a thousand miles away. Everything in my world became unfocused except the tiny, handicapped puppy in the custom-made wheelchair.

"Tiny...Ti-Ti-Tim," I squeaked out, tears blurring my eyes. "No. Not you, little buddy. Not you..." I sobbed once, losing the battle to control my emotions as the purple-eyed puppy approached on excited front paws, his tongue hanging out as he panted. The puppy, whom I had loved more than any other creature in my long life, scrambled on the stone floor in an effort to get to his best friend. I let my gladius wink out as I extended my hands, ready to pick him up and let him attack my face with the ferocity that only puppy kisses could bring.

"It's not him, John! Do NOT fall for their tricks!" Taylor urged. When I didn't respond and Tim inched closer to my open hands, I could hear Taylor sheathing his blade, drawing my attention. As I looked over to him, he nocked an arrow into his bow and let it loose, with it pointed directly at my puppy.

"NO!" I screamed as I sent a whip out from my hand to knock the arrow from the air. Then I picked up Tiny Tim with my left hand and brought him to my face while I willed the manifestation in my right hand to transform. Now I could see how Oberon had been tricked so easily. Lolth knew our hot buttons. I kissed the top of Tim's head and smiled just as he lunged for the skin on my exposed face with tiny teeth laced with the poison of darkness.

Predicting just that, I dropped him in the leather bag I had manifested and cinched it closed while the tears I had been holding back leaped from my eyes. I could hear him struggling as I tied him to my hip. The thing I had loved unconditionally had just been used against me, and I didn't appreciate that. Not. One. Bit.

"Now," I snarled with eyes pluming red and white as my chest heaved with rage, "you fucked up." My gladius sprang to life drenched in a mixture of heavenflame and hellfire.

Oberon's smile vanished in an instant, replaced with a frown of disappointment.

I heard Taylor's bow draw back as I rushed for Oberon. From the corner of my eye, I saw a column of shadow swarm Taylor, who barely dodged out of the way as he fired into the dark tide that was Lolth. I had to trust Taylor could hold his own against Lolth while I faced Oberon.

Our swords clanged, angel gladius on angel gladius, and my worst fears were realized; Oberon was not as weak as on our last meeting, and matched me in strength and speed. Faerie was his plane, and that should have given him the edge to beat me, but Da's armor and my unimpeded vampirism helped close the gap.

We pushed off, sparks flying, and began a delicate dance for the fate of the universe.

He thrusted toward my chest, and I parried by slapping his blade with mine before throwing a counterstrike. He dodged out of the way, narrowly missing the tip of my blade, while an elephant-sized boot kicked me in the Little John. My eyes went wide as the air escaped my lungs, and I was lifted into the air about a foot before Oberon's fist slammed into my face.

I toppled head over feet what felt like a hundred times before my helmeted noggin smashed into stone, abruptly halting my circus act.

I scrambled to my feet just in time to lift my free arm up and summon a shield. Metal clanged on metal, and I swiped at Oberon's feet as he took a step back from having his momentum reversed. My sword connected and etched a line through his shin.

Oberon screamed in rage as a tiny line of blood leaked from the cut in his armor. I sucked in the shield and extended out a whip that I used to lash out at the Faerie king's face. The crack created a small shock wave that disoriented Oberon, and I stepped forward with my sword to stab at his torso. He recovered at the last second and twisted, but not before I gashed another line in his armor. This time, blood spilled freely as Oberon cried out, bringing his sword around as he twisted his body.

Seeing his attack coming, I let the gladius wink out as I ducked and turned in a circle as his blade clanged off the top of my helmet. As I completed my turn, I willed the gladius back and launched myself upward, bringing the blade straight up to the ceiling.

Oberon was still in full swing as I brought the blade up, but countered by leaning toward me while bending at the elbow, smashing it into my face.

My body rag dolled to the ground as I was knocked silly. There were now two Oberons above me, swirling around and around each other. Both of them raised their swords with the tips pointing downward, ready to violate my flesh like a bad prom date.

Then the two attackers coalesced back into one as my vision cleared, and I saw my doom approach in slow motion. My hands were at my sides and would not produce enough momentum to counter this direct, powerful attack.

"Well, I tried," was all I could think as the sword rushed to make my chest its new sheath.

A blur of green passed overhead, followed by a wave of darkness that crashed into Oberon, knocking him off his feet.

He cried out in surprise as I turned to see Lolth feverishly chasing the elusive Taylor, who was much more agile than anyone in the room had anticipated. In her single-mindedness, she had fallen for his maneuver and crashed into Oberon, saving my unlife.

As I lay flat on the ground, I brought my knees up to my chest and then kicked up toward the ceiling, bringing my whole body up to land on my feet in a super cool ninja move, like in the movies. Except this ninja also had a puppy in the leather bag attached to his hip. Must be mindful of my little buddy!

I was aware of the taste of blood in my mouth and instantly knew that son of a bitch had broken my nose.

Oberon recovered and continued his attack. I parried, dodged, ducked, and countered his attacks just as he did mine. I realized this was going to be death by a thousand cuts if I didn't change my tactics.

I was bleeding out of several wounds that matched in number to Oberon's. He had an impressive reach on me, which meant I had to get in closer to effectively strike, whereas all he had to do was keep me just out of range.

As he made a sweeping arc with his sword, a thought struck me, and I let my gladius wink out as I ducked under his attack. I willed two daggers with tanto tips for piercing, and was happy to see they were just as real and celestial as the rest of my manifestations lately.

Oberon's eyes went wide as he tried to slow his power strike, and I moved in.

I jammed both blades into his lead leg, one directly on top of the thigh and the other in the outside of the quadricep. The blades pierced the armor, as the tips had been designed to do, and I immediately began drawing blood into myself.

Oberon was stunned and tried to suck in air, and I began laughing—A dark bull with glowing amethysts for eyes rammed into my side, throwing me across the room with a sickening crunch. While doing my best to not crush Tim in the bag at my side, I bounced off the wall and landed on the ground, knowing several bones were broken. Not only that, I had had the blades ripped from my hands and had lost the energy I had thrown into them, stunning me.

As I lay still, moaning, I heard the ground-shaking thumps of something massive running in my direction. I turned my head and saw Lolth—still in bull form—rushing toward me with head low and sharp horns ready.

I sent the emergency signal from my brain to my limbs to move, move, move! But there was a problem with the connection, and I just lay there, unable to stop the train.

Lolth was a few paces away when a volley of arrows pierced her flesh near the neck. With a scream, she veered off to the side. So instead of piercing me with her horns, all she did was lightly—gently, even—trample me beneath the tonnage of her weight. Bones cracked and joints popped out of sockets as she ran over me, tripping as she went. I was aware of the yipping in my bag, which I desperately tried to shield with my body.

Lolth not only slammed into the wall, but *through* it as well. Though my body was facing the center of the room, my neck had been conveniently positioned to face behind me, so I could watch as the Shadow goddess received a few more arrows in her ass before falling over the edge of the castle.

For some reason, in that moment, even though my body was broken and I was still in very real danger, all I could think about was that it was odd she had fallen to the ground below. I'd thought the throne room had passageways and rooms on all sides. Went to show how much I paid attention.

"My goddess!" Oberon cried as he quickly limped to, then jumped through, the hole she had created. There was a sizable trail of blood following him.

Closing my eyes, I focused on healing my body. Once everything had popped back into place, I grabbed my neck, took a deep breath, and twisted it back into place.

"Owwy!!!!" I cried out like a manly man and not at all like a five-year-old child who had just skinned his knee.

I smacked my lips as I tasted fresh blood.

"That was new," I said as Taylor rushed over to help me up.

"Are you okay?" he asked. I looked him up and down and realized he had had a hell of a battle against Lolth. Blue elven blood leaked from several wounds over his body.

"Yeah, I think so. How did you hit her without light?" I asked.

"Arrows I personally enchanted with the power of the sun," Taylor said, pulling an arrow free. I noticed the gold tip was not metal, but condensed sunlight that I had to squint to look at up close.

"Neat!" I admired.

"Well, I made them for you," Taylor admitted, slightly ashamed.

"Not so neat," I unadmired.

"It kept her from turning once you distracted her for me."

"Yeah. That's what I did. Yup. Yes, sir. I sure distracted her, just like I intended. Yup."

"Thank you for that, John. It changed the tide in our favor. Except…"

"Except we haven't stopped them yet," I finished as I stepped to and then looked out the hole. A strong wind gusted through as I peered down at the cloud cover below. "Holy long fall, Batman! That goes all the way down!"

"Yes. It was exceedingly difficult to position her in such a way that she noticed, and then charged you, from the angle I had drawn her to."

"Um, good job…?" I said, not really knowing what to respond to something so badass that I couldn't fully wrap my head around it. I had always been bad at geometry…and physics…and most things.

I sprouted wings before motioning to Taylor, who nodded as he stepped forward. Another step, and he was falling through the air with me close behind him, my wings tucked in close as I flew like a missile.

As we passed through the cloud cover, I grabbed Taylor's ankle as we searched for any signs of Lolth and Oberon. We were around a hundred feet off the ground when I unfolded my wings to their full width and began soaring.

"There!" Taylor called out as he grabbed his bow and took an arrow from the quiver on his back. I was impressed that, even upside down, the arrows didn't fall out. He nocked the sunlight-tipped arrow, aimed, and let loose one arrow that separated in midflight into several, almost like watching buckshot.

Oberon was pulling the last arrow from Lolth when the volley whistled through the air. The King of Darkness took note and stood with his back to us and arms out to either side as Lolth shrunk down to the size of a cat. Arrows bounced off Oberon's armor, completely missing the now much smaller Lolth. A few found a home in between Oberon's armor, and he dropped to the ground as one of his knees exploded from the strike.

"Note to self: no armor on the back of the knees," I whispered to no one before glancing at my arm, "or front of the elbow."

A few yards above the ground, I let Taylor go, who expertly flipped in the air and landed on his feet with ease like a damn cat. He nocked another arrow while keeping it trained on Oberon, who still tried to shield Lolth.

"Wait," I said gently as I landed and let my wings retract. I made my way over to where Oberon was breathing heavily and trembling with pain. Giving him a wide berth, I walked around to try and spot Lolth, but it appeared as if she had disappeared under Oberon's shadow.

"Fuck," I barked in frustration.

Lolth must have known I was looking for her, because the Shadow goddess appeared in the open field in front of me, rising from the ground like a specter.

I smiled, ready to finish this, when my lips began to tug downward at the corners as what had to be thousands of various Shadow faeries began to emerge from the ground alongside their master.

Incorporeal, featureless monsters stood with stone-faced drow. Supes that had been infected with darkness spilled out from the tree line behind, apparently unable to shadow walk.

Tiny Tim began moving in my leather sack, struggling to get free and join his infected brothers and sisters.

Taylor joined me where I stood, gazing at the hopeless battle in front of us. I was cocky enough to know we could kill hundreds of the Shadow bastards with relative ease, but thousands? Even I knew when to set the measuring tape down and zip up the front of my pants.

"Ready to die?" I asked gravely.

Taylor looked at me and did something I'd never forget: he backhanded the fuck out of my face, to the point where my head was almost facing directly behind us.

My hand went to my face, where the armor had mitigated some of the pain, but I was still very much aware that a truck had just smashed into the side of my head.

Rubbing my cheek, I turned to face the elf, who was freaking *smiling* at me.

"What do we say to the god of death?" Taylor asked.

"Eat my ass? Because, seriously, I'm not going to finish that possibly copyrighted statement. Though I get the meaning," I finished with a wink and smile of my own.

We both looked forward, drawing our respective weapons: Taylor with his bow and sunlight-tipped arrows. Me with my angelic gladius and circular shield, kind of like Captain America's but with a Batman symbol in the middle.

I leaned a little toward my companion and whispered, "I totes didn't know you liked *Game of Thrones*. I would have invited you over for watch parties."

Chuckling, Taylor responded with, "You haven't even seen the spin-off series yet, have you?"

"Oh shit! I forgot all about that. It's been out for, what, eight years? I'm going to have to binge-watch the entire series when I get home."

Taylor's forced smile fell flat as the infected supes made it to the Shadow army. My own mouth mirrored his as the situation became both real and unavoidable.

I took in a deep breath, focused on my flaming gladius, and bellowed a battle cry that could be heard for miles. Taylor, the more subtle type, charged forward, unleashing arrows as he ran smoothly. Watching him reminded me of powerful anime characters when they ran, their features blurring with their speed.

I rushed forward, shifting my focus to the enemy that had began charging as a unified army, while I whispered inward, *Hope you're ready for this,* to Baleius.

In response, I felt my eyes begin to glow a fierce red that mixed with the white plumes billowing up my forehead. My fangs flexed so hard they almost hurt, and for the first time in my existence, I could feel them poking at my lower gums. My ears and nose felt strange as I ran, as did my fingers, but I would have to worry about that later. The wave was upon me.

I threw my shield like a giant frisbee while willing the edges to sharpen to razors as it flew. I kept my focus on the disc o' death as it lobbed off a row of heads. It took me a moment to realize that I didn't have a physical connection to the weapon but could still *feel* it.

While the shield was in midair, I willed it back at an arc, taking several more heads with it. As I caught the manifestation, the front of the line made contact.

I slashed with the flaming gladius, cutting through several enemies, while blocking with the shield. I bashed a few faces in while dodging attacks. A drow leaped into the air and brought his dagger down, slashing at the exposed flesh of my face. I watched in horrified slow motion as the tip of the blade dragged down my forehead just over my eye, narrowly missing the wide, soft orb, before being caught by the skin covering the cheek.

I reeled back and bent at my waist, willing the shield to form into a length of wound up chain that perfectly fit the shape the shield had just been in. I lashed out with my arm, sending the chain out and in a wide circle around me, before willing impossibly sharp blades down its length.

Torsos were cut in half as heads toppled to the ground and screams of agony roared louder than the din of battle. Over and over, I swung the chain in a circle, until I felt confident that I had regained enough space to strike with my gladius once again.

I willed the chain to solidify into a pike that I hefted and twirled in front of me in dramatic movie fashion.

An enormous ogre with purple eyes and dark skin broke through the line and began charging me. I lashed out with the pike, the tip piercing the ample flesh of the ogre, but had no impact.

"Huh?" was all I could manage before he plowed into me and then tackled me to the ground, forcing the pike out of his back.

Keep focus on it. Keep focus. Don't you drop that weapon, I repeated to myself, knowing that if I lost the energy I had put into the manifestation, the Shadow army on top of me would take full advantage of my stunned state.

I was all but crushed underneath the monster who was pinning me to the ground with his girth, the celestial armor keeping my insides from squeezing out of my assortment of orifices. Only my head was exposed, and for a horrified second, I realized that was my most vulnerable weakness while in my angelic armor.

I struggled, trying to free myself, before accepting that the beast of an ogre had done exactly what he had intended: pacify me.

A handful of drow walked around the ogre to where my head was poking out. One kneeled down with its emotionless face—that was for sure going to give me daymares—and wrapped its fingers under the bottom of my helmet.

I screamed as his intentions became clear. The drow began to tug while I shook my head from side to side as hard as I could.

I sucked in a quick breath in a moment of clarity and released the gladius, which winked out of existence at my command. I then focused on the manifested pike that was piercing straight through the ogre, and willed it to transform into my gladius. As the long pike shrunk into my angelic sword, I focused on the blade, sending ravaging flames up its length and toward the sky. Heavenfire erupted straight through the faerie bruiser like an acetylene torch.

The ogre didn't scream as he was cut in half by the focused flames, but his Shadow friends who were burned by the sudden light of my flaming sword did shriek. The drow, however, remained fixated on their mission of removing my helmet.

As the weight of the ogre lifted, I attempted to roll over, only to have the drow rip my helmet off in the process.

My flaming sword went out as my preternatural strength disappeared, and I became mortal.

I stumbled to my feet, completely aware of how naked I was and pissed off that my extra padding made it difficult to move nimbly. I felt heavy and exposed as my eyes darted around. My flaming attack had provided several yards of room from where the shadow creatures had retreated; well, all except for the drow, who bore down on me.

I lifted my sword, feeling like a child holding a stick against a grizzly bear, and stood my ground.

The first drow charged and I slashed at him with the sword. It passed right through him without the aid of light, and he rammed a shoulder into my chest. I flew back at least ten feet before tumbling to the ground as a whoosh of air was forced from my lungs on impact.

I couldn't breathe, and I *needed* to breathe. My heart pounded so hard I could barely hear the battle around me. After what felt like an eternity of panicked heartbeats, I was able to suck in a sharp lungful of air just before I was about to pass out. I coughed, feeling sharp stabs of pain in my ribs, which were no doubt broken.

"Tay-Tay," I croaked out barely above a hushed tone. It was like someone had their hands wrapped around my throat, preventing air from entering or leaving effectively.

I spun in place while on the verge of hysteria, daring to try and find Taylor as the drow circled me.

There, about thirty yards from where I stood, was my companion. One of his arms was hanging loosely in front of him, with blood cascading from deep gashes in his elven armor. The shadow beasts around him stood still, watching as the darkness slowly flowed up his limb and toward his heart and brain.

I knew then, he was dead.

My ragged breaths of hysteria gave way to heaves of rage as my fists clenched inside my gauntlets.

I dropped the gladius to the ground, which did not fade from existence, and squared off at the drow that approached.

If I was going to die, it would be with swinging fists and kicking feet.

"Come on, then!" I roared.

The drow continued their steady approach with stoic faces.

A hand rested on my shoulder, and I turned to see nothing behind me.

You're still you, John. Even in Faerie, the voice of Da echoed throughout my mind. *Now, what time is it?*

"Wha-what time is it?" I asked between hyperventilating breaths.

A man in parachute pants sidestepping on a dance floor flashed through my mind. My hand reached down and latched around Mjolnir, which had remained by my side even without the celestial powers.

"It's hammer time," I exalted as a smile spread across my face. I felt the power exciting every nerve in my body as I raised Mjolnir skyward and rose into the night.

"Woooo-hoo-hoo-hoooooooo!" I laughed into the air as I sped above the battlefield.

I halted in midflight, oriented on the army below, and shoved the hammer toward the sky above my head. Clouds billowed and churned as if in an Oklahoma-sized tornado while lightning cracked in the sky.

As the power coalesced above me, I spotted Lolth peering up at me with hate-filled eyes; one of which was dimmer than the other from her battle with Magni.

That's when an idea came together, and I focused on every set of purple eyes on the battlefield that was staring up at me. I extended my free hand—relieved that I could still feel the molecules of the air—and focused on the eyes of my enemy.

I willed the power of the clouds to flow through me, utilizing Mjolnir as my focusing wand, and sent merciless forks of lightning to the amethyst targets below.

The elemental magic struck with a ferocity that only a man trying to save the entire Lilith-damned universe could muster. Eyes exploded before the blueish-white electricity jumped to another set of peering, exposed orbs. There were no screams as drow, Shadow faeries, and darkness zombies either faded into mist or dropped to the ground, their muscles writhing from the electricity.

The damaged eye of Lolth exploded, sending out purple shards like a broken prism while she screamed in pain. She had the sense to close her other eye and shield it with her hand before turning away from my storm of power.

As the last of the lightning fizzled out, I descended to the ground, keeping a death grip on Mjolnir knowing a fall from that height would result in my mortal death.

I located my helmet and bent to retrieve it while wincing in pain at my chest. I began walking over to where Lolth kneeled on the ground, one hand over her exploded eye that oozed black sludge to the ground, killing the grass beneath it in an instant.

Returning the helmet to my head, I felt the surge of power rush through me as my vampirism returned in a flood. My chest snapped, crackled, and popped as the bones knitted themselves back together. I could feel the gladius on the ground several yards behind me, and I willed it to fly to my hand, where it ignited on contact.

"You've been beaten, Lolth. Tell me how to reverse the darkness and save Yggdrasil," I demanded confidently, feeling like a superhero after defeating the villain.

Wait a sec, this was the moment when the villain pulled out their last—Lolth whirled on me and started growing at an alarming rate while lashing out at me with a hand that was now the size of a car.

"Shit..." was all I got out before stars swam in my eyes and the feeling of weightlessness took over. I slammed into the ground, plowing a divot for twenty feet before my momentum halted.

"Ow. Ow, ow. Ow...ow," I said as bones began to heal in my now broken back. The nasty thought that, if I hadn't been wearing this armor, she would have probably splattered me across all of Faerie reared its ugly head in my mind. My hand rested on my chest and I was surprised to feel the armor dented. "Hope that's going to buff out," I said between my teeth as I struggled to get to my feet.

"Foolish child," Lolth spoke with a voice that sounded like a mountain talking. "The world tree fuels my power. I will bathe the nine realms in darkness and rule over all of creation."

"Are you still a chick? 'Cause you got, like, a James Earl Jones thing going right now," I called out in reference to her voice. Heck, she'd give even Luke Daniels a run for his money on most impressive narrator ever.

Taylor slumped forward, crashing to the ground face-first as the darkness reached his heart and started spreading exponentially throughout his body. Oberon remained on the ground forty feet behind Taylor in a similar pose. Son of a bitch was lucky he had passed out or my attack would have entered through his eyes and fried him. Then again, if I were somehow able to defeat Lolth and free Oberon, someone *would* have to run Faerie. Maybe it was for the best he didn't die just yet.

Lolth continued to grow, making me a tiny bit nervous, until she reached the size of an apartment building. Her arms stretched out a few hundred feet in either direction, ending in three-fingered ham hocks that could use full-blown semitrailers as Hot Wheels toys.

Her one remaining eye locked onto me as she leaned forward to get a better look at my "Oh, poop" expression. Her grin spread from ear to ear—if she had ears—and each tooth was as large as my entire upper body.

Tim rummaged around in my bag, anxious to join his master in glorious battle.

Lolth let loose with a roar that shook the ground I stood on and bent trees like blades of glass in a strong wind.

Tim stopped rummaging around then. Maybe he was scared. Maybe he smelled fresh shit. And maybe you shouldn't judge me 'cause you weren't there.

Lolth closed her eyes, exuding pleasure at whatever she had just sensed.

"You're too late, child. The black hole is upon Midworld, and Yggdrasil is almost entirely taken over by my sweet darkness. You," she pointed a massive finger in my direction, "have failed." Her laugh made the ground jump with each cascade of sound as the staccato left her abysslike mouth.

I knew she was right. I had failed, and the entire Earth and all the billions of lives on it would be lost. Men, women, children, animals, all lost. Just like my parents.

My...parents.

"Mom...Dad..." I breathed out just below a whisper as I looked at the ground, ashamed I had failed them. I was just getting the hang of being a good guy, too. But there was no way I could erase a *literal* tear through space and time—

Lachesis' words pierced the veil of my mind, "Our doubts are traitors, and make us lose the good we oft might win, by fearing to attempt."

"I can do this. I can do this," I started to whisper to myself before my voice grew in confidence and intensity. "I CAN FUCKING DO THIS!"

My eyes shot up to Lolth, and I smiled back at her as she cackled. While she was distracted, I swiped my flaming gladius in the air next to me, revealing a hole that led precisely in front of where the black hole was about to begin siphoning Earth's atmosphere, oceans, and land.

"Hey, Lolth!" I yelled loud enough to be heard over her hubris. "Do you like baseball?"

Lolth stopped laughing and regarded me with her remaining eye, turning her head slightly to get a better look at me.

I stuck my hand through the tear in space I had created and grabbed the baseball-sized black hole with my celestial glove. I *knew* I could do just that. It hummed and vibrated in my hand, eager to be fed; so, I obliged it.

Lolth tried to pull back as I winked once at her before lobbing the black hole at her like an MLB pitcher.

It soared through the air, sucking in the broken trees that had fallen and all the bodies that littered the battlefield. Oberon was fine where he was, but I could see Taylor's limp arms beginning to lift toward the insatiable cosmic phenomenon.

"Sorry about this, buddy," I said as I willed a javelin into my free hand before throwing it toward where Taylor was now skittering across the grass. It pierced his thigh and lodged deep into the ground, pinning my friend in place.

Lolth cried out in terror that had never before been known to her as the black hole began ripping her body apart like sheet metal from a roof in a hurricane. Layer after layer of flesh was torn from her body and sucked into the blackness until one of her entire arms broke loose. It was beyond fascinating to watch something the size of a crane being compressed into a hole the size of a baseball.

Next, her other arm ripped off and followed the first before her legs and torso were sucked into the nothing. As the bulk of her chest was crushed and compacted, it blocked the hole like your wife's hair down the drain. The wind stopped, and leaves, grass, and tree limbs fell to the ground from the sudden release.

I was waiting for Lolth to say one last nefarious thing before dying—you know, something like, "You haven't won yet!" or, "I'll be back!"—but none came. She only screamed in pure fright at being eaten alive by the very thing she had created. I was disappointed by this because I already had my last words ready. Eh, fuck it.

"Don't worry, Lolth! I bet you'll enjoy the darkness on the other side!" Ah, damn it, I'm funny!

The hungry, hungry hole finished chewing up her torso and made its way to her neck. A single wide purple eye searched around in unbelieving terror while a mouth flapped wordlessly. Then her skull collapsed in on itself while her eye exploded from the pressure, and she was sucked into the void of eternity where her atoms would be torn asunder down to their quarks.

The wind picked up again, almost hungrier than before, and I knew what I had to do.

I sprouted wings and allowed myself to be picked up by the torrent of wind. I couldn't actually see the black hole, but I could sense where it was. As I approached, I could see Taylor stirring where I had pinned him. The darkness drained, starting with his flesh—returning his skin color—and ending with his eyes, which had begun to glow purple before reversing.

"Neat," I said as I neared my destiny.

"John! No!" Taylor screamed when I came within a few yards of the hole. My wings wanted to rip out of their sockets and fly into the void rather than support me any longer.

The Archangel Gabriel's words resonated in my head, "...erase your mistakes."

Still holding my gladius, I lifted it into position and swung for the fences with the flat side of my blade. Just like back at Valenta's when I had first escaped the void, there was a pop as my celestial sword erased the hole through space and time, leaving me to fall toward the ground.

I breathed a sigh of relief as I fell headfirst only to extend my wings, catch the wind, and soar to where I had cut my own hole in space. I landed, admiring the hole that wasn't sucking or blowing the atmosphere, when blinding sunlight bathed my entire body. I jerked my arm up to my face, fully anticipating the familiar agony of Earth's sunlight on vampire flesh. But all I felt was warmth. Hesitantly, I lowered my hand and looked out at the universe. I could stare directly at the sun and feel the life-giving light explore the exposed skin on my face.

Taking a chance, I willed the celestial armor out of existence and felt the sun spread over my entire body, from beanie-covered head to steel-toed boots. I moaned in wonder and delight, turning my hands over and over again to spread the warmth evenly. A tear streamed down my cheek to disappear into my thick beard as I realized how much I had missed the sun. Such a simple thing that mortals took for granted every day of their short lives. My clothes felt warm to the touch, and I wished I could lay in a field under the welcoming rays and just fall asleep. It was different than Faerie's sun in a way I couldn't put into words; but I felt it. Over five centuries had passed since I'd last bathed in the light of our star; I hadn't realized how much I'd missed it until that moment. It was beautiful.

I was snapped out of my trance when Oberon began to stir and cough violently to the point of vomiting. Taylor followed suit. I looked over my shoulder and saw the javelin still in Taylor's leg and decided I needed to focus. The forgotten warmth of the sun would have to wait for another time.

A quick swipe of my blade and the rift was closed, along with the beauty of the star at the center of our solar system.

I turned and flapped my wings, soaring just above the now empty battlefield as I let my gladius wink out.

After landing by Taylor, I removed the javelin from his leg and willed it back into my being. I helped him to his feet before asking, "How are ya, buddy?"

"I-I'm alive. But how?" he asked as he examined the useless and broken arm. Placing my hand on his elbow, I willed my blood to flow over the appendage, willing it to heal while the unmistakable sound of a puppy throwing up tugged at my concentration.

After I finished healing Taylor's arm, he lifted it and gave it a quick flex before I moved to his thigh. I had shattered the bone, and it took a little more focus to fully repair it.

Another bout of a puppy throwing up and I opened my leather bag to see a little brown-eyed puppy staring up at me. He was whining and didn't take long to figure out why. In all my tumbles, poor Tim had broken both of his front paws.

I grabbed him under his belly and lifted him from the bag as it disappeared. He whined in pain but still tried to kiss my face from excitement. Lilith, how I had missed him.

Unclasping the belt that held the wheelchair to his lower half, I let it drop to the ground while whispering, "You won't be needing that anymore, little buddy." I placed my other hand on his back and proceeded to send my blood all around his body, focusing intently on healing everything that was wrong with him.

His front paws were easy to mend, but his spine near his pelvis required more concentration. The nerves were completely severed and had withered apart. Using the enhanced ability that the celestial armor afforded me, I reconnected them and sent life energy into his atrophied muscles. They plumped as if he had been using them all along, and his little tail started wagging. A little at first, then it was an unstoppable windshield wiper of joy and unbridled love.

I retracted my blood, let my armor shimmer away, and hugged him against my chest before letting sobs of happiness flow.

"It's really you, isn't it?" I asked my puppy as I rained a barrage of kisses on his little head. He returned my attack with a volley of tongue lashings against my cheeks and nose. He didn't like my beard very much though, opting to give puppy kisses to my skin instead.

Oberon tried to stand before collapsing to the ground after putting pressure on his exploded knee. He cried out as he fell, bringing me back to the now.

I set Tim down on the ground before giving him a few scratches where his tail met his back. Oh, he liked that. He turned his little head to see what this new feeling was before jumping in little circles while yipping. After falling a few times, he seemed to naturally get the feeling of having four working puppy legs.

"Stay here for a minute, okay, buddy?" Tim stopped jumping in excited circles and looked up at me, his tail wagging so hard I thought his butt was going to fly off.

"You good?" I asked Taylor, who seemed like he was struggling to come out of a daze.

"Yes. Yes, I think so," he answered.

"Good. Let's go check on King Dickhead."

As we began to make our way over to where Oberon clutched his knee, Taylor said, "Remember, he was tricked by Lolth."

"I know. But I also know that he was a prisoner under Mab and wanted revenge. So I doubt it was hard to convince him to join the dark side." I was growing angry at the thought. So much so that I didn't even catch the *Star Wars* reference that I had made.

We stopped a few feet in front of him and he looked at us with bewildered eyes. I scrunched my face in disgust as I peered down my nose at the defeated King of Faerie.

"What...where am I?" he asked with a shaky voice. Oberon looked at Taylor and seemed to collect himself at the sight of something familiar. "TalGoid, what has happened to me?"

"Your Highness..." Taylor explained the entire situation. How Lolth had somehow tricked him into being infected with her darkness, granting the goddess direct influence over him. Taylor explained to a teary-eyed Oberon about how he had killed both Tatiana and Mab, throwing this plane and Midworld into a season of lifeless cold. He told him about the black hole that had been destined for Earth, and how I had just saved his life, Taylor's, and even Yggdrasil's.

"Take off that armor," I demanded as soon as Taylor was finished.

Oberon looked down at himself, as if seeing the armor for the first time, and began removing the pieces one by one, struggling with his bad leg. I smiled as he winced and cried out in pain while removing that which did not belong to him. He sat the pieces in a pile in the center of the circle we created with our bodies, and looked up at us.

"I-I guess I have a lot of work ahead of me. I can make this right. Faerie needs its king, and the Seelie and Unseelie Courts must be governed to maintain balance." He looked at me, daring to speak with someone who was infinitely his superior in every respect, and said, "I'm sorry for all that I have do—" I rushed forward and grabbed him by his pathetic throat. I could feel my eyes spilling red-and-green plumes of hatred as I bared fangs that were too long to be mine. My nose and ears tingled as I squeezed, closing his airway.

"John! What are you doing?" Taylor demanded, but he was miles away right then. All my focus was on this piece of shit that wasn't worth the air he tried so desperately to inhale.

I willed my gladius to life, coating it in red-and-green hellfire, before lifting it above his face. Pointing the blade straight down toward his gaping mouth, I released the tension on his throat and slammed the blade down its new sheath as Oberon sucked in his last breath. The hilt stuck out of his mouth as I began turning the blade back and forth while frantic hands scrambled over my chest and face, trying to push me away. I began a low laugh as the hellfire ate at his insides, with flames erupting out of his mouth like a geyser. Then his nose, ears, and eyes began shooting the green-and-red flames skyward as his body began to crumple. Muscles tightened as water inside boiled and evaporated, shrinking the tendons, ligaments, and muscle fibers until Oberon was reduced to a smoldering ember that looked like beef jerky that had been left to cook for far too long.

I pulled the blade out, letting the flames dance their victory, and ran my tongue up the length of the blade in a show of dominance.

"What have you done?" Taylor asked slowly, covering his mouth with both hands in horror as he took slow steps back.

Turning eyes that were now made of pure hellfire to regard the foolish elf, I said with a voice that was too scratchy and high-pitched to be mine, "How dare you ask what I've done. HOW DARE YOU. I am immortal. I am the savior of all creation. All who has ever lived, and all that will ever be, owes their life to me. Man will bow before their new god and worship *me*," I snarled with a throat that belonged to a horror movie monster.

"John...your face," Taylor said with disgust and terror in his eyes as he stumbled backward.

I gained some semblance of control and lifted a hand to feel my face. My nose was gone, leaving behind slits. My ears still tingled, and I was surprised to find my helmet had created gaps where my now pointy ears extended from my head.

I turned the gleaming blade over to its flat side and willed the flames to spread out so I could see my reflection. What stared back at me was a monster born from a demon and a bat.

"I-I," I stammered before something clicked. I slammed my consciousness inside the control room of my mind and felt dread when a fully clad Baleius smiled at me from under a celestial helmet.

Baleius! Stop! I cried as I reached for his hand on the wheel. With impossibly fast reflexes, he snatched my wrist before throwing me across the room. I slammed into the wall, knocking my favorite *Batman* poster to the ground. The glass shattered as the frame broke.

Wide-eyed, I turned to see the horrifying bat demon striding over to me with a determined look etched into his features.

I am in charge now, puny human. I am the fallen angel Baleius, reunited with armor forged by Father himself. I have the power to bend the universe to my will and force the mortals to cower at my feet.

God will stop you, I said meekly as I tried to get to my feet. Baleius blurred over to where I was and lifted me by my neck. I was but a small child, shadowed by the might and will of a vengeful adult.

Father will not intervene. Look at my brother Samael. What makes you think he will lift a holy finger to stop my reign.

He won't have to. I'll stop you, I said with complete confidence. I was done doubting myself.

Baleius laughed before tossing me to the center of the room, the steering wheel catching me in the gut painfully. Something Lachesis said rang throughout my head like a church bell.

"You are being kept in the dark by those you trust," she had said.

It didn't have to be this way, I said with sadness growing. *I trusted you.*

It was all a game, you naive fool. You did EXACTLY as I wanted you to.

Not everything, I whispered, knowing this was going to be a lose-lose situation.

I placed a hand on the wheel and raced outside the control room and back into my conscious self. Letting the gladius wink out, I placed my hands on either side of my head, and lifted the helmet off.

I sucked in air and felt my heart begin to beat as I broke the connection and erased my vampirism.

Chapter 24

"What just happened?" Taylor asked with concern as I stared at the ground with unfocused, somber eyes.

"I was betrayed," I said weakly, fighting back the nausea I felt in my empty stomach. Dizziness threatened to let me fall to the ground.

Taylor saw something was wrong and rushed to support me.

"I don't understand. Why did you take off the helmet?"

"Baleius was too strong with the armor on. I couldn't stop him. So I did the only thing I could." The words Lachesis had uttered ricocheted in my brain, *"Your greatest strength is also your greatest weakness."*

"Who's Baleius?" Taylor asked, shaking his head and squinting his eyes, trying to understand.

I explained about my Predatory Self and how Ulric had passed a demon into my dying body, forever infusing it with my flesh...and my soul.

"Guess I really will be going to Hell," I said to no one in particular. If Lachesis had been right about the armor and Baleius...oh, Lilith, that also meant I was going to kill Magni.

My knees buckled and only Taylor kept me upright. He began taking me somewhere, but I didn't know where. My head bobbed up and down, with my chin hitting my chest as sorrow kept me in a vegetative state.

I was placed in a warm bed as my armor was removed and replaced with thick blankets. I didn't try and fight sleep, choosing instead to cannonball into unconsciousness like a fat kid at the community pool.

My dreams were random and unfocused, like staring out a windshield while it rained without turning the wipers on.

More than a few times, the gaping maw of Lolth flew toward me from the darkness, swallowing me whole.

Then Baleius was there, sitting on a throne made of decimated carcasses, with bones littering the ground for as far as the eye could see. The sky was blood red, and the black smoke billowing from far away fires strangled the clouds above. Horns grew from my...his head, because it was no longer my body. He looked like a more pronounced version of the bat demon I had seen in the reflection of the gladius.

Magni's innocent face appeared to me. It was no longer childlike, having just reached full maturity. I watched as I bit into his neck and began drinking his precious blood. His face went white and eyes became unfocused as I drained him dry, killing him.

I thought about Godwin and how I had been next on the chopping block after my mother. Ulric had saved me, only to be repaid in fire.

Lily was kissing me, stroking my hair and whispering that everything would be alright. That I should trust her. Then she led me to the gates of Hell and watched as I descended into the fiery pits.

I was falling through the Earth and into the flames of Hell below. I screamed. I screamed in terror. I screamed in pain. I screamed with uncertainty. I screamed for all that I had lost, for all that I had done. I deserved to burn in Hell.

Chapter 25

Taylor gently shook my shoulder until I awoke. I couldn't remember a time when my eyelids had been as heavy as they were at that moment.

I moaned a monosyllabic question that I had intended to sound like, "Pardon me, good sir. I am desperately trying to catch up on the rest I so urgently need. What might I do for you at this moment?" but I'm sure it sounded more like, "Uuuuuuuhhhnnn?"

My lips were cracked and throat was hoarse. Taylor lifted a wooden cup to my face and tilted it until the cool liquid spilled over. As soon as the contents touched my lips, I found renewed energy and tried to gulp the nectar of the gods.

"Slowly, John. You don't want to make yourself sick."

Sick? Who the hell did he think he was talking to? Vampires didn't get sick.

My red-rimmed eyes looked up at Taylor, who had traded his armor for silken clothes that looked modern minus the fabric choice.

He pulled the cup away from me and I reached out with numb hands to try and grab his wrists.

"More," I croaked. "More blood."

Taylor smiled, but there was no humor in his eyes.

"It's water," he said softly.

I turned my attention from the cup to his face to study his expression. He wasn't lying.

"What?" I asked dubiously, shifting my focus back to the cup that now seemed more mysterious than any artifact or relic ever discovered. "How?" My sluggish mind raced to find answers, but it was so hard to think. All I wanted to do was sleep. Yes, sleep. That sounded nice.

My eyes blinked as my head became too heavy to support, and I lay back on the softest pillow I had ever felt. Then sleep took me in its loving embrace.

The sound of footsteps echoed outside the wooden door of the room I was in, prompting me to pop an angry eye open and glare at it. I willed whomever had heavy feet to go away. Before my eye closed again, I wondered how the sun had moved from the ceiling a moment ago to where it now began disappearing on the floor.

A hand rested on my forehead and I awoke with a start. Taylor smiled down at me, holding a bowl of something that was steaming. Oh God, it smelled so irresistibly good!

"Sit up, please. I've brought soup," Taylor announced, setting another pillow against the wall so I could move into an upright, seated position. My body felt like it was filled with heavy tar as I sluggishly moved.

Taylor began spoon-feeding me. My hands were still too uncoordinated to do the job. The hot soup was divine, even as good as most blood I had imbibed over the centuries. Chunks of brown meat floated around, along with vegetables and some sort of flat noodle.

I began to simultaneously cry while eating the delectable food. I felt so helpless, and empty.

Taylor didn't say anything about my sobbing or even acknowledge it, granting me a modicum of dignity.

"Where's Tiny Tim?"

"He's safe," Taylor told me with a smile. "He's waiting for you to get better, so eat up."

As I finished the entire bowl, which warmed my insides, I became sleepy again and began nodding off where I sat upright. I blinked my eyes and Taylor was smiling. Another blink and he was closing the door behind him. A third blink and the room was completely dark with only pale moonlight sneaking through the slit in the stone wall that acted as my window. The air was sweet, like flowers, and cool on my skin. I pulled the thick blankets higher up my chest. I drifted off again.

I was awoken by a familiar pressure below my waistline, and I lifted the blankets off my legs before stepping on the ice-cold stone floor. It almost took my breath away, it was so cold to me.

Looking around the room, I spotted a chamber pot and proceeded to do my business.

I climbed back in bed, moving the pillow that had been keeping me upright, and lay flat on the impossibly soft bed. My body sunk in slowly, like the mattress was trying to hug my body. After pulling the thick blankets up to my chin, I was embraced in warmth that promised everything was going to be okay. Then I was drifting through my dreams again.

It went on like this for an indeterminable amount of time. Taylor brought me water and food as I slept most of the days and nights. I continued to use the chamber pot, wondering when they were going to empty it.

My eyes opened at one point, and I was done sleeping. I couldn't explain it. Sufficed to say that I was just...done. I threw the covers off and rose to a seated position, resting my face in my hands. My beard felt weird against my palms, and my fingers started to inspect my facial hair. It felt dry and scraggly. Continuing to explore, my hands moved across the oily skin of my face.

"What the..." I tried to say, but my throat was dry and it hurt to talk. Looking around, I saw a cup, or maybe it was a chalice, on the nightstand next to my bed. I reached for it and greedily sucked down the now warm water inside. When I had gulped half the liquid, I pulled the cup from my face and inspected the water, wondering why it tasted different than before. It was...a flat, round taste instead of the sharp, refreshing one that had been my first cup.

"Isn't it funny how the taste of water is based largely on its temperature?" Taylor said from the doorway. I turned to see him leaning against the frame with a warm smile on his face. He looked well, with not a scar visible from our battle last night.

I stood, making my way to the chamber pot, and proceeded to empty my human bladder. Pulling my silk pajama bottoms back into place, I turned to see Taylor was no longer smiling.

"What?" I asked innocently.

Taylor wordlessly straightened from the doorframe of my room, walked the few steps directly in front of my entrance, and opened another door. It was a modern bathroom, complete with a porcelain throne and walk-in shower.

I looked from the bathroom to the pot on the ground and back to the bathroom. I pointed an index finger at the pot and said, "Not a chamber pot, is it?"

"No," Taylor sighed.

"It's some sort of priceless heirloom, isn't it?"

Taylor nodded with pursed lips as he stared at the pot with eyes that were almost unfocused.

I felt the need to change the subject, and fast.

"Why don't you have any cuts, bruises, or scars from last night?" I asked while my eyes roamed over his body.

"John, that was two weeks ago," he answered slowly.

"Two..." I tried to say before the world started to spin. My knees decided they didn't want to hold me up anymore, and I began to fall. I was vaguely aware of Taylor catching me and setting me back on the bed as I tried to catch my breath. My heart had begun playing a death metal double bass drum in my ears.

As I caught my breath and began slowing it down with an intense focus of will, my heart slowed with it.

"I-I've been asleep for two goddamned weeks?" I asked Taylor, desperate for an answer that would make my head stop spinning.

"I'm afraid so," he said, fully understanding my predicament. Something in my stomach stabbed just under my belly button, and I hunched over in pain.

"Ow. What the hell?" I asked.

"Why don't you go use the facilities, take a shower, and then we will get this all straightened out, okay?" he asked as if debating with a child about bedtime. In my infantile mortal state, I basically was a child.

"Why does my stomach hurt?" I asked as Taylor helped me across the hall and into the bathroom.

"I left you some reading material on the counter there," Taylor said, nodding toward where a large but thin book rested near the commode.

"O...kay?" I said as he shut the door, leaving me alone with the stabbing pain in my guts.

I shuffled over to where the book was and read the title. *Everyone Poops.*

"Huh?" I asked the empty room before realization struck and I started laughing. It was a welcomed laugh that seemed to invigorate my body and mind. The laugh grew in intensity until I had to place a hand on the counter to keep from doubling over. I took in a deep breath, ready to unleash my loudest and most powerful laugh yet, when I shit my silken pants, halting my laughter with a gasp. My head pivoted slowly, careful to not make matters worse, and I saw my surprised face in the mirror. My mouth was in a frozen O shape and my eyebrows were far north of their usual position. The sight of how ridiculous I looked made me want to laugh with renewed vigor, but I decided it was best to drop dirty trou and sit upon the unfamiliar throne.

Despite my many poop jokes, vampires did not defecate, so I had never sat on a modern toilet before. We did, however, pee out the excess liquid after processing the blood we had consumed. (Happy now, Reddit? Now you know.)

I tried to make myself laugh again, hoping I could coax the remaining waste out, but to no avail. After a few minutes of trying to force the situation, I sighed and let my head fall to the side as my eyes fixated on the children's book.

"Son of a..." I whispered in embarrassment as I lazily grabbed the book and turned to page one.

After two read-throughs, I had finished the job and remembered the important part about flushing. I tried tossing the large rectangular children's book into the small trash can next to the toilet, but it was too big and stuck out comically. It was as if my shame would not be forgotten and there was nothing I could do.

I went to pull up my pants when I noticed that they were, shall we say, not proper? and tossed them on top of the book that stuck out from the trash can.

Standing stark naked, I stepped into the shower and turned on the water. Freezing ice water shot needles into my skin that made me cry out in a pitch no man should ever be able to reach. My body responded on instinct, flattening against the back of the tiled shower while one leg rose as I pivoted, trying to shield my most important of body parts from the cold. I think it was too late, because I felt a strange sensation from Little John.

"Wait! Where are you going!" I cried out to my crotch as my friend began to disappear inside the safety of my pelvis.

I could feel the cords standing out on my neck as trembling hands shot out to turn the knob toward the red sticker. Though it shouldn't have been possible according to modern physics, the water actually became colder, attempting to freeze my very soul!

"AAAAAHHHHHH!" I cried out as I slammed the shower handle in the opposite direction. This was all new shit I had never had to worry about as a damn vampire. Warm water sent pins and needles up my nerves where the water touched, and I began to relax with an, "Aaaahhhhh," escaping my mouth.

Steam began to fill the room, and I noticed my skin was starting to burn like I was near a fire.

"What the..." I started asking the air as I looked at my hands. Then molten lava began jettisoning from the showerhead, and my body did a repeat move from when I first got in. I slammed against the back wall, protecting my junk with my leg and pivoted hips, before a hand dared the inferno and smacked at the knob again. It rested dead center between Pluto and Hell itself.

"Who designed these things?!" I called out as the water began cooling to a tolerable, if not pleasant, temperature.

I tentatively stepped into the water, letting the warmth wash over my entire body. Standing under the stream, I opened my mouth and let it fill before puffing my cheeks and spitting it out like a fountain.

There were three dispensers hanging on the wall at chest level labeled *Body*, *Shampoo*, and *Conditioner*. I turned, letting the water run down my back as I stared at the drain. I had done a supreme job of cleaning with toilet paper, considering I hadn't done it in nearly six centuries. Then the water changed color a tad, and I stopped mentally high-fiving myself for attaining expert status after my first try at something new.

I reached behind and pumped the body dispenser about ten times before running my hand up my crack like a fickle credit card machine. My eyes saw movement and I looked up into the bathroom mirror that was almost fogged over, except for a tiny circle where I could perfectly see my shame.

I gritted my teeth and repeated the process two more times, letting the water clear the soap between each session. I moved on to the rest of my body before first shampooing, and then conditioning, my beard and long hair.

My muscles, which I hadn't noticed felt stiff, relaxed, and the shower became one of the most relaxing moments in my life. Even after I was completely clean, I stood under the stream, letting it beat against my face as my mind remained empty.

I thought of nothing. Not of the battle. Not of how Baleius had betrayed me. Not even how I had saved all of creation from annihilation. None of it mattered. Only the warm, relaxing water mattered.

After what felt like a few hours, I turned the water off, grabbed a white fluffy towel, and dried off. My hands were pruney, and I couldn't stop looking at them. A bout of sneezing came over me as cool air swirled from out of nowhere, mixing with the steam of the shower. I looked around but couldn't find an AC vent.

"Fae magic," I reassured myself as I turned to the foggy mirror.

Using the now damp towel to wipe off a section of condensation on the mirror, I looked at myself as if for the first time.

A thinner man with a wild beard stared back at me with light brown eyes. I wiped at the mirror with more vigor, trying to free up more visible space at which to look over myself.

My stomach was flatter, with only a little pudge around my waist now. The cheeks under my eyes were more pronounced.

"I have cheekbones!" I said to my reflection as I poked at them with an index finger. A fingernail that was longer than I was used to pressed into my skin. I pulled my hand away and looked at the few millimeters of white at the tip of my nails, and scrunched my brow.

I began opening drawers and cabinets until I found a pair of silk boxers, house pants, and a relaxed-fit pullover shirt. Taylor was exceedingly considerate, and I had to give him props.

Making my way out of the bathroom, I noticed a Fae hauling away my priceless heirloom/chamber pot. I wanted to say something, because I thought they were all dead, but then I remembered the small number of Fae that had escaped with Taylor and I when Oberon had first attacked.

I wondered down the hallways, aimless and uncaring of the destination. All I wanted to do was live in the now and see everything that I could.

My bare toes stepped over the moss that was once again growing across the floor, staking its claim and proclaiming its victory over the cold, dead stone. Where the moss grew, I could see living wood underneath.

I glanced out a window onto a bright, sunlit scene. I could see on the ground that small puffs of shadows grew along the skeleton limbs of Yggdrasil. Leaning out the window, I turned to look straight up and saw green patches of leaves growing on the once nearly dead tree. And it made me feel warm inside my chest. I knew then that Faerie was going to be okay.

After ten or fifteen minutes of walking around, I found Taylor in an impressive bedroom at the end of a long hallway. He was hunched over a table covered in scrolls with an inkwell and quill near the edge. I could tell by his face that he was concentrating intently on the document in front of him.

I leaned against the doorframe and crossed my arms with a smile. The silk felt ridiculously good against my freshly cleaned skin.

When Taylor didn't notice, I brought a fist up to my mouth and pretended to clear my throat. He looked up at me, startled, before his features relaxed.

"How was your shower? Refreshing, I hope."

"Thanks for the book," I said sincerely. I would always remember how Taylor had treated me with respect and dignity when I was at my most vulnerable.

"It's been a few years since you've had to deal with the human condition," he said with a gleam in his eye before looking me up and down. "I see you found the clothing I chose for you."

"Yes, it's very comfortable. Thank you," I said as I walked to where Taylor stood. "What are you looking at?"

Taylor looked down at the scroll and said, "I'm trying to figure out how to best rebuild the throne, now that I am king of all Faerie."

"Whoa, there. King?" I asked, placing a hand on his shoulder with a shit-eating grin plastered across my face. I was beyond excited for my friend.

"Someone has to do it, and I'm afraid there aren't many of my kind left."

"Well, I know Faerie is in good hands, then." I patted his shoulder twice before lowering my hand to regard the scroll. "Anything wrong with the throne? You seemed engrossed in whatever you had found."

Taylor pointed to a section above the throne that connected to the portal above. "See this? This was supposed to only be a window—a vanity window if you will. Not some portal to Mab's prison." Taylor tapped on the parchment a few times as he thought. "Someone made it like this on purpose. They *knew* it could—and would—be used as a doorway to the Shadow Court." Taylor stood up while keeping his eyes on the scroll, as if doing so might provide a different vantage point.

"Why would someone do that?" I asked, crossing my arms.

"That's the thing that has been bugging me," Taylor said as he locked eyes with me. "I can't figure that out."

We looked at each other before he returned his eyes to the throne room blueprints.

"Well, the good news is that you'll fix that now, won't you?"

"Hmm? Oh yes, without a doubt. Without a doubt," he repeated.

I decided it was best to leave him to his mystery.

"I'm going to find something to eat and then go lie naked in the grass," I said as I turned to try and find the kitchen.

"Hmm? Right...naked..." Taylor mimicked the words without absorbing what I had said.

It took another twenty minutes before I found the kitchen in the enormous castle. Once I passed a hallway with the smell of cooking meat, all I had to do was follow it from there.

There were two dwarves cooking a small feast inside the industrial-sized kitchen. It felt empty with only the three of us in the room that was meant to house an entire staff. I wondered, then, how many Fae were left alive. It made my heart feel cold and heavy the longer I thought about it.

One of the dwarves walked up to me, holding a plate of grilled meat and baked veggies.

"Thank you for saving Faerie. Thank you for saving Yggdrasil and the nine realms. You're a hero," the dwarf said with a deep, gruff voice. As I took the plate, he lightly grabbed my wrists, squeezing once before nodding and releasing them to return to his duties. I didn't know what to say. I know what you're thinking. "You? John the Vampire doesn't know what to say?" And I'm here to confirm the myth as being true: I, John Cook, couldn't come up with anything humorous or witty…and that was okay right then.

I didn't feel like myself because I was missing a huge part of my identity that had been with me since 1480. I felt like a boat drifting in the ocean without an engine or even a paddle. I was simply letting the current take me where it may.

I stepped through the kitchen and into a long dining hall. Like, it was really long, meant to house several hundred guests at a time.

Sitting at the end of the table closest to the kitchen, I took the metal fork and knife and began cutting into the meat. It was a strange motion, and I had to talk myself through it. Insert fork near edge, use knife to cut around fork, put food into mouth, and this is the important part: chew. I learned that last one really quickly as I choked on my first big bite. I also might have bitten my tongue once or ten times.

The meat was juicy and warm on my throbbing tongue, and I moaned in ecstasy. My fork pierced through some carrots that had been cooked in some sort of oil or butter with herbs on top. I inserted them into my mouth and began chewing. They were crunchy and delicious.

A female elf in a tight purple dress similar to a maid's outfit approached with a chalice. She set it down, touched my hand gingerly, and said, "Thank you, hero," before giving me a light peck on the cheek and turning to exit the room and leave me alone with her words. Her lips, though brief as the contact had been, had felt amazing against my cheek.

I watched after her, my chewing slowing as I replayed what she had said in my mind over and over on a loop. I didn't feel like a hero right now. I felt…empty and alone, which was fitting considering Batman was my favorite character.

I looked at the chalice that had a dark red liquid inside, picked it up, and smelled the contents. It wasn't blood, like I was accustomed to. It was…wine, I think. I had always wanted to taste wine. It had been a luxury we could never afford on the farm. Only water and goat's milk were readily available.

I put my lips on the cup and let the wine slowly enter my mouth. I savored it for a few moments before letting it slide down my throat. It burned a little and left an odd aftertaste. Plus, it was really sweet and bitter at the same time.

"I don't think I like wine," I said to the room after I swallowed another mouthful to test my hypothesis.

After a few minutes, I had eaten my entire plate and was still hungry. I also noticed I had consumed the entire glass of wine, all except for one last little mouthful. Shrugging my shoulders, I tilted the cup back and drank the remaining liquid before setting the cup on the table. I missed, and it clattered to the ground.

My head reflexively shot to follow the cup, and I noticed how light-headed I had become.

"Maybe...maybe I like wine," I said again before little titters of laughter escaped my mouth.

The weight of the world seemed to melt from my shoulders, and I pushed back on my chair to get up. I was in the pleasant valley of being tipsy rather than drunk, and felt wonderful.

After making my way through the castle, I exited through the open gates and into the city. Yggdrasil was in the process of taking back the land from the stone that had swallowed it, and I smiled without really thinking about why. I just felt...*good*, right now.

I walked down the streets with my arms out to my sides, feeling the warm rays of the Faerie sun kissing my skin. I even closed my eyes, tilting my face skyward as I walked. I could have tripped if I had kept my eyes closed, but right then, nothing mattered.

As I made my way outside the city and into the open fields beyond, I took off all my clothes and lay in the blades of grass as they swayed in the gentle breeze. Flowers were blooming and I could smell their sweet aroma coaxing me like a perfume.

I lay there, naked in the field, soaking up the sun with my eyes closed, when a shadow formed above me. I squinted an eye open and saw the outline of a fit female figure standing above me, blocking the rays.

"Hello, lover," Lily purred in greeting.

My stomach dropped and I told the guards on the ice wall I had built around my heart to remain vigilant. We had prepared for this and nothing would stop us.

Lily's clothes disappeared into the breeze as if they had been made of sand and stepped on either side of my hips, offering me a view of the holy grail.

I gulped as she crouched over me, resting her most intimates on top of mine.

I immediately sent a signal to my member, commanding it to not respond. "Don't you do it!" I screamed inwardly.

He must not have had his headphones on, because my emergency radio message wasn't received.

"Oh, eager, I see," Lily cooed with fluttering eyes as she began rocking back and forth, forcing my soldier to commit treason.

The ice wall around my heart was torn free and cast into a violent volcano, leaving it defenseless, while a ball gag muffled the protests of my mind.

My mouth became dry, and I could hear my heart in my ears again as we became one. Then she couldn't hold back anymore and began passionately kissing me. I didn't even try and resist, nor did I really care at that moment. I hated her. I loved her. And I hated that I loved her.

While in the throes of passion, I felt a connection to someone familiar, and it made my tears flow. They streamed to my ears before disappearing into my thick hair.

Either Lily didn't notice or she gave me the respect to not mention my tears as we made sweet, passionate love. In those moments, I realized somewhere deep in my mind that I had never actually made love until this moment.

My body yearned for her touch while my mind became a dark void while we made love. Even though it was silent, I knew there was going to be Hell to pay after we were done. Even during the passionate lovemaking, I could feel the cold anger emanating from inside my disapproving, calculating mind, distracting me with the battle between my heads.

After a few minutes of this, I told my brain to shut the hell up, and began focusing on the moment. My return kisses became passionate, matching Lily's hunger. I pulled on her long, wavy hair as she rode on top of me before letting my fingernails glide down her back, leaving marks. She moaned as I planted my feet and began bucking my hips while gently kneading her sensitive breasts. I pulled on her hair, hard, moving her head to the side and exposing her neck. I bit down, but not in my usual attempt to draw blood. My goal was to provide as much sensual bliss as I could to my partner, who was helping to distract me from my self-loathing and despair.

Once it was obvious she was about to climax, I focused on joining her, and we cried out together in that grassy field.

She lay on top of me, breathing hard, while lightly kissing the skin around my face with me still inside her. Her body glistened with sweat in the sunlight, and she smelled sweeter than any flower could ever hope to be.

"I...I lo..." I started to say, feeling the tears returning as my throat tightened.

She lifted her head to stare at me directly in the eyes, worry in her expression. There was a twinkle there, too, signifying a deep eagerness for me to finish what I had started to say.

"What's wrong, John? What do you want to tell me?" she asked with a sweet, soft voice made entirely of silk.

"I...wish I could trust you," I said, wiping the warm streams that ran on either side of my eyes.

Her features softened as she looked from my right eye to my left and back again. "I wish you could, too," she replied, lifting her hips slightly so that we separated. "All you need to know is that I have your best interests in mind. I will do anything to help keep you safe, even from yourself." As she finished, she kissed each of my tear-filled eyelids and then vanished, leaving me alone in the field.

My mind ferociously regained control, chastising me for opening myself up for further heartache. My heart and body, having achieved the connection they had so desperately desired, cowered in the corner, all the energy sapped from them.

I sobbed in that field. I sobbed as the breeze tried to console me by caressing my skin. I sobbed as the blades of grass attempted to embrace me, letting me know everything was going to be okay. I sobbed...because I was alone.

Baleius had been with me since Ulric had spilled his blood down my throat. For over five hundred years, I had relied on him to keep me safe while aiding in the hunt. Now, I was afraid to face him again in the real world. Baleius had shown his true colors when he had thought he had the upper hand with the celestial armor. It had only been by sheer luck and his own hubris that I had been able to disarm him...and myself. "*Your greatest strength...*" Lachesis echoed through my mind. The most significant gift I had ever received from someone that had been like a father to me, and I would never be able to wear it again.

Da had sacrificed himself so that I might live, and now remained only as a whisper in my mind that I didn't even know if it was real or just hopeful wishing. Da—the angel Raziel—who had set me down the path of salvation, was gone.

Continuing down the road of self-pity, I thought about Lily...oh, Lily. She had my heart hostage, and knew it. My love for her was caged in barbed wire; the more it grew, the more it pierced and tore at my scarred heart.

A beam of light pierced the dark clouds of sorrow. Depweg. Depweg had been, and would always be, there for me. The sentiment was mutual. I would do anything for my best friend and brother. I wanted to rush right now and see him, but I think he needed his own space for now. He had been through a lot, losing Dawson and Joey—

"Joey!" I cried out, sitting up straight. My mind raced to replay what Lolth had said through Dawson's mouth. "We turned him to the dark side," she had said. Even if he had been taken by the darkness, Lolth was dead, and that had freed those that had been infected.

I lay back down in the grass, letting my heart settle again as I thought. Joey was fine, I was sure of it. He was fine.

Something tickled the back of my mind, and I realized what I could do to help Depweg out when I returned.

"But when will I return?" I asked lackadaisically, my words disappearing with the breeze. My mortal mind had had enough self-punishment for today and had decided it was best to take a nap in the warm field. "Guess I'll know...when I know."

Chapter 26

Six months passed. Six months of clean food, bright sun, and manual labor with the Fae as we rebuilt the throne. It took so long to do because Taylor added runes, sigils, and other protective markings which—as Ludvig had taught me—took time. Even with Taylor's unparalleled craftsmanship, it was a labor of love.

Time was odd for me in Faerie. Not because of any time dilation—that was the least of my concerns during my stay—but because my memory was dulled. I could remember some events of the last six months, but mostly, everything ran together except a few key moments. I couldn't recall every moment of every day like I could as a vampire, but I could remember how I'd felt. It's funny. I'd never realized how much time and effort I spent sorting and filing memories in my information city until I didn't have to anymore. God, humans had it so easy sometimes.

My skin darkened to a healthy tan. My reddish beard and black hair grew wild and long. Thick, defined muscles could be seen through skin laced with bulging veins that formed a road map over my body. I even had a six pack for the first time, well, ever.

Tiny Tim was with me almost every second of every day, content to oblige my request for puppy kisses and cuddles whenever I wanted. It warmed my beating heart to see how happy he was, and he brought me true joy when I needed it most.

A lot of time was spent with Lily as we intimately got to know one another, and for the first time, not just carnally. Though my icy heart walls had melted, my dubious mind kept its defenses on high alert; always doubting, always questioning Lily's every action.

We did yoga together every morning as the sun came up before running through the beautiful nature trails of Faerie. Often, we stopped in the middle of the run to make passionate love against a tree or a few paces off the beaten path. One morbid advantage about having most of the citizens of Faerie gone was privacy, even in the open.

She spent every night with me, alternating who was the big and little spoon as we slept. Tim, who slept near my feet, would growl if she got too close to him. His loyalty was to me, and he could probably sense my indecision about the woman I shared my bed with. Lily paid Tim no mind when he was being a little poo-head, but I could see her look at me with hurt eyes every time the puppy vocalized his dislike of her. We both knew Tim was reading my hidden emotions like an open book. I knew I loved her, but I also knew I was a fool for doing so. It was an ever-raging war between my heart and brain.

However, I remember one night when I woke up after a dream where I had lost her and just staring at Lily's breathing form under the moonlight. It had been a dream that had felt real, and I had watched her die in front of me. The pain had felt real, and I think my mind opened the gate of possibility and acceptance a little that night.

As time went on, Tiny Tim began to accept Lily as a part of my life, though he still showed his displeasure from time to time. Part of me was worried that meant I was speeding down the highway of love in the rain and without my seat belt on.

When I wasn't with Lily, I spent time wondering the castle and reading everything I could get my hands on. Not having Wi-Fi—or was it Wu-Fi…Wo-Fi? I couldn't remember that fine detail as a human—gave me all the time in the world to improve my body and mind.

I practiced combat with the Fae every chance I got. I became proficient at bows, swords, pikes, and a multitude of other weapons that I had relied on my vampirism—and Baleius—to control. Now I was confident I could hold the wheel on my own.

I trained close-quarter combat with Taylor when he wasn't busy running a kingdom and both High Courts.

Elves taught me agility, balance, and proficiency with different bows such as cross, recurve, compound, and long.

Dwarves increased my strength and muscle mass, as well as increasing my toughness. When we had first started, I had been scared to break a thin plank of wood with my mortal hands. Before I left, I was shattering cinder blocks.

Trolls showed me speed, reconnaissance, and javelin skills; both long-distance throwing and close-quarter deflections and attacks. After months of training, I was able to twirl a bow staff better than any movie could portray.

And one morning I woke up, looked in the mirror, and knew I was ready to stop doubting myself. It was time to face my fears.

One of the portals had been reconstructed, and Taylor and I stood amidst a small gathering to bid me farewell.

I had my gray beanie and trench coat on, but everything else was custom-made clothing because what I used to wear would no longer fit my lean frame. The Doc Martens were still fine, but Taylor had offered me some elven-crafted boots. Not only did they look cool as hell, but they felt indescribably comfortable. The material for the pants and long sleeve shirt had been made from the silk of Faerie spiders that lived somewhere deep in the forbidden forest. Taylor had told me that, though soft and malleable, the clothing would protect me from most nonmagical attacks, including modern human weapons. They also breathed like cotton, which was a bonus.

My hair and beard had been groomed and shaped to the point where people were bound to ask, "Maybe he was born with it?" to which I would respond, "Maybe you should mind your own business and shut up," while being secretly flattered. Not to toot my own horn, but I felt like I could be a romance cover model. Then again, I had felt like that my entire life, so not much of a point of reference to go on.

I felt good. I felt confident. I was John Cook, the Vampire, and I was ready to wear that mantle with a renewed pride.

"Thank you, everyone," I said as I spoke to the room. Then I stepped forward and embraced my friend. Taylor had been there for me when I'd needed him most. He had been by my side when we had stared down Armageddon. He had given me purpose when I had been nothing but a simple mortal. Faerie had rebounded, and under Taylor's leadership, I was sure it would thrive.

"Ready, lover?" Lily asked, placing her hand in mine and lacing our fingers. I set down the large bag that contained the celestial armor as I looked into her beautiful purple eyes and planted a kiss on her forehead.

"I need to do this alone," I explained with warm eyes and a slight smile that I hoped conveyed to her that everything was going to be alright.

She nodded in understanding before throwing her arms around my neck and kissing me deeply. To her, I might as well have been a soldier going off to a war that I might not come home from.

"Make sure Tim gets home, would ya?" I asked as I kissed the top of her head.

"Of course," she said softly. I knew it was asking a lot from her to travel to my home, but the guys would have to understand. Or not. I supposed I really didn't care either way.

She lifted her head and stared into my eyes, as if she were waiting for something.

"What?" I asked with a little laugh. I loved it when she was cute and coy.

"Say it for me, just once," she asked with a voice that was half cute, half sincere.

"You first," I responded through a smile.

She took a breath right as Tiny Tim ran up and put his front paws up on my calves, yipping his excitement.

Lily looked at me, smiled, and planted a kiss on the tip of my nose.

We broke our embrace, letting our fingertips hold one another for a few moments, desperate for more time, before I consciously pulled away. I knew we could have stood there for an eternity and not said what the other so desperately wanted to hear.

Picking up the bag of armor, I turned to face the portal which shimmered to life, took a deep breath, and prepared to face the mess beyond the door that I had run away from.

Chapter 27

I stepped through the portal and felt the immediate rush of ancient power flooding back into me. I clenched my teeth and balled my hands into fists as I fought to maintain control.

I willed myself inside the control room of my mind and saw a bewildered Baleius frantically searching his body for the armor that was no longer there.

What have you done?! Baleius demanded on the verge of madness. His eyes were wild, and spittle flew as he yelled.

I stared at him, unmoving, with an emotionless face.

Say something, you fool! Where is my armor!

I remained motionless, which apparently pissed him off because he charged forward with red eyes and elongated fangs.

I pivoted to the side and leaned back, letting him sail through the air where I had just been standing. Baleius landed on the ground on all fours, turned, and leaped again. This time, I allowed him to get close before grabbing both of his wrists, falling to my back with my feet planted on his midsection, and launching him with my legs to the wall as I rolled backward and onto my feet. He landed upside down, cracking his head on the floor as he fell.

Baleius scrambled to his feet, cursing in hellion as he did.

You are nothing without me. NOTHING! How many times have I saved your pathetic life, mortal? HOW MANY?!

Countless, I admitted calmly.

This threw Baleius off, who stood a little straighter as I relented to his point.

Then you know I mustn't be stopped. Give me the armor, and I will take control and keep us alive, Baleius asserted hesitantly as he approached the steering wheel of my mind. He lifted both hands to place them on the wheel. I let him.

Once they touched it, the wheel vanished from existence. There had been no dramatic element to it. No puff of smoke or blinding flash; it was simply, gone.

Baleius shrieked, letting his features that had once perfectly mirrored mine to morph into the bat demon I had seen on the battlefield.

Through a voice that was no longer similar to mine, the monster snarled, *Death it is then, mortal. One way or the other, I will have that armor and rule over the cosmos. It is my destiny.*

Baleius, now in full demon form, leaped at me with his imposing claws outstretched. Lifting my hand palm up, the demon Baleius froze in midair. Confused, he tried struggling while crying out in frustration and rage.

Thing is, I began with complete ease in my voice, *this is my body. I thought I needed you, but that was before. I was weak. I doubted myself. I relied on you, demon, to do the heavy lifting. But no more.*

As I finished, I held my free hand, palm up, in front of me. The Lament Configuration from *Hellraiser* appeared, otherwise known as the puzzle box.

My fingers wrapped around the golden-and-black cube and began a specific pattern of movement across its surface. The box hissed and began to open as if made from two identical parts that had been slid together, interlacing seamlessly. They sat, one on top of the other, before the top part turned forty-five degrees and collapsed. Instead of a cube, the Configuration made more of a Celtic cross that opened at the top.

Baleius struggled to pull away as an unseen force began pulling him into the cube I had manifested. Batlike ears flapped forward as if blown from behind by a jet engine's exhaust. Baleius fought to keep from being sucked into his iconic horror movie prison, but this was my mind. I no longer needed him. Just as my fear of losing him after returning from Faerie the first time had given him strength, now my assuredness siphoned the stolen power back into me.

You...need...me! he cried out as his legs were pulled into the void, followed by his hips. His torso elongated before disappearing into the Configuration, then his arms. Panicked eyes searched desperately for a way out before his head vanished and the cube closed behind him.

The puzzle box lifted, rotated, and became a solid cube once again, a satisfying hiss sounding as it closed. I tossed the prison in the air once, caught it, and set it down on the coffee table that had appeared in front of my brand-new reclining couch. The wheel was no longer needed now that I—and I alone—was in control.

As I plopped onto the black leather couch, a form appeared sitting next to me.

My limbs shot out in front of me as if I were falling before a familiar laugh calmed my nerves.

"Dear me, John. Bloody took you long enough," Da said. He was normal human size as he sat next to me.

"Da?" I asked, disbelieving. My air of badassery and confidence gave way to childlike wonder. "How can—Is it...is it really you?"

"Did you or did you not take me into your own essence when you drank my blood."

"I did what you told me to!" I protested.

"That you did," Da said, resting a hand on my arm in appreciation. His smile was welcoming, like a relative that you respected saying how proud they were of you.

"Why are you only just now showing yourself? What was with all the Obi-Wan guidance?"

"Baleius kept me at bay with his indomitable determination. I also didn't need to manifest inside your mind to influence you, now did I?"

"I used the force just like you told me to," I joked.

"Precisely why I didn't feel the need to fight Baleius. It was also advantageous to let him think he was winning the battle. I was afraid that once he had my armor, he could overtake your mind. His constant focus on me kept him distracted," Da admitted with a wink.

"Then why let me have your armor and gladius?" I asked, knowing it was a stupid question once it had left my mouth and entered my own ears.

"I never doubted you could beat him, John," Da said sincerely.

I leaned over and embraced my friend in an awkward sitting-on-the-couch hug.

"So, does this mean you are here, with me, for like, ever?" I asked hopeful as I pulled away. A tear ran down my cheek in joy.

"No, I'm afraid not. Though I will always be with you in spirit, my road ends here. Your journey, on the other hand, has just begun."

"But why can't you come with me?" I asked, feeling my chest constrict as my vision became blurry.

"Because you don't need me to," Da said with a soft, compassionate voice. He began turning translucent, the air twinkling where his skin faded.

"I believe in you, John. I always have," he said as he beamed a smile at me. "Remember, I won't always be here, but I'll always be with you," were his last words as he disappeared and the air went still.

Warm tears ran down my cheeks as I smiled at my friend and mentor's words. Then I placed my face in my hands and sobbed my goodbyes for the angel who had always seen the good in me.

Chapter 28

I sent my consciousness through the window of my soul, probably for the last time, regaining control over my body.

Looking around, I was surprised to see that I was not in the same cave as before. Recognition hit me like a brick to the face when I figured out I was in the mausoleum above my lair. There, in the center of the room, was the throne that was the hidden door. It had been fixed and left as good as new after Oberon had all but destroyed it.

Holding the bag of angelic armor, I pressed on the hidden switch and made my way to the front door underground. Raising my hand to knock, I pfft'ed myself and opened *my* door aggressively.

"Honey, I'm hoooooome!" I called into the illuminated lair. I noticed there were some new doors along the side.

"John? John, is that you?!" Locke called out from the recliner he was resting on with an old book on his lap. He slammed the book closed, set it on the coffee table, and rushed to greet me.

Tiny Tim scampered up to me, cutting in front of Locke and prompting me to drop to my knees and scoop him up in my arms. He wriggled with pure joy against my chest as I kissed the top of his little head. Tiny Tim, not Locke, by the way. Just wanted that to be clear.

"Who's this, then?" Locke asked as he approached.

"This wittle puppers is Tiny Tim. Can you say hewwo to the little warlock? Yes. Hewwo."

Locke fidgeted on his feet and then rushed to embrace me in an awkward holding-a-puppy hug. I guess he was grateful that the universe hadn't, you know, ended.

Locke was taller than I remembered, almost up to my own height now; the thought as to why created a small shadow in my mind.

"How long has it been this time?" I asked somberly as we embraced.

He pulled back, looked me in the eye, and said, "Three years."

"Oh. That's not *that* bad, all things considered," I said with a sigh of relief. "What's with the doors?" I asked, pointing around the room.

Joey exited one of them and regarded me with emotionless eyes. Then he saw Tiny Tim and I saw the briefest sparkle of light in them. I set the puppy down—who of course was no longer an actual puppy, but I shall keep calling him that because he was tiny—and watched as he rushed to Joey. They bonded immediately, and it was truly awesome to watch Joey's stiff demeanor melt in an instant.

Ludvig and Magni came through two more of the doors, answering my previous question. Magni was a full-grown man now, no longer a child. He had a thick five-o'clock shadow that accentuated his face nicely. In my absence, he had also been lifting weights with Ludvig, apparently, because he was no longer the skinny, scared kid from our battles with the darkness.

Magni nodded once while Ludvig crossed his arms.

"Where have you been?" Ludvig asked. "And how come you look...different? I didn't fink vampires could change deir appearance."

I felt the eyes of everyone in the room roam over my body, stopping at various points to acknowledge Ludvig's observation.

"Dude..." Locke started, letting his arms fall from around my narrow waist to poke at my stomach, "you're skinny now."

"Lean is the appropriate term," I corrected. No one who had spent months and months working out incredibly hard and maintaining a strict diet of organic food wanted to be called "skinny."

Joey smelled the air around me and said, "You're different."

"I've gone through some...changes," I said, finding the right words.

I caught the room up on the events of my time in Faerie: the final epic battle with Lolth, training with the Fae, spending time with Lily (much to Locke's disapproving expression), and becoming one with myself after battling Baleius for complete control.

"Let me get this straight," Locke began, pacing the room as he thought out loud. "The first time you went to Faerie was only for a few hours, but ten years passed here. Now you're telling me that you were there for six months, but only three years passed here? None of this adds up."

A picture of Lily lying in bed next to me, asleep and bathed in moonlight, flashed through my head.

"I don't know what to tell you, man. Parallel dimensions and all that jazz," I answered.

"What are you going to do with the armor?" Locke asked, careful not to offend.

I looked down at the bag next to me, feeling the power it represented practically radiating from it.

"I need to keep it safe. Store it."

"Store it where?" Locke asked, looking around the now tight confines of the Fortress of Solitaire.

"With Val," I answered. "He will probably want this back, too." As I finished, Mjolnir, which I had always felt on my hip, shimmered into existence before flying into my outstretched hand. Everyone in the room made an "Oooh" sound in amazement; all except Ludvig, who stared intently at the Nordic weapon.

"I'm going to see him now, and then Father Thomes. Do you know how he is, by the way?" I asked Locke as Mjolnir flew back to my hip before winking back out of existence.

"He's fine. Doc has been providing his aging solution, though the price went up for some reason," Locke said.

"Yeah, about that. A lot of enchantments and whatnot are about to get super pricey and rare. Most of the Fae are dead, so there's not a lot of supply anymore."

"Oh. That's unfortunate," Locke said, lowering his head to stare at the ground. I assumed a lot of what he did as a warlock involved enchantments, spells, and other hocus-pocus mumbo jumbo.

I could feel Ludvig continued to stare at my hip.

"Welp, look at the time. I really must be off to Val and then Papa T," I said as I hoisted the bag over my shoulder and began walking to the door.

"Wait," Locke said quickly. I turned to look at him and quickly took in the expression of anxiety on his face.

"What?" I asked, my eyes shifting from person to person, seeking any clue I could find. My gaze lingered on Joey, who stared at the ground and shook his head slowly, not wanting to believe what Locke was about to tell me.

"What?!" I demanded. Then the missing puzzle piece fell into place. "Where's Depweg?" I asked angrily, letting the bag drop to the ground as I squared my body to the room.

"We don't know," Locke said slowly.

"What the fuck do you mean you don't fucking know?!" I bellowed, losing my temper. When my own ferocity took me by surprise, I began to look inward and tell Baleius to knock it off, then I remembered...

I closed my eyes, took a deep breath, and cleared my throat. "Where is he?" I asked calmly, with a degree of effort.

Ludvig stepped forward, braving the danger that was my wrath, and said, "I tracked him for a while, but lost the scent somewhere over de Mexican border where I stood out among de locals."

"John, there have been reports of vicious maulings all across Mexico," Locke informed me with a steady voice, as if one wrong syllable might set me off.

"He-he's probably just letting off some steam. You know, killing the cartels and stuff," I said hesitantly, knowing my words were bullshit.

"He's killed innocents. The news are saying entire families related to known offenders, like those from the cartels, are being targeted by the unknown animals."

"It makes sense if you think about it," I pleaded lamely. "If you remove all the pieces from the board, there will be no cartels left."

"*Entire* families, John. Women and children with the misfortune of having a male in the immediate family be a part of a cartel. Even the elderly who live with their children. Jonathan has...Jonathan has lost his mind."

"No. *NO*," I yelled, vehemently shaking my head. "I don't believe you. I don't...bel-believe...ya-you," I began to hyperventilate as my world spun. My face and fingers went numb as I collapsed to my knees.

"It's true," Joey said. "He's gone feral." That stopped me in my tracks.

"Recently, a video briefly showing him surfaced," Locke told me as he made an L shape with his left-hand index finger and thumb. I noticed the screen was bigger than last time.

"So? All the supes are dead, right? No one will hunt him down except the humans," I said with a modicum of hope.

"Look," Locke instructed as he walked next to me to show me his screen.

What I saw took my breath away. A blood-covered werewolf crouched to enter a doorway. He walked on two legs, with muscular arms ending in clawed fingers instead of paws.

"That's not him," I said, pointing a shaking finger at the bipedal monster. "Depweg's got four legs, not two."

Joey stepped forward, "His mind and body have fused. Depweg is no longer Depweg."

"I-I-I don't understand," I stammered.

"His mind broke, John," Locke said softly.

Joey added, "Allowing the wolf to take over. A feral wolf is a real problem. Entire countrysides were wiped out in the old days. Now that there's a video, it won't take long for the humans to try silver."

"Where is he now?" I queried flatly, depressed at the situation unfolding.

"We'll get you the information while you are out and try at an approximate location," Locke said as he closed his hand, clearing the picture of my brother as a monster. "Once you get to that area, I'll do a tracking spell using one of the teeth he left in the Hummer."

"Three years and you kept those, huh?" I asked, getting to my feet. I didn't really care why, I just wanted to poke fun at him. I picked up the bag and turned to face the door.

"When he didn't come back, I thought it pertinent..."

"I'm just fucking with you. Now fix my room up nice while I'm out, would ya?" I called back to the room as I opened the front door and made my way up the stairs.

I walked through the cemetery—the bag of armor clanking with every step—alone with my thoughts on what was to come. Would I be able to save Depweg? Or would I have to put him down like a rabid dog. Father Thomes would know what to do.

At Valenta's Saloon, I caught Val up on the entire story just as I had done with my friends. Once done, I followed Val into the basement where an empty box waited at the end of the line from the others. Val opened the lid and revealed cutouts in the black foam that seemed to fit the angelic armor perfectly, as if it had been made for it.

"Where's the other set?" Val asked without his accent.

"Taylor and I agreed to keep them separate," I said.

"Hmph," Val responded with a slight nod of the head. He didn't like it, but knew it was probably the smartest thing to do.

"Oh, what about this?" I said, poking out my hip and letting the Nordic hammer of the gods shimmer to life.

Val regarded it for a moment before looking up at me.

"Keep it. I think you've earned it."

"Neat!" I said, picking up the hammer and waving it around.

"Be warned," Val started with a serious tone to his voice.

"Of course, here it comes," I said melodramatically while rolling my eyes. "Are you going to say, 'With great power comes great taxes,' or some other sentiment that may or may not be trademarked?"

"Showing your full hand may invite challenge from those that think they can beat you."

"And that means?" I waved my hand in a "come on" gesture.

"You are dense, aren't you? I don't know how much clearer I can be. Did you trade brain cells for muscles or something?" Val chided before shaking his head in exhaustion. "Just be careful with how you use items like that. I'm trusting you, John. Don't make me regret that."

"I won't," I said honestly. "Probably."

Val closed the lid on the armor, placed it on the shelf, and turned to make his way out of the basement.

While standing near the kitchen door, Val extended a hand out to me. I looked down at it and back up to him before grasping his hand in mine. We shook then, and I knew I had done the right thing with the armor.

"You did good. Raziel would be proud."

"I know," I said softly with a warm, knowing smile.

Outside, I extended my wings and was disappointed to see they were comprised of my blood again. Though they felt and performed like the real deal, it just wasn't the same.

I flapped once and flew the short distance to the church. Knowing I had lost the pendant, I decided it was best to go down the chimney again.

"Ugh," I complained as I wiped soot from my custom-made elvish clothing as I stepped into the parlor. I took off my gray beanie and shook my head back and forth quickly, sending a shower of white ash to the ground in front of the fireplace.

After replacing my beanie and patting my trench coat clean, I looked at the ground and realized I had made a mess.

"Eh, I'll let Father—"

"You'll let Father Thomes do what, exactly?" a familiar elderly voice called out from behind me.

I jumped three feet in the air and turned to land facing a very annoyed Father Thomes, who was reading a book in his favorite chair.

"Oh, ah, hi, Papa T!" I said, waving a hand back and forth quickly. More soot flew from my gesture, and I quickly grabbed my waving hand and brought it to my chest. "Um, it was like that when I got here."

Closing his book and setting it beside the lamp on the table next to him, Father Thomes looked at me and asked, "Where's the pendant?"

"Lost it," I lied but also kind of told the truth.

"Mm-hmm. And where have you been?"

"On vacation."

"John..." Father Thomes said, removing his glasses and giving me the "don't you dare lie to me" look.

Sighing, I told him the whole story, which felt like I had told a million times already. I was getting good at acting out all the important parts.

"And then I said, 'Don't worry, Lolth! I bet you'll enjoy the darkness on the other side!' And-and-and she died." As I finished, I plopped back in the chair next to him, letting my feet fly up for a second before crashing back to the ground in dramatic fashion—which was my favorite kind of fashion.

Father Thomes didn't seem amused by my now usual antics and asked with a slightly annoyed tone, "You've had quite the adventure, haven't you?"

"Everything...um...okay?" I asked, unsure of what I had done.

Father Thomes leaned forward in his chair, and I noticed for the first time that he looked rejuvenated, sprier than the last time I'd seen him. I'd have to thank Doc for his help. Maybe give him a fat ol' bonus.

"What part of 'if you die, the apocalypse will happen' do you not seem to fully comprehend, my son?"

I. Got. Mad.

"Oh, I don't know," I exploded. "Maybe the part about a fucking black hole coming to eat Earth, all while a Lilith-damned plague ate at the world tree." I finished by slamming my hands down on the armrests of the chair, audibly breaking them with the sound of splintering wood.

I shook my head in disbelief, refusing to make eye contact with the priest.

After a few moments of uncomfortable silence, I aggressively added, "You're welcome, by the way."

"Something is different about you," Father Thomes said. I turned to see him staring at me with narrowed eyes.

I took a deep breath, held it, and let it out while saying, "Yeah. There's been some personnel changes upstairs, and I'm still dealing with the fallout."

"Hmm," Father Thomes hummed, still inspecting me. Then I remembered something important I had wanted to ask my old friend.

"Oh, I need your help with Depweg," I said, changing the subject. Father Thomes shifted his facial features and became concerned.

"What is it?" he asked. I caught him up on the situation Locke had just dropped on me.

"I don't know what I'm going to have to do, Father. If I can't talk him down...I-I-I," I stammered.

"Will have to put him down," Father Thomes finished for me.

Tears threatened to leap from my eyes. "I can't kill him, man. Not Depweg. He's my brother! I-I can't! I just...can't."

"When the time is right, you will know what must be done," Father Thomes said, clasping his hands in his lap as he sat back against his chair and stared into the room with unfocused eyes. "I will pray for him. And for you, my son."

"Thanks," was all I could manage as I wiped snot and tears from my face while sniffling.

After about five minutes of silent contemplation on both our parts, which allowed me to collect my emotions, I asked, "Oh, can you get me another pendant? I kind of liked that old one. It saved my ass once."

"What did happen to the one I gave you, John?"

My mind sprang to action, debating the pros and cons of the situation. If I told him the truth, he would probably ask about what the seer had said, and I didn't want to have to explain that she had seen the gates of Hell open. I also didn't want to admit that she had seen me kill Magni in her visions. Father Thomes hadn't been too happy with me when I'd murdered Magni's mother in a blood rage, and had actually imprisoned me for it. I wasn't confident he would let me off with a slap on the wrist if he knew what was coming.

But if I lied, then I would be lying to my friend and confidant. To compound this side of the coin: if he were to discover I hadn't been truthful, how much worse would that be?

"You know what? I just remembered where it is," I said as I snapped a finger and held up my index finger to the sky. I had decided on the edge of the coin, where I neither lied nor revealed the entire truth. I did, in fact, know where the pendant was.

"I'm glad to hear it," Father Thomes said with subtle doubt in his tone.

I stood to go, walking by his chair and toward the stairs, when he gently grabbed my arm. I looked down at him as he did.

"Remember, the only thing necessary for the triumph of evil is for good men to do nothing," he said with sorrowful eyes. I broke eye contact the second I understood what he meant.

"I know," I croaked around a tight throat. He held on for a few significant seconds before letting his arm slide down mine and back to his armrest. I continued moving toward the stairs, glancing at Ulric's prison as I did. Normally, the physical presence of my maker's prison—which had once held me—would draw on my attention more, but right now, my mind was consumed with what was to come.

I stepped onto the landing, confident the church's defenses would not attack if I was exiting, and felt a warm breeze kiss my face. Closing my eyes, I pictured Taylor sitting on the throne, controlling the two main courts and the lesser courts under their rule. The world was returning to normal right as mine was falling apart.

Could I kill my best friend and brother? Or was it possible to pull him back from the mouth of madness?

Sprouting my bloodwings, I looked up to the cloudless night and was bathed in the pale light of the full moon. Setting my jaw, I shot into the sky and toward my inevitable, and undeniable, destiny.

THE END

Epilogue

I returned to my lair where Locke was breaking the cellophane seal on a brand-new phone. He helped me set it up before sending me Depweg's last-known coordinates. We shared access so he could make live changes to my phone as needed, like the map. I was amazed to see how responsive the hologram screen was as I opened and closed my index and thumb in rapid succession.

"Are you sure you can do this?" Locke asked, placing a hand on my shoulder. It was easier for him to do with how tall he had gotten in my absence.

"No," I answered honestly, feeling my face drag down into a frown. "But what choice do I have? I only hope I can talk him into coming back with me."

Joey stepped out of his room with an unreadable, stony expression. He had grown hard since I'd first met him back at Val's. Now he was in his midthirties and had lost his twin brother and his pack leader. Though weres aged incredibly slow compared to mortals, he still had frown lines between his eyebrows. It made my heart heavy for him.

"How are you going to do that, vampire?" Joey asked coldly with arms crossed over his chest. I didn't take offense to the implied disrespect because I understood both what he was going through and what he meant. If Depweg's human mind was compromised, or even gone, how could I hope to communicate with him.

An impulsive idea lurched to the forefront of my brain, and my mouth reacted before the rest of my consciousness understood what I was about to ask. "Do you want to come with me?"

Joey uncrossed his arms and softened his expression as I caught him off guard.

"Yeah. Yeah, I do," he said with a conversational tone, all aggression washed away with such a simple question.

Of course, that simple question also held a world of danger and responsibility for Joey. From what I had seen, Depweg was a terrifying monster now, and I honestly couldn't say if I was going to be able to stop him.

"Grab your bug-out bag and let's go," I instructed. Joey complied by retreating to his room with a hustle in his step. Locke looked down at his phone, pretending to fine-tune our sync.

"What is it?" I asked, fully knowing what he was going to say.

"Nothing," Locke replied, though he stopped pretending to work on his phone and instead stared through it with unfocused eyes.

I leaned in close enough so Joey couldn't hear us, and whispered, "Come on, man."

Locke looked at me with dread in his eyes and admitted, "If he fights Depweg, Joey will die. If you manage to kill Depweg, what's to stop Joey from losing his own mind and going feral? The situation is stacked against you, John. Surely you must see that."

I nodded my head as it was my turn to stare into oblivion with eyes that didn't see the now. Instead, I saw the exact likely events Locke had just laid out fly in front of my eyes in a millisecond.

"I need to respect his decision. He has a right to try and save Depweg just as much as I do."

"Just as long as you understand the risks," Locke relented, returning his focus to his phone while letting his eyebrows rise slightly in a gesture that said, "I said what I needed to say; now it's on you."

I placed a hand on his shoulder and was about to say something along the lines of, "I appreciate your input," before my bare forearm cut me off. A scowl spread on my face as my eyes followed the path up my arm to where my trench coat had been torn just above the elbow. The usual disappointment at seeing my trusty coat in tatters was dominated by the realization that Da was no longer around to fix it. My scowl transitioned into a frown as tears formed at the bottom of my eyelids like a wave about to crash.

Locke looked up from the phone to study my face and then followed my gaze to the coat. His eyebrows knitted together in an expression of understanding before surprise shot them to his hairline.

"Oh!" he exclaimed, excited. "John, go in my room where you found the gauntlet. There's...there's something there for you." His voice was soft as he spoke, signifying he knew something of vast importance to me.

My eyes, on the verge of spilling tears, drifted to his room, and I made my way to his door. I stared at the knob, knowing whatever was behind that door would change things forever.

Eventually, my hand grasped the knob and turned. As I stood in the doorway, the H. R. Giger picture hung, ready to give up its secret.

I walked to it with painfully slow steps, placed my hand on the edge of the frame, and swung it open with a gentle creaking sound.

On the bottom shelf was the rectangular box with the bow on it. I stood frozen for several seconds as I just stared at it. It looked old, like it had been there for years.

After what felt like an eternity, I found the will to grab the box and set it gingerly on Locke's bed. I lifted the lid and was met with thin white sheets with a card on top. I picked up the card with shaking hands and read it.

John,

If you are reading this rather than me presenting it to you in person, then I am probably back with Father.

You've been gone for some time—two years to be exact—and it behooves me to go in search of you. However, should I not make it back, I wanted to leave you a gift that each of your dear friends had a hand in making. We were all so proud of how you not only defeated Ulric, but your own pride. Plus, quite frankly, I have grown tired of keeping your beef jerky of a trench coat alive. There's only so much magic even I can do, so I made you a new one.

It gives me great pleasure to introduce you to your new coat.

I opened the paper sheets encasing the garment, pulled the coat out, let it drop to full length, and then set it gently on the bed. I looked back at the note, the words getting hard to read as the tears resurged in a tidal wave.

> *Taylor provided the material, which is substantially stronger than anything I could have procured. Valenta crafted the buttons from wood taken directly from his bar; and yes, it did reside in Valhalla at one point—not sure why Val told me this, but he assured me that you would know what he meant. Father Thomes provided the silver crosses on the collar that will protect you from both divination and ranged attacks. Depweg, with a great deal of convincing, let us buzz his were-pelt to place along the inner lining. Locke, the twins, and myself had a heyday with him until he pounced on Locke. You know Depweg!*

My mind shifted from Da to Depweg, compounding the anguish, and my silent tears became full-on sobs as I covered my mouth with my free hand.

> *John, I don't know where you are, but it is safe to assume you are in one piece, considering the world has not yet ended. Depweg and the twins are working with Father Thomes to carry on the good work in your absence. They are doing amazing things. You would be so proud of them.*

> *Oh, you won't believe this, but even Locke and I have grown, shall we say, "not hostile" toward one another. You made the right decision letting him on the team.*

> *Well, that's enough of that, as I fully plan on returning to present you with your unique outerwear in person. So, until we meet again.*

Ta-ta,

—*Da*

He had signed it with the name I had bestowed upon him, like a badge of honor. Tears coated the letter, smearing some of the ink, and I fell to my knees as I clutched the page to my chest. I heaved with a perfect balance of indescribable sorrow and undeserving love. I shoved my face into Locke's thick comforter, and cried out as my lungs expelled every square inch of air. I sucked in again and repeated the process three more times, until I had cried my last tear. I lifted my wet face and looked at the coat my friends had made for me.

Sniffling, I stood up, wiping my nose on my burnt shirt, and took in the sheer magnificence of the most beautiful thing I had ever seen.

My fingers ran gingerly over the black Fae silk that I knew was preternaturally resilient. Wooden buttons lined the edge of one of the flaps, and I squinted to see impossible details etched into all six. Each told the tale of how I had met my friends. I lifted the coat and looked at them one by one, starting at the bottom.

The first showed the twins sitting at a table, Dawson with an animated toothy smile and Joey with a shit-eating, closed-mouth grin. A pang of sadness thumped against my chest as I stared at Dawson's grin.

"Rest easy, buddy. I'll take care of your brother for you," I whispered to Dawson.

Above that was Locke's head in a box with a surprised look on its face. I chuckled at the memory.

The fourth from the top showed Father Thomes waving in front of his church. I could even make out the detail of his little collar in the wood.

Next was me sitting at a bar with my hand in the air, mid wave, as Val rolled his eyes. I could actually see the detail of the eye roll, and barked out in laughter.

The button above that showed a bridge over a flowing river. Da was floating in midair with a welcoming smile on his face. My throat constricted at the memory.

I was paralyzed on the second to top button, knowing what the topmost one would hold.

I took in a deep breath, held it, and exhaled as I willed my eyes to the first wooden button. A moan escaped my throat as I saw Depweg and I clasping forearms, signifying the beginnings of a long and fruitful brotherhood.

I let my thumb slide over the button as my fingers glided over the soft fur lining on the inside. I let my eyes slide to the brown fur, and let out a burst of laughter that sent snot sliding down my face. The image of a buzzed Depweg in were form was too much!

"I'm coming to save you, brother," I promised Depweg.

A glint on the collar caught my attention, and once again, I wiped my face clean on my shirt as I looked at the silver crosses. They were gorgeous in their simplicity.

"You and I...weren't that close when this was done," Locke said softly from behind. "I didn't have anything to contribute, so, instead, I offered to hold it for you until you came back."

I looked over my shoulder with wet eyes, and said, "Thank you, Locke. I-I can't begin to tell you how much this means to me."

Locke smiled and nodded his head, having a strong idea of what impact the gesture had had.

I removed my WWII trench coat, which had been with me for almost a full century, and set it on the bed next to the one Da had made for me.

Picking up the most epic trench coat in the history of *ever*, I slipped my hands through the sleeves and felt the comfort from the thin layer of fur. It wasn't puffy like a traditional fur coat. Instead, it was more akin to thick suede.

I ran my fingers down the Fae silk, basking in the wonderment of something that was beyond soft, yet could deflect bullets.

Feeling a rush of joy, I twirled in place, letting the long flaps extend out, and stopped to orient on Locke.

"How do I look?" I asked with a huge smile.

"Like a badass," Locke said admiringly. I couldn't tell if he was just saying it because the moment dictated such sentiment or if it was genuine; but I also didn't care. I would wear this trench coat until the day I died, and then drag it into whatever eternity I was sucked into.

I walked to Locke, who stood with his arms crossed as he leaned against the doorway, and wrapped my arms around him in a bear hug. I lifted him up and bounced him as he said, "Okay, okay. I get it." He paused for a moment before he commented with his face squished against my chest, "Wow, that really *is* soft."

"I know, right?" I said, putting him down. He turned and made his way into the living room with me in tow.

Joey came out, slinging a tactical backpack over his shoulders and clasping the straps across his chest. He eyed my trench and said in an even tone, "Nice coat."

"Are you ready, dude?" I asked Joey.

He lifted his chin and nodded at me once.

We made our way to the door, ready to do whatever must be done.

"Good luck," Locke said as we stepped outside. I grabbed Joey, pulling him close to my chest, sprouted my bloodwings, and we were off.

"When did you get those?" Joey asked over his shoulder, nodding at my massive flapping wings.

"K-Mart. Blue light special," I said in my announcer voice.

Joey returned his gaze to the ground below, unimpressed. Damn kids and their MTV.

I headed north, and I could see Joey looking around at the city for markers.

"Mexico is south, dude," Joey called over his shoulder loud enough to be heard over the wind. It comforted me to notice how much warmer it was this time around.

"I need to make a stop first," I called back.

Within a few minutes, we were descending next to an old ramshackle of a house with a sign out front.

"Psychic? Really, dude?" Joey criticized.

"I know, I know. I said the same thing," I responded slowly, as if in a dream. I was terrified to see Lachesis again.

We approached the stoop, and I turned to Joey as I said, "She will probably want you to wait here."

"Fine by me," Joey responded, crossing his arms and leaning against the house to stare out at the road.

The door began to slowly creak open like we were in a horror movie. Which to me, we freaking were.

When it opened all the way, the doorway was empty. I peered inside, searching left and right.

A familiar voice called out from the back room. The room where my fate had been exposed to me.

"Come in," said the woman with the African accent. I took a step inside when she continued, "Both of you."

I stopped, dead in my tracks, and regarded Joey. He leaned off the house, uncrossed his arms, and walked past me and into the darkness. I watched after him, surprised at his confidence; but then I reminded myself that he didn't know what awaited us.

Taking a deep breath, I willed my nerves to steady, and followed Joey inside and to the back room.

Lachesis sat in her chair as if waiting for us. Which, of course, she was. She had to have known we were coming, which meant she also already knew what we were going to ask.

I cut to the chase, dispensing with the pleasantries. "What's your price, seer?" As soon as it left my mouth, I understood that calling her "seer" was a pathetic attempt to siphon control of the situation that I was powerless in.

"Blood," she answered curtly as she pulled out an ornate silver knife. It looked like it had been made for sacrificial purposes.

Now, I may not have been the sharpest crayon in the cabinet, but I knew giving my blood to a supernatural was not a good idea. Especially one as seemingly powerful and proficient as Lachesis.

When I didn't respond, opting to look at my hands as I debated the price, she countered, "Or maybe the hammer hanging about your waist. Mmm." She was all but purring as she spoke.

I held out my hand with a furrowed brow as she lifted the knife. Funny how the request for blood, which had been so emphatically a bad idea, suddenly became as menial as asking for a dollar bill when Mjolnir was brought into the mix.

She made a show of pretending to cut my hand wide open before she stopped midstrike and simply poked the tip of my index finger as she said, "Boop."

"Ow," I said with more annoyance than pain as a tiny bubble of blood left my finger to rest on the tip of the blade.

"What are you going to do with that?" I asked, licking my finger.

"Not your concern," she answered swiftly.

"Eh, it kinda is," I countered. Lachesis ignored this as the blade disappeared under the table.

"As for you," Lachesis began, turning to Joey, who immediately stiffened. She inspected him up and down with a scowl, her milky eyes roaming intently. Then her expression went slack. "I require nothing from you."

"Wh-why?" Joey asked, taken aback.

"Dude, shut up!" I hissed at him.

"Because, child, you have paid enough." I turned with a scrunched up face to regard Lachesis, who showed such compassion in that moment that it left me speechless—*me*. I hoped this wasn't becoming a habit of mine.

Seeing this side of Lachesis, I asked, "So, are you a heartless seer toying with people by revealing vague futures, or do you actually care about those who seek your guidance? I don't understand."

"I know you don't, fool," she said coldly.

"Aaaaand, there it is. Can we get on with it, then?" I asked, rolling my eyes.

"You must ask your question so that the universe might hear it."

"You already know what my question is."

Lachesis turned to Joey with hands out to her sides and palms up. "Does he seriously not ever listen?"

"Hey!" I called out.

"No, he really doesn't," Joey answered as easily and in the same tone as if he were telling someone the time after they'd asked.

"Alrighty then," I said, pulling the chair out and slamming my (actually) fit butt down on it aggressively. "Can we continue?" I let my hands fall on the table with a smack, just to make sure they knew how much fun I was having.

Lachesis looked at me, expectantly.

"What?" I asked, throwing my hands up.

"Dude, ask the damn question," Joey said as he sat down in a more respectable fashion than I had. You know, not dragging the chair across the floor and plopping down. That kind of thing.

I shot daggers at Lachesis, annoyed that she was making me ask.

The picture of Monster Depweg, covered in the blood of the innocent, flashed through my mind. I sobered up immediately, letting my pride deflate.

"What is the name of the boy Depweg was tricked into killing during World War II?" I asked, leaning forward in my seat.

Lachesis looked up, letting her milky eyes shift back and forth as if the answer was written on the ceiling.

Her eyes locked on a spot before growing wide. "Benji Silver," she said slowly, enunciating the words as clearly as she could manage with her thick accent. I was half expecting her to freak out and go all poltergeist again.

As she finished, she dropped her eyes from the ceiling back down to me and sat silently for a few weird moments.

"Is-is that it?" I asked. "Benji Silver? That's not much to go on."

"From all da death around dat time, it's a miracle I could get anything at all. But know this, vampire; you asked the universe a question, now the universe knows the answer."

"Okay, that's not a weird thing to say at all," I said facetiously.

"I think she means others will know who Depweg killed now," Joey suggested.

"Only da ones who know how ta listen," Lachesis added prophetically. I was starting to get sick of that.

Throwing on my best Ace Ventura, I said, "Foreshadowing much?"

Not wanting to spend another second there, I promptly stood and said, "Thanks for nothing. Don't suppose I could get a refund on that blood you took from me? No? Didn't think so. Joey, let's go. Now."

I strode down the hallway and out the front door to stand in the warm night. Extending my hand into an L, I checked the time and decided we could probably get a few hundred miles south of the border before dawn. I sprouted my bloodwings and turned to see the empty doorway.

"Joey! Lilith damn it, come on!" I called into the house.

Joey appeared in the hallway, walking slowly while staring at the ground with a scowl on his face. He almost tripped walking off the stoop to stand next to me.

"What is it, man?" I asked softly, trying my best to mask my annoyance. I knew—I fucking *knew*—Lachesis had said something to him after I'd left.

"No-nothing," Joey said, shaking his head to clear the thought. He set his jaw, and I immediately respected his strength more.

He walked around to stand in front of me, and I reached under his arms to clasp my hands around his chest before taking off into the night with a whoosh of air.

I threw on my best airline captain voice, and said, "Ah, this is your, ah, captain, ah, speaking. Our next stop, ah, will be somewhere in Mexicooooahhh. We know you don't have a choice when flying, ah, so we here at John Air, ah, would like you to know, ah, we don't care about you. Thanks for the money, chumps. No smoking."

Joey ignored my supremely hilarious commentary on today's world of corporate airlines, opting to sulk in silence instead. Or maybe he was taking the situation a little more seriously than I was. Without his return banter, I was forced inside the swirling din of anxiety that was my mind. Every conceivable bad scenario stood in a line and played out one by one in pulse-pounding high definition.

"Ready or not, here we come, brother," I whispered through a sigh to myself.

Afterword

Final words from the author

If you enjoyed this Urban Fantasy eulogy for Sir John Cook*, would you consider leaving an honest review? Click **here** to go straight to the Amazon review page.

On the next page I have created links so you can:

- Preview a few pages of the next book in the series right from the Amazon Kindle platform

- Check out the Audible page and listen to samples of Audible Hall of Fame narrator, Luke Daniels, as he brings John to life with his amazing performance!

- I also left a link for Facebook, Goodreads, and BookBub

Thank you for giving John *unlife* after death. The series dedicated to my bromego will be 13 full novels with a handful of novellas and short stories for good measure. So until next time, John On!

*not actually knighted

Click here for a free preview of the next book in the series

Audible: Series page, listen to free samples here

Connect with Me

T-shirts, signed books, and more await at

www.HunterBlain.com

Facebook Author Page

Goodreads Author Page

BookBub Author Page

Also By Hunter Blain

THE PRETERNATURAL CHRONICLES
I'm Glad You're Dead
Dawn and Quartered
Shadow of a Doubt
Moonlight Equilibrium- Book 3.5
Mouth of Madness
What the Hell
Holy Sheoly
Those Wonderful Toys
Crack the Sky
Fall From Grace

THE SOL SAGA
Dawn's Light
Midday's Sun- Q4 release, 2023
Dusk's Night- coming soon

THE CHRONOS PARADOX
Wielding an Hourglass

Sands of Time

Made in United States
North Haven, CT
25 May 2025